Further praise for the Bobby Girls series

'Written with warmth and compassion, *The Bobby Girls* gives fascinating insights into the lives of three courageous young women.'   Margaret Kaine, RNA award-winning author of *Ring of Clay*

'This is a story that needed to be told. As a former Special Constable, I love Johanna Bell from the bottom of my heart for giving a voice to the women who first made a way for me and countless others like me – to work as real police officers in the service of our communities. Let us not forget the fight that these women had just to be allowed to put on the uniform and do what was right; in their own small way, the first Bobby Girls changed the world for women every-where.'   Penny Thorpe, bestselling author of *The Quality Street Girls*

'A well-researched and interesting story giving a great insight into early women's policing.'   Anna Jacobs, bestselling author of the Ellindale series

'A lovely story! The author has researched the era and the theme very well. The characters stood out on the page and through their eyes you are transported back to a different age.'   AnneMarie Brear, author of *Beneath a Stormy Sky*

'I really did enjoy *The Bobby Girls*. It has a lovely warm feeling about it and is excellently written.'
Maureen Lee, RNA award-winning author of *Dancing in the Dark*

Johanna Bell cut her teeth on local newspapers in Essex, eventually branching into magazine journalism with stints as a features writer and then commissioning editor at *Full House* magazine. She now has more than sixteen years' experience in print media. Her freelance life has seen her working on juicy real-life stories for the women's weekly magazine market, as well as hard-hitting news stories for national newspapers and prepping her case studies for TV interviews. When she's not writing, Johanna can be found walking her dog with her husband or playing peek-a-boo with her daughter.

To hear more from Johanna, follow her on Twitter, @JoBellAuthor and on Facebook, /johannabellauthor.

Christmas with the Bobby Girls

Book Three in the Bobby Girls series

JOHANNA BELL

HODDER

First published in Great Britain in 2020 by Hodder & Stoughton
An Hachette UK company

3

Copyright © Johanna Bell 2020

A CIP catalogue record for this title is available from the British Library

Paperback ISBN 978 1 529 33422 7
eBook ISBN 978 1 529 33423 4

Typeset in Plantin Light by Palimpsest Book Production Limited,
Falkirk, Stirlingshire

Printed and bound in Great Britain by Clays Ltd, Elcograf S.p.A.

Hodder & Stoughton policy is to use papers that are natural, renewable and
recyclable products and made from wood grown in sustainable forests.
The logging and manufacturing processes are expected to conform to the
environmental regulations of the country of origin.

Hodder & Stoughton Ltd
Carmelite House
50 Victoria Embankment
London EC4Y 0DZ

www.hodder.co.uk

For Emma and Georgia x

Dear reader,

I can't quite believe I'm sitting down to write to you for a third time. We're back in London for *Christmas with the Bobby Girls,* and this book follows Annie as she faces some tough challenges during her spell with the WPS. Though it has been a difficult time to write a book this time around, it was great to be able to escape into the world of my Bobby Girls for a little while every day. The girls really have become a part of my life now and I feel like I'm living through their adventures with them when I sit down at my computer to type. Working on the book during these strange times also granted me a good sense of perspective; no matter how hard I felt things were in my own life, I knew it was nothing compared to what women like Annie, Maggie, Poppy and Irene went through during WW1. And reading about life in the trenches during my research really hammered home to me just how lucky we all are to have the freedom we do, despite current restrictions.

The research for *Christmas with the Bobby Girls* has, as always, kept me fascinated. My favourite nugget of information I came across this time was an anecdote about how the WPS recruits used to help drunken soldiers sober up before escorting them back to their barracks. I also had to laugh when I read about a tactic some of the prostitutes used to try and sneak men past the female police. I enjoyed both of those so much that I just had to write them into Annie's story, and I hope you enjoy them too.

I'd like to finish this letter by thanking you, reader,

for continuing on this journey with me and my Bobby Girls. I hope you stick with us for the next instalment, too: *The Bobby Girls' War* – which is available to order now.

Johanna Bell, June 2020

Christmas with the Bobby Girls

I

Annie Beckett felt a rush of wind as she and her colleagues started their descent down the steps. The warm air billowing over her told her that a tube train was about to make its way into Whitechapel Station. Sure enough, only seconds later she heard the familiar sounds of carriages pulling up and doors opening to spit out Londoners eager to get on with their journeys. Annie, Maggie and Poppy were halfway down the steps when the crowd surged around the corner and started clambering up the stairs towards them at speed.

Annie stopped and stepped to the side to let everyone past. She had learned the hard way that it wasn't worth trying to fight your way through the hordes of passengers desperate to escape the stuffy station and get out into the fresh air. Maggie and Poppy followed suit and the three of them stood firm so as not to get knocked off their feet.

Once the worst of the crowd had passed, the girls made their way down the steps once more. Annie spotted a young lad in uniform loitering at the bottom of the stairwell. She slowed down and watched carefully as he looked shiftily around him and scratched his head nervously. She was about to mention him to her friends when he appeared to pull out an imaginary rifle and fix it into place. The second he started his advance up the staircase, Annie leapt into action. She had to do something before he hurt somebody. His mind had clearly transported him back to the battlefields and it was anyone's guess what he would do if some poor blighter – a German to him – got in his way.

The soldier had only made it up a few of the steps when Annie, Maggie and Poppy sprung forwards in unison to block his path. As bemused members of the public veered to the side to watch the drama unfold, the girls braced themselves to take his weight. They made it into position just before the man reached them. He tried to charge through the human wall they had created but they stood firm. Annie was in the middle, so she took the brunt of the force, but she stood in a ju-jitsu pose with her hands and arms out protecting her body so that she wasn't knocked off her feet. When the soldier bounced back off the trio, they all grabbed him, catching him before he fell back down the staircase. The movement seemed to jolt the man back to reality. Annie was relieved. Blinded by rage and fear, he could have hurt a lot of people by charging through the crowd at speed with all his force if they hadn't stopped him. Not to mention how his actions would likely have caused a dangerous panic and crush.

'I . . . I . . . where am I?' the man stuttered. The girls loosened their grips on him and he looked around, dazed, as another surge of tube passengers made their way past them up the steps, unaware of what had just happened.

'You're back in London. You're safe,' Annie said firmly as the soldier leant against the wall for support. The relief that swept over his face as her words registered winded Annie like a punch to the stomach. She hated what this war was doing to men like this – like her fiancé, Richard. Would any of them ever be able to get over what they had seen and been forced to do to protect the country? Annie quickly pushed her anguish aside to deal with the matter in hand.

She found that if she thought about things like this too much then she lost all focus, and she needed to get through this patrol as smoothly as possible.

'Let's get you out of here and into the air, and then we can help get you home,' she offered, taking the soldier's hand in hers as Poppy placed her own gently on his shoulder. Together, they guided him up the stairs. Out on the street, they all took a moment to adjust to the early September sunshine. Annie pulled her hefty jacket tighter around her – there was only a slight nip in the air but she always struggled switching from the warm and stuffy atmosphere in tube stations to the fresh air outside.

The soldier, however, seemed to be a lot more comfortable in his surroundings. He took some deep breaths before muttering, 'I'm sorry. I don't know what happened back there, but I felt like I was back in the trenches.' The usual London hustle and bustle swept past them all, unaware of the major panic and crush that had been averted below them.

'Don't worry,' Maggie said kindly. 'It's not the first time we've been in a situation like that. That's why we stepped in to help you so quickly.'

In the early days of the war, there had been no organisation responsible for meeting leave trains at the mainline stations where they pulled in after transporting troops from the front, so a lot of the recruits had found themselves helping confused soldiers find their bearings. The onwards journey was tricky for a lot of them and busy, stifling tube stations were the worst places for the men to be when they were trying to get themselves home while at the same time dealing with what they had seen on the front line. Officials were meant to meet them off the trains at the main stations now and escort them on the rest of their journey but every now and then one slipped through the net and the girls found that they could spot the ones who were struggling with the transition a mile off. Just as they had done today.

When Maggie started jumping up and down and gesticulating wildly, Annie realised she had spotted a police car. The officer pulled up beside them with a stern look on his face and Maggie stepped forward to speak to him.

'He'll take you home,' Maggie declared, turning back around to face the group and wave the soldier over. He thanked the girls, took off his backpack and made his way to the car.

'Make sure you get some rest,' Poppy called out as he climbed into the back seat. 'Let your mother look after you, won't you?'

As the oldest of the three recruits, it was typical of Poppy to show this type of concern. The soldier looked back at her with tears in his eyes and nodded sadly. Annie felt a pang in her chest for this stranger and found herself wishing he could stay at home with his mother looking after him for as long as he needed, instead of having to go back out into the line of fire in a matter of days.

'That policeman was a right miserable so-and-so. He didn't even thank me for our help,' sniffed Maggie as they watched the car drive away. 'I would have given him a piece of my mind if I wasn't so concerned about that poor lad getting home.'

Annie laughed to herself. She loved how feisty Maggie Smyth was. She didn't stand for any nonsense from anybody – whether they were her superior or not. She had really helped Annie come out of her shell in the last year or so. Annie had been so timid when they had first met while training for the Women Police Service; so much so that at first Annie had been horrified by Maggie's self-assured attitude and confidence. But they had been through an awful lot together during their training and subsequent placement together at Bethnal Green Police Station. Annie knew she had Maggie and their other friend and original patrol partner Irene Wilson to thank for the fact she was such a strong and independent woman now, even if she did go through occasional moments of self-doubt.

Although the threesome had patrolled together to begin with – and cracked the biggest burglary case the station had seen in years – Irene had been transferred to Grantham back in May and they both missed her dearly. The male officers hadn't taken too kindly to their arrival in the beginning, but their success with the burglary had helped them to be accepted. There were still a few officers who made it clear they didn't agree with women patrolling the streets and taking on 'men's work', but as the war had raged on longer than anybody had expected and more men had signed up to fight, the WPS recruits across the country had become an ever more valuable resource for the struggling police service. Annie assumed the chap who had driven the soldier away wasn't one of their biggest fans.

Poppy Davis had been sent to join Annie and Maggie on the beat when Irene had left for Grantham and, although being in her thirties made her quite a bit older than them both – Annie was twenty-three and Maggie just nineteen – she had fitted in well to their little set-up – even moving in to the flat they shared in Camberwell Green. She had already been patrolling in another part of London before she joined the girls and Annie had been relieved to have been sent someone with experience rather than a recruit fresh out of training. Maggie had been convinced Poppy would use her age to boss them both around, and Annie had been ready for the pair of them to clash. But it turned out that Poppy was young at heart, and she made sure her extra years of life-experience benefited the whole group. Now it was like she had always been a part of their life together, although Annie wished Irene could still be with them, too.

'What were you thinking back there?' Maggie asked suddenly.

Confused, Annie looked round at her to check who she was addressing.

'What do you mean?' Annie asked when she found Maggie staring at her expectantly.

'I mean, how could you take such a big risk so close to the wedding? You leapt straight in there and plonked yourself in the middle, right in the line of fire. I wish you'd taken a step back and let me or Poppy do that.'

Annie blinked. She hadn't thought before she had acted. It all came naturally now. 'It happened so quickly,' she explained. 'I didn't even get a chance to make sure you had both seen what I'd seen and were going to back me up.'

'Well, thank goodness we did,' Maggie sighed. 'What if we hadn't realised and left you to take him on alone? He could have knocked you straight off your feet. Your mother would kill me if I dragged you along to the dress fitting with a head wound, and don't get me started on Richard's reaction to a bruised and bloody bride!'

Annie could see now that Maggie was joking around with her. 'Well, it's a good job we're all so in tune then, isn't it?' she said, smiling. 'I know you've always got my back.'

She gave her friend a playful pat on her back and the three of them giggled. And that was the truth; she had dived straight in without checking Maggie and Poppy were behind her because she always trusted that they were. They had never once let her down, and she was confident they never would. Just like she knew she would always be there to help them, no matter what the situation was. That was one of the reasons their bond was so strong.

'We'd better hurry back to the station,' Maggie declared suddenly, checking her watch. 'I don't know where the afternoon has gone, but we're cutting it fine to meet your mother at the dress shop and I don't want to upset Mrs Beckett!'

Annie rolled her eyes playfully. Her mother was as relaxed as they come and certainly wouldn't moan at them being late to meet her with such good reason. She wondered if Maggie had one of her grand plans in place and secretly hoped she didn't. She didn't want any big surprises over the next few days. All that mattered was that she got to see Richard again, and become his wife at last. He was due back on leave the next day and this final dress fitting was the last piece of wedding preparation she had left to do before the ceremony. She rushed along the street with Maggie and Poppy. She had to admit, she was rather desperate to try her dress on one last time before the big day.

2

Wrapped up in their excitement, the three girls ran practically all the way back to the police station and changed back into their everyday clothes without pausing to catch their breath. Making her way to the dress shop with two of her best friends by her side, Annie couldn't quite believe that this was one of her final days as a spinster. Walking into the store, she smiled when her eyes fell upon her mother. She had been so busy with the WPS lately that she had hardly had any time to see her, and all the time they had spent together had been consumed with last-minute wedding planning following Richard's re-proposal the previous month. As she walked towards her mother for what suddenly felt like a much-needed hug, she noticed a tall, slim figure standing just behind her. She had to stop and take a second look as her heart caught in her throat. Annie rubbed her eyes dramatically.

'I can't believe it's really you!' she cried as her mother stepped to the side to allow the two of them to embrace. Annie threw herself at Irene so hard that she nearly knocked her friend off her feet. She hadn't seen Irene since she had popped back from Grantham to tell her and Maggie that she had broken things off with her terrible fiancé, Charles. Annie had since learned through letters that Irene was courting Jack, the deserter she had discovered on her new beat. They were even planning on getting married – with Maggie and Annie as bridesmaids – although they hadn't set a date yet as they were both busy working in Grantham. Irene had helped Jack to get the medical care he needed for his shell shock, and when he was better he had returned to Grantham for her. He now had an office job at the army camp there. Irene's letters to the girls were always brief as she wasn't one for expressing her feelings, but it was clear that she was the happiest she had ever been, and Annie was so happy for her friend.

'What are you doing here? I wasn't expecting to see you until the wedding,' Annie gasped. Then realisation dawned on her and she pulled away to seek out Maggie. 'So, this was your grand plan,' she exclaimed joyfully. 'I knew you were up to something!' Maggie shrugged her shoulders and grinned from ear to ear before running up to give Irene a hug herself. Annie looked over and saw Poppy standing awkwardly on her own. She had only met Irene once before, and very briefly. She was trying to think of a way to involve Poppy when Irene stepped in.

'Your fitter is still busy with her previous client, so why don't we all sit down and catch up?' she suggested, gesturing for Poppy to join them. They moved to the waiting area and Annie sat with her mother and Irene on either side of her, holding a hand of each of them in her own.

'I have to know more about this re-proposal,' Irene gushed, squeezing Annie's hand affectionately and looking excited. 'It was such a romantic thing for Richard to do.' Annie hadn't gone into much detail when she'd written to Irene to break the news, and she was glad because it meant she got to relive the whole thing with her in person now.

'I was so surprised,' Annie squealed. 'As you know, Richard signed up the minute war was declared, and we'd always planned on getting married once it was all over. But that was when we thought it would done and dusted very quickly.' Annie paused for a moment, thinking back to the time when everyone had believed all the fighting would come to an end within a few months and everything would be back to normal before they knew it. How full of hope they had all been, she thought wistfully – and how silly and naive. 'If we'd known then that it would still be dragging on now – well, we would have made sure we'd exchanged those rings before Richard left.'

'No one could have known, dear,' Annie's mother said quietly. Annie nodded, thinking of all the lives that had been lost and families that had been ripped apart since that time.

'Richard surprised you with a visit while he was back on official duty, didn't he, dear?' Annie's mother prompted her, pulling her out of the reflective lull she had fallen into.

'Yes.' Annie grinned, the mention of the special visit perking her up again. 'The last time I'd seen him was when he had that home-leave back when we'd only just started patrolling,' she explained. 'He was so withdrawn and quiet during that visit, I feared that whatever he'd witnessed during his time away had changed him forever. I remember telling Maggie about it and getting so upset. I was convinced I'd never get the old Richard back. But then that Richard turned up a month ago!'

'He managed to get word to me and Mr Beckett beforehand to say he was going to be in London for a matter of hours dropping off a top-secret package,' Mrs Beckett cut in, unable to restrain herself. 'We still don't know any more about that official business, but I sent one of Annie's sisters along to tell Maggie and Poppy, and they made sure Annie came to see us for lunch that day. It was all so rushed and last-minute, and it could have so easily gone wrong. But I know those two are meant to be as it worked out perfectly.' She smiled fondly at her daughter. Annie was beaming now, and she looked across at Maggie who was looking rather pleased with herself.

'I've never been as shocked in my life as I was when I opened the front door and found my handsome Richard on the doorstep down on one knee,' Annie gushed. Tears welled in her eyes as she remembered the flood of emotion that had swept over her. 'He was *my* Richard again. He looked happy instead of haunted. He told me he couldn't wait any longer to make me his wife. Everything he'd seen while he'd been away had made him realise what was important in life and he told me he wouldn't be able to go back out to war after his next lot of leave unless it was as a married man. He didn't propose properly the first time around – it was more of an agreement between us – so this was even more special. We decided there and then that we would get married a month later when he was due back home for a few days' rest. And then I heard a big cheer from behind me and realised my whole family had crept up behind me to listen in from the hallway!'

All the girls laughed at the lovely ending to her story.

'That's wonderful,' sighed Irene. 'I take it you didn't get to spend long with him, though, if he was in London on official business?'

'He'd managed to drop the package off early and he had just under an hour until he had to leave and get his train,' Annie said.

'Oh, so did he stay for lunch with the family?' Irene asked innocently.

Annie felt her cheeks flush. 'No,' she said hesitantly. 'We went for a nice walk together and—'

To Annie's relief, the fitter chose that moment to pop her head around the corner. 'I'm ready for you now, love,' she said, and Annie jumped up and scurried off, glad to leave the topic behind. As they entered the fitting room, the woman unveiled Annie's dress and her previous embarrassment was replaced by an overwhelming feeling of happiness. She was suddenly aware that getting into that outfit and marrying Richard was what she had been destined to do from the moment she was born. Everything felt so right. Her mother joined her in the changing room and as she stepped into the plain white, floor-length gown, both their eyes filled with tears.

When she stepped out, all three of her friends gasped in unison. Annie was relieved. She had gone for an understated dress; with everything that was going on it would have felt wrong to opt for anything extravagant, even if her father was willing to pay for it. Plus, there hadn't been time to get anything too fancy. But her friends' reactions told her she had made the right choice.

'I don't think there's too much more that needs doing,' the fitter said, standing back to allow Annie to do some twirls for her adoring audience. When she stopped to look at herself in the full-length mirror, Annie put her hand over her mouth as she took in her reflection. She had been worried about the dress being too revealing, but her curves seemed to fill it out perfectly. Her womanly frame was on show without giving away too much. She had always been a little on the fuller side, but all the hours walking around on patrol had slimmed her body down somewhat. She was still what some would call 'plump' compared to the likes of Irene, Poppy and Maggie, but she found that she didn't feel as self-conscious about her size anymore. And this dress certainly complimented her figure.

As she admired her reflection, Annie couldn't help but think about the suggestion her mother had made a few weeks before when she had decided on her outfit. Mrs Beckett had told her it would be perfect for making into a christening gown when Annie and Richard started a family together. She took a moment to appreciate all the wonderful things she had to look forward to at such a terrible time. In a few days' time she would be Richard's wife. And then just a few months later, she would be spending her first Christmas as a married woman. She had always loved that time of year, but this year it was going to be even more special. Then, once the war was over, she and Richard would be able to start a family together.

Finally taking her hand away from her mouth to smooth down the delicate material, Annie realised with a start that for the first time in her life, she felt beautiful. She couldn't wait to walk down the aisle and for Richard to see her in this dress. As she reluctantly took it off to get changed back into her normal clothes, all she could think about was how the next time that she stepped into it, it would be her wedding day.

Leaving the shop with the gown draped over her arm and her mother and her best friends by her side, Annie felt so lucky that her future was full of such hope and happiness.

3

The next morning, Annie woke very early, anticipation and excitement rushing through her veins. She felt the same way she had always felt on Christmas Eve as a child, only it wasn't Father Christmas and a stocking full of presents she was hungry for; it was Richard and the start of their new life together as husband and wife.

She was staying with her parents until the wedding day, which meant things were a little cramped. One of the reasons she had been so keen to move into the flat with her friends was because her aunt and cousins had moved into the family home indefinitely when her uncle had gone off to fight in the war. Annie's aunt had been struggling at home without him. As Annie tossed and turned in the bed she was sharing with her sister Maria, she became worried about waking her sibling and crept downstairs.

In the living room, she tiptoed past her aunt who was snoring on the sofa and quietly made herself a cup of tea in the kitchen before settling down in the dining room. Her dress was hanging up in there and she felt calm again as she sat and stared at it, drinking in all the promise it held as she sipped her tea. She knew her life wouldn't change dramatically once she became Richard's wife – he'd be back on the front line and she would be back on patrol within a few days. But she knew somehow that she would feel different.

Before she knew it, the house was alive, and Annie sighed

as she prepared herself for all the chaos that came with having so many young women under one roof. With her three sisters and two cousins, there was never a moment's peace. She stayed in the dining room as noise travelled through the house. She wanted to enjoy her moment of solitude for as long as she could.

Then, suddenly, the front door slammed and it all went quiet. The dining room door creaked open and Annie looked around to see her mother beaming at her.

'I thought you'd want some space to get ready for Richard's arrival so I've sent the rabble out on various wedding errands,' she explained. 'And your father's gone to work, so the house is all ours.'

'Thank you,' Annie sighed, taking one last look at the wedding dress before getting to her feet.

'Let's get to work on freshening you up – your husband-to-be is due to arrive in an hour,' Mrs Beckett said with a glint in her eye, and Annie's stomach flipped like a pancake.

An hour and a half later, Annie was anxiously pacing the living room. She had put on her long-sleeved dark-red dress – normally reserved for Sunday-best – and her mother had styled her loose, mousey curls into tight ringlets that bobbed around on her shoulders and swung into her face annoyingly every time she turned to change direction.

'Please sit down,' her mother urged. 'Your hair looks perfect and I don't want it to fall out before Richard gets here. And you're going to make yourself all agitated and sweaty.' She stepped forward to block Annie's path. Startled, Annie stared into her mother's face. She hadn't even realised she'd been pacing up and down. 'Come, sit down with me,' Mrs Beckett soothed, guiding her to the sofa.

'Where is he?' Annie asked anxiously as she wrung her hands. 'He should be here by now!' She didn't want to panic, but she had so much nervous energy rushing around her body.

'He'll be here, we just have to be patient. He could have come across all sorts of delays – there is a war on, you know!' Mrs Beckett laughed lightly and rubbed her hand up and down Annie's back. Annie relaxed a little and let out a nervous giggle. Her mother always knew how to calm her down when she was getting herself in a state. Annie took a deep breath and put on her biggest smile.

'That's my girl,' Mrs Beckett said cheerfully. 'Nice, cheering thoughts, my dear.'

As soon as the words had left her mother's mouth, Annie spotted a man's silhouette move past the window. She felt a sharp hammering in her chest, and then she heard hammering on the front door. She leapt up and rushed to the hallway, ready to greet Richard and fall into his arms. Seeing a khaki-coloured, military-style cap behind the stained glass, her hand trembled as she pulled the handle.

But when she swung the door open, her heart sank. Instead of Richard stood a man in uniform who she didn't recognise.

'Oh,' Annie spluttered, trying and failing to hide her disappointment. 'Who . . . who are you?' she asked cautiously, looking behind him for her fiancé.

'I'm Jeremy. I'm one of Richard's friends,' he explained, taking his cap off and nodding politely. Annie smiled at him bemusedly and peered out behind him again and into the street. Maybe Richard had fallen behind or sent his friend on ahead to distract her ahead of a grand arrival? But that didn't sound very much like her Richard. Looking at this stranger again, she saw his face drop.

'My goodness. You don't know, do you?' Jeremy said quietly as she desperately searched his face for answers.

'Know what? What are you talking about? And where's

Richard?' Annie demanded, agitation making her voice uncharacteristically sharp.

'What's going on? Who is this?' Annie's mother's voice called out from behind her.

'Ma'am, may I come in?' Jeremy asked in a shaky voice.

Annie felt her mother's arm guiding her back into the living room and before she knew it, she was sitting on the sofa beside her again, with the stranger in uniform sitting opposite them on her father's favourite armchair. Annie stared at him as he leaned forward and rested his elbows on his knees, clasping his hands together.

Worry surged through her as she tried to work out why this man was here instead of her fiancé. Had Richard's leave been cancelled or delayed? That would be all right – they could move the wedding day. It would be a hassle, but people would understand at a time like this. Or maybe there had been an accident and Richard was injured. Oh no, her poor Richard. The thought of him in pain made her want to burst into tears.

As Jeremy picked up his cap and started fiddling with it, Annie wondered if he was so anxious because he was here to break the news that Richard wasn't coming because he had changed his mind about the wedding. Had he decided he didn't want her to be his wife, after all? Maybe being stuck in a trench halfway between life and death had made him reassess what they had. Annie's panicked and anxious musings were interrupted when Jeremy finally spoke up.

'I'm sorry to have to tell you this. I honestly thought you would know by now. I can't believe his parents didn't come straight here when they got the telegram,' he said nervously. 'Although, maybe they haven't got it yet, there's all sorts of delays with them at the moment.'

At the mention of a telegram, both Annie and her mother sat up straight. A shot of fear mixed with nerves raced straight up Annie's spine and pooled in her head, making it spin. Of all the possible reasons for Richard's absence today, the one that was now staring her straight in the face was not an option. She refused to listen to any longer. This wasn't happening.

'No!' she cried, getting to her feet. She started grappling with the sleeves on her dress, trying to pull them up. She felt so hot and bothered all of a sudden. Why hadn't her mother opened a window in this room?

'I'm sorry, but—' Jeremy started as Mrs Beckett reached for Annie's hand.

Annie heard someone scream. She looked around the room, startled, before realising the high-pitched sound had left her own mouth. She took a deep breath and tried to compose herself. 'Please, I think you must have this wrong. It's probably best that you leave so I'm not too upset when Richard gets here.'

'He's not coming. He's dead,' Jeremy said matter-of-factly. 'I'm so sorry, Annie.'

'No, he's on his way home now for our wedding,' Annie said calmly, walking over to the living-room door to show Jeremy out. 'So, if you don't mind . . .' She gestured to the hallway. She grew impatient when Jeremy stayed sitting, looking over to her mother helplessly. Why was her mother crying? Surely, she didn't believe this nonsense? Annie knew Richard wasn't dead. They were so close that she would have known if something had happened to him, like when a twin feels the pain their sibling experiences. This man obviously meant well, but she was certain he was mistaken.

'I know it's hard for you to take in,' Jeremy started as Annie tried to block out the distressed sobbing she could now hear coming from her mother. 'But I saw him die with my own eyes.' His eyes were welling up now, and suddenly Annie felt trapped in a bad dream. 'I was there when he took his final breath, Annie. That's why I'm here. There was something he wanted me to give you.'

Annie didn't hear anything else. Her head was spinning again – it was like she was standing on a merry-go-round that she couldn't get off. And then everything went black.

4

When Annie came to, she was lying on the sofa with her mother by her side. For a blissful few seconds she forgot what had happened and she was back living a life where Richard was on his way home and they were soon to be married. But then she looked over to her father's armchair and saw Jeremy. As soon as their eyes met, the cruel reality crashed down on her like waves battering rocks in a storm. Annie's heart plummeted to the pit of her stomach and she closed her eyes and wished more than anything that she could stay living in the world she had woken up in.

'Maybe I should leave.' Jeremy's words cut the silence in the room like a knife. 'I can come back when you've had time to take it all in.'

'No, stay,' Annie said, more firmly than she had intended. 'I need to know what happened to my Richard.' His name lingered on her lips as she realised that he was no longer hers. Her Richard no longer existed. He was . . . gone.

'If you're sure you're ready, I have a message he wanted me to pass on,' Jeremy said quietly, looking at Mrs Beckett for reassurance. Annie's mother nodded her head sadly.

'I need to know what happened to him first,' Annie said. She knew she was torturing herself, but she couldn't live the rest of her life not knowing. The truth was going to be hard to bear, but it would surely be easier than constantly imagining what he had been through in his final moments. She was certain her imagination could dream up a far worse end for him than he had probably met, which she prayed had been quick and painless.

'I think . . . it's best if you don't know,' Jeremy said. He looked terrified now and Annie felt for him. She knew that she was asking a lot of him. But she stood firm.

'Please,' she begged, rising up into a sitting position. 'Or else I'll always wonder.'

Jeremy looked to Mrs Beckett for guidance again. She took Annie's hand in hers and gave Jeremy a solemn nod, and after a few agonising moments of silence, he began.

'We were meant to be repairing and cleaning the firing trench, but it was one of the wettest days we'd seen. It poured all day and all night. The water rose steadily until it was knee-deep. Even at that point, Richard was laughing and joking.'

Annie smiled at the thought. One of things she'd always loved about Richard was his ability to grin through anything. Even when he'd lost his first job soon after they started courting, he had managed to laugh at the situation he found himself in and ended up turning it into a good thing when he landed a better-paid role just days later. He always said if you kept your spirits up, then good things would happen. That's why it had been so hard to see him so downtrodden on his first visit home after joining the army.

'So, he was happy despite the awful conditions?' Annie asked hopefully.

'Oh yes,' Jeremy smiled. 'I don't think Richard had it in him to be down for too long. He sometimes went in on himself, but I always assumed that was when he was longing for home, and for you.'

Annie's heart ached. She was so happy to know Richard had found his old spark again, even if she would never enjoy it again. She had seen a glimmer of it on the day he had returned to propose, of course. But they hadn't been able to spend much time together and they had been preoccupied during that short time.

'Anyway,' Jeremy continued, growing sombre again. 'Once the water reached knee height we were given orders to retire to our trenches. Richard had planned on writing letters home, but he'd spotted some barbed wire he wasn't happy with while we'd been in the firing trench. He wanted to stay on to fix it. I tried to talk him out of it as I didn't think it was worth the risk. I told him he was more likely to be taken out by a sniper than a Fritz managing to get through the gap and into the trench. I said he should wait until dark as that was when we normally did jobs like that. But he was worried we'd get attacked beforehand and said it was better to have one casualty than a whole group of us.'

It sounded just like Richard to put his comrades' safety before his own. Annie felt proud of him, but at the same time furious with him for not being selfish for once.

'I was going to stay and help but then I got put on sewer guard, so I said I'd meet him back at our trench when we were both finished,' Jeremy explained. 'Only, when I got back, he wasn't there.'

Annie felt sick. She nearly told Jeremy to stop. She was pretty sure she knew what happened next. But the little voice in her head reminded her that she needed to know for certain, and she looked at Jeremy expectantly.

He sighed before continuing. 'Lofty was nursing a leg wound so I went to find out what happened to him, and he told me Richard had been shot while fixing the barbed wire. He'd hardly made it up over the top before they got him, the ruthless bastards. Lofty went straight over to help him and they got him too. But the bullet only grazed his leg, so he managed to crawl back down without getting hit again. The officers ruled it was too dangerous to send anyone else over to help Richard. I begged them to let me try.' Jeremy was crying now, and Annie found herself sobbing, too. She could feel her mother shaking next to her.

'They just left him there?' Annie whispered in shock. She was devastated at the thought of Richard lying there all on his own and in pain. Worse still, he would have been a sitting duck for the German snipers.

'I know it sounds terrible, but what other choice was there? I was desperate to try and get to him, but I probably would have ended up dead, too. Those snipers were hitting anything that moved. I probably would have got my head blown off as soon as I raised it above the parapet. It seems callous but the officers were making sure no one else was killed.'

'You said you spoke to him before he died?' Annie's mother cut in. Annie was glad of the change in direction pulling her away from thoughts of Richard being left to suffer on his own. Jeremy looked relieved, too.

'Once night fell, we were allowed to go over the top and get him. I was so happy when he looked up at me and smiled – I thought he was going to be all right. He'd managed to get his jacket off and hold it against the wound to stem the bleeding. It was dark so I didn't realise how saturated his jacket was with blood until I touched it. That's when all my hope vanished. I don't even know how he was still breathing at that point, let alone smiling. But he knew. He knew he didn't have long left. I could see it in his eyes when he watched the realisation hit me. Even though he was smiling, he had accepted he wasn't going to make it home.

'We got him to the medical post where they made him comfortable, but there was nothing anybody could do to save him. He'd taken a bullet to the gut and lost so much blood already. I sat with him while Lofty went off to get him a sneaky rum ration. Richard joked that he didn't want to waste it – he found the thought of it pouring out of the hole in his stomach hilarious.'

Annie winced.

'Trench humour.' Jeremy shrugged apologetically.

'He started getting weaker as the evening wore on and, like I said, he knew he didn't have long left. Once we were on our own, he asked me to make sure I got a message to you. We'd both talked about writing final letters that we could swap to give to the other's loved ones if the worst happened. But I suppose his attitude rubbed off on me as I never got around to it. I felt like we would make it home together.' He paused and Annie saw tears well up in the corners of his eyes. 'I hadn't realised he'd written his letter until he handed me this.'

Jeremy reached into his breast pocket and pulled out a tatty-looking envelope. He held it out to Annie with one hand and used the other to wipe the tears from his eyes.

Annie took the envelope and the room fell silent as she stared at it in her shaking hands. She wasn't sure she was strong enough to do this right now. She was still reeling from the fact that Richard was gone. She felt as though she had lost a limb and now she had to find the strength to read his final words to her.

Taking a deep breath, she ripped open the envelope and started to read.

To my dearest Annie,

If you're reading this then I'm afraid the worst has happened, my love. Please know that I thought about you every moment I was away fighting this wretched bloody war. It was my memories of you and our time together that kept me going through my darkest moments. And there have been many of those.

I'm so sorry I didn't get the chance to make you my wife. I dreamed of having a family with you. Doing that would have made me the happiest and luckiest man in the world. I know you would have been the perfect mother to our children. It pains me that we didn't get the chance to make our family complete, but I'm grateful to you for making my life complete up until now. There has never been another woman for me from the moment I met you, Annie. Even if I'd managed to live to be one hundred, there would never be anyone else who could hold a candle to you.

Love and pain rushed through Annie as she took in the beautiful words. Richard had always made her feel so special. She couldn't believe he had managed to do it in his final days, too. Even in the midst of war his priority had been making her feel better instead of dwelling on his uncertain fate. Annie suddenly became aware of the sound of sobbing and she looked around, confused. Her mother and Jeremy were both watching her intently, concern etched over their faces. She realised with a start that the sobs were coming from her own mouth. She took a deep, steadying breath, wiped her eyes and got back to reading Richard's letter.

I've been so proud of your police work, Annie. I must admit, when you first signed up I didn't believe you had something like that in you. But my, how you proved me wrong! I'm so sorry for ever having doubted you. I've been able to tell from your letters that your confidence and self-assurance have grown by the day. Just ask Jeremy and he'll tell you how I was always harping on about what a great policewoman you are.

Annie found herself smiling through her tears and reached out to squeeze her mother's hand. She had been the one to push her into signing up for the WPS – Annie had been terrified at the prospect and very nearly didn't join the service at all. She remembered her mother's words: 'You have to remember that your future is by no means certain any more.' If only she hadn't been right. She'd give up her life with the WPS in a heartbeat if it meant having Richard home safe and their dream of a future together safely laid out in front of them. Annie turned the piece of paper over to reveal Richard's final sentence.

> *Remember, Annie, you were as good as my wife and I want you to remember that. I hoped to be able to give this to you on our wedding day, but if that's not to be then I hope that this small token of my love will help you remember and keep me close.*
>
> *Yours, always and forever,*
> *Richard*

Annie read the last sentence again and again, growing more confused each time. Finally, she looked up at Jeremy, her eyebrows furrowed.

'There's something else in the envelope,' he whispered.

She picked up the tear-stained envelope and peered inside. Her heart skipped a beat when she saw something glistening at the bottom. She tipped it upside down and a ring fell out into her palm. It was a plain gold band that took Annie's breath away.

'It was his grandmother's,' Jeremy explained as Annie turned it over and over between her fingers. Her whole body tingled as she thought about the fact the ring had probably been the last thing Richard had handled before taking his final breath. She slipped it straight on to her wedding finger. Her hand looked complete now. When they had first agreed to get married before Richard went off to fight, it had all been so rushed and unofficial that there hadn't been an engagement ring. And when he re-proposed there had been no question of a ring – where would he have managed to get one? Annie hadn't even been expecting to get a wedding band at their ceremony, assuming Richard would buy one when the war was over. It was enough to have the paperwork to confirm she was his wife. She was overwhelmed by the thought of him having carried this ring around for her. As she stared at it on her finger, she knew that she would never take it off. She was as good as his wife – he'd said so himself.

'He wanted you to be happy and to keep going with the police work. He wanted me to make sure you didn't give up on it after losing him,' Jeremy added. Annie twisted the ring around on her finger. She felt closer to him again just by touching it.

'I'll keep going for you,' she whispered as she stared at her finger. After a few minutes of reflection, she looked to Jeremy again.

'He died in my arms shortly after handing me the letter,' he said, quickly switching his gaze to the floor. Annie took a deep breath and nodded.

'I'm glad you were there with him,' she said before lying back down on the sofa and turning over to face away from him. She was desperate to read over Richard's final words to her over and over. She didn't want to do anything else until they were ingrained in her memory so that she was certain she could never forget them – or him.

5

Though it was mid-afternoon, Annie was lying on her bed. Playing absently with the wedding band on her finger, she went over the scene of Richard's dying moments she had conjured up in her mind through everything Jeremy had told her. It had been three weeks since he'd turned up at the house instead of her beloved husband-to-be and the scenario had been playing in her head on a loop pretty much constantly. She still couldn't believe so much time had passed since that terrible day. They would be entering October soon, which would mark a full month since she had been at the flat she shared with Poppy and Maggie. She had insisted on staying at her parents' house. It was so crowded here that it meant she was never alone. Even though she locked herself away in her old bedroom every day – which she now shared permanently with Maria – she found the sound of the constant hustle and bustle that travelled around the place comforting and she liked the fact that there was always someone around if she decided she needed company.

Maggie and Poppy had visited a few times – according to Annie's mother, anyway; Annie had refused to see anyone. She didn't even speak to Maria when she came up to join her in bed every evening. Everything from those first few days was a bit of a blur. She had a vague recollection of standing at the top of the stairs and staring down unseeingly at Richard's parents in the hallway when they had visited to break the news of their son's death soon after Jeremy had left. She could only remember being consumed with grief and rage for the cruel way she had learned of Richard's passing and being unable to bring herself to face them properly, instead retreating back to her bedroom and leaving her mother to speak with them.

She knew it wasn't Richard's parents' fault that she had answered the door expecting to find him and been met with the news of his death instead, but she couldn't stop herself from blaming them for not coming to tell her sooner and sparing her that dreadful moment. She knew she was being unreasonable: they must have been in as much pain as her at losing their only son, and it was possible the telegram hadn't even reached them by the time Jeremy had turned up at her door. But it felt good to have an outlet for her rage and grief.

Annie stopped playing with the ring. She could hear footsteps approaching her bedroom. Rolling over to turn her back to the door and face the wall, she prepared to send away whoever it was. And if they were foolish enough to bring her food again, well, they could come back later and take it away untouched.

When the door was pushed open without the visitor knocking first, Annie knew it was her mother. She had given up knocking on the door when Annie had started ignoring the polite gesture.

'Your friends are here to see you,' Mrs Beckett said gently, approaching the bed. Annie knew it would be Maggie and Poppy trying to see her again. Everyone else had stopped bothering, but those two kept on persevering.

'No,' Annie said firmly. Why couldn't they leave her alone? There were a few moments of silence as Annie waited for her mother to retreat. But then she felt her weight bearing down on the edge of the bed. Before she knew it, her mother was lying beside her with her arms wrapped around her.

Annie stiffened: she still wasn't ready to let anyone in and talk about Richard's death. That would make it too real, and it would mean people would expect her to start trying to move on.

'You can't keep putting it off, darling,' Mrs Beckett whispered into Annie's ear. 'Richard wouldn't have wanted you to carry on like this.'

The sound of his name jolted Annie out of her trance. She hadn't heard it spoken for so long. She turned around to face her mother and she was shocked by the pain that was etched across her face. 'I can't stand seeing you like this,' she told Annie, brushing the stray hair away from her face. 'It's time,' she added firmly.

Tears welled in Annie's eyes as she tried to imagine a life without Richard – something she hadn't been able to manage since she had lost him. 'I'm not ready,' she sniffed.

'You're never going to feel ready. But the sooner you get back out there and start helping people again, the sooner you'll start feeling better. It will take time, and it will be hard. But Maggie and Poppy are the best possible friends to see you through this.' Annie closed her eyes. She wished she could stay in her room with her memories of Richard forever. 'He wanted you to carry on with the WPS. Don't you want to continue making him proud?'

Met with silence, Mrs Beckett tried a different approach. 'Remember how scared you were when you first signed up?' Annie nodded. 'I know what's good for you, Annie. I pushed you then and it ended up being the best thing for you. I'm only doing it again now because I know this is what you need to do in order to heal. And I'm afraid I'm not taking no for an answer.'

With that, Mrs Beckett sprung to her feet and held out her hand to her daughter. Reluctantly, Annie let her mother slowly help her to her feet. She couldn't deny that her mother knew what was best for her, so maybe it was time to listen to her. She stood in silence as Mrs Beckett brushed her hair and slipped a dress over the top of the slip she'd been wearing since the last time she'd managed to have a wash. She wasn't sure when that was.

Walking into the drawing room, Annie felt a sense of relief when she laid eyes on Maggie and Poppy. In that moment she realised that the two of them felt like 'home' to her more than the house she was standing in or even the flat they all shared. She smiled weakly, but then she frowned at the expressions on their faces.

'Whatever's the matter?' she asked, looking behind her to see what it was that had them both looking so shocked.

'Oh, Annie, there's nothing left of you,' Maggie breathed, walking over and drawing her in for a hug.

Annie knew she'd been struggling with food over the last few weeks, but she hadn't really been keeping an eye on the effect skipping all those meals had had on her figure. The reactions on her friends' faces told her she looked quite different to how she had done the last time she'd seen them. Smoothing down her dress to take a seat at the table, she was startled to find her curves had all but disappeared.

'How have you been?' Poppy asked gently once they were all sitting down.

'I don't know,' Annie replied weakly. 'I can't even remember Richard's memorial. Was it a nice service?'

Richard's body had been buried close to the front line where he'd been shot, but his parents had held a memorial for him at their family church so that everybody could say a final goodbye. Annie knew that she'd attended but she had no recollection of any of it. She hoped she had made amends with his parents. She made a note to check in with her mother on that later.

'It was beautiful,' Maggie told her. 'There were so many

people there – he was obviously a great man.' Annie felt another wave of sadness hit her. Her closest friends never even had the chance to meet the man she loved. 'Irene and Jack send their apologies for having to rush off so soon afterwards,' Maggie continued. 'Irene tried to come and see you before they had to go back to Grantham but—'

'I wasn't ready to see anyone,' Annie cut in.

'It's all right, she understands,' Maggie said, her voice soft as lamb's wool. Annie smiled gratefully as Poppy handed her a tissue. It was only then that Annie realised she was crying.

'Sorry, I don't even know when it's happening anymore,' she muttered through her tears.

'Don't be silly, you've no need to apologise,' Maggie said, leaning over and taking Annie's hand in hers. After wiping her eyes, Annie looked to Poppy to thank her for the tissue and felt a sudden rush of guilt.

'Look at me breaking down in front of you,' she chided herself. 'Richard and I weren't even married, yet you lost your husband of ten years to this war.' She couldn't believe she was being so insensitive. Poppy had opened up to Maggie and Annie about losing her sweetheart at the beginning of the war soon after she had joined them in Bethnal Green. Annie could remember thinking at the time that she wasn't sure how Poppy was still going on after suffering such a loss – and wondering what she would do if she ever lost Richard. She had naively assumed it would never happen to her. Now she wished she had taken more time to prepare herself for the worst instead of burying her head in the sand.

'Nonsense,' Poppy said, waving away Annie's concerns.

'But, how did you survive it?' Annie asked. 'It's as much as I can do to get out of bed every day, and most days I don't even manage that.'

'I survived it because I had to,' Poppy said gently. 'I had no choice. He was gone and I was still here, and there were people relying on me. He'd been so excited when I started my training that I felt like I had to see it through for him. And do you know what? It was probably the best thing I could have done as it gave me something else to focus on other than my misery and grief. And every time I reached a milestone or helped someone, I thought about him looking down on me and smiling.' She paused and Annie wondered if she was picturing her husband's face. 'The world keeps turning, Annie, even if you feel like yours has crumbled. And you have to keep turning with it, eventually.' Poppy gave her a sad smile.

'And maybe it's time for you to get back out there,' Maggie said hopefully, giving Annie's hand a light squeeze.

Annie thought back to Richard's letter and how proud he had been of her work with the WPS. She didn't want to give it all up and disappoint him. But could she face putting the uniform back on and acting as if none of this had happened? She didn't feel as strong as Poppy.

'A patrol has come up with E division in Holborn,' Maggie continued cautiously. 'The chief there has accepted that some female officers might help ease the burden on his stretched force. A lot of his officers have joined up to fight and the ones left are so busy they don't have time to focus on prostitution and looking out for vulnerable women and children. Frosty called us in a few days ago to offer the patrol to us – the three of us.' Maggie had come up with the nickname 'Frosty' for their sub-commandant on their first day of training and it had turned from a joke into a loving nickname and stuck.

'Being a bit more central, it's likely to be a lot more challenging than Bethnal Green,' Poppy added. 'We thought the fresh start might be good for you, and we both really fancy a new challenge.'

Annie suddenly felt like she was the young woman she

had been when she had first joined the police, timid and lacking in the self-confidence to take on a new role like this. *Is this what grief does to you?* she wondered. It was like losing Richard had transported her back and erased all the self-assurance and skills she had built up since becoming a police officer.

'I'm sorry but I can't face leaving the house at the moment, let alone going out on patrol,' she whispered, staring down at the table. She hated letting her friends down, and she stopped herself from looking at their faces to save herself having to witness the disappointment she knew would be plastered across them both. She couldn't even think about how she was going to break the news to her mother. Maybe she could get away with keeping the offer to herself.

Back in her bedroom after her disheartened friends had left, Annie lay on her bed and played with her wedding band again. She imagined Richard in the trenches, telling Jeremy how proud he was of his fiancé for everything she was doing for the WPS. There was no way he would have imagined she would go to pieces like this and give it all up, she was sure. Before she knew it, tears were streaming down her face.

'I'm sorry, my love, but I can't do it. Not yet,' she whispered through sobs. 'I will make you proud again, I promise. Just not yet.'

6

Two days later, Mrs Beckett tried to get Annie to join her and her other daughters for a stroll around the local park, but Annie dismissed her as usual. Lying on her bed, she wondered when her mother would finally give up on her and found herself hoping it would be soon. Ten minutes after hearing them all leave the house, she groaned when she heard a knock on the front door. Her father was at work and she had heard her aunt and her cousins leaving earlier that morning, so it would be down to her to answer it. Annie's heart started racing as she thought back to the last time she had answered the door and what had been waiting for her on the other side. She had refused to answer it since, finding the memories of Jeremy's visit too upsetting to cope with. If there was ever a visitor while she was home alone, they were left standing on the doorstep.

Trying to calm her breathing now as panic washed through her veins, Annie decided to ignore this visitor like she had all previous ones. If it was that important then they would leave a note or come back another time like everyone else had. It wasn't likely to be for her, anyway; she didn't actually live here anymore, after all.

Just as Annie started feeling calmer, another knock made her jump. Pulling the covers up over her head, she willed the unexpected and unwanted visitor to go away and leave her alone. She had started thinking they had finally left when a third knock – more of a bang this time – rang out through the quiet house. Annie huffed and threw the covers off herself before sulkily putting on acceptable clothing and making her way down the stairs. Whoever this was, they clearly weren't going to leave her alone until she had seen them off.

Annie found she was too annoyed with whoever had dragged her out of bed to let the memories of Jeremy's visit shake her up again now. As she reached the door, she could make out official uniform on the other side through the stained glass. Sighing, she assumed Poppy or Maggie had come back to try and convince her to join them back on the beat. Why wouldn't anybody listen to her when she told them she needed time?

Annie yanked the door open angrily, ready to give her friend, whichever one it was, a short shrift. But she was left speechless when she took in the figure before her. She froze for a few seconds, unsure if she was in line for a big telling-off, but then Frosty's stern expression softened into a smile and Annie relaxed a little.

'Good morning, sir,' Annie said formally, instinctively straightening her back. 'Would you like to come in?'

'First of all, there's no need to call me "sir" when you're off-duty,' Frosty said firmly but kindly. 'And, second of all, we're well into the afternoon now, Annie. My goodness, when your friends said you were in need of a gentle nudge, I didn't realise things would be quite this bad.' She stepped in past Annie, who was flushing red with embarrassment, and saw herself into the sitting room. 'I'll have a cup of tea, thank you,' Frosty called back as Annie closed the front door and rushed in after her.

Annie shuffled off into the kitchen, silently cursing her friends' interference and feeling mortified at her slip-up in front of Frosty. What must she think of her answering the door in such a state and thinking it was still morning when it was the middle of the day? Annie ran her fingers through her hair in an effort to make it look presentable and tapped her cheeks to try and get some colour into them while she waited for the water for the tea to boil on the stove. When she joined Frosty in the sitting room, the older woman was sitting on Annie's father's favourite armchair, admiring a framed photograph of Richard and Annie together. Her mother had insisted on keeping the thing out since Richard's death despite her daughter's protestations, and Annie's heart sunk as she saw it in Frosty's hands.

'He was a very handsome man, and from what I hear he adored you,' Frosty said softly, placing the frame back on the windowsill then turning to face Annie.

Annie smiled sadly as she laid the tea out on the coffee table and sat down on the sofa opposite her superior. Was she still her superior? Perhaps she was here to tell her not to bother coming back to the WPS. It wouldn't surprise her; it was an extremely professional organisation and she had just dropped her role without informing anybody. She had assumed her friends would update all the relevant people for her but still, that wasn't very mature of her.

And now she thought about it, somebody as strong and independent as Frosty was probably disgusted at the pathetic way Annie had reacted to her fiancé's death. Shame hovered over her like a dark cloud as she thought back over the last few weeks. Just look at Poppy! Now, that was the way a proper recruit dealt with grief. Annie wondered if she should save Frosty the bother of trying to break the news to her that they were letting her go and tell her she wanted to quit right now.

'You're doing well,' Frosty said. Annie couldn't help but scrunch up her forehead in confusion. 'I expect you thought I was here to reprimand you,' Frosty said, laughing gently. Even though she was smiling, her stern demeanour was still shining through and Annie found herself confused and unsure how to react.

'Well, yes,' Annie replied cautiously.

'I didn't get out of bed for six weeks when my sister died. And here you are, answering the door to an unexpected guest and making me tea,' Frosty said. Annie squirmed when she thought back to her original plan of ignoring the knock at the door. 'It may have taken a few attempts to get you down here, but my perseverance paid off,' Frosty continued as if she were reading Annie's mind.

'Six weeks?' Annie asked, pouring out their tea. Frosty nodded. 'But, how could somebody like you let losing someone affect you for so long?' she asked. She was genuinely astonished at the thought.

'Grief affects different people in different ways,' Frosty said matter-of-factly. 'Just because I don't show a lot of emotion in my day-to-day life, and especially in my professional role, doesn't mean to say I don't have feelings like everybody else. In the same vein, someone sensitive who gets upset at the littlest things in everyday life may well be able to carry on regardless when something big happens, like the death of a loved one. It can affect us all differently and there is no way of knowing which way you'll go until it happens to you.'

Annie pondered Frosty's words while she sipped her tea. She felt better knowing that someone like her, with her imposing presence and strong personality, had suffered like she had after losing someone – suffered more, even.

'I lost my sister a couple of months before we set up the WPS,' Frosty went on. 'Sally and I had lived together all our adult lives and I was lost when she died. She had been ill for quite some time and I'd known it was coming, but that didn't ease the shock when it happened.' She paused to take a sip of tea before continuing. 'It was a good job everything was happening with the WPS, to be honest, because it gave me a reason to rise up out of the grief in the end. When we were suffragettes, Sally's main passion and focus was on combatting the white slave trade, and this was my chance to carry on her good work – along with all the other aims of the WPS, of course. If I hadn't had it to focus on, I'm not sure how much longer it would have taken me to get back out into the world.'

Annie was dismayed. She had been one of the first sets of recruits to go through the training process, meaning Frosty had been fresh out of her bed of grief when she'd met her, Maggie and Irene. Annie would never have guessed Frosty was struggling with such a big loss at the time.

'I found that by helping so many women better themselves and giving them the skills to protect our streets just as well as any man can do, I felt a lot better than when I had simply sat around pining for Sally,' Frosty explained. 'I felt like I was part of something even bigger than my grief. Every time I wanted to give up I thought about how Sally would have loved to have been doing it herself, and that pushed me through. It felt good to get patrols out at the big train stations to look out for the refugees coming in and help get them to the dispersal centres before the awful white slavers got them in their clutches – and in time, Sally's passion became mine.'

Annie thought back to the man who had thrown Maggie in front of a moving car all those months ago . . .

'I was pleasantly surprised when you and your friends entered the process,' Frosty continued, snapping Annie back to the present and wiping the horrible memories of Maggie's attack from her thoughts. 'It was wonderful to watch you come out of your shell. And Maggie reminded me of a younger version of Sally, and it made me happy to see her tackling all the training head-on.'

She was smiling to herself now, as if conjuring up a picture of her sister in her mind. Annie wondered when she would be able to smile when she thought of Richard instead of being overcome with sadness.

'Anyway, I suppose I wanted to let you know that there is a great opportunity waiting for you in Holborn, with two very supportive friends. More and more chief constables are coming around to the idea of our patrols and this is an important patch, so I want to make sure I send a good team. I need to be confident they can prove we're worth having around. You're a good recruit, Annie, and I have faith that this challenge will help you overcome your grief.'

Annie avoided Frosty's gaze. She was flattered, but not convinced. Frosty was a stronger woman than she was. How could she be sure that she would feel better by getting back out on patrol?

'I know it doesn't feel like it now, but once you have something else to focus on, the pain will start fading,' Frosty said, watching the unsure expression on Annie's face. 'And there could be more opportunities after this. I'm sure you've heard about the deal we've struck with the munitions factories? We're sending more and more recruits to police the workers there.' She paused for a moment before continuing, 'The pain of losing him will never go completely, that much I can promise you. I still think of Sally every day and I hate that she's not here. But it will get better.'

Annie finally met Frosty's eyes and saw in them a vulnerability that she would never have dreamed existed. But was she as strong as her?

'I can't seem to think of a life without Richard in it, let alone live one,' Annie admitted as tears welled in her eyes again.

'You're already living that life,' Frosty replied. Her tone was back to its usual firmness and the switch in demeanour caught Annie off-guard. 'You need to decide if you're going to waste it languishing in your childhood bedroom and wishing he was still here, or accept that he's gone and live it to the full and make him proud of you. Either way, you're still here and he's not and nothing you do can change that.'

Annie felt strangely lifted by the forceful tone of Frosty's voice. Everyone else had been tiptoeing around her and indulging her need to take her time with her grief, but Frosty's refreshing frankness made Annie realise that she at least needed to try to find meaning in her life again.

Something had snapped inside of her and she was desperate to stop feeling so sad all the time. 'You're right,' she said with a confidence that left her shocked. It was the first time in weeks that she had felt sure of anything. 'I don't want to waste any more time. Richard wanted me to carry on with the WPS, so that's what I need to do. It won't bring him back, but neither will lying in bed all day crying.'

'Exactly,' Frosty agreed, bestowing on Annie a rare smile. She got to her feet. 'I'll make the necessary arrangements and let your friends know. I'll send word to let you know your start date with the E Division.'

As Frosty made her way out of the room towards the front door, Annie jumped up and rushed after her.

'Thank you,' she called as Frosty let herself out. The older woman paused on the threshold and turned back around to face Annie.

'Be sure to take advantage of some home cooking before you come back,' she said, regarding Annie steadily. 'We need you back to full strength before you get back on the beat.' With that, she turned around and left without another word.

Annie stood on the doorstep, staring after her. Had she imagined the first part of their conversation, where Frosty had come across as so warm and caring? It was like she had spoken to two completely different women. But it didn't matter. Frosty had made her see that she needed to pick herself up, get back to work and make Richard proud. It was going to be hard, but with Maggie and Poppy by her side she was in with a good chance of success. And she had to try, at least.

A week later, Maggie and Poppy were back at the Beckett family home to help Annie pack up the few belongings she had taken with her when she'd left their flat ahead of the wedding. They weren't due to start patrolling in Holborn for a few more days, but the girls had convinced Annie to come back early and join them on their final shift in Bethnal Green. Annie hadn't been keen at first as she had been looking forward to the fresh start on a new patch – somewhere where nobody knew about her dead fiancé. But when her friends had told her how many of the locals had been asking after her, she had to relent. She would have felt terrible leaving without saying goodbye to the people who had made them feel so welcome.

There wasn't much to pack – she had lived in bed clothes for most of her time away – so they were finished quickly. Poppy looked around the bedroom awkwardly when Annie picked up her bag ready to leave.

'What's the matter?' Annie asked her.

'Well, it's just . . .' Poppy started. 'We didn't pack much and I just . . . I don't know. I wondered . . .'

'What are you doing about your wedding dress?' Maggie cut in. Poppy looked over at her gratefully.

'Should we be taking it with us?' Poppy added cautiously.

'I don't think so,' Annie said, suddenly deflated as her thoughts switched from an exciting new start back to the loss of Richard. She rubbed her wedding band before continuing. 'My mother put it in her wardrobe after Jeremy left and we haven't spoken about it since. I can't bring myself to look at it. I'm not entirely sure what I should do with it.'

'Don't worry,' Poppy said, putting a comforting arm around her shoulder. 'I'm sure your mother will keep hold of it for as long as you need her to. She won't do anything with it until you ask her to – if you get to the point where you're ready for that.'

'I'd dreamed of holding on to it for our first-born's christening. I wanted to make a smaller gown out of the material,' Annie confessed. Poppy squeezed her shoulder lightly. 'It's all right, I'm not upset,' Annie assured her. 'I feel stronger already and it's nice to talk about it instead of keeping it in my head.'

'We're always happy to listen,' Maggie said, and Poppy nodded fervently in agreement.

'Right, let's get you home!' Poppy declared in a determinedly cheery voice, and they set off down the stairs to bid farewell to Annie's family.

As Annie hugged her mother, she felt proud of herself. A week ago she had felt destined to live out her days as a sad 'widow' in her childhood bedroom while everyone else moved on with their lives. She still missed Richard intensely, but she knew now that pining for him wasn't doing her any good. Her still-frail frame was proof of that. She had tried to start eating properly again after Frosty's advice, but she couldn't seem to handle much before feeling sick. Grief seemed to be making her feel constantly nauseous.

Making her way back to the flat with Maggie and Poppy, Annie felt ready for this new chapter in her life. She gave her wedding band a comforting rub and smiled to herself before linking arms with each of her friends.

7

The following day, Annie felt a mix of nerves and excitement as she got ready to head into Bethnal Green with Poppy and Maggie for their afternoon shift. She had been away for so long she worried she might have forgotten how to be a WPS recruit. But as soon as they got off the bus and the station came into sight, she relaxed and felt like one of the team again. When she spotted Witchy – an officer nicknamed so by the girls because of his pointy nose and nasty demeanour – sneering at them from behind the reception desk, she had to laugh to herself.

'I definitely feel at home now I've had a Witchy glare,' she whispered to her friends as they approached the desk. Witchy was one of the officers who still hadn't accepted the girls despite the fact they had proved themselves by solving the burglary case and helping so many other people in the area. Instead of letting his terrible attitude get them down, they joked about it. Maggie always said that they could save Witchy from a burning building and he would still insist that they weren't cut out for police work.

'Don't think you can slack off today just because it's your last patrol here,' Witchy snapped as they reached him. They all gave a curt nod and walked straight past him. 'And make sure you're back here on time this evening,' he shouted down the corridor after them. 'The chief has paperwork for you to sign before you can go!'

Being the only women at the station, the girls had a small

room they were allowed to use to get changed into their uniform. Annie wondered if they would be afforded the same luxury at their new station, or if they would have to make do with getting changed in the lavatory as they had done when they had first arrived here.

'I thought Witchy might at least wish us well,' she grumbled once they were in their room with the door closed.

'Oh, just ignore the miserable so-and-so,' Maggie replied, shrugging her shoulders. 'Once we're gone, he'll have to deal with all the drunkenness and shenanigans until they send replacements, then maybe he'll finally appreciate how hard we've been working all this time.'

'But that doesn't help us now,' Annie huffed.

'No, but it will hopefully mean he'll go a little easier on whoever's stationed here next,' Poppy said.

'I wouldn't count on it,' Annie sighed. She was putting on her uniform now, and she was shocked at how it hung off her slight frame. Suddenly, Witchy's stinking attitude didn't seem like such a big issue to her.

'I'm sure Florence could take that in for you if we can work out a way to get it to her without my father knowing,' Maggie offered, looking Annie up and down with concern on her face. Since her abusive father had thrown her out of the family home in Kensington, Maggie had started meeting up with her mother in secret. Sometimes she also got to see the family cook, Florence, who was more like an aunt to her.

'Oh no, I wouldn't dream of putting you all in such a risky position,' Annie replied. Maggie was always putting her friends before herself and Annie felt lucky to have such a selfless companion. 'Besides, I'll soon be back to my best,' she added determinedly. This frail frame didn't feel right on her. She had always been on the larger side and had always rather resented the fact, but now they were gone she realised that she missed her curves. Being like this reminded her of the darkest days of the grief she had endured after Richard's death. Although the loss still gaped within her like a chasm, she was determined to move past it, and she wanted her body back to the way it had been when she was happy.

'Well, if you're sure . . .' Maggie replied, sounding unconvinced.

'Leave the poor girl alone,' Poppy chided affectionately. 'She just needs some decent meals inside her to get her back to good health. I'll take care of that, don't you worry.'

Annie gave her friends a grateful smile. Poppy fitted in so well with Maggie and Annie that she sometimes forgot she was a good ten years older than them. She was only reminded of the age gap when she showed her maternal side like this.

Once they were all ready, they headed out on their Bethnal Green beat for the final time. They decided to visit the Boundary Estate first. It had been the main focus of their patrols and they had got to know a number of the families well because the mothers tended to call on them to guide their children in the right direction. With so many men off training or fighting, and the sense of freedom that a lack of male presence in the household led to, a lot of the women on the estate were struggling to keep their little ones in check. They had also found a great many of the local women, young and old, were overwhelmed with gratitude towards the soldiers when they returned home on leave – and in this area in particular, the women didn't have anything to give to show that appreciation apart from themselves. And then there were others who were desperate to make a living in the only way they knew how and saw the lonely soldiers with their pay burning holes in their pockets as the perfect source for their soliciting.

Annie, Maggie and Poppy were always sympathetic towards the prostitutes. They would never judge anybody for selling their bodies to survive and they weren't there to punish the women. Their role was simply to warn them of the risks of their activities and move them on before the real police caught up with them and arrested them. They also tended to try to educate the soldiers on the dangers of paying for sex, especially now that venereal diseases were putting so many members of the army out of action for months at a time.

The Boundary Estate was Annie's favourite part of their patrol. A big slum called the Old Nichol had been demolished around twenty years before to make way for a host of red-brick tenement blocks. It had taken the girls quite some time to get to grips with the estate, as every tree-lined street and building looked the same. But they had put together a map and over time built up good relationships with a great number of the tenants.

As they entered the first street, it struck Annie how much had changed since she had last been on patrol. Now they were into October, the leaves on the trees had started to turn brown and fall away. A whole new season had started while she had been hiding away at her parents' home. She noticed, too, that the atmosphere on the estate felt a little more subdued than when she had last visited. The British Army had lost fifty thousand troops in the Battle of Loos at the end of September, and many of the families here were anxiously awaiting news of their loved ones. It broke Annie's heart to think about all those people going through the same devastation and heartbreak that she was. Just like her, they wouldn't get a chance to say a proper goodbye. She was grateful every day that Richard had written her a letter from the trenches. At least she would always have that, as well as his wedding band.

The girls wanted to visit Sal first, as she was going to be the hardest person to say goodbye to. As the matron's assistant at the estate's central laundry, Sal seemed to know everyone and always had a fresh piece of information for the girls when they dropped by to see her. Annie had grown to love her rough-and-ready personality and she always looked forward to a chat with her and her assistant Mary, who Sal had taken in when the girls had asked for help in getting her away from a life of prostitution. They took along some jellied eels for Sal every now and then as the kind-hearted gossip tended to reveal more if she was devouring her favourite snack. They weren't supposed to carry anything while they were on duty, especially not packages of jellied eels, but they always felt like Sal was worth taking the risk for, and today was no exception.

'Awwww, me favourite girls! What will I do without these regular treats?' Sal boomed as they approached her standing outside the laundry in the weak, early October sunshine. It was decidedly chilly so she had a shawl on over her uniform of a long black skirt and white blouse. She was clutching a mug of warm tea, as she always did on her breaks. 'Mary! Make another pot up!' she yelled through the open window she was stood next to.

'Don't worry, we've told one of the men at the station to let the next lot of recruits know about your love for jellied eels,' Poppy said as she handed over the package to Sal, who was beaming at the sight of it. Poppy had told Annie the night before that she'd had a talk with Frank, the only officer who had welcomed them when they had first arrived and went on to have a short-lived courtship with Irene before her move up north. Poppy and Maggie had made sure he had an extensive list of all their best contacts and the places that needed the most patrolling.

'Always looking out for me, you girls,' Sal replied gratefully as she unwrapped the brown paper and immediately started guzzling her snack. 'Arthur's due along any minute. When I told him it was your last shift this afternoon he insisted on popping over every couple of hours to make sure he got to see you. We knew you'd come by at some point.'

'Oh, it'll be lovely to see him,' Annie said, catching Sal's eye for the first time. She noticed the sympathy pass over the older woman's face straight away and it made her heart sink. She wondered when people would stop feeling sorry for her and thinking of her as 'Annie the war widow'. How was she supposed to move on when she was reminded of what she had lost every time she spoke to someone?

'How are you coping, love?' Sal asked. Although she sounded genuinely concerned, her mouth was full of slimy eels, so the question came out quite muffled. Annie had to laugh to herself and her spirits were immediately lifted. She would certainly miss this character. But she felt instantly guilty when she realised it was the first time she had properly laughed since learning the news about Richard.

'It's not been easy, but these two are helping me through,' she replied quietly, her right hand instinctively reaching for her wedding band on her left. She was relieved when Mary emerged with a fresh pot of tea and mugs for them all. As the subject naturally changed, she found herself drawn into the conversation instead of being stuck in her own head going over her memories of Richard. Although being back with the WPS felt tough so far, she realised that it was definitely going to help pull her out of her grief by keeping her busy and distracted.

Before long, Arthur turned up. The girls had met the elderly gentleman on their first day patrolling the estate, and he had tipped them off about Sal's love of eels as well as given them the idea of drawing up a map to help them find their bearings. He had grown to be a good friend since then and had sent them in the direction of grieving mothers and widows in need of their help, both practical and emotional, on more than one occasion.

'I was sorry to hear about your young man,' Arthur said to Annie once they had all greeted him. She nodded her thanks and looked around anxiously, willing somebody to step in and say something so she wouldn't have to talk about Richard.

'What have you got there?' Maggie asked Arthur, pointing to the piece of card in his hand. Annie silently thanked her friend.

'Oh, some of the younger ones made you a card to say farewell,' he said, handing it over to her. Maggie held it up. There were what looked to be three policewomen, obviously drawn by children, on the front. Annie moved closer so she could peer over Maggie's shoulder as she opened it up. The message inside read:

We will miss you lady pollies. Good luck!

A whole host of scribbled names and scrawls took up the rest of the page. Annie couldn't make out many of them. A lot were just squiggles, but she could picture all the little faces of the children responsible for them and tears clouded her eyes.

'They're all at school this afternoon, which makes a change,' Arthur joked. 'But they wanted me to pass it on.'

'We love it,' Maggie gushed as Annie and Poppy nodded their agreement. There were certainly some cheeky youngsters on the estate, but Annie had always found them to be good kids at heart. She was so touched at the thoughtfulness behind the gesture.

The group enjoyed a brew together before the girls had to head off on the rest of their patrol. Annie was desperate to spend a little longer with Arthur, Sal and Mary, but they all knew it wouldn't be wise to risk getting caught out on their final day, and especially not after Witchy's warning.

They managed to stop in and see almost everybody that they had intended on saying goodbye to over the course of the afternoon, and there were also a few amorous couples to move on from alleyways as the early evening drew in. They stopped off at The Lamb on their way back to the station and were happy to see the landlord, Bob, serving behind the bar. Annie was relieved when he failed to mention Richard or offer her any condolences. The pub was beginning to fill up as locals clocked off from work so Bob quickly wished the girls well and they went on their way, which worked out well as it meant they arrived back at the station just in time for the end of their shift.

'I suppose we'd better go straight to the chief's office to sign this paperwork,' Poppy suggested as they made their way up the front steps to the station entrance. Chief Constable Sadwell hadn't been very welcoming when Maggie, Annie and Irene had first arrived at Bethnal Green. But Frosty had made them all keep a diary of their duties and after seeing the first instalment he had warmed to them. The daily log had seemed to make him realise how hard they worked to protect the women and children in the area, freeing up his over-stretched men for bigger tasks.

Annie sighed. It had been a long day and her body was really feeling the surge in physical activity after spending so long idle and without proper nourishment. She was desperate to get home and get some rest. But when she looked up towards the reception desk, she gasped. All three of the girls stopped in their tracks to take in the sight in front of them. There were about fifteen officers stood in the reception area, with a banner stretching out between them all. It read GOOD LUCK.

As the girls tried to gather their composure, the group started clapping and cheering. Annie looked along the line of men and smiled when she saw Frank and Chief Constable

Sadwell grinning back at her. She was almost floored when she spotted Witchy standing in the middle of the crowd. He wasn't quite smiling, but the corners of his mouth were slightly upturned. All three girls looked at each other and started laughing. Annie assumed her friends felt as over-whelmed as she did at the unexpected display of affection.

'We wanted to let you know what a great job you've done here,' Frank said as the clapping died down and the three of them made their way over to the crowd.

'E division will be lucky to have you,' Chief Constable Sadwell added. 'It's no secret the men here were a little scep-tical at first,' he continued. There was a bit of a guffaw from someone in the back and Maggie laughed out loud and did her signature eye roll, but playfully. 'Thank you, back there!' Chief Constable Sadwell laughed, before going on. 'You've thoroughly won us over – well, most of us anyway! And we're looking forward to welcoming your replacements soon.'

The three of them made their way down the line-up shaking hands with each officer and thanking them for their good luck wishes. Annie noticed Witchy had disappeared by that point, but she still felt like his presence, however brief, had been a victory.

As they got changed back in their room, Annie felt a jolt when she realised that she hadn't thought about Richard since they'd left the pub, and although she was exhausted from her day on the beat, she was feeling something close to happiness again.

'Thank you,' she suddenly said out loud, making Maggie and Poppy look over at her in confusion.

'For what?' Maggie asked her.

'For bringing me back and making me a Bobby Girl again,' Annie explained.

'You never stopped being one,' Maggie said softly as she walked over and drew both her and Poppy in for a hug.

8

Two days later, the threesome set off on the bus for their new adventure in Central London. Their flat in Camberwell Green had been around five miles away from Bethnal Green Police Station, so they were used to having to travel in. The Hunter Street Police Station, where they were to be based now, was around the same distance away from their home, so they had no plans to relocate.

The moment they stepped off the bus, Annie was struck by how much busier this part of the city was compared to their previous patch. 'We're not that far from Bethnal Green, so I didn't expect it to be quite so different,' she muttered as they negotiated their way through the crowds of people.

As the girls followed the directions Frosty had sent them to help them make their way to the police station, Annie couldn't help but notice the impact the war had had on the area. Before losing Richard, Annie had been so busy with the WPS that she hadn't ventured out of Bethnal Green and Camberwell since joining and hadn't seen the changes the rest of London had been through since the war effort had ramped up.

It hadn't been as obvious in Bethnal Green as it was a poorer area but here, surrounded by businesses and important buildings, there were many more motor cars than she was used to seeing and hordes of smartly dressed women rushed past the group where once the streets would have been filled with men in their suits. Annie knew that women were starting to take on more of the men's jobs now – she had read in the paper that the Bank of England had recruited more than three hundred female clerks since August 1914, and over half the clerks at Barings were now women. She found that the streets here seemed brighter, somehow, despite the gloom of a war raging on all around them. She wondered if it was down to the rise in women in work, wearing colourful outfits so the streets were no longer saturated by the dull, black suits favoured by men.

The group also passed by a lot of men in army uniform on their journey. They knew from Frosty that Gray's Inn was being used to house and train hundreds of troops, and they had decided that was going to be one of their main focuses when it came to keeping an eye on vulnerable women and prostitutes looking to help soldiers spend their wages. But these streets were also being used by hundreds of soldiers passing through on their way back from the front line to get home and enjoy a few days of precious leave before returning back to the battlefields. Those men were easy to spot as they wore long trench coats and were weighed down with bags, hard hats and water bottles dangling from their backs

'It's positively heaving,' Maggie cried as they rounded a corner on to Judd Street, where the police station was situated. It had originally been built on Hunter Street – hence the name – but over the years further buildings had been purchased on Judd Street in order to extend the site. So, although the station's address was actually 53–57 Judd Street, Brunswick Square, it had carried on with its name of Hunter Street Police Station.

'As well as all the extra women going to work now, there's an awful lot more men on the streets in general,' Poppy commented as she stopped to glance over the directions one more time. 'The government has dealt with labour shortages by clearing out the night hostels and workhouses and getting everybody who was using them into jobs left open by men leaving for the front. Some of the workhouses are being used to put up Belgian refugees or as overspill military hospitals. And they're not sending men to prison for smaller offences now as they'd rather keep them working to help with the industrial boom.'

Annie marvelled at Poppy's knowledge. It really made a difference to be patrolling with somebody with more life experience than she and Maggie held. She resolved to engage more with the world from now on.

'This is it,' Poppy declared when they reached a large five-storey building made of red brick and Portland stone. It was taller than the adjoining buildings and the top floor was triangle-shaped with a round window right at the top, which stood out from all the rectangular windows throughout the rest of the station. Annie noticed Maggie taking a deep breath as they stood and took in the size of the building, which looked to her to be about three times the size of Bethnal Green Police Station. She was relieved that she wasn't the only one finding it overwhelming.

'Come on, you two,' Poppy said loudly, her voice full of determined positivity. 'I know we're all a little apprehensive about how we're going to be received here. But you both know as well as I do that we don't need approval from any of the officers to do well here. We've done the training and we did a brilliant job in Bethnal Green without a lot of support from our colleagues there. The two of you and Irene were responsible for that, remember.'

Annie nodded nervously. Poppy certainly made a good point, but she still couldn't help but feel anxious about what kind of reaction they were going to get from the male officers. She thought back to the hostility they had been shown when they were first stationed in east London and found her fingers rubbing her wedding band for comfort.

'You're right,' Maggie pitched in. 'We can do this with or without their support.'

'That's right,' Annie agreed, trying her best to sound like she meant it, but she could feel her legs shaking as she started walking again.

'Ah, ladies, you're right on time – that's what I like to see!' They looked around and saw a tubby man standing next to the reception desk, looking over at them. They walked over to him. Annie felt a wave of relief rush over her as he smiled and held his hand out to Poppy. Perhaps here in Holborn the officers were more welcoming. He was quite short, and Annie imagined he would only just have scraped through selection. It felt strange to be looking down at their superior.

'I'm Chief Constable Green. Welcome to E Division,' he said, shaking each of their hands in turn. There was an officer behind the reception desk who completely ignored them even as his chief welcomed them so enthusiastically. Annie found that his steely glare wiped out any of her fleeting confidence.

As Chief Constable Green led them down the corridor to his office, they passed a group of officers who all stared at the girls with passive faces after greeting their boss in passing.

'The lads will get used to you in time,' Chief Constable Green said, sitting down at his desk and motioning them all to take seats on the other side. He took off his cap to reveal dark, thinning hair. Annie thought she spotted a bald patch on his crown when he lowered his head to look at some paperwork before turning it over and directing his attention back to them. 'They've never worked with women before, so it might take them a little while to get used to you. But your commandant assures me you'll be doing your own thing, and I've talked to some of the chaps at your old station, who spoke very highly of you.'

Annie thought he must have spoken to Frank.

'We're very happy to get on and do our own thing,' Maggie confirmed. 'And I'm sure you're aware that we'll be focusing on the women and children in the area – looking out for the most vulnerable and keeping an eye on the prostitution.'

'Yes.' He nodded solemnly. 'I'm afraid to say there has been a boom in the last year or so and my men are struggling to keep things under control. We were overstretched as it was, and then when so many of the force decided to sign up to fight . . .' He shook his head, seemingly disappointed to have lost members of his team to such a cause. 'The women don't take too kindly to officers stepping in and ruining their trade, and the men have so much to do already that arguing with those harlots takes up too much valuable time. Then there are the soldiers who are desperate to let off steam with drink and . . . well, you know. But the public see them as heroes so as soon as my men step in to try and get them under control, they're harassed and heckled until they let them go.' His voice was growing passionate now and his chubby cheeks were wobbling. 'That's one of the reasons I agreed to get you lot in. I'd heard you're good at bringing it all under control so that my men can get on and do proper police work.'

Annie bristled at the comment, and she sensed both her friends doing the same. But they all nodded politely. This was the kind of attitude they had learned to take on the chin. It was much better to prove themselves to men like this out on the streets. And this was definitely somebody they needed to keep on side.

'Right, well, you have a big area to explore so I'll show you to your room and you can get changed and get on with it,' he said cheerfully.

'Oh, erm, will there be anybody free to show us around?' Annie asked. She thought back to the first day at Bethnal Green and how helpful it had been to have Frank showing them the patch.

'You're all big girls, I'm sure you can work it out for yourself,' Chief Constable Green replied. 'Just make sure you steer clear of King's Cross Station. My men have that area under control.' He was already on his feet and making his way around his desk to show them out of his office. Panic surged through Annie, but she tried to stay calm. Where were they going to start?

'What about our shifts?' Poppy asked as they followed him back down the corridor to a tiny, empty room where their uniforms hung from a hook behind the door – sent ahead so they didn't have to lug them home on the bus and then back out here.

'Do as you see fit,' he replied, shrugging his shoulders. 'Look, girls,' he sighed, sounding a bit annoyed now. 'Obviously, a lot of the problems you'll be focusing on occur under the cover of darkness, as I'm sure they did on your old patch. So, I imagine you'll want to patrol at night a lot, but I'll leave it up to you. I'm not going to be keeping an eye on your hours or what you get up to. As long as you help with the issues that we've discussed then you can do what you want, as far as I'm concerned. Feel free to ask my men for help if you get stuck or you need an arrest to be made, but apart from that, you're on your own. I brought you here to help me, not make more work for me.' With that, he marched off back down the corridor, leaving the three of them standing in the doorway to their room gawping at each other in silence.

Poppy ushered Annie and Maggie into the room and closed the door. They all fumbled around for a light switch but there didn't seem to be one.

'Do you think this is a . . . cupboard?' Maggie asked incredulously. 'They've stuffed us into a damn cupboard, haven't they!'

Annie's eyes had adjusted to the dark and she could see her friend shaking her head in disbelief. 'At least they've given us our own space,' she reasoned, trying to find a bright side to look on as she took down their uniforms and tried to work out which one was hers. 'We had to leave our uniforms behind reception and get changed in the lavatories when we started at Bethnal Green, remember?'

'I suppose it's better than nothing,' Maggie said, sighing. 'And at least they cleared it out for us.'

The three of them changed in silence, fumbling with all their various buttons in the darkness, and emerged from the cupboard squinting in the sudden light.

'Let's head out and take a look around,' Poppy said, turning to face the other two. 'It won't take us long to get our bearings, and we know exactly what to look out for. We can work this out for ourselves – we don't need any men telling us what to do, anyway. I'd put money on us knowing a lot more about how the soldiers and the women operate than any of them.'

'I think you're absolutely right,' Maggie chipped in, sounding a lot more optimistic now.

Annie couldn't help but feel buoyed up by her friends' obvious confidence. And she had to admit that it felt quite liberating to not be relying on one of the men to show them the ropes. She knew that they were more than capable of getting the lay of the land themselves. After all, one of the reasons that Frosty had sent them here was because they were seasoned recruits who she could rely upon to make a difference. They didn't need their hands holding like they had done when they had turned up in Bethnal Green fresh from training. This was their chance to make the patch their own and develop their very own patrol.

'I say we start with Brunswick Square Gardens,' Annie said with renewed confidence. 'We're right on the doorstep and I'm sure it's a prime location for soliciting.' She pulled open the door and strode down the corridor, and her friends hurried after her. All of a sudden, she couldn't wait to get started – and make her Richard proud.

9

Brunswick Square Gardens were surrounded on three sides by townhouses. Trees and bushes lined the gardens and there were groups of children playing on the grass when the girls arrived, despite the October chill. Maggie stopped by the signpost at the entrance, staring at the name and rubbing her chin with a thoughtful look on her face.

'Come on, daydreamer,' Poppy teased after realising Maggie had fallen behind.

'I knew it!' Maggie declared triumphantly. She clenched her fist and threw it in the air in celebration.

'Whatever are you talking about?' Annie asked as her friend ran to catch up with her and Poppy.

'This square was in *Emma*. It's one of the Jane Austen books that Irene left for me to read before she went to Grantham. Brunswick Square was where Emma's sister and her husband, Mr Knightley's brother, lived. I knew I recognised the name, but I was struggling to place it. I'll have to write to Irene to tell her that I've seen the real thing! It's just how I'd imagined, you know.'

Annie smiled. Irene was so passionate about books and she got so frustrated with the slow pace at which her friends read as she was always so eager to discuss them. She knew she'd be delighted to hear about this.

As they made their way around the gardens, people seemed comfortable with their presence, despite the fact that there had been no WPS patrols in the area before them.

'I expected people to be a little thrown by the sight of women in police uniform, like they were when we first arrived in Bethnal Green,' Annie commented when a gentleman passed by and tipped his hat in greeting.

'I suppose everyone has had time to get used to the idea now,' Maggie mused. 'There's been a lot of talk about ladies in blue, after all.'

'Plus, they've had National Union of Women Workers patrols around here for a while, although I'm sure they've been about as useless as they have been everywhere else,' Poppy chipped in. 'If they were any good, then the chief here wouldn't have asked Frosty to send us over.'

Annie quickly thought back to what she knew about the NUWW. She had heard about their patrols, but they hadn't come across any of them in Bethnal Green. She knew there was a great deal of rivalry between them and the WPS, though. One of the main reasons went back to when the WPS was first established – back when it was named the WPV. The NUWW had named their patrols the Women Voluntary Patrols and so their acronym of a WVP was so similar that the public, and the press, often got the two organisations mixed up. WPV recruits didn't take too kindly to WVP patrols claiming the credit for their hard work, and vice versa. That had settled down when the WPV had changed to the WPS, but another bone of contention between the two groups were their differing attitudes towards the future of the female police. The NUWW were clear that they only expected the WVP to operate until the end of the war, whereas the WPS saw their patrolling as a stepping-stone to women being accepted into the police force for good. Annie knew that the WVP patrols only worked two nights a week, which was nothing in comparison to the gruelling hours the WPS recruits put in across the country, and she thought maybe that was another reason why her colleagues looked down on them.

'I came across the WVP now and then on my old patch,' said Poppy, and the other two looked around at her with interest. 'They're happy to blend into the background. They don't want to step on any toes and they lurk on the sidelines. They're a waste of space, if you ask me.'

Annie thought that there must be some truth in the statement, otherwise why would they be needed here when the NUWW women were already in place?

'We might come across them at some point, although I very much doubt it given how infrequently they actually do anything,' Poppy added, her voice full of disdain. 'I'm certain some of them joined up purely so they could say they were "doing their bit" without actually doing much of anything at all.' They had reached the far end of the gardens now, and Annie noticed women in formal-looking clothes playing with young children on some of the grass in front of a rather impressive-looking building.

'I wonder if they're from that big building,' Maggie commented, and Annie saw that she was looking at the same group.

'I think that must be the Foundling Hospital,' Poppy replied, leading them over to one of the women, who had waved them over.

'They don't look sick,' Annie commented.

'It's a home for abandoned children and babies,' Poppy explained. 'They're brought in as babies and sent away to live with a nurse or foster family in the country. Then they're sent back aged four or five to live there, and they receive schooling until they reach fifteen.'

Annie thought it was a grand idea. One thing she had struggled with seeing since joining the WPS was the number of illegitimate children discarded by mothers too young or too poor – or too ashamed – to be able to cope with them. It broke her heart, and the numbers seemed to be rising recently. Irene had told her it was due to women playing away while their husbands were off fighting, and then needing to be rid of the baby so their scandalous behaviour wasn't exposed. It sounded like there was a lot more of it happening in Grantham, which was likely due to the army camp there. Irene had even told them about a poor baby she had discovered abandoned on a train.

'Ah, WPS,' the woman who had waved them over commented cheerfully as the threesome approached her. She was looking at the silver *WPS* lettering on Poppy's shoulder. 'My name's Sara. I was hoping we'd see some of you soon. It's about time they sent some proper patrols out around here.' She motioned to one of her colleagues and then stepped away from the laughter and chatter of the children and their carers. 'We don't like to talk about it in front of the little ones,' she said in a hushed voice. Then, once they were far enough away, she continued in a normal voice. 'There's a lot of funny business goes on in these gardens, as well as the others around here from what I can tell.'

'Well, that's what we're here to help with,' Annie said confidently. They were finding their feet already and she realised she was rubbing the wedding band on her finger again. *I knew you could do it*, she imagined Richard saying, with a big, proud smile on his face. She smiled at the thought and then pushed it away – she needed to focus. She tuned back into what Sara was saying, and she caught the fact that prostitutes tended to start hanging around in the gardens after dusk.

'The soldiers from Gray's Inn know where to head if they're after some company,' Sara said, raising her eyebrows. 'Thankfully, we have all the children inside for tea by that time of the day, but some of the women have started coming out earlier and I don't want the little ones to see anything untoward. It also means that these gardens are not a proper place for a lady to be walking on her own at any time of the day now.'

'We can keep an eye on things from now on,' Maggie told her.

'We'll soon be a constant presence around here. We can move the women on but once they get used to the fact that we'll be hanging around regularly, our presence should act as a deterrent,' Annie added.

'That's good news,' Sara said gratefully. 'Thank you so much.'

'Feel free to let us know about anything else you might be concerned about,' Poppy offered before Sara bade them farewell and made her way back to the group of youngsters.

'It sounds like we need to focus on all the gardens around here to begin with,' Poppy said as they continued on their way.

'Gray's Inn will be worth a visit, too,' Annie suggested.

'Agreed.' Maggie nodded. 'See, who needs a stuffy policeman to show us the best places to patrol? We've worked it out already!' she cried triumphantly. 'I bet the men at the station don't even realise what's going on round here.'

Annie thought she was probably right.

Over the next few hours the girls made their way around as many of the gardens in the area as they could, to help them find their bearings. They covered St George's Gardens, Regent Square Gardens, St Andrew's Gardens, Russell Square, Tavistock Square Gardens and Gordon Square. They also popped into Hotel Russell on Russell Square. Annie thought the building looked almost like a palace with its terracotta walls and fancy exterior. There were life-size statues of four British Queens – Elizabeth I, Mary II, Anne and Victoria – above the main entrance, and a marble staircase inside. After a quick wander around the reception and lounge areas, they decided they had nothing to worry about with the upper-class patrons.

'It might be worth us showing ourselves every now and then, though,' Poppy said. 'I don't imagine there will be any brawls or scraps to break up here, but just because the women we normally look out for would stick out like a sore thumb in here, doesn't mean to say that they might not try their luck.'

'Yes, I agree,' Annie said. 'And just because the men are fancier, it doesn't mean to say that they won't be tempted to spend some of the cash they have on a bit of fun. It isn't only soldiers who take advantage of the Toms.' Maggie got her notebook out and added the hotel to their list of places of interest, as well as its sister hotel, the Imperial, which stood on the east side of the square. Finally, they made their way down to Gray's Inn.

As soon as they stepped into the gardens, Annie was struck by the sight of the hundreds of soldiers lined up for drill practice against the backdrop of the stately big brick buildings that surrounded them. Maggie and Poppy had spoken to Frosty in a lot more detail about the area, and they had passed on what they had learned to her. Gray's Inn Gardens had been transformed into a barrack square when the 1st London Welsh Battalion, Royal Welsh Fusiliers was formed in the autumn of 1914 to recruit men for Lord Kitchener's New Army. They used the buildings as headquarters to raise the unit and the historic gardens and the ancient squares of the Inn were used for drilling and exercise of the battalion. As many as nine hundred would sometimes gather to drill and train. The 2nd London Welsh Battalion had been formed in early 1915 as a service battalion, and a volunteer training corps, Holborn Battalion, had also been established at around the same time.

'Let's try and find a sergeant to talk to,' Poppy suggested

as row upon row of men in uniform marched past them carrying rifles. They were all so serious-looking. Of course, Annie couldn't help but think of Richard. He had never really spoken about what his training had entailed, but he had been so excited to get started when he'd signed up at the beginning of the war. She hated the fact that something he had been so passionate about had ended up being his downfall. She wondered how many of these men would return home after serving their duty, and how many would be stuck buried under no man's land for eternity like her darling Richard. It still haunted her that she hadn't been given a chance to say a proper goodbye to him, to hold his hand or touch his face one final time.

'Are you all right?' Poppy asked, putting a comforting arm on Annie's shoulder.

Annie was pulled back from her own thoughts. 'I'm sorry, I was lost there for a moment,' she muttered, shaking her head lightly.

'Don't worry about it. It's tough. I couldn't stand the sight of soldiers when I first lost John,' Poppy said quietly. Her normal bright and confident tone had softened. 'Seeing so many in one place like this so soon after Richard's death is bound to be overwhelming.'

'I can't stop thinking about how many of them won't come back,' Annie whispered. Then she remembered Maggie's situation and silently scolded herself. She looked over at her friend, who appeared to be deep in thought herself now. Maggie's brother Eddie had been serving in France with the Duke of Cornwall's Light Infantry and she knew Richard's death must have brought home to her the very real possibility that she could lose him in the blink of an eye, although neither of them had brought up the topic. 'I'm sorry, I didn't think,' she spluttered.

'Don't be silly,' Maggie said with a false cheerfulness.

'There's no use trying to protect me from anything. I know how much danger Eddie is facing. I'm counting down the days until he's back on leave.'

'Do you have a date?' Annie asked, happy that the conversation had taken a positive turn.

'He's due in a couple of weeks,' Maggie said excitedly. 'I kept meaning to tell you, but with everything you've been through I wasn't sure—'

'I understand,' Annie cut in. She felt bad that Maggie hadn't felt comfortable sharing her news with her, but she thought she probably would have been treading lightly herself if the roles had been reversed. Then a thought hit her. 'Where will he stay?' she asked. 'I would imagine he's not welcome at your parents'?'

When Maggie and Eddie's father had thrown Maggie out on to the streets following her attack, pregnancy and subsequent miscarriage, Eddie had returned home from training to confront him. After years of putting up with the man's abuse, Eddie had bitten his tongue far too long and he'd finally lost his rag at the cruel treatment of his sister, punching his father in the face before returning to training. Neither Maggie nor Eddie had spoken to their father since the confrontation.

'Well, I was rather hoping—' Maggie started, before Annie and Poppy spoke over her in unison.

'He can stay with us,' they both said together, then looked at each other and laughed.

'Well, I'm glad that's all right with everyone,' Maggie said, beaming.

They had reached the officer's mess now, so all three girls composed themselves ahead of what they were sure would be a serious conversation. After knocking on the door, they were met by a tall and slim officer with curly black hair, who introduced himself as Sergeant Eccles.

'I hope you'll help us keep our men healthy,' he declared

after they had all introduced themselves. 'A man has needs, as I'm sure you understand, but there are ways of doing things and I've heard about some nasty diseases doing the rounds with the ladies of the night around here.'

'Are you doing anything to stop the men seeking out these women?' Poppy asked.

Annie had bristled at Sergeant Eccles' comments and she was glad Poppy had thrown that back at him. She was sick and tired of women getting the blame for all of this when there were always two parties involved.

'We have a curfew, but they're grown men,' Sergeant Eccles sighed. 'You try keeping a virile young chap who's been kept from his wife or lover for months and is fighting his natural urges from sneaking out and taking what's on offer down the road. It's a hotbed of immorality out there, I assure you. Add to that the fact that these men are preparing to go out and fight in a war that they're very aware they might not survive, and I'm sure you can understand that I need all the help I can get keeping them tucked up in their beds at night and away from temptation.' He paused to take in their distinctly unimpressed expressions before adding, 'Don't get me wrong – I do appreciate it's a shared responsibility and my men need to be held to account when they step out of line. But a lot of them are weak and they need help keeping on the straight and narrow.'

Annie had always felt strongly that the men who sought out prostitutes should take responsibility for their actions, but this sergeant didn't seem to be laying all the blame on the street women, as she found tended to be the case among the army and the regular police. He had a friendly air about him, and she found herself wanting to keep him on-side.

'Well, if you continue to do your best with the men, we'll do ours with the women,' Poppy replied.

'We only arrived today, but we've already got an idea of

where most of the prostitutes are operating,' Annie said. 'So, we'll be keeping an eye on them and we're happy to keep a lookout for any of your men skulking around the usual pick-up haunts.'

'Please do guide them back here when you come across them,' Sergeant Eccles said gratefully. 'As well as any that you find in the pubs who have had a little too much alcohol. Some of the more depraved women encourage them to drink, you know? And they're only too keen to dampen their nerves with strong spirits. I've had men return here robbed of all their money by women they had gone with the night before while in liquor.' He sighed and scratched his head. 'We've tried talking to the landlords about it, but I'm afraid they rather enjoy the income too much. I send some of my men out to round them up when I can, but there's only so much I can do. We have a war to try and win, after all.'

'We'll do what we can, and I'm sure together we can keep your men healthy – and sober – enough to make it out to France,' Poppy assured him.

'Thank you, ladies,' Sergeant Eccles said before shaking each of their hands and showing them out of the main door.

Making her way out of the gardens, Annie was drawn into watching the soldiers going through their drills again. She longed to see Richard among them. *What I wouldn't give for a glimpse of him, alive and healthy, right now*, she thought as she reached for her wedding band again.

'There doesn't seem to be many options for us when it comes to moving the women on around here,' Maggie commented, and Annie forced her concentration back to the job at hand. 'Maybe we can find some factories or small businesses that might be willing to offer them alternative work. And somewhere cheap for them to stay would be helpful, too.'

'I expect it will be more fire-fighting for us; moving them

on so that the problem is shuffled around rather than solved,' Poppy replied glumly. 'But at least we'll be slowing everything down instead of letting it continue at its current pace. We have to protect these women from themselves – and the soldiers – as best we can.'

10

When Annie's stomach started to rumble, she realised they had been so engrossed in finding their way around that they had completely forgotten to stop for lunch. She was about to mention it when it struck her that this was the first time that she'd felt hungry in weeks. She felt buoyed by the realisation, but guilty at the same time. Richard remained near the forefront of her mind, but she was starting to live her life again and she didn't know how to feel about that.

'I need to eat,' Maggie moaned.

'I was thinking the same thing,' Annie replied gratefully.

'All this walking and interaction has been good for you already,' Poppy said happily, flashing Annie a grin. 'Let's stop at a tea room and I'll treat us to a special lunch, to celebrate us being back together properly again and getting to grips with our new beat so well.'

'Oh, I don't know,' Maggie said quietly.

Annie knew she had struggled with taking help from her friends since her family had cut off her allowance. But both she and Poppy were more than willing to help her if it meant she didn't have to work herself into the ground with factory shifts as well as patrolling. Annie was lucky enough to have free-flowing funds from her middle-class family, and Poppy was receiving a widow's pension, which meant she didn't have to worry about money. Maggie refused to give up her factory work entirely, but her friends made sure they gave her a helping hand where they could.

'I'm not taking no for an answer,' Poppy said firmly, grabbing hold of Maggie's jacket and pulling her into a tea room. Maggie huffed and Annie followed them in, laughing. They took off their hats, sat down and ordered tea and sandwiches.

While they were waiting for the food to come, Annie started feeling nauseous. Maybe she would feel better once she had eaten. But when her sandwich was put down in front of her, she felt another wave of sickness hit her. She forced herself to take a bite, but she couldn't stomach any more than that. Finding she could only sip water, she apologised to Poppy and excused herself to wait outside in the fresh air.

Standing on the pavement, she felt slightly better. When her friends joined her again, she apologised to Poppy once more.

'Don't worry. It will take time to get back to normal after everything you've been through,' she soothed. 'And after all her protestations, this one was more than happy to wolf down your lunch as well as her own,' she joked, poking Maggie in the ribs.

'There was no point in letting it go to waste!' Maggie cried, shrugging her shoulders dramatically. Annie was relieved they hadn't made a big deal out of it, and she felt lucky to have such understanding friends.

That afternoon, they decided to do a round of the local pubs. There were quite a number to work through, but thankfully all the landlords were welcoming, and they all seemed keen to keep any illicit liaisons from taking place on their premises. Annie got the impression that they were happy for the soldiers to spend their wages in their businesses, as Sergeant Eccles had advised them was the case, but it was tricky for them to keep the prostitutes from tempting the men away once they were under the influence.

'If I try and say anything, they jump down my throat,' the landlord at The Dolphin Tavern explained as he poured a pint of ale. His name was Wilfred and he was tall and stocky with dark-blond hair. He handed the drink over to the elderly gentleman who was sitting next to the girls at the bar and rubbed his hands together, deep in thought. 'Maybe a quiet word of caution from other women would make a difference? The policeman at your station won't even try anymore. As soon as they go near a soldier the rest of the pub goes mad at 'em. Then while it's all kicking off the women skulk away, and I'm left with a near-on brawl starting. As far as people are concerned round here, the men in army uniform can do no wrong.'

The girls nodded in understanding – that had been their experience in Bethnal Green, too.

'And if I say anything, the women make such a scene it's just not worth it. I don't want to put people off coming in, do I?' It was clear he wasn't turning a blind eye to soliciting taking place under his roof; he really was in a quandry about how to stop it from happening.

'We saw it a lot on our old patch,' Annie told him. 'But you're right – the women do respond to a quiet word from us better than landlords or policemen. And we'll always be as discreet as we can, so we cause as little disruption as possible.'

'It will probably mean we end up escorting a few of the lads back to Gray's Inn a little earlier in the evening than usual,' Poppy warned.

Wilfred sighed. 'That's not ideal.'

'Do you want them fit and healthy to fight the enemy, or do you want them stuck here with hangovers and VD?' Poppy asked sternly.

Wilfred stood up straight and looked shocked. Even Annie felt a bit flustered by her friend's sudden change in tone. But it obviously did the trick as he threw up his hands in resignation. 'I see your point,' he admitted sheepishly.

'Wonderful. We'll be on our way, then. And we'll see you again very soon,' Poppy replied.

Stepping back out on to Red Lion Street, Annie was beginning to feel the strain of spending so long on her feet without any nourishment.

'Can we call it a day soon?' she asked meekly. They had been patrolling for hours now and she was feeling shaky.

'I think that's a good idea,' Poppy replied. 'We can come back tomorrow evening and make a start on advising the prostitutes hanging around all the gardens.

'You've gone very pale,' Maggie commented, rushing to Annie's side. 'You need to eat something, please.'

Annie nodded her agreement. She let Maggie help her over to a bench and she sat and waited while she rushed off to find her something. Poppy sat with Annie, who tried to stop her head from spinning. When Maggie returned, she was clutching a brown paper bag.

'Please tell me that's not jellied eels,' Annie groaned. She could feel bile rising up her throat at the thought of it.

'Don't be silly,' Maggie scoffed. 'I don't want to make you vomit!' She pulled out a small, hard, light green object. 'Suck on this,' she ordered. 'It's a pear drop. The sugar should help give you a bit of a boost until we can get you home for a proper meal.'

The sweet had a funny taste, but Annie had to admit the sugar made her feel instantly more energised, and the constant sucking seemed to take away the feeling of nausea that had overtaken her body. When the dizziness had subsided, she stood up slowly, and Maggie passed her another pear drop. She smiled gratefully, knowing how precious spare cash was to her friend. She made a mental note to repay her generosity in some way soon.

Ten minutes later, they were almost back at Hunter Street Police Station. Just as they were passing Brunswick Square Gardens, they heard raised voices behind them.

'It sounds like it's coming from outside The Lamb,' Maggie commented as they stopped to try and follow the noise. They had just passed the pub on Lamb's Conduit Street and everything had appeared quiet and calm, but clearly something had happened. 'Are you all right to come with us?' she asked Annie, concern etched on her face. 'You can carry on back to the station and wait for us there if you'd rather?'

'No, I'll come with you,' Annie replied, already heading back in the direction of the pub. The pear drops had given her a welcome boost and now a rush of excitement was carrying her towards the commotion with no thought of the weakness her body had been riddled with just minutes before.

Approaching the pub, they could see a small crowd of people had gathered outside.

'Come on now! What's so interesting?' Poppy shouted in her most authoritative tone. A couple of people at the back turned around and when they saw the threesome, they tapped the shoulders of the people in front of them in warning. As the crowd parted, Annie could make out an army uniform and a police uniform. The soldier swayed suddenly to the left and two men leapt forward to grab him and hold him upright while the policeman staggered a few feet away. He brushed down and rearranged his clothes – it looked as though he had been pulled around by the crowd. He was red in the face and flustered, although he was obviously trying to keep an air of calm.

'Tell 'im 'e can't arrest a serviceman!' someone yelled as the girls reached the gathering. When the policeman looked up and saw their uniforms, he looked relieved. Annie wasn't used to that kind of reaction from officers.

'We'll get him sobered up and back to his barracks, or wherever he's meant to be,' Annie said confidently. The sorrowful soldier didn't appear to have any bags with him, so she assumed he was from Gray's Inn and not on his way to the front line or travelling home on leave. But they would need to get some coffee into him before they could get any sense out of him, to make sure.

'Well done, ladies. These lads need looking after, what with everything they're doing for us!' shouted a middle-aged woman holding the hand of a young girl from the middle of the furore.

Satisfied now, the crowd dispersed, and Maggie and Poppy took over from the two men who were propping the soldier up. Annie looked around for the policeman, but he was nowhere to be seen. She thought he could have at least thanked them, but she reasoned that he probably felt quite ashamed that they had been forced to step in. The public's staunch protectiveness over servicemen wasn't any good for the WPS recruits' relationship with the police force.

They stopped into a YMCA service canteen on the way to Gray's Inn. The girls had spotted the building earlier in the day and knew it was sure to become a regular haunt for them on patrol. The staff at the canteens were used to dealing with inebriated soldiers and a young man helped them get their charge into a seat.

'Two black coffees with the usual sober powder,' Poppy instructed him, and he rushed off to fulfil the order while the serviceman groaned and let his head fall on to the table with a loud thud. None of the other customers batted an eyelid – it was such a common sight. The 'sober powder' Poppy had ordered with the coffee was bicarbonate of soda. When she had first joined Annie and Maggie on patrol, she'd shared the trick with them. The concoction made a drunk violently sick, but it sobered him up enough so that he was able to reveal where his bed lay for that night. It meant the girls were able to guide him back to where he needed to be instead of dragging him between them all, and if he was meant to be at barracks it saved the soldier from a big rollicking for turning up blind drunk.

The waiter returned with Poppy's order, along with a big metal bowl. Between them, they managed to get the soldier to drink both drinks and then they swiftly guided him out on to the street as soon as he had finished. Within minutes, the cocktail had worked its magic. Knowing the bowl wouldn't be nearly sufficient enough, the group had left it behind on the table. As the man started retching, they led him towards a bush and then stood back as he emptied the contents of his stomach. Annie had to walk some way down the street. She normally had a strong disposition when it came to these situations, but today she was struggling. When she was certain he was finished, she rejoined the group.

'He's from Gray's Inn,' Poppy revealed, and they walked with him back to the barracks. It wasn't yet evening, so there were still troops out in the gardens being drilled.

'You're in for it!' one of them yelled as the group passed. The soldier had been ashen-faced and silent for the whole walk and he made no reaction to the comment or the jeers that followed. Annie heard an officer calling the troops to order as they made it to the officers' mess. Sergeant Eccles was still on duty and looked surprised to them again. Then he took in the sorry state of the soldier standing behind them.

'This one started early, then,' he said, his voice dripping with disdain.

'We managed to step in before he got himself arrested,' Poppy said.

'Thank you, ladies,' Sergeant Eccles replied, looking

extremely grateful. 'You're doing quite the job already. I'll get some extra cleaning duties sorted for this one as soon as possible.'

The soldier groaned and Annie had to stifle a laugh as they bade them both farewell.

Once they were finally back at the station, Annie noticed the policeman from the commotion standing in front of the reception desk. He had a thick, black moustache and a fat, round nose on which circular spectacles were perched. Although she had only seen him briefly before, his was a distinctive look and so there was no doubt in her mind that it was the same officer.

Annie braced herself for a nasty comment as he tried to cover up for the shame that he surely must have felt at having been saved by three women, but he avoided eye contact with them and let them pass without any trouble. She was just opening the door to their cupboard – they refused to call it a room – when she heard footsteps hurrying along the corridor towards them. The three women turned to see the same officer holding up his hand and smiling.

'I wanted to thank you for stepping in back there,' he muttered, looking around shiftily. It was so far from the reaction that Annie had expected that you could have knocked her down with a feather. Poppy and Maggie obviously felt the same, as they were both staring at the man, dumbstruck. 'Can I come in?' he asked.

'Yes, but we'll have to keep the door open – the cupboard doesn't have a light,' Maggie said sarcastically.

The officer looked uncomfortable. 'I can have a word with the chief,' he offered as they stepped into the tiny space and away from inquisitive ears.

'That would be most agreeable,' Maggie replied smugly.

'Look, I'm sorry I disappeared earlier,' he said. 'It's just . . . well, I'm grateful to you for stepping in – that crowd was getting vicious. But . . . it doesn't make me look very good, does it? Having to be rescued by three lady coppers?'

'We can appreciate how uncomfortable it must have made you feel,' Poppy said. 'And we're not looking to undermine you and your colleagues. But hopefully this has shown that the chief was right to get us in?'

'Oh definitely,' he agreed. 'I must admit, I wasn't convinced when I heard they were sending women over. A lot of the men feel the same.' Annie had to work hard not to roll her eyes, and she was certain her friends would be feeling the same. 'But in situations like that, you could be worth your weight in gold,' he added. 'We can't touch the soldiers around here. They have them up on a pedestal and they'd let them get away with murder as long as they were a member of the army. It makes it really difficult for us. But they don't seem so against you lot stepping in.'

'Hopefully we can all help each other out a little bit,' Annie said, feeling reassured by his words. 'I know you all think we're going to be calling on you to pull us out of demanding situations, especially as we're not able to make arrests. I promise you we can handle ourselves very well. But now and then we might need an arrest to be made, and it would be good if we could call on you and your colleagues with confidence.'

'Of course.' He nodded. 'I'll have a talk with as many of the other men as I can. I'll let them know how impressive you were today.'

'We'd appreciate that.' Poppy smiled, holding out her hand. 'I'm Miss Davis and this is Miss Smyth and Miss Beckett.'

'I'm PC Samuel Miller. But everyone calls me Miller,' he said. He stayed to talk a little longer, and he was impressed when they explained how they had sobered up the soldier before getting him back to Gray's Inn.

'You must be exhausted after all that,' he commented. He

was shocked when they revealed they now had to get back
to Camberwell Green. His reaction reminded Annie of the
fact she needed to get home to eat properly, and she willed
the conversation to end. She was beginning to feel weak
again. She rummaged in her pocket and pulled out another
pear drop as Miller started telling them about nearby quar-
ters for police officers. Apparently, there was accommodation
on site for a married inspector and fifteen married and fifteen
unmarried constables. The rooms were all on the top floor
of the station.

'As far as I'm aware, it's all full,' he added. 'But a new
section house was built a few years ago. That houses eighty
unmarried men at one shilling a week and I know there are
still rooms free since the last lot signed up to fight and moved
out.'

'Would they let women move in, though?' Maggie asked
doubtfully.

'It would be worth asking the chief,' Miller said contem-
platively. He rubbed his moustache, deep in thought. 'Would
you like me to suggest it? It would be the least I can do after
the help you gave me earlier.'

Annie thought it was a great idea. One shilling a week was
less than they were each paying at the moment, and on top
of that they would save on the bus fares to and from the
police station. Maybe Maggie could even be convinced to
give up her factory work if she could be persuaded to accept
a little bit of financial help from her friends. Annie's mother
had such a soft spot for her friend. She was certain that if
she explained the situation to her then her parents would be
happy to make up the shortfall. They were grateful to her
friends for getting her back into life on the beat, so maybe
this could be a way for them to return the kindness.

'Yes please,' Annie said confidently. She saw Maggie's face
drop and knew she would be panicking about moving too

11

That evening, Annie ate most of the vegetable stew that Poppy served up to her and Maggie. She even managed half a bread roll with it. She talked her two friends through her idea for making the lodgings at the section house work and, to her delight, they were both keen to give it a go. Maggie was reluctant at first, but Poppy firmly assured her that with the rent covered by Annie's parents there wouldn't be a lot left to pay out for – and she had more than enough to take care of both of them.

Annie was delighted Maggie would be able to give up her factory work. She hated how exhausted the double shifts were making her. They agreed that, provided they got the go-ahead from Chief Constable Green, they would stay on in Camberwell Green for another couple of weeks before moving. They wanted to make sure they had enough space for Eddie to stay without it being too much of a squeeze. They would have been able to make it work in the new accommodation, but in their current flat there was room for him to sleep on the sofa instead of having to kip on the floor in Maggie's room.

Annie felt a bit queasy again when she lay in bed that evening. She tossed and turned as she tried to get to sleep. As usual, terrible thoughts of Richard in pain penetrated her mind as she struggled to drift off but, in the end, she was so worn out from the day on her feet that sleep won, and she ended up getting a better night's rest than she had enjoyed in weeks. And she got to take advantage of a lie-in, too, because they had agreed to go in for a night shift the following day.

I'm sorry for not seeing you and Jack before you left. I had been so looking forward to meeting him. We're patrolling a new area now and I'm starting to feel stronger every day, she wrote in her letter to Irene that morning. It was the first time she had put pen to paper since losing Richard, and she was glad to have so much to update Irene on and therefore not to have to write about how she was feeling. She got so carried away that Maggie had to give her a nudge to remind her to get ready to head into Holborn in the afternoon. She couldn't believe she had lost a whole morning to letter-writing!

On the bus journey, Annie couldn't help but overhear the ladies sat in front of them talking about Zeppelins. It sounded as if there had been another air raid the night before. Before Annie had a chance to ask for more information, Maggie had leaned forward to request it herself.

'Oh, it sounds just awful,' one of the ladies said, turning around to face them. 'A whole family – mother, father and three children – were killed in their own home in Deptford.' The girls listened in grave silence as she explained that eighteen people had died in total. Annie was surprised she hadn't heard anything, even from their distance, but then she remembered how tired she had been the previous day and how deeply she had slept.

The three of them were rather subdued for the rest of the journey. Things like this brought the realities of war crashing home to them. Just because they weren't on the front line didn't mean to say they were safe from the Germans. And the same went for everyone they loved. There was an ever-present threat since the Kaiser had started sending the Zeppelins out over the city. And the three of them weren't able to run to the safety of a tube station or take shelter in a cellar or basement if bombs started dropping while they were on duty. They were to stay above ground, in very real danger, and do their best to protect members of the public. It was a terrifying thought, but it was part of their role, and Annie consoled herself with the fact that the Zeppelins were unlikely to attack two nights in a row.

At the police station, they were instructed to go and see Chief Constable Green as soon as they were in their uniform. It was five o'clock and he was about to go home for the day when they knocked nervously on his door.

'Ah, it's just a quick reminder,' he said as he walked off down the corridor and motioned for them to walk with him. 'In light of last night's air raid your commandant has asked me to remind you that you need to keep use of your torches to a minimum if there's word of another taking place.' They had been given electric torches to use on night patrols and they had come in handy in the parks and dark alleys the prostitutes liked to hang out in during the darkest hours.

'Yes, sir,' they all echoed together, and he gave them a smart nod before leaving the building. Following the first attack on London at the end of May, instructions had been issued on what to do in the event of a raid, but they were only imposed when a Zeppelin was known to be en route. All lights were to be subdued or dimmed, street lights were left unlit and the brightness of lights on trams, buses and trains were to be reduced or extinguished during a raid. Just thinking about it all made Annie anxious again.

'They won't be back so soon,' Poppy said confidently, and Annie hoped she was right. They headed straight out to the gardens they had explored the previous day, planning on visiting each one again but in a different order. They found all of them quiet and were wondering if their assumptions about how the women in this area worked had been completely wrong when they entered Brunswick Square Gardens and immediately spotted a young girl standing on her own. It had become dark, but they didn't tend to switch their torches on unless absolutely necessary as they found the approaching dancing lights gave people too much warning. Sometimes that was useful – it was good for splitting up a brawl or an indecent liaison without having to confront anybody. But tonight, they were keen to talk to anybody they encountered in the hope that word would spread about their presence and deter further inappropriate behaviour. Annie found that her eyes became accustomed to the dark very quickly now, so that she hardly ever felt the need for her torch anyway.

'Good evening,' she said cheerily as they approached the girl. The poor thing jumped out of her skin at the sound of a voice so close to her – she obviously hadn't heard or seen them approaching.

'Goodness!' she shouted, looking round and putting a hand up to her chest in shock.

'Sorry,' Annie laughed. 'We didn't mean to startle you.'

'Well, you ruddy well did,' she replied, regaining her composure and straightening her back as she took in their uniforms. 'I'm doing nothing wrong standing here,' she said defensively, turning her head away from them. 'You can't arrest me for taking an evening stroll. You can't arrest me, full stop.'

Annie sighed. Gone were the days when they could pretend that they had more powers than they actually did to try and get people to behave. They had to work harder now that everyone knew for certain they had no powers of arrest.

'You're right,' Maggie said evenly. 'But if you're hoping for the company of a lonely man then you're going to be disappointed. No one will come near you while we're around.'

The girl's head snapped back around to face the group. 'But I'm not doing anything wrong,' she spluttered.

'You won't mind us joining you on your stroll, then?' Poppy asked.

The girl's face dropped. Now she was able to get a closer look, Annie realised she must only be a teenager. Her heart ached for her being in this situation. She hated that they didn't have any way of helping her properly and all they could do was move her along and hope she didn't fall into the wrong hands.

'Please,' the girl begged, all bravado vanishing. 'My family have struggled so much since my dad died. I want to get a bit of cash together so my mum has one less thing to worry about.'

'And you don't think she'll worry about you being dragged into some awful slavery ring, or catching VD?' Poppy replied.

The girl looked away again. 'I don't have much choice but to risk it,' she whispered.

'What if we could help you find some work?' Annie offered.

'I tried that a few months ago, but I'm only young,' she said sadly.

'I'm not sure that matters much anymore,' Annie replied.

With as much manpower being freed up for the army as possible, employers were turning to children to bulk out their workforces. Few seemed worried by the fact they were exploiting youngsters and they were happily aware that enforcement of the 1908 Children Act, which tried to regulate child labour and prevent children working in dangerous trades, was now pretty much impossible. The WPS recruits had been instructed to turn to teachers and parents and ask them to keep a closer eye on their children. But parents were beginning to rely on their children's extra income, and schools were closing or operating on reduced hours, so teachers were often too far removed to help. It wasn't an ideal solution – and Annie knew she could get into a lot of trouble for encouraging it – but it seemed a lot safer than the alternative.

Annie waited anxiously for Poppy or Maggie to shoot down her idea, but she could see them nodding their agreement out of the corner of her eye. Encouraged by this, she carried on, 'You're best off heading home now as we're going to be around for the rest of the evening. But try some of the factories tomorrow.'

'Just don't tell them we sent you,' Maggie chipped in.

The girl sighed and walked away with her head hung low.

They spotted another figure in the shadows as they continued walking around the gardens, but whoever it was scarpered as they drew nearer. Out on the streets, they were surprised to find little groups of soldiers at every turn. They all seemed in good spirits, so the girls nodded hello and let them get on with their evenings, knowing they would probably be escorting a few of them to the tea room near Gray's Inn for a special coffee later in the evening. Members of the public seemed to react positively to the WPS uniforms, and Annie felt comfortable on their new patch even though it was just their second day.

'I honestly thought it would be harder than this, especially when the chief left us to find our own way around,' she commented once they had agreed to get started on public house duty. They were making their way along Eagle Street towards Red Lion Street when a sudden explosion of noise made them all stop dead in their tracks. It normally didn't take them long to follow the noise to its source, but this time was different. There was panic all around them.

'What's happening?' Maggie whispered. She sounded as frightened as Annie felt. Annie's hands started trembling as she looked around desperately, trying to work out what was going on. Some people were running out of their houses and pointing to the sky, while others were dashing past them, fear written all over their faces. Annie looked to Poppy, hoping for some guidance. She found her rooted to the spot, staring up towards St Paul's Cathedral in the distance. Annie moved her gaze in the same direction, and her heart caught in her mouth when she spotted the object that was making everyone so terrified.

Floating high over the historical landmark, silent and eerie, was a sleek, cigar-shaped silver aircraft.

12

Annie was mesmerised by the Zeppelin. She couldn't help but think of one of the science-fiction novels Irene had encouraged her to read. It was so different to the love stories her friend usually pushed on her that it had stayed strong in her memory. *The War in the Air* – that was it! In the book, Germany had dispatched a herd of airships in a surprise bombing raid against New York. At the time, Annie hadn't thought it possible that she would ever see anything like it in real life. She stood staring up at the aircraft in wonder, but she was suddenly jolted back to the present when Poppy grabbed her arm.

'We need to get everybody indoors,' Poppy instructed.

Annie nodded and her moment of fascination with the deadly Zeppelin was suddenly replaced by deep fear. 'They need us to keep calm,' Poppy said. 'If anyone is more than a few minutes away from home then we should direct them to Holborn tube station.' She turned to Annie and Maggie and looked each of them in the eye. 'You can do this,' she assured them firmly. Annie felt Maggie's hand in her own and suddenly she felt strong enough to face the menace in the sky.

'They're here again!' a small voice shouted. Annie spun around and saw a young girl standing on her doorstep, pointing up at the Zeppelin.

'You need to stay inside!' Annie yelled, running towards the girl. 'Quickly! Turn off all the lights and close the curtains.

Don't come out until someone knocks to tell you it's safe.' When she turned back around, she found Maggie and Poppy instructing passers-by in the same manner. A whistle started sounding, and a policeman cycled past.

'In your houses! In your houses! Now! Put your lights out!' he shouted in between long blasts.

A horrified-looking woman pushing a pram came out of nowhere and Annie was suddenly reminded of the nickname the Zeppelins had been given since a whole family was killed by one: 'baby killers'. She felt a sudden, desperate need to protect this mother and her child.

'Where do you live?' Annie asked urgently, placing an arm around her shoulders to try and comfort her as chaos reigned all around them.

'Miles away. I went for a walk to get the baby to sleep,' the woman whispered. She was so scared her voice was shaking and she had tears in her eyes. 'I didn't think they'd come back again tonight.'

'Pick up your baby and come with me,' Annie instructed.

'What about the pram?' the woman stuttered.

'Leave it,' Annie barked. She was determined to get them both to safety and time was of the essence. Her sudden change in tone snapped the woman into action and she scooped up her now-screaming child and rushed after Annie, who had started banging on a door.

'Can you take this woman and her baby in? And turn off all your lights!' she cried when the door was answered by an elderly man. He nodded and quickly ushered the woman inside before slamming the door shut.

'Take cover! Take cover!' Annie shouted as hordes of people rushed past her. 'Get yourself to the tube station if you don't live nearby!'

As the street suddenly grew quiet, Annie breathed a sigh of relief. She could no longer see any stragglers wandering around. She stood still for a moment and looked to the sky to locate the Zeppelin again, and she shuddered at the thought of the damage it could do. It was all the more ominous for the glacial speed at which it moved. She willed it to keep going, far away from Holborn – far away from anywhere containing innocent civilians.

Suddenly, she was aware of an eerie throbbing sound, followed shortly afterwards by the deafening sound of explosions. It was like nothing she had heard before in her life. The ground beneath her seemed to shake and she looked around frantically for Poppy and Maggie. As the sound of breaking glass reached her, she spotted her friends and ran towards them. It was only when she reached them and let out a sigh of relief that she realised she had been holding her breath ever since she had seen the aircraft in the sky again.

Before she could say anything, the darkness was lit up in flashes as searchlights hunted out the Zeppelin and guns were trained on it. The girls watched in awe as London's artillery opened fire. Annie felt light-headed with relief, thinking that this meant it would soon be over. But that feeling turned to horror when it became apparent none of the shots were making it anywhere near the deadly aircraft. Little flashes of flame danced around it, but none made it close enough to hit it.

All Annie wanted to do was knock on the nearest front door and rush inside to hide along with the occupants, or run to the tube station for shelter as fast as her legs could carry her. But she forced herself to breathe through her fear. She had to remain brave and check there were no more members of the public outside and in danger. Annie's ears were ringing, but with Poppy and Maggie by her side she continued along the road to make sure that no one was lurking about and putting themselves at risk.

As another throbbing sound penetrated the air, meaning that another explosion was surely seconds away, Annie instinctively grabbed hold of Poppy and Maggie and dragged them both into the garden of the nearest house. They crouched down and cowered next to the small brick wall, and she had never felt more vulnerable in all her life. She shook with terror as she realised that they may as well be stood out in the middle of the street, arms outstretched, inviting the bombs to find them, for all the shelter and protection the wall was giving them.

Waiting for the inevitable explosion, Annie squeezed her eyes shut. *Is this what it was like for Richard in the trenches?* she wondered as she reached for the comforting feel of her wedding band. Forced to sit and wait it out as all around him gunfire raged and shells dropped from the sky with nothing to do but trust that they would all miss him? It seemed so utterly hopeless. Would she end up dying at the hands of the Germans, too? Faced with that fate a few weeks ago, she probably would have shrugged and accepted it gladly – anything to escape the grief she was feeling. But something inside her now was willing her to fight back, begging her to make it out of this alive.

The revelation that she felt like she had something to live for again had barely hit her before another BOOM rang out – this one considerably closer than the last. Annie let out a yelp and grabbed hold of Maggie as the ground shook violently. Looking up, she could see debris flying through the air as clouds of smoke engulfed everything in sight. It looked as though the bomb had landed just a few streets away from where they were crouching. There were a few moments of complete silence before the guns started up again, continuing their futile attack as the Zeppelin sluggishly floated on.

Suddenly, screaming and shouting pierced the air.

'We've got to help,' Poppy said, rising to her feet and putting out both her hands to help Maggie and Annie up. Together they ran down the street towards the site of the explosion. Annie's heart fell when they turned into Red Lion Street. Although it was still some distance away and there wasn't much light, the fire was burning bright from The Dolphin Tavern and some of the surrounding houses – bright enough for her to know that the pub had been devastated by the bomb. Her thoughts went immediately to Wilfred and she felt a sick swoop of fear for him. They hadn't got to know the landlord very well, but the thought of anyone she knew perishing in such a terrible way sent shivers up her spine. She willed him to be safe.

When they got closer, she could see that the back part of the pub was still standing and was filled with hope that Wilfred hadn't been harmed in the blast. She crossed her fingers and made a quick wish that he and all his customers had made it out and found shelter in time instead of hunkering down inside.

'Over there!' Poppy cried, suddenly picking up speed. As Annie followed, she could see the shape of a body splayed out on the ground. There was a man crouched down next to the still figure. He looked up as the three of them approached.

'He's gone,' he said sadly. 'He was working on the gas lamp over there.' Annie followed his hand to where the stump of a gas lamp now remained. The poor man had been blown quite some distance. 'I was in the pub when the commotion started. I came past him to get inside my house and I told him to come with me and take shelter, but he refused. Poor sod didn't stand a chance.'

Subdued, the three girls turned back towards the pub and took in the chaotic scene in front of them. There was a massive crater on the ground in the street outside The

Dolphin – it looked as if the bomb had landed just in front of the pub.

'Where do we go first?' Maggie asked, all three of them watching as people stumbled out of their houses in panic and horror. There was already a crowd of people gathered on the street, and a handful of men were throwing buckets of water over the burning houses – though it didn't seem to be doing much good.

'Everyone's out of the houses!' one of the men yelled over his shoulder as he ran to refill his bucket. Annie looked over at a woman who was standing on the pavement, covered in a shawl. She was staring up at one of the houses, tears streaming down her face. Three young children were gathered at her feet; one of them, a girl of about four or five, was clutching on to her leg and shaking visibly.

Annie's mind was clouded by the shrieking and shouting all around, but now she knew that there was nobody trapped in the houses, she did her best to focus on the pub. All the windows were smashed and the entrance had been blown out, but Annie knew she had to get inside to help. Poppy had already walked around the crater and was making her way towards the rubble that lay in front of the bar, which was now visible from the street.

Another explosion rang out; this one sounded like it was a mile or so away. Annie shuddered as she thought of all the new devastation that was being caused because of it. But she also felt a tinge of guilty relief that it had moved on. She could still hear the guns shooting at the Zeppelin – it had become like background noise. A sudden panic flashed through her mind: now the Zeppelin was moving away from her, were her family about to be in danger? But she pushed it away. Now was not the time to dwell on it.

'I'd wait for the fire brigade!' someone yelled, but Poppy ignored it and Annie and Maggie followed her in. They picked their way carefully over the fallen beams and bricks and pieces of broken furniture. A fire was raging at the back of the building, and Annie felt the surge of heat as soon as she got close to the bar.

'We need to be quick,' Maggie shouted over all the noise.

'I'm down here!' Wilfred's voice came from behind the bar. It was a barely audible croak, and they followed it and found him lying on the floor, clutching his arm.

'Some shrapnel hit me,' he said, his voice quivering. There was a pool of blood on the floor next to him. Annie grabbed a towel that was hanging next to her and wrapped it around his wound. She heard a whooshing of water and assumed the fire service had arrived and started work on the burning houses.

'How busy was the pub when the bomb hit?' Poppy asked Wilfred urgently as the three of them helped him to his feet. 'We need to search for any other survivors before that fire gets too out of control or what's left of this place collapses.'

'I sent most of the customers home or to the tube station,' Wilfred said. He stumbled as his foot got caught on a chair leg sticking up from the ground, but managed to right himself. 'But Bob refused to go. Last time I saw him, he was standing in the doorway smoking. That was just before the blast. I loved that stubborn old mule.' His voice broke on the last word and Annie trembled at the thought of what must have happened to Wilfred's last remaining customer. He would have been in the direct line of fire, judging from where the crater was. She was relieved Wilfred had managed to clear the rest of the pub in time – it could have been so much worse.

'Are you going to be all right getting to the hospital?' Poppy asked him once they were outside in the street. The fires blazing from the various surrounding buildings had brought a flickering orange glow to the dark night. Normally they would have escorted him to St Bartholomew's, but it was a good mile away and there was still so much to be done here. Annie, for one, was eager to help the mother and child she had spotted outside one of the burning houses. She held her breath as she heard another explosion rocking the city.

'Over here!' Maggie shouted, waving her arms frantically in the air. A police car pulled over. It was filled with people covered in blood. All of them looked completely overcome with shock and they sat, wide-eyed, staring at the girls through the car's open roof as Maggie bent to speak to the officer behind the wheel. 'Have you got room for one more? He's lost a lot of blood,' she told him. The constable in the front passenger seat got out and let Wilfred take his place.

'I'll round up more casualties while you drop this lot off at the hospital,' he told his colleague. Once the car had driven away, he turned to the girls. 'Ladies, bring anyone in need of urgent medical assistance back to this spot. We'll drive backwards and forwards collecting them and dropping them off for as long as it takes.'

They nodded dutifully and made off in the opposite direction to him. The fire brigade had brought most of the house fires under control and they all appeared to have been relatively small. But one was still raging, along with the fire at the pub.

'Can we do anything to help?' Annie asked one of the crew. His long jacket was covered in dust and he looked exhausted.

'Take care of that lot over there,' he said, pointing to the woman Annie had spotted previously. She was sitting on the side of the road now, with her three dumbstruck children standing next to her as she wailed and rocked backwards and forwards. 'Her husband's in there somewhere,' he explained, nodding towards the only house still burning. Annie's heart dropped.

'I thought all the houses were clear?' Poppy breathed.

'They were, but the silly fool went in to collect some kind of family heirloom. Apparently, he thought he'd got the fire under control before we arrived, but the back of the house collapsed just after he went in and he hasn't been seen since. Now one of my men is in there trying to get him out.' He shook his head and walked off towards the fire engine, where an officer was aiming the water hose at the building. The explosions were moving further and further away now, and more and more people were emerging from their hiding places to survey the damage the Zeppelin had left in its wake.

'Let's get her away from here,' Annie suggested. She knew more than anybody that the woman would be desperate to learn what had happened to her husband as soon as possible – but judging by the state of the house, she was certain the fire brigade would be pulling his lifeless body out of the wreckage. It was bad enough for his wife to see that, but Annie couldn't cope with the thought of his poor children bearing witness to it.

'We can take her to the YMCA tea room, get her a strong coffee,' Maggie suggested.

As they approached her, the woman glared at them. 'No! I already told them, I'm not leaving until Geoff's out!' she shouted, backing away from them. Her poor children looked terrified.

'You can't stay here,' Poppy said, her voice kind but firm. 'Maggie, help me get her to her feet. Annie, you take care of the children.'

Annie rushed forward and put her arms around all three little ones. 'It's all right,' she said calmly. 'We're going to get you and your mother somewhere safe and warm while they try to find your father.'

None of them said anything but they allowed her to guide them off along the street. She made sure she stayed ahead of her colleagues so that the children wouldn't have to watch their mother resisting as she was led away. She hoped all the noise would drown her out so that they wouldn't have to hear it.

On the way, Annie had time to think about her family. There was a basement at home, and she convinced herself they would have all made their way there in time if the Zeppelin had unloaded anything near the house. She couldn't bear to think of the possibility that any of them had been out tonight and caught up in all of this. She couldn't deal with any more loss or with the prospect of being denied the chance to say goodbye to another of her loved ones.

The woman had stopped fighting Maggie and Poppy by the time they reached the tea room. The staff had opened up again and the place was filling up with people. Some had minor injuries while others looked like they were in a trance. A woman called across the room when they entered, and it turned out she knew the family the girls had escorted there. They handed them over to her care and headed back into the night.

Being so close to Gray's Inn, Annie wasn't surprised to see groups of soldiers emerging looking for people to help.

'A big one landed at the hospital,' one of the troops shouted out to them as he and five others hurried past them in the direction of St Bartholomew's.

Annie instantly felt bile rising in her throat, and she looked over at Poppy and Maggie who had both turned a ghostly shade of white. She knew they were all thinking the same thing: *Wilfred*. And that carload of people. They had all been making their way to the hospital before the next lot of bombs had landed. Putting the friendly landlord in a motor car to the hospital had seemed like the best thing to do at the time, somewhere safe where he could be looked after and his injury would be treated before he lost too much blood. But now Annie wondered if they had actually sent him towards more danger – and possibly to his death.

13

During the one-mile journey to St Bartholomew's, Annie thought only of Wilfred and the other casualties they had sent to the bomb-hit hospital. Incendiary bombs had been dropped at various places along the route without causing too much damage, but there were small fires burning at what seemed like every turn. Every time the girls spotted one, they slowed down to assess the situation. They were anxious to get to the hospital but didn't want to pass by anybody who needed help. On each occasion they were thankful to find police officers or soldiers dealing with the carnage and so they sped up again, focused on their final destination.

The guns and searchlights had all stopped now, so people seemed to be feeling brave enough to come out and investigate. More and more were emerging from their shelters, keen to seek out the blast sites and either help where they could or gawp at the damage. There were a lot of children running around, marvelling at how they had seen one of the 'baby killers' in real life, and Annie wondered if any of them realised how much danger they had been in only minutes before. The raid must have only lasted around twenty minutes, but it had felt like hours.

Once the hospital was in sight, the girls all slowed down. Annie couldn't understand it – the building looked untouched. She felt relieved but at the same time confused. They made their way around the side of the hospital and the further they got, the noisier it became. They could hear yelling and calls for help, along with the sounds of big objects being moved. Annie took a deep breath and then broke into a run again.

A massive bomb, along with three incendiaries, had landed on Bartholomew Close, which backed on to the hospital. The biggest bomb had exploded with such force that it had made an eight-foot crater in the ground and flattened the buildings in the immediate vicinity. One of the hospital walls had been damaged by the shrapnel and hundreds of windows smashed, but apart from that the building was untouched

From speaking to a woman passing by, they established that nobody inside had suffered any injuries. Knowing Wilfred and his companions wouldn't have reached this side of the hospital, Annie felt hugely relieved. However, taking in the collapsed buildings, crater, and ground littered with huge pieces of debris, she prayed that others had been lucky, too. Everywhere she looked, people were moving large bits of debris and checking to see if anyone was stuck underneath. She couldn't see anybody with injuries, which seemed unbelievable given the extent of the damage caused.

'I think we've got all the casualties,' a smartly dressed man said.

Annie looked up and found he was addressing the three of them. She wasn't sure how long they had been stood staring at the devastation in silence. The man was wearing a waistcoat and his long jacket was covered in dirt and dust. He even had specks of it on his moustache. He took his glasses off to wipe away the muck that was smeared all over the lenses. 'From what I can tell, there's no one unaccounted for. The buildings that were destroyed were businesses, so they were all empty.' He frowned at the dirt on his glasses, which seemed unwilling to budge.

'Has anyone been killed?' Annie asked.

'I'm afraid there's two men dead so far,' he replied grimly. He put his glasses back on – they were as clean as he was going to get them. 'It sounds as though they were leaving the Admiral Carter when the bombs struck. Most of the residents were in basements or cellars, thank goodness. It's hard to believe so many made it out alive when you look at all this damage,' he added before tipping his hat and wandering off into the night.

'I can't believe it,' Maggie whispered. 'Just look at it.'

Poppy put a hand on her shoulder. 'We have to keep going,' she said calmly. When she started picking her way across the rubble in front of them, Annie and Maggie followed behind her in silence.

Annie was grateful Poppy had taken charge. Everyone was working well together so soon after something so terrible had happened. One thing Annie had become aware of during this war was the fact that Londoners tended to stick together in such trying times and they refused to let the enemy break them down – even when everything around them was collapsed or burning. It made her proud to have grown up here. Her thoughts flashed back to her family again, but she shut them out of her mind quickly. There was nothing she could do for them at this moment, so she was better off training her energy on helping the people in front of her. She would check in on her family later.

Poppy stopped abruptly and turned to face Annie and Maggie.

'We'll leave the heavy lifting to the men and focus on comforting anyone struggling to deal with what's happened. And we should look out for anyone with injuries, too. Looking at all this, I find it hard to believe no one else was harmed,' she said, gesturing to the chaos that surrounded them.

They were passing an alley when Annie heard moaning – and not the kind of moaning she was used to hearing when they were on patrol.

'Down here,' she cried, heading down the alley with Maggie

and Poppy hot on her heels. Sure enough, they found a woman crouched in the corner, holding her head. She looked over as the girls approached, and Annie could see she was a lot older than all of them – possibly old enough to be her grandmother.

'What are you doing down here on your own?' Annie asked, her voice full of concern. She crouched down next to the woman and took her hand away from her head to reveal a gaping wound. Annie couldn't help but flinch before putting the woman's hand back where it had been. 'Keep as much pressure on there as you can,' she said, trying to keep her voice even. She turned to her friends. 'We need to get her to the hospital.'

They worked together to get the woman to her feet. By the time they got back on to Bartholomew Close it was clear she was extremely confused. They hadn't even managed to get a first name out of her. At the hospital they flagged down a nurse who was rushing down the corridor and handed the injured woman straight over.

'I think shrapnel must have struck her. She couldn't even tell us her name,' Annie told the nurse as she quickly guided her away.

On the way out they saw a police car pulling up outside. The driver was the same officer who had driven Wilfred away from The Dolphin. The girls rushed over and as Maggie and Poppy started helping a fresh wave of injured passengers out of the car and into the hospital, Annie took the chance to check in with the constable. She was relieved to hear that Wilfred and the rest of the passengers had made it into the building unscathed by any of the bombs.

'I think we're finished up over there now,' the officer said. 'We're going to drive around the other sites and see if there's anyone who needs to get to a hospital urgently. It's sounds as if Liverpool Street took a battering.'

'How about we come with you and help round up casualties?' Annie suggested.

The situation seemed to be in hand on Bartholomew Close
– there were people everywhere. At least this way they would
be able to get the injured to hospital a lot quicker. He nodded
straight away, and Annie ran into the hospital to collect Poppy
and Maggie.

As they made their way towards Liverpool Street Station,
the officer, a sergeant who went by the name of Turner, filled
them in on what he had learned so far.

'There's four children dead from a tenement block at
Portpool Lane,' he said sadly as he took a route to avoid the
area. 'There's enough soldiers there helping out and we won't
get the car close enough anyway,' he added by way of explanation for the detour. The three girls digested the terrible
news in silence. Annie didn't know what you could say in
response to something so heart-breaking. Was it not enough
that this war was taking good men away from the people of
this country? Why couldn't the poor, innocent children be
left out of it? It didn't seem fair.

'The lads have told me that there were four bombs dropped
on Liverpool Street. One hit the railway lines but two of
them struck motor buses still working their routes. They were
pulling bodies out the last I heard, so we'll go over that way
and see if there's anyone who needs transporting to hospital.'

The girls nodded, still in a stunned silence. Annie wasn't
sure if she was ready to see the scenes at Liverpool Street,
but she knew she had to pull herself together before they
got there. So many people were already out on the streets
throwing themselves into rescue efforts. She couldn't shy
away from her duty through fear of getting upset by what
she was about to witness. It was nothing compared to what
Richard must have been forced to face every day on the
front line. As her thoughts wandered to her family again, she

did her best to assure herself that they would all be safe at home. None of them had cause to be catching a bus at this time of night, and especially not in this area, so there was no reason that they would have been on one this evening.

Turner got them as close to Liverpool Street as he could. The surrounding roads were littered with a sea of glass, shrapnel and debris. Picking their way through it all and keeping an eye out for anyone in need of medical care, they eventually made it to the station. Annie gasped in shock when she saw one of the buses that had fallen victim to the Zeppelin's bomb. The fire brigade had drenched the flames, and all that was left was a shell of the vehicle. Annie felt sick when she thought about the poor people who had been sitting on it at the wrong time. Imagine sitting on the bus of an evening, happily making your way home, and then *wham!* – you're wiped out by a bomb, just like that.

'No one made it out alive,' a voice quietly informed the girls as they surveyed the scene. Annie turned around to find a young soldier shaking his head. 'It's a good job the raids are at night, otherwise both buses would likely have been full. As it was, they only got nine crew, passengers and bystanders. At least it missed the station, I suppose,' he added, shrugging.

Annie was surprised by how matter of fact he was being about witnessing such a huge loss of life in such awful circumstances. But then she thought about what he must have seen on the front line and realised that this was probably nothing compared to watching your friends being blown to pieces right in front of you.

Determined not to dwell on the horror of the situation any longer, Annie looked around for anybody who needed some help and she led Poppy and Maggie away when she spotted a young boy wandering around on his own.

'You should be at home in bed,' she told him.

'Aww, but miss, I've never seen anything like it!' he cried, looking around in awe at all the destruction.

'Come on now, son. Your mother must be worried sick,' Poppy said, taking a firm grip of his hand. After some persuasion, he told them his address and they escorted him home to a very anxious mother. They spent the next few hours getting groups of the injured together ready for Turner to drive them to the London Hospital, which was about a mile away. They took the casualties with less severe injuries to one of the Red Cross centres, and Annie was surprised to find there were a number of private houses that had been offered up as hospitals and convalescent homes for soldiers, where they were able to drop off a few patients.

The girls found they worked really well with Turner and Annie felt hopeful the experience might help some of the other officers at the station warm to them. It seemed a shame it had taken such a catastrophe to bring them together – she was certain this wouldn't have happened had there not been an ongoing emergency – but it felt like a positive step, nonetheless. When Turner finally dropped them back at Hunter Street Police Station, the sun was beginning to rise and they were all exhausted.

'Maybe we could lie down in our cupboard for a few hours,' Maggie groaned. Annie had to smile. Even after a night like they had just experienced, Maggie was sparky enough to be offering up her usual jokes. 'I don't think I have the energy to make it home,' Maggie added sleepily.

'I'm that tired, I could easily fall asleep in there,' Annie sighed. Poppy nodded her agreement; it seemed she was beyond even being able to speak.

'Ladies!' a voice boomed out along the corridor as they dragged themselves towards their room. Annie recognised the chief's voice straight away, but she kept shuffling along, hopeful that one of the others would deal with him or that he would see they were shattered beyond comprehension and leave them be.

Sadly, it was not to be. She heard his footsteps running along the corridor and she silently groaned. They were all too tired and affected by what they had seen to try and build themselves up in front of him so they turned and waited for him.

'Don't worry, I don't have any work for you,' he said, rubbing his chubby cheeks, which were bright red from the dash along the corridor. 'I hear you've been out helping my men with the aftermath of the air raid.'

'That's right, sir,' Poppy said quietly.

'Your commandant said you would be willing to get stuck in, but I must admit that I wasn't convinced. You've proven me wrong.' The three of them nodded and smiled, desperate to get their heads down for some rest. But he continued talking. 'I bumped into Miller on my way out to survey the damage. He said you might be after rooms in the section house accommodation. Well, there's three rooms waiting for you. You can go and use them now if you wish – you must be impatient for some rest. Just move your things in when you're ready and we'll organise the rent from then.'

The three girls perked up. The thought of a proper bed to sleep in without having to traipse home on the bus certainly gave Annie a welcome boost, especially after the scenes they had witnessed at Liverpool Street. She wasn't sure when she might be brave enough to set foot on a bus again.

'Thank you, sir,' she said as relief washed over her.

'You're obviously dedicated to the task at hand. It will be good to have you nearby so you can spend more time on your duties. I'll send an officer along to show you to your rooms,' he said before giving them a formal nod of his head and walking away. 'Oh, and I've had a light fitted in your cupboard – I mean, room!' he shouted back behind him.

'This is very good news,' Maggie whispered excitedly as they closed the door to their room and quickly got changed out of their uniforms – able to see, for a change. 'We can hand our notice in at the flat and then move to the section house as soon as Eddie has visited.'

'Let's wait until we've seen what the rooms are like before we get too carried away,' Poppy said evenly. 'We need to make sure we're not going to be expected to share a bathroom with twenty men before we give up the flat.'

They needn't have worried. When they were walked over to the section house at the end of the road and shown to their rooms, they were delighted to discover that each one had its own sink and toilet. There was a communal kitchen assigned to their block as well as a dining area, which they would share with the other officers.

Despite her exhaustion, Annie wanted to go straight to her parents' house to check everyone was safe and well, but Poppy pointed out that they had all been on their feet for more than twelve hours and she really needed to lie down before she collapsed. So, reluctantly, she agreed to get some rest first.

It turned out that was right, because as soon as her head hit the bed in her room, Annie was fast asleep.

14

When Annie woke up ten hours later, she was astonished. She couldn't remember the last time she had slept for that long. She got herself dressed and put her ear first to Maggie's door and then Poppy's. There was no sign of life behind either so she set out to her parents' house, leaving her friends a note to say she would see them back at the flat when she was done.

It was afternoon now, but the streets were still full of people marvelling at the desolation across the city as Annie made her way north towards her family home. When she passed by Queen's Square, she saw the spot where the first bomb of the night had fallen – the one she had heard as she was trying to get people under cover. She stopped to take in the glass-covered ground and breathed a sigh of relief that the device had fallen right in the middle of the square. It had shattered all the windows of the buildings surrounding the square but luckily that was as far as the damage went. This was even more fortunate because the square was surrounded by hospital buildings including the Alexandra Hospital for Children, the Home for Working Boys, the Examination Hall of the Royal College of Physicians and Surgeons, and the National Hospital for the Paralysed and Epileptic. There must have been at least a thousand adults and children tucked up in bed when that first bomb landed, and Annie shuddered to think of how many could have died if it had drifted even slightly off in either direction.

When Annie finally made it home, her mother swept her up in her arms before she was even able to say hello. She had clearly been as worried about her daughter as Annie had been about them all. Annie was happy to learn that everyone had been at home the previous evening and had made it to the basement when word of the attack reached them, although the Zeppelin didn't come anywhere near their part of town in the end.

'We're very proud of you,' her father said stiffly once Annie had told them about the events of the evening. Annie felt tears welling in her eyes, but she made sure she held them back. Her father wasn't a very emotional man, so declarations like that were rare. After catching up with her sisters and cousins, Annie was feeling tired again.

'I thought you said you slept for ten hours,' her mother laughed when she explained that she was going back to the flat for a lie-down.

'I think all the physical activity and stress and worry has really taken it out of me,' Annie sighed.

'You certainly don't look yourself,' her mother commented, peering into her face with a frown. 'I thought getting back out on patrol would be good for you, but you look even more drained than when you left us.'

'It's because of last night,' Annie assured her. 'Being back with Maggie and Poppy on duty was making me feel more like myself already. I just need an early night and I'll be back to making progress again.'

Her mother smiled in response, and Annie quickly took the opportunity to tell her and her father about the section house accommodation. They were so happy for her to make the move they didn't even react when she tentatively asked if she could have a little more money to cover Maggie's rent, too. They were so relieved she didn't have to travel to Holborn and back for every shift that the money wasn't an issue.

Annie left feeling exhausted but excited about what a difference she and her friends could make in Holborn now they were going to be based there.

Over the next couple of weeks, Annie, Maggie and Poppy got into a good routine with their patrols. Bulgaria had joined the war by declaring battle on Serbia and it felt like the fighting might never end. Annie was glad to have her WPS work to focus on, to take her mind off everything that was going on.

The girls started every shift with a wander around all the gardens, then stopped at all the pubs before checking in on some of the more hidden alleyways where they now knew prostitutes tended to carry out their business with soldiers home on leave or based at Gray's Inn. The nights were drawing in earlier now winter was beginning to settle around them, giving the women more opportunity to operate under the cover of darkness and keeping the group busy – despite the increasingly low temperatures.

Annie always had a heavy heart when they walked past The Dolphin Tavern. The building was heavily damaged, but Wilfred had told them he wasn't going to repair any of the damage until the war was over. They had bumped into him salvaging what he could from the wreckage on their first patrol following the air raids. He had needed stitches and his arm was bandaged up, but apart from that he was grateful to have made it out alive. He had even managed to retrieve the clock that had been on the wall that night. It was a little battered, but it was still in one piece and it had stopped at the exact time the bomb hit the building – 10.40 p.m.

Some of the houses nearby that they had seen burning the night of the raid had been made habitable again, but it was obvious from the outside that they had been badly damaged that night. Others sat empty, sad shells of their former selves. The fireman who had gone in to try and rescue the husband of the woman the girls ushered off to the tea room had died from his injuries in the end. Annie wondered if the heirloom the man had rushed back in to save had been worth his own and the fireman's lives.

During this time, Eddie made it home from the front line and spent two precious evenings at the flat in Camberwell with them all. The day he returned, Poppy and Annie patrolled together without Maggie, allowing her some one-to-one time with her brother. The siblings managed to sneak home to Kensington to see their mother and the family cook, Florence, while their father was at work. The following day, they all took some time out from WPS duties to go for a walk with Eddie, and they stopped off for tea and cake in the afternoon.

Although Eddie seemed quiet, Annie could tell straight away that he wasn't struggling with everything he had seen in the line of duty quite so much as Richard had been when he had first returned home. She was happy for him, and relieved that it meant Maggie wouldn't have to endure the turmoil she had been through when Richard returned to the front line. There was enough to worry about when someone you loved was out there, without that extra burden.

After Eddie's visit, they moved into the police section house and Annie found she was grateful to have her own space. She had loved living with her friends before losing Richard, but something had changed since his death. She still enjoyed spending time with them, and she was incredibly grateful to have them by her side on patrols. But she found that when they were off duty, more often than not she wanted to be alone. It wasn't that she didn't enjoy Maggie and Poppy's company, but she was always so tired. One of them always commented when she spent too long in her bedroom on her own when they were living in the flat – they liked to spend spare time together in the living room. This set-up made it easier for her to sneak away for a rest without her friends worrying about her for it.

Annie couldn't work out why she was so tired all the time. They were putting in the same kind of hours as they had done in Bethnal Green and covering about the same amount of ground. She thought maybe the pain she still felt at losing Richard might be draining her energy more than she realised, and she was hopeful that would ease off with time. She was still struggling to eat like she used to, but she put that down to a lack of time and energy rather than grief. When it came down to it, she would rather crawl into bed after a shift, especially a night patrol, than spend precious sleeping time preparing food. Poppy did most of the cooking, but she liked to put together big, hearty meals and Annie was normally asleep by the time they were ready. Poppy always left some for her, which she picked at when she was feeling up to it.

Once October had turned to November, the girls felt so comfortable with their new patch that Annie felt like it might be time to venture a little further.

'I'd like to take a look around King's Cross this afternoon,' she announced to her friends as they made their way around all the gardens on their usual patrol. They had noticed a drop in the number of women hanging around late at night since they had made their presence a regular thing. They had switched things up over the last week and started alternating between afternoon and evening patrols. Evenings had always been better for keeping on top of suspicious activity between prostitutes and soldiers and rounding up youngsters who were out and about on the streets at a time when they would be a lot safer tucked up at home in bed. But they were wary of simply pushing the problems from the evening to the afternoon and didn't want anyone getting too familiar with their routine and working around it. Today they were carrying out a daytime patrol, so Annie thought it would be a perfect time to explore the station.

'But the chief told us to steer clear of King's Cross,' Maggie replied.

'Yes, I'd rather not get on his bad side,' Poppy added.

'He told us to stay away because his men cover the station,' Annie explained. 'Do you really think they're going to be concerned with the issues we want to help with? They don't know the warning signs to look out for – and what's more, they don't care. We won't be stepping on any toes.'

'Well, when you put it like that . . .' Maggie said thoughtfully. Annie smiled gratefully as Poppy also nodded her agreement. They decided to go after lunch, when they'd finished their usual patrol.

As they headed off, the other two chatting merrily, Annie took a quiet moment to think. She wasn't sure why she felt such a strong desire to expand their patrol to take in King's Cross. All she knew was that she needed to be kept busy to stop her mind from constantly drifting back to Richard and the misery she was feeling underneath everything. The train station was bound to be a hive of activity so it seemed like the perfect distraction now they had the rest of the patch under relative control.

Annie was full of anticipation when they made their way to the train station that afternoon, but as they got near a woman stopped them in the street. Her dress was shabby-looking and her hair was bedraggled; she had obviously done her best to try and look presentable but it was clear she didn't have the necessary means. Annie hated to make assumptions about other women but sometimes these things were clear-cut. She could tell straight away that she was a woman of the streets and that intrigued her because it wasn't normal for prostitutes to seek them out.

'I need your help,' the woman said quietly. She self-consciously patted down her hair when she saw Annie looking at it, and Annie felt instantly terrible for making her feel judged. 'Well, it's not me who needs help,' she added, looking around her cautiously. 'I'm afraid I'm past that.' She sighed and stared at her feet. She must have been in her fifties and Annie wondered how long she had been selling herself on the streets to survive.

'How can we help?' Poppy asked sympathetically.

'I'm worried about one of the younger girls. She turned up a few days ago. I've no inkling where she came from or what brought her here, but she's terribly naive. Keeps trying to talk to men out in the busy streets in the middle of the day for everyone to see.'

Annie didn't like the sound of that. It was surprising the girl hadn't yet been arrested and hauled before the courts for soliciting . And once she was in the court system, which always went in favour of men and treated women despicably, she would be on a downward spiral.

'Me and a few of the others, we've tried talking to her, but she won't listen to us. I want to save her from herself.' The woman sighed again but this time instead of staring at her feet, she looked them all in the face one by one. 'She's so young. I don't even think she has anywhere to stay – I've caught her sleeping in Regent Square Gardens a few times. Please do something. I can't stand the thought of her being stuck in this life until she's my age. I wish there had been someone to help me.'

'We can try,' Maggie said, but she didn't sound very convincing. Annie wasn't sure what they could do, aside from warning the girl to be more discreet in her endeavours. They knew from experience that, as much as they wanted to, they were stuck when it came to rescuing these girls and women. They could try and encourage her into paid work like they had the girl in the gardens all those weeks ago. But the truth was that prostitution made women a lot more money than factory work ever could and once they had fallen into it, it was difficult to pull them back out – especially when there was no family around, as with this poor girl.

'She's tall and slim with blond hair, and she normally carries a big bag around with her,' the woman said. She was whispering now and looking around again. She obviously didn't want anyone to see her talking to them in their uniforms. 'I think she must carry her life around in that bag,' she added sadly. 'There's a lodging house near here, so you could always try and get her a bed there.'

'That's a good idea,' Annie said. 'Do you stay there?'

'I did,' the woman replied, suddenly looking shamefaced. She refused to look any of them in the eye as she hurriedly explained. 'I was asked to leave. Something to do with some silly rules that means they don't tolerate drunkards.' Her cheeks burned red and Annie felt bad for her.

'How much is it per night?' she asked, wanting to change the topic and spare the woman her blushes.

'All the charges are low,' she replied. 'The price of a cubicle is sixpence per night, and you can get a really good breakfast or dinner for fourpence. I've tried to tell the young girl about it, but she runs away every time I approach her. I think she's worried I'm going to give her a telling off for working on my patch.'

'Hopefully she'll listen to us,' Poppy said kindly. 'Where is this place?'

'It's the Mary Curzon Hostel, over on King's Cross Road,' the woman said, pointing back behind her in that general direction.

'Thank you . . . we don't know your name?' Poppy said in reply.

'Oh, that don't matter,' the woman said, and before any

of them had a chance to say anything else to her, she had darted off down the street.

'The train station can wait,' Annie declared. She was happy to delay that when they had a refreshing challenge like this one to focus on. This was exactly the kind of distraction she needed. Plus, she couldn't stand the thought of the young girl sleeping out in the open in the current weather. The air had turned positively icy over the last few days.

'I agree,' Maggie nodded.

'All right. Let's head to the lodging house and see if they have any room for the next couple of nights,' Poppy suggested. 'Then we can track this girl down and try and get her to agree to a few nights in a safe place. If she doesn't have the funds, I can loan her enough for the first couple of nights. I can't stand the thought of a young girl sleeping out on the streets.'

Annie was impressed by her friend's generosity once more. She felt lucky to have such caring companions – and excited to have a purpose again, even if it might only last for a couple of patrols.

15

Although she had heard of them, Annie hadn't been to any lodging houses before, so she was interested to see inside one. The woman in charge – a thin, wiry matron in her seventies who wore her grey hair tied back in a bun – introduced herself as Mildred.

'We don't allow any funny business here,' she said stoutly as Annie, Maggie and Poppy stood on the doorstep. 'The women aren't permitted to have any guests, and you'll find that no man has been over this threshold since the place opened three years ago,' she added proudly.

'That's not why we're here,' Poppy assured her.

'That's what you women police are concerned with, though. Isn't it?' Mildred's voice dripped with suspicion and she narrowed her eyes at them.

'Well, yes, but mostly we want to look out for the welfare of vulnerable women, and we think there's a young girl you might be able to help before she falls too far into the wrong way of life,' Poppy explained.

'Oh. Well, in that case, you had better come in,' Mildred said much more enthusiastically, standing back and opening the door wider for them. She led them to a large living area where a cook was preparing vegetables. 'This is where the women can cook and eat meals, or they can have it made for them,' Mildred explained as she motioned towards the busy woman. 'Violet here gets all the food ready while the women are out. Their cubicles have to be vacated by nine in the morning and they're not allowed back up until seven thirty at night. They can use the day room if they wish, but most spend the day at work.'

They sat down together in the bright day room and Poppy took Mildred through the conversation they'd just had with the prostitute and their subsequent concerns for the young girl.

'You understand she'll need to pay to stay here?' Mildred asked. 'And that I can't allow her to fund her lodgings with immoral activity?'

'Yes, I was planning on covering her first few nights if we can find her and she's happy to be helped,' Poppy replied. 'And then we were hoping to find her some work so that she can support herself. We wanted to talk to you first to make sure you had space for her.'

Mildred nodded.

'You said most of the women who stay here are in work?' Annie asked her.

'Yes, dear. There are teachers, typists, clerks. These hostels were set up to help poorer women – in fact, they are described as being for "the respectable poor" – but I'm afraid the likes of factory workers have been priced out.'

Annie's heart dropped. She couldn't think of many options for this girl other than factory work or helping out at a greengrocer's or bakery – all of which didn't pay very handsomely. She knew that some of the chemists, oil shops, drapers and butchers were in the habit of using very young children as errand-boys and -girls but, again, the pay wouldn't be nearly enough.

'We have forty cubicles and it's rare for any of them to be free,' Mildred continued. 'But if your girl is quick then she might be in luck. I've had two become available. We don't ask any questions or demand any references, but the women must stick to a small list of rules. No beer or spirits are allowed on the premises, smoking is forbidden and, of course, there are to be no visitors or immoral activity at all.'

The three of them nodded hopefully and agreed to bring the girl back that evening if they could locate her in time.

They were due to have the night off, but agreed time was of the essence. It sounded as if the free cubicles at the hostel might not stay vacant for very long, and none of them could stand the thought of the poor girl spending another night sleeping outside under the cold November skies.

Knowing that their best hope of finding her was if she decided to spend the night in Regent Square Gardens, they decided to go back to the section house and get a few hours' sleep before heading back out on their quest. Annie was relieved; she was feeling overcome with tiredness yet again. She skipped dinner – she was feeling a little queasy anyway – and went straight to bed.

Annie woke a few hours later to someone gently shaking her arm. She looked up drowsily and was confused when she saw Maggie's face. It was the middle of the night, why was she waking her up? Then she remembered their plan to head back out that evening. She groaned and asked for a few more minutes to get herself together. She closed her eyes again after watching Maggie's concerned face backing away, and when she woke again, it was daylight.

Realising that she must have slept through, Annie went to jump out of bed to go and find out what she had missed. Why had her friends not come in to wake her again? But her limbs felt so heavy, it took her a lot longer to haul herself out of bed than usual. Once she was on her feet, the room started to spin and suddenly she felt nauseous. She managed to stumble to her toilet just in time. As she emptied the contents of her stomach – which wasn't a great deal – she wondered what on earth was the matter with her.

Annie cleaned herself up, then checked the time. It was

still early, and she knew that if her friends had been out late last night then they wouldn't be up and about for a while yet. So, she got herself back into bed, grateful for the fact she had her own space now. When she woke again a few hours later, she felt better. Venturing tentatively to Maggie's room, she knocked gently. She found her friend sitting up in bed reading a book.

'I was about to come and check on you,' Maggie said, beckoning her over to join her. 'How are you feeling?'

'Did you go back out without me?' Annie asked, sitting down on the bed next to her.

'We did try to rouse you again, but you were sleeping so deeply we thought it best to leave you. How are you feeling now?'

Annie's cheeks flushed crimson. She felt ashamed. 'I'm fine now, thank you. How did you and Poppy get on? Did you find the girl?' she asked, keen to change the subject and take the attention away from herself.

Maggie explained that they had waited in the gardens for two hours before a tall, slim figure entered. 'She tried to run away at first but it was so dark that we were nearly on top of her by the time she spotted us, so Poppy grabbed her and pulled her back. It took some convincing that we wanted to help her and not get her into trouble, but she calmed down in the end.'

'How old is she?' Annie asked.

'She's only thirteen,' Maggie replied, hanging her head. 'It doesn't bear thinking about, does it? I mean, the thought of being in that position at any age is dreadful, but to have to do what she's been doing that young . . .'

Annie thought about her sisters, the youngest of whom was just thirteen. The idea of her sleeping on the streets and being forced to sell herself to survive made her heart ache.

'Anyway, Tilly – that's her name – she was cautious at

first. I think she thought we would be after something in return for helping her. But we managed to get her to the hostel in the end and Poppy has paid for her first few nights. We said we'd go back later today and try and come up with some ideas for work for her, but it's going to be hard given her age.'

'What about her family?' Annie asked. 'Is there no chance of her going home?'

Maggie let out a sigh. 'I'm afraid not. The poor thing's an orphan. She was sent to live with her uncle when her parents died, but he's a hopeless drunk who started beating her almost as soon as she walked through the door. She packed a bag that first night and left and has been doing what she can to get by ever since. She's a determined little thing for someone so young. I don't know how she's kept going.'

Annie was reminded of how lucky she had been to grow up in such a loving family, with no need to ever worry about money. Would she have known what to say to this girl if she had been there last night? It was at times like these that she really missed Irene. She knew for certain that she would have known exactly the right things to do and say to help.

'Anyway, enough about Tilly for now,' Maggie said, pulling Annie back to the present. 'You did very well to keep avoiding my question there but I'm afraid I won't give up until you've given me an answer. How are you feeling now?'

Annie couldn't help but smile. There was no fooling Maggie. 'The only thing it can be is tiredness. But I haven't done anything more than you and Poppy. I feel so silly,' she whispered, playing with her hands in her lap. She didn't want to confess to having been sick for fear of worrying her friend even more than she obviously already was.

'Don't feel silly,' Maggie said softly, laying down her book and taking one of Annie's hands in her own. 'You've been through a lot these last few weeks. It was a big step for you to come back – and to a new area, as well. It's been a big change after going through something so awful. And then you had the air raid to deal with before you had even settled back in to patrolling. It's probably all caught up with you a little.' Annie nodded gratefully. She hoped Maggie was right. 'Poppy and I thought it might be best if you took a few days off – maybe go and stay with your family again? Just until you feel a bit better. No one would think any less of you for taking some time out for yourself.'

'No,' Annie said firmly. Just the thought of it filled her with dread. 'I need to keep busy. All I think about when I'm not patrolling is Richard and how I no longer have anything to look forward to once this damned war is over. I need to keep busy. I need to help. Please.'

'Of course,' Maggie replied, pulling her in for a hug. 'But you must let us know if it gets too much again. Promise?'

'Bobby Girls' promise,' Annie whispered. She so longed to go back to the day when they had come up with that name for their little group. She'd had so much to live for and look forward to back then. Now so much had changed that she didn't even recognise her own life anymore.

'Bobby Girls forever,' Maggie whispered back, squeezing Annie tight. Annie held on to her friend for as long as possible, knowing that if she ended the embrace too soon the tears streaming down her face would give away her sadness.

16

Later that day, Annie, Maggie and Poppy finally made it to King's Cross Station to look around. The first thing Annie noticed was that there wasn't a police uniform in sight.

'I knew it,' Annie said, feeling vindicated. 'I knew there was no way the men from the station were keeping an eye on things here.'

'I wonder what they're telling the chief,' Poppy pondered, looking around the vast concourse. 'They could well be telling him they have it all under control while not bothering to come here very often.'

'Yes. And they might not keep an eye on things all the time,' Maggie added. 'They might only come at certain times so I still think we should be careful about treading on any toes.'

However, after speaking to a few of the train guards on duty, it became apparent that policemen were not a regular sight at the station.

'It would be good if you could come for a wander every now and then. There are a few suspicious-looking characters who tend to hang around at certain times, but of course there's nothing we can do,' one of the female guards explained.

Just as they were bidding her farewell, a group of young boys appeared out of nowhere and headed towards Platform One. 'There's a train due in from the front soon. They'll be after the men and begging for money,' the guard explained.

The girls thanked her and followed the group of children.

They often stepped in when youngsters started begging on the streets. They had even come across little ones who got around on go-carts and followed behind coal-carts carrying old sacks in order to pilfer lumps of coal as they toppled off the back. They rarely escorted them home now, preferring to simply warn them and move them on. They found that the parents tended to plead a total lack of control when it was obvious they were encouraging the behaviour.

Sure enough, a train pulled into the platform just as the group arrived there. As soon as the first army-issued boot was on the ground, one of the boys rushed up to the soldier.

'Please, sir, help us keep our families fed,' he pleaded.

Annie, Poppy and Maggie watched the boy's three companions filter along the platform, each picking off a carriage door to target. Annie shook her head in disbelief. She had never seen youngsters working so systematically before. Some of the men walked on as if the boys weren't there, others gave them a knowing smile and patted them on the head, and a select few dug around in their pockets and handed them change.

'This is what happens when there's no one here to keep an eye on them,' Poppy commented. 'That's enough of that now, let's take one each.'

Annie went after the first boy, who was now following a soldier along the platform. She grabbed him by the scruff of his neck and pulled him back towards her. The look of utter shock on his face when he took in her uniform confirmed to her that he was used to operating in a lawless train station. The girls wordlessly escorted a child each back to the entrance at King's Cross, where they congregated together under the big arched windows and clock tower.

'We're not doing no harm, miss,' one of the boys protested as Annie, Maggie and Poppy stood around them in a circle. They had managed to get hold of one youngster each but the fourth lad had run off when he'd spotted his friends being hauled away.

'Begging is no way to make a living,' Annie said gently. She didn't want to come down too hard on the boys, but they had to try and stop them from carrying on the way they were. She understood that times were hard and they were probably acting out of desperation – maybe even encouraged by their families – but that didn't make it an acceptable activity.

'Me mam won't care a jot if you take me home and tell her,' one of them boasted. He was the smallest of the three and there was a gaping hole in the front of his shoe where Annie could see a toe poking out.

'She won't care you've been begging but she'll slap you for getting caught, Jim!' his friend cried with glee. He was wearing a flat cap that looked as though it belonged to his father and his face was covered in dirt. He started laughing as the smaller boy's cheeks flushed red with shame.

'At least mine will be at home and not out getting a soldier of her own to fleece,' Jim snapped. He looked momentarily pleased with himself for the retort, until he saw the boy with the flat cap's expression change in an instant, his laughing face replaced by one filled with rage. Jim ducked behind Annie for cover, and the boy with the flat cap launched himself in their direction. Annie thrust her arms out and caught the lad's hands in her own before they connected with Jim, who was now cowering behind her. Then she quickly twisted him around so that his arms were pinned firmly behind his back.

Annie took a moment to take a deep breath before smiling across at Maggie and Poppy. She may have been feeling out of sorts lately, but she definitely hadn't lost her WPS instincts. Two men in suits walked past the group and gave a dramatic round of applause.

'Impressive skills, there,' one of them remarked to the other as they rounded the corner. It helped to ease the tension, and Annie released her grip on the boy with the flat cap, who thankfully had calmed down. Maggie had run behind her and now had her arm comfortingly around Jim, while their companion, who had stayed silent for the whole exchange, stood in front of Poppy looking completely shocked.

'Have you calmed down enough to speak sensibly to us?' Poppy asked evenly. All three boys nodded. 'Right. Well, we're not interested in dragging you home and telling your mothers what you've been up to. We realise they probably told you to come in the first place.'

Annie could tell from the sheepish looks on all their faces that Poppy was correct.

'There are better ways you can help your mothers,' Maggie said. 'I imagine they've been desperate to get you out of the house as you're forever under their feet. So why don't you give them some help with the chores, or look after your brothers and sisters for a little while?'

'My mother was always grateful to have an extra pair of hands,' Annie chimed in, hoping that they wouldn't point out that she was clearly from a more privileged background than they were and would never have struggled for money. When nobody made a sarcastic comment, she continued, 'Your help will be worth a lot more to them than a few pieces of loose change you've managed to scrape together from the men who are already giving so much to protect you all.'

'My mam's always on at me about taking my sisters out to play so she can do some cleaning,' admitted the boy who had so far not said a word.

'There you go, then,' Annie said happily. 'Just think how grateful she would be if you kept them occupied for an hour or two so she could get some important things done.'

'Off you go, then,' Poppy said firmly. 'Home to help your

mothers – and remember to leave the soldiers alone. They're already doing enough for you.'

All three boys nodded obediently and scurried away. Annie wasn't sure how long their new helpful attitudes would last, but she was confident that they weren't going to be hassling any more soldiers for a day or two, at least.

The girls walked around the station again to get used to the layout and see if they could spot any of the suspicious activity the guard had mentioned. They didn't see anything they felt they should be concerned about, even after waiting for a number of incoming trains.

Just as they were leaving, Annie caught sight of a man who made her stop in her tracks. He was walking away from one of the platforms with his head hung low, but Annie caught a glimpse of his face and a strange thrill of recognition went through her. He was walking towards the group, and Annie stayed glued to the spot as she tried to get a better look at his features and place where she had seen him before. Maggie and Poppy walked on ahead, oblivious. Even as the man passed right beside Annie, she couldn't for the life of her work out where she recognised him from. The possibilities were endless, given the number of people she had encountered over the last few months after starting work with the WPS.

After racking her brains for a little longer, Annie admitted defeat and ran on to catch up with Maggie and Poppy before they realised that she had lagged behind them. But she made sure to file away a mental image of the man's face in her mind. She knew she wouldn't rest until she had remembered where it was that she had seen him before.

Outside the station, the girls discussed the apparent lack of police presence inside.

'I'm a little nervous about including it on our patrol after the chief warned us off it,' Poppy said anxiously.

Normally Annie would have agreed with her, but she still had a burning sensation to do something more on their patrols. And from what the train guard had said, it sounded like they could do a lot of good here.

'Remember how much everyone's attitudes towards us changed after we cracked the burglary case in Bethnal Green?' she asked, looking meaningfully at Maggie. She knew her friend could be easily persuaded with the correct motivation.

Suddenly, Maggie's eyes lit up. 'Oh, I'd love to show those men exactly what we can do,' she said, full of excitement.

'I bet there's a hive of mischief we can help bring order to taking place here while the other officers are turning a blind eye. If we keep a log and show the chief exactly what we can do, imagine how impressed he'll be,' Annie added, glad her idea was going to plan.

'You're right. Those boys probably represented a small fraction of what's really going on here,' Maggie declared determinedly, looking to Poppy for validation.

Poppy sighed heavily. 'It looks as though I've been outvoted,' she said, defeated, but smiled as she said it.

Annie beamed.

'But first, let's check in on Tilly,' Poppy added. 'We need to organise some work for her before she falls back into her old ways.'

Back at the hostel, they were greeted by a cheery Mildred.

'That Tilly is a gift from God,' she announced as she showed the group in again. 'I've been having some problems with my back recently, and when she saw me struggling to clean one of the bathrooms earlier this morning, she stepped in. She didn't just help me out, she insisted on taking over and I have to say she's doing a fine job. She's still down there now – would you like to see her?'

The girls nodded eagerly and Mildred led them down to

the basement, where they could hear beautiful singing ringing out. They followed the graceful voice into one of the many bathrooms, where a young girl jumped up in surprise when Mildred knocked on the door. She stopped singing immediately and turned a deep shade of pink as she took in her visitors and laid down her cleaning cloth. Annie was surprised by how young Tilly looked. Her blond hair was tied back in a neat plait, and her brown eyes glistened with life even in the dim light. Annie felt a pang in her heart as she thought about everything the girl had already been through.

'Tilly, your friends are back,' Mildred said kindly.

'Hello,' Tilly said, her voice tremulous. 'I didn't hear you coming, sorry.'

'No need to apologise,' Annie said, stepping forward and offering her hand. 'I'm Annie, it's good to meet you. You have a wonderful voice.'

Tilly blushed again as she shook Annie's hand. 'Thank you,' she muttered.

'We came by to have a talk about finding some kind of work for you,' Poppy said.

Tilly looked pleased at first that the attention had been taken away from her singing, but then her face darkened. 'I've already told you, there's nothing out there for someone like me,' she said, quietly but firmly. 'I'm really very grateful for the help you've given me, but I'll be moving on from here once the money you gave Mildred runs out. Until that time comes, I'm happy to help out around here as a way of saying thank you.' She went to pick up the cloth again, obviously not keen to discuss the topic any further.

'Let's not be hasty,' Mildred said slowly. It sounded as though she was turning an idea over in her head. Tilly got back to cleaning the basin she had been tackling when the group had arrived, but Annie, Maggie and Poppy turned to Mildred, keen to hear what she was about to suggest.

She paused for a moment, deep in thought. 'I've been umming and ahhing about getting a maid in recently, but I wasn't sure about how to cover the costs. Tilly saw how I struggled with the cleaning and, I have to admit, even changing the bedsheets is a feat for me these days.'

Annie looked Mildred up and down carefully. Yes, she was certainly past her prime, but she seemed to be in good health, and she would have described her as sprightly had anyone asked for her first impressions of the woman. But she liked where this was going, so she kept her thoughts to herself. Tilly stopped what she was doing and started listening intently.

'I couldn't pay you to keep helping me out,' Mildred went on. 'But I could certainly keep one of the rooms aside for you. And there's always a bit of soup and bread left over after the other women have eaten every evening. Sometimes there's even a slab of cheese. I could make sure you wouldn't go hungry. And, of course, you would have free use of all the facilities.'

There was a silence as everyone digested what Mildred was suggesting.

'So, I could be your maid, and you would let me stay here for free?' Tilly asked cautiously.

'In a way, yes. You would be working for your board, so not free as such. But I think that type of arrangement would benefit us both, so it would be silly not to try. What do you think?'

Tilly's face flushed with relief and she dropped her cloth and flung herself at the matron. As Mildred returned the embrace, she laughed and looked over at Annie, Maggie and Poppy. Tilly had seemed timid and reserved when they had first walked in, but this kind offer had clearly overwhelmed her to the point that it had broken down the front she had been trying to put on.

'I think that's a yes,' Maggie commented brightly and Annie delighted in the rare moment of joy. This was the kind of thing she loved about patrolling. It was difficult not being able to help everybody and having to make do with offering advice and guidance instead of solutions. But things like this made it all worthwhile.

'Thank you,' Tilly whispered, still holding on to Mildred tightly. When she eventually let go, Mildred took them all up to the kitchen for a cup of tea before the girls got back to patrolling and Tilly got back to her chores. As Mildred talked them through the history of the hostel and explained where the funding for the project had come from, Annie's mind wandered off. She couldn't stop thinking about the man at King's Cross. Who was he, and where had she come across him before? Why couldn't she get him out of her mind?

When Maggie and Poppy got up to leave, she jumped. She had been so lost in thought she hadn't taken in any of the conversation.

'Well, that was a lot easier than I anticipated,' Poppy said brightly as they made their way back towards the police station.

'I'm so glad Tilly has a safe place to stay,' Maggie said.

Annie smiled and nodded in agreement, but she was only half-listening as she continued to desperately rack her brain to work out where she knew the man at the station from.

17

Over the next few days, Annie struggled to get the image of the man at the station out of her head. She tried desperately to shrug it off, but something kept pulling her mind back to him, and it was bothering her to the point of distraction. She managed to convince Poppy and Maggie to go back to the train station on a couple of occasions, but each time she failed to spot the stranger again. She was reluctant to share what she had seen with them in case they thought she was being silly. After all, she had no idea herself why she was so fixated on him.

A few days later, they had decided to head back to the King's Cross area halfway through a night patrol when they were distracted by a couple of very tall, bulky-looking women wandering along the street, trailing behind a more petite lady. Annie recognised the smaller figure straight away – it was Alice, a prostitute who they had got to know through their regular patrols of the gardens. They had stepped in on a number of occasions after finding her in compromising positions with soldiers. She no choice but to do what she was doing to make money and Annie found it frustrating that they didn't have any way of helping her out of the fix she found herself in.

'It's nice to see Alice in an innocent situation for once,' Maggie whispered lightly as the threesome drew closer. Annie nodded but she couldn't take her eyes off Alice's companions. One was wearing a hat and had her head bowed low, while the other had mostly hidden her face with a shawl. It was dark so she couldn't see their faces through the shields they had put up, but she was fascinated by the size of them. They both appeared very broad and stocky for women. Alice nodded a quick hello and rushed past the group.

'That was odd,' Maggie commented.

Annie had to agree that it was strange behaviour for Alice. Whenever they had come across her doing anything that they weren't obliged to advise her against, she would revel in the fact that she was playing the part of an innocent civilian for once, and she normally kept them in conversation for a long time.

Poppy stopped walking and turned around to stare after the strange-looking group. Then she suddenly stormed off after them. Confused, Annie looked at Maggie, who simply shrugged her shoulders and followed after Poppy. Annie did the same and the pair of them reached Alice and her companions just as Poppy was reaching her hand up and pulling the shawl off one of the women's heads. Annie gasped, wondering what on earth Poppy was playing at. But when the woman spun around and tried to grab the shawl back, Annie was astounded. Despite the darkness she could now see clearly that it wasn't a woman at all – it was a man.

'I knew it!' Poppy declared triumphantly, and the man's face dropped with the realisation that his ruse had been uncovered. Alice twirled around, and her face filled with disappointment when she took in the sight before her. The man stopped grabbing for the shawl and instead grabbed the arm of the other 'woman', and they both sprinted off back in the direction they had come from.

'That's it, back to the barracks you go!' Poppy called after them. The second man's hat flew off and he continued running without a backwards glance, leaving it sitting sadly in the middle of the road. 'We'll be telling Sergeant Eccles all about this!'

'I had better get those jackets back,' Alice huffed.

'Where did you get ladies' garments so big?' Annie asked. She was amazed she had found any large enough to fit the pair. They had been baggy enough that they had fooled her – in the dark, at least.

'My mam was a big woman,' Alice sighed. 'If only I'd found a couple of men a bit smaller . . .'

'It wasn't the coats that gave them away. And just so you know, the whole disguise was terrible,' Poppy said good-humouredly. 'But I admire your determination.' Alice grinned, looking pleased with herself. 'Did you really think you could sneak them past us like that?' Poppy added, seriously this time.

Alice looked to Maggie and Annie. 'These two didn't seem to notice,' she sniffed.

Annie shifted uncomfortably on the spot and hoped the darkness was covering up her blushes. She had certainly picked up on the fact there was something up with the duo, but she hadn't for one moment suspected they were men dressed up as women. And she was confident Maggie was in the same position.

'You can be assured we won't be fooled again,' Maggie declared robustly. Annie nodded fervently and Alice smirked at them both.

'This has got to stop,' Poppy said firmly. Alice's face clouded over and all her previous bravado vanished. 'There's only so many times we can warn you before we have to get one of the officers out to arrest you.'

'Oh, come on. I'm not doing no harm. These men need a bit of cheering up just as much as I need the money that they're so happy to part with. Surely it's better than them drowning their sorrows with liquor all night?' Alice replied.

Annie looked at Poppy, hoping she would come up with a suitable answer. She herself found it hard to disagree with these arguments. When it came to protecting the younger and more vulnerable women, she found it more clear-cut – but Alice clearly wasn't being taken advantage of. She was a mature woman who knew exactly what she was doing and, quite frankly, had no other choice. And the men were more than willing to hand over their cash for a bit of fun with her, so why was it only Alice who was looking at a possible arrest? It seemed so unfair.

Poppy sighed. 'You know that as long as you're being careful, we don't see an issue with what you're doing,' she explained. 'We understand that you don't have much choice in order to keep a roof over your head. But you have to be more discreet or else it puts us in a very difficult situation. We can't be seen to keep pulling you up without taking it further. And if we keep catching you, then what's to stop a policeman catching you at it? Once they get their hands on you and throw you into the court system, you're done for. We want to avoid that. The justice system isn't kind to women, no matter the circumstances. You need to take more care, Alice.'

'That's what the disguises were for,' she said sheepishly. Annie couldn't help but let out a small giggle at the memory of the man's face as he turned around and desperately tried to grab hold of his shawl. She was certain that had it not been so dark, she would have cottoned on to the disguises even quicker than Poppy had. Annie's giggle set Maggie off, and the two of them looked to Poppy as they tried to contain their amusement. It was no good – she sniggered along with them before bursting into a fit of laughter, too. Looking relieved, Alice joined in.

'I can't believe you thought they would pass for ladies,' Maggie managed between giggles.

'It nearly worked,' Alice replied.

'Only because it was dark!' Poppy cried through her laughter. 'Off with you now and behave yourself for the rest of the night at least.'

Alice gave them all a wave and wandered off.

After recovering from their laughing fit, the group continued on their way to King's Cross. They were waiting on the kerb opposite the station to allow a car to pass when a man ran into the road from the other side. They all looked on in shock as he darted out just ahead of the motor. Annie's breath caught in her throat as she panicked that he wasn't going to make it across in time – and the car didn't look to be slowing down. The gentleman had made it only a few steps into the road before he realised his mistake. Annie was about to call out to warn him when he swiftly jumped back out of the path of the car.

'That was close,' Maggie sighed, sounding relieved as she and Poppy stepped into the road together once it was clear to cross. But Annie didn't hear what her friend had said. She was rooted to the spot as memories of one of the worst nights of her life flashed back through her mind. As the car's headlights had passed over the man's face just before he jumped back out of the way, everything had come crashing back to her. She knew where she recognised the stranger from the train station now. She wouldn't have been able to recall or describe the man before, but his features had obviously been buried in her memory from when she had glimpsed them in the car's headlights on that awful night, and the way the light had moved over this random man's face this evening must have made the connection her brain had been trying so hard to make for days. It had triggered her memory somehow as it was all playing out in her mind now.

Annie took a deep breath as the realisation dawned on her. The man at the station whose identity had been niggling at

Annie for the last few days was Maggie's attacker – the man who had left her so badly injured in the middle of the road that she had lost the baby growing inside her. She had caught sight of his face in the headlights of the car he had thrown Maggie in front of in Bethnal Green. Annie's throat felt as if it was constricting and her heart started pounding.

'What are you waiting for?' Maggie's voice called out playfully from the other side of the road. Annie snapped back to the present and looked up to see her friend laughing and waving at her below the lights from the station. She quickly checked for cars again and dashed across the road, trying to compose herself as she went. Her mind was racing, and she needed it to slow down for a minute.

'What's the matter?' Poppy asked, sounding concerned.

After a moment's hesitation, Annie waved the question away and continued walking to the station entrance. 'I remembered something I need to talk to my mother about,' she replied as casually as she could manage. Maggie was doing so well at the moment that she didn't want to risk bringing that awful time up again and upsetting her. She had rebuilt her life since that night and all the terrible consequences it had brought for her. It was best not to mention it – for now, at least.

As they made their way around the train station, Annie couldn't stop thinking about Maggie's attacker and what seeing him there could have meant. She was suddenly reminded of her visit from Frosty and what she had told her about white-slavers. Frosty had been clear on the fact there was a concern around men trying to accost women and refugees at the big train stations and force them into a life of prostitution through the white-slave trade.

The girls had originally come across Maggie's attacker in Bethnal Green after being tipped off about a gang of men who were trying to do just that in the area at the time. And it had been clear from the way he had been trying to wrestle the woman that Maggie had saved into a car that his intentions were not good. Had he moved on to King's Cross station now? Was that what he had been up to when Annie had spotted him: scouting for potential victims?

When Poppy and Maggie stopped to talk to a group of women, Annie tried to get involved in the conversation. But she came away having no idea what had been discussed as her head had been too wrapped up in trying to work out what her realisation about Maggie's attacker meant. If she was right, then she would surely see the man at the station again. In that case, she would have to try to keep track of him without alerting her friends to it. She needed to make sure she was right about this before she caused any upset. And she couldn't very well go up and confront him without having evidence – especially not when she knew how dangerous he might be.

Once she was sure, she would need to figure out what to do about it. She certainly wasn't going to let him get away with what he had done to Maggie, and she would also need to act quickly in order to save more women from falling into his evil clutches.

18

It was another week until Annie spotted Maggie's attacker at the station again. As soon as she laid eyes on him, her heart leapt and her palms became clammy. It was a busy Saturday afternoon and the concourse was bustling, but she had been keeping a beady eye out and this time she recognised him instantly. There was no doubt now about where she knew him from. Rage coursed through her as she remembered once more the terrible way he had treated her friend.

Annie knew in that instant that she had to find a way to deal with this without involving Maggie. If Annie felt this strongly about the man on sight, then there was no telling what her friend would do if she found out he was walking around without a care in the world, right under her nose. Annie was struggling to stop herself from walking straight up to him and punching his lights out, so Maggie's reaction was bound to be extreme. Or even worse, it might undo all the brilliant progress Maggie had been making in rebuilding her life.

She briefly considered confiding in Poppy but decided against it. She loved Poppy but she was far too sensible to get involved with something like this without insisting on informing their superiors, and there would be no way of protecting Maggie from it that way. No, Annie would have to come up with a way to get him behind bars without involving her friends.

She was surprised to find that, although she felt guilty for keeping something so big from her friends, the thought of taking on this man on her own also made her feel a little excited. Part of her was crying out for a bit of danger and more of a challenge. She had always been so timid and shy that the feeling was completely new to her. She was struggling to understand it all herself. She had certainly grown in confidence since joining the WPS, but not so much that it had made her fearless. But they had fallen into such a regular routine with their patrols in Holborn, and the more monotonous the days and evenings were, the more she found her mind drifted to Richard and what she had lost.

The night of the air raids had been terrifying yet also exhilarating. She had felt like she had more of a purpose, and all the activity had left her so exhausted she had enjoyed her best night's sleep in a long time. Annie wondered if she was craving more danger and excitement in order to tear her thoughts away from the misery she was feeling deep inside. They came across the odd tricky situation on patrol, of course, but nothing that cleared her mind quite like the night of the air raids. She felt bad wishing for more danger, but she couldn't help it – normal patrols weren't distracting her enough. She needed more to focus on, and this could turn out to be just the medicine she was after.

Fresh from that revelation, Annie peered around for Maggie's attacker again. She had spotted the man's face through the crowds and she found him now standing near to Platform Two with another man who she definitely didn't recognise. Whereas Maggie's attacker was tall and beefy-looking with hardly any hair, his companion was short and skinny with a thick head of dark hair. Despite the circumstances, she couldn't help but notice how funny they looked standing next to each other. Two complete opposites.

The two men didn't speak a word to each other the whole time they stood there. They seemed to be scanning the crowds intently, and every now and then the shorter of the pair would give his companion a subtle nudge before nodding his head in a certain direction. Annie followed both their gazes on one such occasion, and her skin crawled as she took in what – who – they were looking at. A young girl was in their sights. She appeared to be lost as she wandered past them slowly. Annie wanted to run after the girl and pull her into her arms. But she couldn't risk causing a scene or alerting the men to the fact that she was on to them.

Annie made sure to keep her eyes on the pair as much as she could while she followed Poppy and Maggie around and they spoke to various people. The men stayed in the same spot for such a long time that she started panicking that they might not make a move before her friends decided to leave the train station. How was she going to convince Maggie and Poppy to stay on at the station for any longer without giving anything away?

Just as Annie was trying to think up tactics to prolong their patrol at King's Cross, both men started heading purposefully towards one of the exits. Poppy was deep in conversation with an older lady who was tipping her off about a neighbour she suspected was entertaining soldiers in her home.

Annie tapped Poppy lightly on the shoulder. 'I'm sorry to interrupt, but I've come over all giddy all of a sudden. I think I had better head back and lie down. I'll leave you and Maggie to it.'

Poppy searched Annie's face. 'Oh dear, is it the same thing you experienced before?' Poppy asked, sounding concerned.

Annie tried her best to look as if she were about to faint and she hoped that showed on her face rather than the guilt she was actually feeling. Annie felt terrible for lying to her friends and taking advantage of their good nature, but she assured herself that it was justified. She looked away from

Poppy and down at the ground, nodding her head sadly. But no matter how hard she tried to reassure herself, shame kept pulsing angrily through her.

'I'll go back with you,' Maggie offered, stepping forward to put a comforting arm around Annie, who instinctively shrunk in on herself. This was getting worse by the second. Annie had been hopeful Poppy would accept her excuse and wave her off without question. This was the price she paid for having such loyal and caring friends, she thought to herself. She knew it wasn't something she should complain about, but she couldn't help but wish they would leave her to it for once.

'We should all go. It's best to stick together,' Poppy declared, then wrapped up the conversation with the older lady. Annie panicked. She glanced behind her and saw the two men disappearing out of the exit. She had to act quickly before she lost them. She hadn't seen Maggie's attacker for so long since that first sighting, she had no idea when she would get another chance like this again.

'Honestly, I'll be fine. I just need some rest,' she managed to splutter, gently removing Maggie's arm from her shoulder. Before either of the others had a chance to respond, she turned and fled, hoping that they didn't notice that she was heading towards the wrong exit.

Annie made it outside just in time to see Maggie's attacker and his companion shepherding three battered-looking women to a car, locking them in and driving them away. She had only caught a glimpse of the women, but she thought she recognised one of them from the station – the young girl the men had watched together.

Annie's head spun as she tried to work out how Maggie's attacker and his friend had managed to round up the three women so quickly; the men had definitely been alone when she'd seen them leaving the station, and she hadn't taken her eyes off them for very long at all. How on earth had they managed to pick up the women and convince them to willingly leave in the car with them in a matter of a minute or two? And it had been quite a while since she had watched the young girl walking past them, so how had they caught up with her and brought her back while Annie had been keeping tabs on them? It seemed impossible.

One thing she was certain about, however, was what the men wanted with the women. As far as she was concerned, she now had evidence that Maggie's attacker was targeting King's Cross – and this time, he was somehow managing to persuade the women to leave with him instead of resorting to forcing them into a car. Whether they knew what their fate was when they agreed to go, she wasn't sure. But she was confident the women she had seen leave with him and his companion were about to start a very unhappy new chapter in their lives.

Glad that she had some time to herself to mull everything over and try to come up with a plan of action, Annie made her way back to the section house. She pulled her jacket tight around her body to keep out the freezing weather. There was still a touch of frost on the ground and she longed to have warm sunny days back. While she walked, a wave of tiredness and nausea swept over her. Stopping briefly to steady herself, she felt a little less guilty for lying to her friends. Maybe this funny spell was her punishment for misleading them? She had felt waves of this feeling on and off recently, but she was slowly getting her appetite back, so she hadn't been overly concerned. It took her longer than usual to get back to Hunter Street Police Station, and once back she stopped for a rest before changing out of her uniform and back into her normal clothes.

Back at the section house, Annie crept into the comfort

of her bed, ready to come up with a plan with a clear head and no distractions once she had had some sleep. She couldn't help but think that this was the type of thing she would have written to Richard about in what now seemed like a previous life. He didn't always get a chance to write back in time, and that probably would have been the case with this, too. He didn't always have the answers; sometimes he didn't even address the issue in his reply. But she missed the feeling of sharing a problem with him. Maybe she should write it all down, as if she was writing it in a letter to Richard? The act of getting everything down on paper might help.

But the next thing she knew, she was stirring from a deep sleep. She looked drowsily out of her window and her heart dropped when she saw that it was dark outside. Realising she must have fallen asleep almost immediately and slept through the rest of the afternoon, she got up slowly and headed to the communal kitchen in hopes of finding her friends. She certainly felt better after her nap and her stomach was rumbling, which she reasoned was a good sign. She shivered as she stepped out of bed and the cold air hit her body. Pulling on her thickest jumper, she couldn't believe the year was almost over. She was meant to be ending it as a happily married woman but as Christmas crept closer and closer, her heart filled with dread instead of joy. She didn't know how she was going to cope with the festive season without her soulmate by her side.

'Ah, there you are. We weren't sure if we should come and check on you. We didn't want to disturb you,' Maggie said when Annie walked into the kitchen. Maggie was sitting at the big table in the middle of the room while Poppy stood next to the stove stirring a big pot, which was simmering invitingly. Annie felt another sudden twinge of guilt for misleading her friends, but she was soon distracted by the amazing smell that was filling the air.

'I'm making some bean soup, and we managed to get some bread. Will you join us for dinner?' Poppy asked.

'I'd love to,' Annie replied, suddenly ravenous. Both her friends smiled – they were obviously as relieved as she was that she was feeling better at last. If she could kick the tiredness then she was certain she would be completely back to normal.

As they ate, Poppy and Maggie filled Annie in on what they had got up to for the remainder of the patrol without her. But Annie was only half-listening. Her mind was consumed with Maggie's attacker and what the poor women he had driven away with must have in store for them. This was so much more dangerous than she had realised when she had first recognised the man at the station.

Any doubts she might have had about going it alone disappeared from her mind. It wasn't that she doubted her friends' abilities, but this was now more than taking on one man with a history of trafficking and violence. Maggie's attacker was working from the station with an accomplice, and they also had a driver on board. Could there be more people involved that she didn't know about yet? For all Annie knew, she was barely scratching the surface, and she knew for certain that at least one of these men was very dangerous.

Annie was well aware of the lengths Maggie's attacker was prepared to go to in order to evade capture. The chances were the people he was working with would act just as recklessly when confronted by the police – especially female officers. It felt careless to put herself and her two friends in such a treacherous situation before at least trying to find another, safer, way. She was also worried that Maggie's emotions would take over if she was faced with her attacker again. Would she be able to stop herself from lashing out at him and getting in trouble herself – or worse, getting hurt again?

Annie's thoughts were interrupted when a couple of officers walked into the kitchen. They were in their everyday clothes, but Annie recognised them from around the station. They had never been unpleasant to the three girls, but she couldn't remember them being particularly welcoming, either.

The girls tended to do so many night patrols that they hardly ever bumped into the male officers back at the section house; their long hours and strange mealtimes meant that they often tended to have the communal kitchen to themselves. But Poppy had been talking about cooking up extra food when they were around at normal hours, such as now. She had won her husband over with cooking, she had previously confided to Annie and Maggie, and she thought it was worth trying to get some of their new, sceptical colleagues on their side in the same manner.

Both the men's stern-looking expressions softened when they saw the sight in front of them.

'Well, we're not used to these kinds of smells in here,' the first one said, smiling at the group who were now finishing off their soup. Annie had enjoyed hers so much that she'd been hoping to go back for a second portion, but she hung back now as she remembered Poppy's plan.

'There's more than enough to go around,' Poppy assured them, getting to her feet, going back to the stove and picking up the ladle. 'Can I tempt you?' she asked casually as she stirred the delicious stew and more steam wafted up into the air, sending the gorgeous smell drifting around the room.

Both men seemed to take a moment to enjoy the lovely aroma before shifting uncomfortably. This was clearly not a situation they were used to. Annie wondered if they were worried their colleagues might think them traitors for spending time with the girls. Although nobody at Hunter Street Police Station had been quite as openly negative towards them as they had been when they had started at

Bethnal Green, they weren't exactly treating them as equals, either. It was more of a begrudging acceptance, on the most part. Nobody had been as friendly towards them as Miller or Sergeant Turner.

Poppy must have been having the same thoughts, as she offered up a solution before Annie could even think of one. 'We were on our way to bed, so I'll leave the rest of the soup here,' she said, placing the ladle back in the pot. Annie's mouth watered in longing for just one more mouthful of the delectable dish, but she held herself back. 'Please, do help yourselves so it doesn't go to waste. It would be such a shame to have to throw it out in the morning. Goodnight.' With that, she swept past the men and straight out of the kitchen door.

Annie looked at Maggie, who shrugged before quickly getting up from her seat and gathering their dishes together. The officers stood in silence as she rinsed them off, and then Annie followed her out of the room, giving the men a quick nod as she did so. Poppy was waiting for them further down the corridor.

'Do you think it worked?' she whispered anxiously. The three of them stood still for a moment, and then Annie felt a jolt of excitement as she heard the clatter of dishes being pulled out of the cupboard. Moments later, chairs were being dragged out from under the table. It certainly sounded as though they had helped themselves to some of the stew.

'Once they taste that, they'll be falling over themselves to support us,' Maggie whispered excitedly.

'I wouldn't go that far,' Poppy giggled. 'But it's certainly a step in the right direction.'

Back in her bedroom, Annie wondered if she would be able to sleep after having had such a long afternoon nap. But she found herself starting to doze off just minutes after getting under the sheets. Before succumbing, she racked her brain one more time to try and come up with a plan for finally apprehending Maggie's attacker. She felt in over her head.

Annie found herself, not for the first time, wishing that Irene hadn't moved to Grantham. If she were here, this was something they would be tackling together. She contemplated writing her a letter to ask for advice – it was the kind of thing Irene would know exactly how best to deal with. But she sighed in frustration when she thought about how long it would take to receive a reply. Even if Irene wrote back to her as soon as her letter arrived, she didn't have time to waste waiting for the unpredictable and lengthy postal service.

After much to-ing and fro-ing, she decided to visit Chief Constable Green the following morning and share her suspicions about what the men were up to at King's Cross Station. It was a risky move – he had warned the three of them off patrolling in the area, after all. But surely he would be grateful that she had managed to spot the problem? She wasn't looking to undermine his men or show them up for not patrolling the station properly themselves. This kind of activity was subtle, and she had only spotted it herself because of her previous run-in with Maggie's attacker. She would probably be none the wiser had she not recognised him that first time at the station.

This was definitely the best course of action, she reasoned as she drifted off to sleep. She was reluctant to hand a job over to the men after so long doing so well at not having to rely on them. It went against everything they had been building towards to ask for backup in this way. But these were exceptional circumstances, and this seemed like the best thing to do in this situation. Allowing herself to give in to yet more sleep, Annie smiled as she thought about how good it was going to feel to be able to tell Maggie that her attacker was finally where he belonged – locked up in a prison cell.

19

Annie struggled to find an opportunity to visit Chief Constable Green alone over the next few days. The girls always patrolled together, and they didn't often take time off. The time they did enjoy out of uniform was normally spent eating, sleeping or doing something else together. So, it was difficult to slip away unnoticed, even for a short period of time. When they agreed to take a much-needed day off a week after Annie had seen Maggie's attacker, she knew she couldn't waste the opportunity. Maggie was keen to go out for an afternoon tea – since meeting Poppy, she had enjoyed spending time in a tea room. And Poppy was keen on a trip to the picture house in the early evening. Annie knew she wouldn't be able to get out of either activity without raising suspicion, so she decided to sneak off on her own first thing in the morning.

'I'm going to go over and see my mother and sisters this morning, and then I'll meet you at the tea room for afternoon tea,' Annie told Maggie and Poppy over breakfast. It wasn't a complete lie. She was indeed going to go and see her family, but she had left out her plan to visit the chief beforehand. She had no idea if he would be at the station, or even if he would agree to see her, but she had to try. And if she had no luck before visiting her family, then she would try again on the way back.

Annie was worried Maggie would ask to join her on her visit home. Maggie got on well with Annie's mother and enjoyed spending time with her, especially since being unable to see her own mother often or very easily. And she was aware that her friend was keen to thank her parents for their financial help. Thankfully, Maggie was deep into the latest book Irene had recommended, so she hardly even looked up from it when Annie filled her and Poppy in on her plan for the morning.

Annie was doubly relieved – not only was she keeping the visit to the chief from her friends, but Christmas was still slowly but surely approaching and she knew her mother would be looking to lock down her plans to spend the day together as a family. It was something Annie couldn't bring herself to think about now Richard was no longer here. But they were into the last week of November now so she knew she would have to face it soon enough. She wanted a little more time, so she decided to change the subject as soon as her mother brought it up – something she knew wouldn't be so easy if Maggie was with her.

At the police station, Annie was relieved to find Miller manning the reception desk. And, even better, he was talking to one of the officers the girls had seen in the kitchen a few evenings before.

'Makes a damn tasty stew, this one does!' the officer from the section house roared as Annie approached them. She smiled nervously. Poppy's idea had worked.

'It's my colleague who does the cooking,' Annie explained. 'And I agree, all her dishes are delicious.'

'I keep popping into the kitchen hoping to find something on the hob,' the officer replied cheekily.

'We're often out in the evenings on night patrols, but I'll have a word with Poppy for you. Perhaps she can rustle something up one afternoon and leave it out for you to warm up when you finish for the day.' His eyes lit up at the suggestion. Annie would have to find a way to pass this exchange on to Poppy without telling her about her secret, lone visit to the station, but she would think about that later.

'Do you work most nights, then?' he asked. He looked genuinely shocked at the revelation.

'The WPS girls hardly ever stop,' Miller said fondly, and Annie threw him a grateful smile. 'I don't know why everyone seems to think they're anything but hard-working. Just ask Turner and he'll tell you how hard they went at it the night of the air raids. He told me he would have been stuck without them.'

The officer looked embarrassed, but Annie flashed him an understanding smile. 'Don't worry, we're used to it,' she said. 'But we're keen to prove how good we are at this.'

'It sounds like you're doing a very good job,' he replied.

Annie mentioned that she needed to speak to the chief, so while Miller went off to see if he was available, she filled the section house officer in on what the WPS recruits got up to on a daily basis. PC Lewis, as he finally revealed he was called, seemed surprised at how busy they kept themselves.

'I think most of the male officers expect us to make a big song and dance of it all, and come running for backup every five minutes, but we really are very capable,' Annie informed him.

'It sounds as if you are,' PC Lewis replied, looking thoughtful. 'As well as being great cooks,' he added, his eyes lighting up again. Annie could see Miller coming back along the corridor now.

'Don't worry, I won't forget to put in your request to Poppy,' she said, laughing lightly. 'Keep checking the kitchen and I'm sure you'll find something tasty waiting for you soon.' PC Lewis grinned, tipped his hat and then made his way out of the station.

'The chief can see you now, but he doesn't have long,' Miller said as he got back to the reception desk.

'Thank you.' Annie smiled, suddenly feeling nervous. 'Erm, would you mind not mentioning my meeting with him in front of the other two, please?' She couldn't risk him innocently asking her how it had gone the next time they bumped into him. He gave her a wink and tapped his nose with his finger, which she took as a yes, so she rushed a thank you and shuffled off down the corridor towards the chief's office.

Chief Constable Green looked deep in concentration as he pored over a pile of paperwork on his desk when Annie walked into his office. He waved her in and motioned for her to sit down. His full cheeks were burning red and he was rubbing a hand over the top of his head. Annie wasn't sure if he was aware that it was making a horrible mess of his thinning hair, and she tried not to look at it for too long. She waited patiently while he made some notes on the piece of paper in front of him. As soon as he put the pen down on the table, she became aware of his gaze taking in her clothing.

Annie suddenly felt very aware of the fact she wasn't in uniform, and she wondered if she could get into trouble for coming in to see him looking so casual. She had been so worried about getting into bother for disobeying his orders to stay away from King's Cross that she hadn't even considered the possibility that this might be an issue. But when he gave her a big, welcoming smile, she relaxed. After a little small talk, Annie got to the point of her visit.

'I know your men are taking care of King's Cross Station, but we ended up following one of our more prolific ladies on to the concourse and we came across some activity I thought you should know about,' she said.

He had raised his chin and narrowed his eyes at her when she had mentioned King's Cross. Annie felt her heart race at the reaction, but she kept going and he seemed to soften as she continued.

He listened intently as she told him about her concerns regarding the men at the station. She mentioned that they had come across one of them previously in Bethnal Green and that they knew from that encounter that he was dangerous and most certainly behind some form of trafficking. Chief Constable Green looked shocked when Annie revealed what the man had done to Maggie.

'So, I think he's doing something similar at the train station,' she explained. 'It seems as though him and his companion are—'

'The authorities are well aware that slavery rings are popping up, especially in London,' he cut in. 'Women are being kidnapped and forced into prostitution.' Annie nodded her head in reply. 'It's mainly foreign refugees but they're also targeting younger and more naive local women,' he added.

Annie felt overwhelmed with relief that she wasn't in trouble for going against the chief's orders, and that he understood exactly what she was concerned about. She had been so worried he would dismiss her concerns. The meeting was going far better than she had expected it would.

'What can we do about it?' she asked, full of hope that she would be allowed to help. Maybe there was an undercover operation she could get involved in to help save these women? But Chief Constable Green's face hardened, and she felt her smile freeze on her face.

Taking in her disappointed expression, he softened a little and appeared to take the following few moments of silence to think. 'I'm afraid that unless there is hard evidence, which as I'm sure you can imagine is pretty much impossible to gather, then the law favours the men,' he explained sadly while studying Annie's face intently. 'Even if we manage to find out where they are holding these women and determine that they are forcing them into these disreputable acts, it's the women who end up being prosecuted, rather than the animals who gave them no choice but to do it.'

Annie dropped her gaze, feeling hopeless and useless, but Chief Constable Green straightened his back, seemingly satisfied. 'It's all very sad,' he sighed, shuffling the papers on his desk and picking up his pen again, 'but we don't have the resources to investigate it properly at the moment. I mean, we're taking help from women to keep the streets in order so it should be obvious that we don't have the manpower to tackle something big like this.'

Annie's shoulders sagged as his words sunk in. She had hoped for so much more from this conversation. He looked down at his papers and started making notes again, but Annie couldn't stop herself from trying once more.

'So, they just have to suffer?' she asked. She had switched from feeling dejected to angry – how could he just dismiss these poor women like this? But she hadn't meant to make such an outburst, especially when Chief Constable Green was now making it obvious that he had things to be getting on with. He placed the pen back down with such force, the noise made Annie jump. His cheeks were red again and he stared at her, looking as outraged as a hungry infant.

Normally, Annie would have scurried straight out of his office without another word, but something was pushing her to give it one last try, so she sat tight. This wasn't just about saving innocent women. Of course, that reason alone would have motivated her to risk getting into trouble, but something was burning in her belly and she realised that it was a fierce need to get justice for Maggie. She was also desperate to get her friend's attacker behind bars to eliminate the risk of Maggie bumping into him herself while they were out on patrol. She had no idea how Maggie would react if she came face to face with the man who done her such harm and had set such a terrible chain of events into motion for her. Would she even recognise him? One thing was for certain: if she did remember his face then the outcome would not be a good one for either of them.

'If you must insist on patrolling the station on your route, then do what you can to steer the women away from these men,' Chief Constable Green said finally, through somewhat gritted teeth.

Annie knew she was pushing her luck here, but she had to try harder. That wouldn't work because in order to do that she would have to reveal everything to Maggie and Poppy. The reason she had come to the chief was because she wanted to keep this from Maggie until her attacker was safely locked up and unable to harm her or anybody else again.

'Could I have your permission to investigate this myself?' she asked with all the confidence she could muster. She felt ashamed at how weak the words sounded when she heard them out loud, but she quickly reminded herself that just months before she wouldn't have had the courage to so much as approach the chief on her own, let alone make such a request. She coughed to clear her throat and then added, 'I can gather all the evidence needed to stop this slavery ring in its tracks.' Then, with a lot more confidence she said, 'Once I have everything we need, I can lead your men to wherever these slavers are holding their victims so they can arrest them.'

Chief Constable Green remained silent. Annie searched his eyes, looking for some kind of positive reaction. But all of a sudden his stern expression changed and he started to laugh. Annie looked around the room uncomfortably, waiting for him to stop.

'The brass would have my job for suggesting I let any woman – let alone a young, unmarried one – be involved in such a compromising and dangerous investigation!' he spluttered, shaking his head and rubbing the back of his neck.

Annie instinctively rubbed her wedding band. Strangers assumed she was married when they spotted it and she had thought the policemen at the station had come to the same conclusion; she had certainly never discussed it with anybody. But she realised Frosty would probably have filled the chief in on her background before her and her friends had arrived. She found herself shocked at how upset she felt to be referred to as 'unmarried'. She had come to think of herself as a widow over the last couple of months. She hoped against all hope that the chief hadn't shared his knowledge of her with any of his men.

'And you expect me to send you out to do all this on your own?' Chief Constable Green added, interrupting her thoughts.

Annie shrugged nervously. 'I would be following them undercover, so I could stay out of danger,' she tried, but she knew it was hopeless.

He laughed again, this time more lightly, as if she had made some kind of joke that they were both expected to delight in. 'I don't think so, my dear,' he scoffed. His patronising tone told her that this conversation was definitely over. Chief Constable Green picked up his pen again and waved her away with his other hand. He started shuffling through the papers in front of him again and Annie slowly got to her feet and left the room without another word.

On her way to see her parents, Annie had to fight back tears. She had been so determined to crack this and get those horrible men off the streets, but that possibility had been snatched away from her. She couldn't stop the tears from stinging her eyes when she thought of the cruel way the chief had laughed in her face.

Her hand flew to her wedding band once more, and as her thumb rubbed it for comfort, she realised something. When the chief had mentioned the fact that she wasn't married and she had instinctively reached for the ring, it had been the first time she had turned to it for reassurance since she had spotted Maggie's attacker at King's Cross. She had come to rely on it for comfort since losing Richard. Rubbing it and thinking of her lost love had become second nature whenever she was feeling anything less than positive.

The action and the feelings it brought with it kept her going when she found herself struggling. Annie could see now that her grand plan to bring down the slavery ring had been helping her move on from her grief. Was it a coincidence that her appetite had been getting back to normal lately, too? She shook her head sadly. It was a deep shame that she had been stopped in her tracks, she thought – not only because she wouldn't be able to help Maggie now, but she had also been stopped from helping herself.

20

During her visit to her parents, Annie managed to avoid the inevitable discussion about Christmas by asking her father about his work as soon as her mother broached the subject. She could see from her mother's face that she knew exactly what she was up to. That was the problem with being so close to someone – they knew all your tricks and could tell just by looking at you exactly what you were feeling. Thankfully, Mrs Beckett didn't push it. Annie knew her mother hadn't given up entirely, but she was off the hook for now, at least.

The truth was, Annie would be quite happy to lock herself away in her room at the section house for the whole of the festive season and not speak to another soul. She didn't see the point in celebrating now that Richard was gone.

On her way to meet her friends, Annie decided to tell Poppy she had bumped into PC Lewis on her morning travels. She figured that would enable her to reveal the discussion about the stew without raising any suspicions with her friends. It wasn't too much of a fib, and there was no way she could keep the good news from her friend, who she knew would be delighted that her plan to get some of the officers on-side had worked a treat. In the end, she was so nervous about the lie that she blurted out a summary of the conversation as soon as the group sat down for tea that afternoon.

'That's wonderful!' Poppy exclaimed, rubbing her hands together in glee. She was beaming from ear to ear. Then, suddenly, her eyes glazed over and became misty. Panicked, Annie wondered what on earth she could have said to illicit such an extreme reaction – she had thought she was passing on such good news.

Poppy wiped away a tear. 'I'm sorry,' she whispered. 'Please don't feel bad because these are good tears, honestly.' Annie's face was obviously still full of concern as Poppy reached out her hand and squeezed her arm in an act of reassurance. 'Honestly,' she repeated, then took a sip of her tea.

Annie and Maggie waited patiently while Poppy composed herself. When she was ready, she took a deep breath. 'I only learned to cook properly when I met John,' she explained.

Annie felt a sudden rush of sympathy for her friend. She always seemed to be keeping things together so well, and Annie assumed she was a lot stronger than herself because of that. But she clearly struggled too – it wasn't just Annie who was getting constant cruel reminders of what she had lost because of this war. It was comforting, in a way, to know she wasn't the only one going through this nightmare while trying to live her life with some kind of degree of normality.

'How did you meet John?' Maggie asked. Annie felt bad that even after all this time living together, she didn't know the full story of Poppy and her dead husband. She knew a lot about John, and she knew he had been killed in action, but Poppy had never gone into their history together and it wasn't something you tended to ask about. But Maggie's question had come at a natural time, and Poppy seemed keen to talk about him.

While Poppy smilingly recounted the tale of how she met John, Annie found herself thinking about Richard and their early courtship. She had been such a different person back then, and it still wounded her when she thought about the fact that he would never get the chance to get to know the new, confident, assertive Annie. He had certainly picked up hints of her in her letters to him on the front, though – he had said as much in his replies. He loved hearing about her police work, especially the occasions when she stood up for herself, which was something the old Annie never did. And he was delighted to learn that she was fully versed in ju-jitsu to protect herself on the streets.

But they had spent so little time together since she had joined the WPS that Richard hadn't had the opportunity to get to know her new personality properly and in the flesh. She knew, though, that he would have loved the new Annie even more than he loved the old one. At least she would always have that one last special afternoon.

'And John's eyes would light up whenever he talked about food, so I just knew that was the way to his heart. So I learnt how to cook,' Poppy was saying as Annie tuned back into the conversation that had been happening at the table while she had been daydreaming. She mirrored Maggie's actions and nodded along with a sympathetic smile, feeling extremely guilty for not listening properly to what seemed to have been a heart-warming story that obviously meant a lot to Poppy.

A few days later, Poppy went out of her way to prepare another meal before the girls headed out on night patrol.

'At least PC Lewis and his chums won't go hungry tonight,' Maggie groaned sarcastically while pointedly staring at the pot sitting on the stove. Annie couldn't help but grin. She was feeling exactly the same way as Maggie, but she would never have dreamed of complaining to Poppy about it. She knew she could always rely on Maggie to speak her mind in these situations, though.

Poppy didn't say a word in reply, but instead she silently laid three bowls out on the table before offering the ladle up to Maggie with a raised eyebrow. Maggie didn't need telling twice and she leapt forward, grabbed the ladle and served up three generous portions of stew.

As they all sat down to enjoy it together, Annie felt grateful once more for the return of her appetite. She was feeling more tired than usual, but at least she was able to take on extra food to help power her through patrols now. And she knew that it was showing on her figure, because her uniform was starting to fit better again. Even her mother had commented on her recent visit home that she was looking 'healthy' – which Annie knew was a kind way of saying she was getting plumper again. Such a comment would have upset her previously, but now she didn't mind because she had come to learn that she preferred to have a bit of meat on her bones. She hadn't felt womanly at all when all that weight had fallen off, and it was something she had never appreciated before. She understood now that her body was built to be a little fuller, and she was happy with that.

'You're sure they'll know to help themselves?' Poppy asked Annie when the three of them went to leave the kitchen, a generous helping of the stew still simmering on the hob and filling the room with a delicious aroma.

Annie nodded. 'I made it very clear, but we could always leave them a note, just in case?' she suggested. 'We don't want it going to waste.'

'Good idea,' Poppy agreed, and Maggie fetched her letter-writing kit and scrawled a quick message on a fresh piece of paper before they made their way to Hunter Street Police Station.

Out on patrol, they started on their usual rounds. Brunswick Square Gardens was quiet, then in St George's Gardens they spotted an older woman talking to a man on one of the benches. The couple scarpered in different directions as soon as they spotted the girls approaching them. Maggie smiled and nodded knowingly at Annie and Poppy. Their reactions were a clear indicator that they had been up to no good. Annie was pleased they had been able to move the couple on without a confrontation.

In Regent Square Gardens, they spotted a lone figure and immediately started making their way towards it. It was hard to tell in the dark and from a distance if it was a man or a woman, and while they were still quite far away, Poppy stopped walking and indicated to Annie and Maggie to pause, too.

'Look at the way they're lingering,' she muttered. Annie looked over again and, although she couldn't see the person clearly, she could see that they were looking around themselves a lot, and occasionally pacing up and down. She could just about make out now that it was a man – when he walked up and down, she could see the outline of trousers as opposed to a dress or skirt. Whoever he was, his behaviour was typical of a man scouting around for a prostitute to have a good time with.

'Let's not give him a chance to run away,' Maggie whispered. 'I'd like to listen to the excuse he comes up with.'

Even in the moonlight, Annie could see the glint in her friend's eyes when she spoke. She and Poppy nodded their agreement. Although confrontation often wasn't pleasant, it was the best way to deal with things as it normally meant the culprit was less likely to offend again – at least not in the same place, anyway. It was widely known that the WPS didn't have powers of arrest, but also common knowledge that they were able to call on the male officers to make an arrest on their behalf, as well as an ability to escort an offender to the police station to be dealt with.

But, as the girls got closer, Annie's heart started racing. She could see now that it was most definitely a man, and a man who had the same outline – from what she could tell – as the one she had seen with Maggie's attacker just a few days before. Poppy quickly signalled to them both to stay quiet and pointed in his direction. Annie realised her friend wanted to creep up on him and surprise him.

The man was facing away from them, oblivious to their presence, and he still appeared to be waiting for somebody or looking out for someone coming from the other direction. He was so preoccupied with that, he didn't hear Annie, Maggie and Poppy approaching until they were just a few feet away.

Now Annie could see it was definitely who she had thought it was. Panic rushed through her as she thought of all the ways that surprising him could go wrong. This wasn't just an average chap who was going to get flustered and embarrassed when he realised the girls knew what he was up to. If he was anything like his companion – and Annie would bet her wedding ring he was – he would lash out when confronted. Especially if taken by surprise.

They might have been in a safer environment than they had been when Maggie was attacked, but who knew if he had a weapon with him? Maybe that was how he convinced women to leave with him. Or maybe Maggie's attacker was nearby, ready to jump in and help him if he ran into trouble. Even if this man ran when he saw them, Annie knew that her friends would give chase. And she couldn't let that happen. She had to protect them. But how?

Before she'd had time to think it through properly, Annie pretended to trip. She let out an almighty yelp as she threw herself dramatically to the ground. Both her friends took their eyes off the target and leapt to her aid. As she clutched her ankle and pretended to writhe in agony, Annie risked a glance up and saw, to her relief, that the man had disappeared. She couldn't even see the back of him as he ran off into the distance. He must have fled as soon as he'd heard the commotion. Annie calmed her dramatics a little and allowed her friends to help her to her feet, pretending to be unsteady on one foot.

'Well, that put an end to whatever he was up to,' Maggie commented ruefully.

Annie smiled to herself. She had managed to get rid of him and her friends didn't suspect a thing, and neither were they annoyed with her about it. She pretended to hobble for the next hour or so, wincing every now and then for added effect. The hobbling slowed her down sufficiently enough that she was able to keep a keen eye out for the man in case he was lingering around nearby. She hoped against hope that she had managed to scare him away for the rest of the evening at the very least. But one thing she knew for certain was that he had been there scouting for his next victim.

She needed to do something to bring his and Maggie's attacker's little operation down as soon as possible. She couldn't spend every patrol looking over her shoulder and fearing they would bump into him. Now she knew he was operating in areas other than the train station it felt like it would be impossible to avoid a run-in with him or Maggie's attacker at some point. But the surge of protectiveness she had felt when her friends had been so close to the brute reconfirmed to her that she couldn't risk getting them involved. It was far too dangerous.

Annie wasn't sure why she was happy to put herself in such a perilous situation. Perhaps she didn't care so much about her own safety? It was true that since losing Richard she had felt braver. But was that feeling one of bravery or did she no longer care so much about whether she lived or died? After all, she'd had the most precious thing in her life taken away from her in the blink of an eye, along with all her hopes and plans for the future. It was true that coming so close to danger during the air raid had made her realise how much she had to live for. Maybe she was looking for a similar brush with death to recreate that feeling and reassure her that she was, in fact, better off alive.

The rush of feelings running through her made her see just how numb and empty she had been feeling all this time. That was why she had been longing for more action, she realised – even if that came in the form of more air raids to deal with. Just the thought of bringing down these two men was making Annie feel energised in a way she hadn't felt since the last time she'd seen Richard. She suddenly felt alive again, full of purpose. She was going to do this on her own, she just had to work out the best way to do it.

She would have to carry out her secret operation behind the chief's back, as well as keeping it from her friends. That thought worried her for a moment. She knew she could get into a lot of trouble for defying Chief Constable Green's very clear orders. It was another reason not to get Maggie and Poppy involved in her plan: she didn't want to bring them down with her if she was caught. But, then, Annie remembered how adamant the chief had been that his men were keeping things in order at the train station. His officers quite clearly hadn't set foot inside the place for a long time and he was none the wiser, so how was he going to find out that she was tailing these men to confirm what they were up to? And he had said they could try and warn vulnerable women away from the pair. Annie suddenly felt confident that she could do this without being found out.

Annie wondered briefly whether she should go to Frosty with her findings, but she decided she needed firmer evidence before doing that. All she had at the moment was her suspicions and Chief Constable Green had been very clear that they would need firm evidence that the women were being forced into prostitution against their will. No, she would have to investigate this further herself and get a stronger case together before going to anybody for help.

As the thought of getting justice for Maggie crossed Annie's mind once more, she made a promise to herself. She may well be dreading Christmas this year, but one thing that could turn things around for her would be succeeding at this before the holiday came around. Time was tight: Christmas was only a few weeks away, but she was determined to bring down the gang by then. The best present she could give Maggie this year – as well as all the current and potential victims of these men – was seeing the brutes behind bars once and for all. Setting herself that deadline, she decided she was going to do this for all those women, as well as for herself – because getting this done would also be a way of making Richard proud of her as he watched over her from wherever it was his spirit had gone when his life had been so cruelly snatched away.

21

The following day Annie awoke feeling exhilarated about her new secret mission. She wanted to devise a detailed plan of action straight away, but she had to stay focused on her patrol with Maggie and Poppy. She didn't want to raise suspicions by acting oddly. They both knew her so well that they would start asking questions the minute she started behaving as though her mind was somewhere else rather than on the job in hand.

'Have you had any thoughts about Christmas?' Maggie asked as they passed a small group of children carrying sprigs of holly and mistletoe stuffed into sacks. It was early evening and they must have picked up the haul on their way home from school. Annie's heart dropped. Setting herself the deadline to get the traffickers behind bars before Christmas Day had helped, but apart from that she had been trying to pretend the festive season wasn't creeping closer and closer. They were into the first week of December now, though, and as well as her mother bringing it up at every opportunity, little reminders like this were popping up all around them. There may have been a war raging on, but Londoners were determined to find joy where they could.

Annie felt a rush of sadness when she looked over at Maggie's unsure face. While dealing with her grief, she had forgotten the fact that this would be Maggie's first Christmas since being disowned by her cruel father. She realised there was no way Maggie would get an opportunity to see her

mother over the festive period, and she was facing the prospect of spending what should be a special time all on her
own. Maggie hadn't mentioned it before, but now Annie
thought about it, she understood that she must have been
dreading Christmas Day just as much as she was. She had
been so caught up in her own angst that she hadn't even
thought about the fact her friend was likely to be feeling
desperately sad as the big day approached.

And then there was Poppy. She had opened up to them
about John, but she had never mentioned any of her family.
Did she have anybody to celebrate with, or was she in just
as sad a situation as her two friends? The fact that Poppy
hadn't mentioned any plans for Christmas made Annie think
she didn't have any and that she was doing exactly what she
was doing – living in denial of the fact that it was happening
and quietly hoping life would just go on as normal without
the usual festive fanfare. Maybe they could all help each
other through this difficult time?

'Well?' Maggie pushed, and Annie snapped out of her
thoughts.

'Sorry, I was just thinking about inviting you both to spend
the day with me and my family,' she said before she had
even had a chance to think it through properly.

Maggie's face flooded with relief, and then she broke into
the biggest grin. 'That would be wonderful!' she cried.

Annie felt a slight sense of panic. What if her mother
didn't want any more guests for Christmas? They were
already hosting her aunt and cousins, after all. But then
Mrs Beckett loved bringing people together, and Annie
knew her mother had a soft spot for Maggie. She was certain
her mother wouldn't mind. Besides, looking at her friend's
face now, she knew there was no way she could go back
on the offer. They would have to make it work.

'Good, because my mother can't wait to see you,' Annie

lied. She felt her sense of dread for the day lift slightly. Maybe it wouldn't be so bad if she was with her closest friends and her family. Added to that, the more people she surrounded herself with, the less chance she would have of getting any time to herself – and therefore any time to think about how much she was missing Richard and what the day should have been like for the two of them. Maybe this was actually a better idea than locking herself away to wallow in her sadness on her own for the day.

'How about you, Poppy?' Annie asked. 'Would you like to join us?'

Poppy smiled warmly and nodded. 'That is so kind, thank you. I'd been so worried about spending the day all alone, to be honest with you.'

So, she didn't have anybody to celebrate with. Annie wanted to find out more, but she stopped herself from prying. Poppy would tell them in her own time, just like she had told them more about John eventually. Knowing that Maggie wouldn't be able to show such self-restraint, Annie quickly glanced over at her friend, who appeared to be preparing to ask Poppy a follow-up question.

'Right, shall we start a round of the pubs? They'll be getting busy by now,' Annie said quickly. She knew Maggie's natural inquisitiveness would be eating away at her and she would be annoyed at Annie for changing the subject before she'd had the chance to ask Poppy for more information. But she knew better than anybody that it was better to let somebody share sensitive information in their own time, without being pushed on it. The group walked off towards the nearest public house, and Maggie shot Annie a look of annoyance. 'She'll tell us in her own time,' Annie hissed under her breath. Understanding spread over Maggie's face and her expression softened as she gave Annie an apologetic nod.

'What was that?' Poppy asked.

'I was just saying that my ankle is still a little sore,' Annie said innocently, and she stopped and reached down to give it a gentle rub. Poppy didn't look convinced, but she didn't say anything, and Annie breathed a sigh of relief that at least one of her friends knew when to let something go.

They visited a few of the local pubs and escorted some worse-for-wear soldiers back to Gray's Inn. One was so drunk that he thought Poppy was his mother and started telling her how much he had missed her while he had been away, and how he thought of her face every time he was in danger. Annie expected Poppy to correct the poor chap, but she listened intently as they ambled along the street, and she stopped to give him a comforting cuddle when he broke down in tears. It was strangely moving, and Annie found herself wiping away a tear or two from her own eyes.

Once back at the section house, Annie was feeling wide awake despite all the evening's activities. Her body was exhausted, but her mind was alive. She decided to sit down on her bed with her writing pad and a pencil to jot down some ideas before getting some much-needed rest.

In the end, she concluded the most sensible thing to do would be to tail the men on her own as soon as an opportunity arose, and work out where they were operating from. Once she knew where the brothel was, she could decide what action to take next. It was best to take this one step at a time, Annie thought as she drifted off to sleep.

Over the next couple of days Annie sneaked off whenever the chance arose and tried to find one or both of the men. Living in separate rooms at the section house rather than together in the flat in Camberwell meant she could head out to search on her own without having to make up excuses for her friends, for the most part. It also meant she was closer to where she knew the men were operating, so she saved precious time on travelling.

Annie went out looking at every opportunity. She had only seen the men on a handful of occasions so far, so she knew she was going to have to strike lucky to find one of them again so soon. She felt more confident about trying to tail the pair under the cover of darkness and she was relieved when she managed to convince Poppy and Maggie to go for a week-long stint of day patrols rather than their preferred night patrols. Annie told her friends it would be good to change their routine a little and catch out anyone who had got used to the fact they were only around when it was dark. She felt guilty for the deception, but then she would remind herself of the reason for it. Working this way meant she could go back out searching once her friends were tucked up in bed for the night. She was going to be exhausted from working flat-out, but she was certain whatever activities the men were up to would peak at night-time so she had no choice.

Halfway through the week, Annie was beginning to feel disheartened by her lack of progress. Her Christmas deadline was looming ever closer and she was no nearer to finding the men, let alone bringing them down. She was reminded of the impending festivities at every turn, with shops adorned with homemade decorations and drunken soldiers singing carols as they stumbled along the street. Someone at the section house had even strung up paper chains in the kitchen. Annie was convinced it had been Maggie, although her friend denied being involved.

Annie was also exhausted from the lack of sleep and struggling to hide it from her friends. She was beginning to wonder if the traffickers had moved on to a different area. She had first come across Maggie's attacker in Bethnal Green, so it was possible that they worked their way around an area for a few weeks before moving on. Maybe she was too late to catch them. Crestfallen, Annie decided it might be best to admit defeat and get some well-needed rest. She had tried her best, but it seemed like she was just too late to make a difference.

Annie found herself feeling relieved she hadn't said anything to her friends about the men. She was distraught at having to let her plan go, so she couldn't imagine how upset Maggie would have felt to have come so close to getting justice and then having to give up on it.

The following day, the three girls were walking around King's Cross Station when Annie spotted Maggie's attacker making his way through the crowds with a woman by his side. She couldn't believe her eyes – she had searched so hard and been convinced she would never see him again, and now here he was right in front of her. Thankfully, Maggie had her eyes set on a group of children gathered by Platform Two, so she was none the wiser. Annie hadn't wanted to do this in uniform or indeed in daylight, but she had to act now. Who knew how long it would be before she would find him or his companion again?

'I'm feeling poorly again,' she said quickly, trying to sound convincing. She was so full of nervous energy that her voice had an authentic wobble to it. She had to get away quickly before she lost sight of the couple, and before Maggie and Poppy had a chance to offer to escort her back to the section house. 'I need a lie down. I'll catch up with you both later.'

She dashed away, hoping to goodness that neither of them gave chase, but bracing herself just in case. When she was halfway across the concourse she slowed and took a quick look back and found her friends talking to the group of boys they had spotted before she had fled.

The man had left through the same exit as before. Annie

realised he was probably going to leave in a car again, but she couldn't let him get away. She burst into the freezing air and, sure enough, he was there guiding the woman she had just seen him with into a waiting red car. It looked to be the same as the one used previously.

Annie peered around looking for another car, and felt a burst of triumph when one drove up and came to a halt right next to her. Annie felt grateful to be in her uniform now. The car she needed to tail was pulling away, so she didn't have much time. She pulled out her WPS identity card and banged on the passenger window of the car that had just stopped. The man in the driver's seat jumped and looked over at her, startled. He seemed to relax when he took in the WPS card. Annie threw open the passenger door and got into the seat next to him.

'I'm on patrol and I need to see where that car goes,' she said firmly, pointing to the vehicle now approaching the end of the road.

The man looked perplexed. 'But . . . my boss, I'm meant to pick him up—'

'He can wait. And they shouldn't be going far so you won't be long. Now, go!' Annie barked, trying to sound as authoritative as she could despite the panic raging through her body. If she had picked the wrong man, then he was likely to laugh in her face and kick her out of his car. And if he mentioned this to anybody with links to a police officer and her actions got back to the chief then she could get into a hell of a lot of trouble. This was well beyond what she was allowed to do while on duty.

Annie kept her eyes firmly on the attacker's red car, which was about to make a right turn at the end of the road. This was it. She had to hold her nerve. If she started begging this man for help, then he would cotton on to the fact that something was up. She had to make him believe she had the right to commandeer his vehicle. Annie silently willed him to pull out and give chase, knowing full well she wouldn't be able to find the brothel any other way now. When the man pulled away without saying another word, it took Annie everything she had not to cry out in joy. She felt alive again as excitement mixed with fear inside her belly.

Annie kept her eyes fixed firmly on the road ahead. She couldn't risk losing that car. As they crossed the canal, though, she grew a little nervous. This was outside of her patch and she wasn't sure if that was good or bad. On the one hand, it would mean she would be free to investigate without constantly looking over her shoulder for Maggie and Poppy. She knew they never ventured this way. But she also wasn't sure if there were any other WPS patrols working in this area. She was likely to have heard of them if there were, but she would need to check.

'So, who might be in this car you've got me following, miss?' the driver finally asked.

'That's on a need-to-know basis,' Annie replied firmly. That was something she'd heard one of the male officers saying a few weeks before, and she had been itching to use it ever since. It seemed to do the trick as he fell silent again.

'They've just turned right. There – into Copenhagen Street,' Annie said, pointing at the road ahead and trying to sound calmer than she was feeling. 'Stay back. Slow down,' she ordered. There were no other vehicles between the two cars and now they were on a small street she didn't want them to notice the car driving so closely behind them. Even more importantly, she couldn't risk them spotting her obvious uniform in the passenger seat.

The red car slowed and pulled in to park next to a row of houses, and Annie's driver started to slow down too. 'No, keep going,' she said firmly. 'But slowly.' She risked a glance to the side as they passed the parked car and she saw her suspect getting out. 'You can drop me here,' she said once they reached the end of the street. The driver pulled in.

'Is that it?' he asked, as Annie opened the door and got out.

'Sorry it wasn't more exciting,' she said lightly. 'I hope you're not late for your boss.'

The driver shrugged and pulled away.

Annie took a moment to gather her thoughts. She had to work out which house the men were operating from without being seen, and then she would be ready to get into the investigation properly as soon as she was out of her uniform. She was so close to success she could almost smell it.

'Nearly there,' she whispered, rubbing her wedding band and feeling her stomach fizz with anticipation.

22

Annie was in a quandary. The man and his victim had disappeared before she'd had a chance to see which house they entered. Had she been in normal clothes, it would have been easy to inconspicuously wander past the row of houses a few times until she spotted some suspicious activity or saw one of the suspects coming or going. But she stuck out like a sore thumb in her uniform and if, as she suspected, there were no WPS patrols based in this area, then she was at risk of causing a stir with her presence there. She didn't want anyone linked to the brothel to see her. These were dangerous men and goodness knew what they might do if they got spooked by a police uniform outside.

Annie started to wish she had got the driver to take her back to King's Cross with him. It would have made much more sense to come back another time when she was in her everyday clothes. But it was too late now, so she figured that she may as well stay put and try to work out which house was the brothel before heading back to Holborn.

The street was quiet, and one of the houses near to where she had been dropped had cardboard over all the windows. Assuming the home must have been abandoned, Annie decided to sit on the doorstep where she could discreetly keep an eye out without drawing attention to herself. From that spot she had a clear view of the row of houses in question. But as soon as she had settled on to the cold ledge, the door behind her swung open.

'Oh!' Annie cried, jumping to her feet. She turned around to see an elderly man staring at her. His expression switched from angry to only slightly annoyed when he took in the shock written all over her own face. 'I'm so sorry – I didn't think anybody lived here,' Annie explained, taking a step back and smoothing down her heavy WPS skirt.

'Well, that's the idea,' the man snapped. He clutched the walking stick tightly in his hand as his right leg wobbled slightly. He was short and his top half was stooped right over. 'Now bugger off before they realise I'm still here,' he hissed under his breath, motioning with his head to further down the street.

'Wait, who?' Annie asked. She jumped forward and gently placed her hand on the door as the man went to close it on her.

He looked angry again, but he took a step back. His thin lips were shut tight and he glared at her for a few moments. Then he glanced up and down the street quickly. 'If you insist on discussing this then you had better come in,' he snarled, grabbing her hand and pulling her over the threshold with more strength than Annie would have expected from his frail frame.

Once inside with the door closed, Annie took in the surroundings. The house was run down. He definitely lived alone; no woman would live in this squalor, she thought as she peered into the kitchen and saw pots, pans, cups and plates piled high and plastered with all sorts of dried-on muck. Annie wouldn't normally have felt safe going into a strange man's home on her own like this, but she was glad to be out off the street, and despite this chap's obvious tetchiness, she didn't feel threatened by him. His big, round face was home to a fat nose on which perched a pair of round spectacles. Although he was glaring out at Annie from behind the glasses, the hostility just didn't seem to come naturally to him.

'I'm sorry to have bothered you,' Annie said. 'It's just, well, I think one of your neighbours might be up to something terrible, but I need to check what house it is before I can investigate further.'

Understanding swept over his face and it softened instantly. 'At last! I'd given up complaining about that awful place!' he exclaimed.

Annie was glad Maggie wasn't with her right now, as she knew her friend would have struggled to hide her reaction to the irony of such a statement coming from a man living in such squalor. Instead of raising her eyebrows and stifling a giggle as she knew Maggie would have done, Annie nodded and silently waited for him to continue She was glad that he had dropped the hard-man pretence, which didn't suit him one bit.

'The last time I filed a report about the place my windows got smashed in, and don't think I don't know the two are related,' he went on, his voice growing louder as he spoke. 'Bloody bent coppers!'

Annie nodded again but she was beginning to think he might be letting his imagination run away with him a little. He was clearly paranoid if he thought the men running the brothel were in cahoots with the police.

'They thought they could silence me, but they were wrong. I've been lying low ever since so they think I've scurried away and left the house empty, but I've been keeping an eye on their movements. Wait there,' he said firmly before hobbling off into a back room. He came back clutching a pile of grotty-looking pieces of paper with scrawls all over them.

'There's a constant turnover of women, but they never go in on their own,' he explained as Annie glanced over the top sheet, speechless at her luck. 'They're always escorted by the men in charge, and more often than not they have a soldier or some other man who should be acting more respectfully with them. Sometimes smarter-looking men turn up on their own and stay for a short while before leaving. It certainly wasn't like this in my day,' he said, sighing heavily. 'It almost makes me glad my Martha has passed now. It would have tortured her to know what was going on just a few doors down.'

He closed his eyes and Annie saw his lip quiver. Martha must have been his wife, and the mess surrounding them made sense now. Annie felt a pang of sympathy for this man and her hand reached instinctively for the ring on her wedding finger. He opened his eyes again and thrust the pile of papers towards Annie and she immediately took a mental note of the address at the top: *83 Copenhagen Street.* She had her target now.

'I've noted how long each fella stays for,' he said, pointing to the list. Annie shuddered; she dreaded to think what was going on during the visits. Some only lasted ten to fifteen minutes while others continued for hours.

'I'm Bert, by the way,' the man offered as Annie studied his scrawls.

'I'm Annie,' she replied, looking up and smiling. 'I'm with the WPS.'

'Oh, so they've finally decided to send you lot out here, then,' he said. 'It makes sense, what with the men at the station not wanting to shut it down.'

His face had softened more now, and Annie could see the warmth and kindness behind his eyes shining through like a torch breaking through a dark night. It was risky to admit to a stranger that she was out investigating this without authority, but they clearly both had the same goal when it came to the brothel and she could do with an ally right now. Besides, it was clear that Bert wasn't going to be running to her superiors to tell on her any time soon. She looked into his eyes and decided to trust him.

'I'm here against my chief constable's orders,' she admitted. It was such a relief to tell the truth instead of coming up with another story to cover her lies.

Bert's eyes lit up. 'Well, I've always enjoyed a bit of insubordination,' he said, his voice full of glee. He led Annie through to the kitchen where he picked up a pile of plates from the table and dumped them on the side before offering for her to take a seat. She politely declined his offer of a drink – she didn't imagine he had a clean mug left in his cupboards – and she filled him in on everything that had led to her sitting on his doorstep in her uniform.

'Are you sure you should be doing this alone?' Bert asked, a concerned note to his voice. 'I mean, they seem like very nasty men. And after hearing about what they did to your friend—'

'That's exactly why I have to do this on my own,' Annie said forcefully. 'I want to protect them. Since my fiancé Richard died, everything seemed a little pointless. Then I found out about this and it's given me a new focus. I know it could be very dangerous – but I don't much care.' She couldn't believe she was admitting all of this to Bert, who she had only just met. She hadn't spoken to anybody about this – not even her closest friends. 'It doesn't matter if anything bad happens to me. But the best outcome is that I rescue these women and get justice for Maggie. Maybe I'll feel like my life is a little more worthwhile at the end of it all.' She shrugged.

Annie looked up just in time to see Bert wipe a tear from his eye. That was why she felt so comfortable opening up to him, she realised. He knew exactly how she felt because he was feeling the same way. One glance at his home told her he'd given up on life when his wife died.

Annie ended up telling Bert all about her history with Richard, and how she had opened up the front door just a few months ago expecting to be reunited with him and had instead learned about his death. It felt good to unburden herself, especially to an stranger.

'You have a base here whenever you need it,' Bert said straight away when she had finished, getting to his feet and not meeting her eye. Despite his kind offer, Annie felt a thrill of consternation – she had been expecting more of a sympathetic reaction to her story.

He hobbled over to a box on the side and took out a key. 'Take this,' he said, handing it to Annie. 'It was Martha's door key. You might need to get yourself away quickly at all hours and, as you can see, I'm not quick on my feet anymore. If I'm in bed, then I might not get to the door in time to let you in. I couldn't forgive myself if anything bad happened to you.'

Annie smiled gratefully and took the key. Bert obviously didn't know how to react to her heart-wrenching tale, but this gesture was his way of saying he understood and he wanted to help her. Annie was humbled by his kindness, but unsure of how she could pay him back.

'Just get those vermin behind bars,' Bert said kindly. It was as if he could read her mind.

'So, how are you going to collar them?' he asked, sitting back down, and Annie detected a glint of life in his tired old eyes. She was happy to have somebody to discuss her ideas with, but if she was going to sit and discuss this at length with Bert, she would definitely need a cup of tea. She was worried about offending her new confidant, but she could not drink from any of his cups unless she did a big clean-up first. She stood up, took off her jacket and hung it over the back of her chair.

'You've already helped me so much. Now I'm going to help you,' she declared. She hoped her gesture wouldn't go down in the wrong way. 'This kitchen is in need of a woman's touch,' she said gently.

Bert nodded thoughtfully. 'Martha used to take care of it all,' he muttered, not meeting her gaze.

'Well, we can do it together while we work out how I'm going to bring down those terrible men at number eighty-three,' Annie replied. 'I'll wash and you can dry. And then we'll reward ourselves with a nice cup of tea.' Bert nodded and followed her over to the sink.

By the time the pair of them had tackled the mountain of washing-up, Annie had a firm plan in place to gather evidence against the men running the brothel. It was a relief to learn that they were sending some of the women out on to the streets to pick up new clients as well as clearly holding appointments at the house with regular ones. Sending the women out meant that Annie had a chance to try and speak to some of them.

She and Bert had decided that she was going to pretend to be a streetwalker and attempt to make contact with some of the prostitutes working in the area. Once she had gained their trust, she would be able to try and persuade them to give evidence against the men forcing them to sell themselves at number 83.

Bert was still concerned the idea was too risky. He was certain the men must operate by lurking in the shadows while the women picked up men to take back to the brothel. He couldn't understand why they didn't run away if they were left to their own devices once they were out of the house. But Annie had reminded him that the women they targeted didn't have anywhere else to go, and they were probably frightened the men would track them down if they ran. Bert was worried they might try and get their hands on Annie in the same way if she approached any of the girls while the men were watching, but she assured him she would keep her wits about her.

'They can't be everywhere at once,' she told her new friend. 'I'll make sure I only approach the women who aren't being watched.' She had to admit that the thought of it all was making her a little nervous – but at the same time she was feeling a rush of excitement similar to the one she had felt during the air raid. It was the feeling she had been so keen to replicate ever since. The danger was making her feel alive, and that was pushing her on to do this more than the fear was holding her back.

Annie would have to work around her WPS shifts, and she was tired just thinking about how little sleep she was going to get. When she thought she'd dealt with all the obstacles to her plan, Bert added yet another just as they were sitting down to drink their tea. He told her that the NUWW sometimes had patrols operating in the area.

Annie's heart sank into her boots. It was going to be hard enough to dodge the dangerous men in order to get some of the prostitutes onside, but it would be ten times harder if she was trying to avoid being pulled up by one of the patrols at the same time. She couldn't even begin to imagine how she would explain that one away if she was hauled into Hunter Street Police Station.

'They don't seem too switched on, if I'm honest,' he assured her after seeing her face drop at the unwelcome news. 'I think the fact they're so useless is why these men set the brothel up in this area in the first place.'

Annie smiled in response. She had to admit that such a thing would never have gone unnoticed on her patch – so maybe Bert had a point. Still, at least she was forewarned.

Annie was bursting to get going on with her operation now. The clean kitchen seemed to have lifted Bert's spirits and she was pleased to have been able to help him in some small way. When they finished their drinks, they washed up the cups and teapot together and Annie went on her way.

It was dark now, so she was able to slip past number 83 without worrying about raising any suspicions. She needn't have worried – Bert had already told her the curtains stayed drawn all day every day and she noted that there wasn't even a glimmer of light shining through when she passed by.

Once Annie reached the end of Copenhagen Street she ran the rest of the way back to the section house because she needed to get tucked up in bed before Poppy and Maggie finished their patrol and knocked on her door to check on her. As she lay in bed, physically exhausted, her mind still whirred. The excitement she was feeling at her breakthroughs seemed to cancel out her tiredness. Her plan to get justice for Maggie was coming together and she couldn't wait to give her friend the best Christmas present ever.

23

The girls had decided on a night patrol for the following day. Annie had tried to argue for a day patrol to leave her free in the evening for her secret mission, but she hadn't done so too strongly as she didn't want to raise suspicions. She would have to find a way to weave more day patrols in now she knew where the brothel was, though. She didn't have long to gather all her evidence if she was going to bring these men down in time for Christmas. She couldn't stand the thought of the women being stuck there doing what they were doing at such a special time.

In the morning, although shattered from all her running around and thinking up plans the previous day, she found herself awake early. She would normally spend time with Maggie and Poppy in the free hours before a night patrol, but Annie wanted to get back to Copenhagen Street in normal clothes so she could start working out which girls would be best to try to speak to. In the end, she joined her friends for breakfast before claiming she had errands to run and would meet them at the station in time for their patrol.

She tapped lightly on Bert's door and stood back ready for him to answer, but the door swung open straight away and she was met with Bert's round face. She laughed to herself, remembering that the grumpy yet friendly old man already had the brothel under his own surveillance and had probably seen her approaching.

'You should have used your key,' he said, ushering her in

quickly. He was obviously still keen for the men in charge to think his house was empty so they would leave him alone. Not that Annie believed they were the ones who had smashed his windows. That would have meant the police tipping them off about his complaint – a ludicrous suggestion, in her opinion. Bert was still dressed in the same clothes as the previous day, but the kitchen was still clean and tidy, and he looked fresh, as though he'd enjoyed a good sleep.

'I thought I had better save the key for emergencies,' Annie explained. 'I don't want to start letting myself in and taking you by surprise.'

Bert gave a bark of laughter. 'You've seen my brothel log. All I do is watch the comings and goings of that place. You think I won't see you coming?' Annie laughed too now. 'And besides, you'll save me the effort of having to get up and down to answer the damn door if you let yourself in.' He sounded annoyed but there was a twinkle in his eye as he spoke, which made Annie relax. She was getting to know his character already.

'Speaking of which, could I take another look at your findings?' Annie asked eagerly. Bert gave a quick nod and led her to the kitchen. Annie had only glanced at the top sheet the night before, but Bert's scribblings could help her work out the comings and goings at the brothel without having to stake it out herself for hours on end. It could save her precious days of surveillance – time she just didn't have to waste.

Bert handed the log over. There were sheets and sheets of notes. Annie skimmed through the first few pages and her spirits lifted when she took in the fact that there was a lot of daytime activity. Maybe she could get this done before Christmas, after all. Of course, it would be easier to do it all under the cover of darkness. But most of her own patrols were at night, so it was a relief to know she was going to get a fair shot at this without having to try and persuade Maggie and Poppy to change their routine. Annie smiled up at Bert – she really had struck lucky by meeting him.

Bert showed her the tiny slit he had made in the cardboard that covered the kitchen window. When he wanted to keep an eye on the brothel he folded the flap down and then put it back up again when he was finished or if he saw anybody approaching his house. The spyhole was perfect. Annie certainly hadn't noticed it on her previous visit or when she had arrived this morning, from outside or inside the house.

The brothel was part of a terrace of houses that ran along the street. Bert's house was larger, and the windows stuck out slightly, giving him a good view down the road. He told Annie he had also cut a spyhole into one of the upstairs bedrooms, but he claimed the kitchen one had a better view. Annie couldn't see how that was true and she was suspicious he wanted to keep her downstairs so that he could have some company. She was more than happy to oblige, but she found herself already feeling sad that she didn't see this little set-up lasting too long. Thanks to Bert's comprehensive log, she was already well ahead on her plan and of course her aim was to be done by Christmas, which was only a couple weeks away. Her heart gave a pang as she thought of Bert in this house all on his own on Christmas Day. Annie quickly pushed the sad thoughts aside and pulled a chair up to the card-board-covered window.

'I'm not quite sure I'll know what to do with myself now you've taken over that job,' Bert commented.

'Take a seat at the table and you can keep me company while I work,' Annie suggested.

Bert sighed heavily but did what he was told. 'If you insist,' he grumbled.

Annie was facing away from him, but she could hear the smile in his voice. This man liked people to think he was happy being a grumpy recluse, but she already knew him better than that.

Over the next couple of days, Annie started tailing the girls as they left the house. Sometimes they were escorted by one of the two men she recognised, and she was surprised to learn that there were two more men in on the action, too. The women never wore so much as a shawl despite the freezing December weather, while the men looked cosy in thick jackets, gloves and hats. Each and every one of the women looked downtrodden and miserable. Annie could see the desperation in their eyes as they followed in the men's footsteps obediently.

They would head out to a nearby park or alleyway in pairs – one captor and one woman. Annie was surprised at first that they didn't frequent any pubs, but then she realised that although they were good places for prostitutes to work alone, it would be hard for the men in charge to keep control over them in such a setting.

Once they had found a suitable spot in the park or alley, the man would keep out of sight while the girl propositioned men who passed through. Some were taken by surprise while others seemed to head in their direction, like they had known they were going to be there and were pleased to see them. The women always tried it on with passing soldiers, but they were more selective about the ordinary men they approached.

If the men weren't interested, the girls would wave them off and then wait for the next one to pass by. All the while the men who had led them there were waiting in the shadows – far enough away that the potential customers couldn't see them but close enough that the girls made sure to stick to the script. They would look nervously over their shoulders in their direction every now and then. Every time she saw that it made Annie shudder. She was more certain than ever now that these poor girls and women were being held against their will and forced into picking up these men to take back to the brothel.

The December afternoons were so cold that Annie found herself willing them to succeed, if only so they could get back to the warmth – despite what they would have to do when they got there. She was used to walking around in the cold with her WPS coat to keep the chill off, so she was struggling standing still in the plummeting temperatures despite the fact she had put two jumpers on underneath her jacket in anticipation of the freezing temperature. Watching from afar, Annie would wrap her jacket tight around her and jump from foot to foot to try and keep warm as her breath froze in the air in front of her. She could see the girls' teeth chattering as they tried to look seductive in their tatty, flimsy dresses and she wanted to rush up to them and envelop them in her arms to heat them up.

When the women found a willing customer they would enter into a short conversation with them before walking them back to number 83 Copenhagen Street. The men in charge would follow behind at a safe distance – close enough to overhear any exchange but far enough away that the customers weren't aware of, or didn't care about, their presence.

Occasionally, one man would head out from the brothel with two women. Once the first was set up in her spot, the second would wander off and hang around nearby to pick up business on her own. Once successful, she would head back to Copenhagen Street with her client alone. It appeared to be the same few women who were trusted to be on their own every time. These were the women Annie needed to target, she decided. Although, she couldn't work out why some of them were trusted on their own over others. What was keeping them there? Why didn't they flee as soon as their captors were out of sight? If she was in their position then she would have made a run for it as soon as she was left to her own devices.

'There have been a few suddenly disappear,' Bert revealed when Annie gave voice to these thoughts one afternoon in his kitchen.

Annie was cutting it fine to get back to Holborn in time for her night patrol, but she was reluctant to leave Bert. She could feel the loneliness emanating out of him no matter how strongly he would deny he was in desperate need of company. He started poring over his notes then thrust one of the sheets in front of Annie and pointed at a section of scribbles. 'This one,' he said, tapping the description of a young girl with short, blond hair. 'She came out twice and then that was it. I never saw her again. There are a few more examples of the same,' he added, shuffling through the piles of paper.

'Maybe they're the ones who don't comply?' Annie mused. She didn't want to think about what happened to the poor girls who refused to take part in the sordid activities behind the doors of number 83.

'Well, that's what you're going to find out,' Bert said, looking up from the sheets of paper and fixing her with a worried stare. 'Of course, there's always the possibility that they are kept in the house, to satisfy the regular customers who turn up for appointments. The men who are too important to pick prostitutes up in the street. The well-dressed gentlemen who have their chosen woman ready and waiting for them when they arrive at the house.'

Annie shuddered at the thought.

Annie only spent a few hours each day tailing the men and women from the brothel, leaving her time to get some more sleep before heading out on patrol with Maggie and Poppy. They tended to do a couple of day patrols a week, and she decided to go undercover as a prostitute as soon as her first free evening came up. The opportunity came around when she had been following the brothel lot for just four days. But Annie felt ready. She knew the girls who were trusted on their own and she had checked with Bert that they also went out with the men in the evenings as well as during the day.

Thankfully, Maggie and Poppy were too tired to suggest doing anything other than dinner together at the section house and an early night following the patrol that day. It had been army pay day so the group had been particularly busy visiting the pubs and parks in Holborn. They had also spent a good chunk of the afternoon tracking down a wayward young girl whose mother was concerned she had run off with a soldier. In fact, it turned out the kind-hearted girl had picked up work delivering bread from one of the local bakeries. She was desperate to help her mother with money but had wanted to surprise her with her first lot of pay.

Sneaking out under the cover of darkness once she was sure her friends were tucked up in bed, Annie shivered as the cold evening air hit her. Keen to blend in as much as possible, she had left her coat behind at the section house. She wanted these women to relate to her and trust her, and in order for that to happen they had to believe she was the same as them. She had considered taking her jacket with her to store at Bert's, but she wasn't sure how she was going to get on time-wise and she wanted to leave herself the option to head straight back to the section house if she needed to.

Despite feeling dead on her feet, she decided to run the mile to Copenhagen Street to get the blood pumping through her veins and warm her up a little. When she got to Bert's house, she pulled out his wife's key to let herself in. She had warned him she would be popping in tonight to watch for her targets leaving the brothel and he had instructed her to use the key, just in case he was in bed when she arrived.

'What have you been up to?' a voice called out as she stood in the hallway. The whole house was in darkness and Annie jumped out of her skin. But she recognised the voice – Bert had obviously decided to wait up for her. She laughed to herself as she realised he must be wondering what all her panting and puffing was about. Annie felt her way to the kitchen and could just make Bert out thanks to the moonlight streaming in through the spyhole that he had left open in anticipation of her arrival.

'It's best to do it with the lights off at night, otherwise the light will stream out of the watch-hole and draw attention to you,' he explained. Annie nodded her understanding, still working to get her breath back. 'You must be freezing,' he said as he took in her appearance, getting to his feet and walking unsteadily to the stove. 'No wonder you ran here,' he huffed.

'I've got to fit in with the girls,' Annie explained. 'None of them ever wear anything over their dresses.' Bert sighed. 'Go on . . .' Annie coaxed. She knew Bert so well already that she had learnt that his signature heavy sigh meant there was something he wanted to share with her, but she had to invite him to do so. 'How else can I make myself look the part?' she asked him.

'Well, they never wear coats, you got that bit right. But their dresses aren't half as fancy as yours,' he said, turning away from the stove now to look her up and down. Annie looked down at her navy blue, ankle-length dress. It was the plainest dress she had with her at the section house. The rest of her dresses were all far too nice for this. While getting ready, she had wished Irene was still living with them all. One of her outfits would have been perfect for this mission, she had thought guiltily at the time. But then she had reminded herself she would never have fit her wholesome curves into one of Irene's dresses. The pair of them couldn't have had more opposite figures, especially now that Annie had filled out again. She hadn't worn this particular dress in a few weeks and she had been shocked when she'd struggled to button it up. Her bosom and her belly both seemed to have expanded despite all the hours she was spending walking the streets and shivering in the cold – both of which she had assumed would burn off all the food she had been eating and keep her slim.

'This is the simplest dress I have with me. In fact, I don't think I have anything more sedate at home, even,' she explained. 'Oh, darn it!' Annie cried, throwing herself down into a chair and putting her head into her hands in exasperation. 'I need to get out and start talking to these girls; I'm running out of time. But what's the point if they won't trust me?'

'Stand up again,' Bert said firmly. Annie looked up and was taken aback to see a sharp knife in the old man's hand. Her eyes widened in fear. Had her outburst angered him? She hadn't known him long, but she thought she knew him better than this. Annie sat rooted to the spot as she tried to think of the best thing to do. Should she try to talk him round or just get up and run for the door? She could definitely outrun him . . .

Bert's voice cut into her thoughts. 'I'm going to rip your dress you silly girl.' He tutted. Annie was terrified now. 'Have you seen any of those girls in an outfit without at least one tear or hole in it?' he added.

Annie laughed in relief. Then she felt a wave of guilt for having doubted her new friend. Bert was as harmless as they come. She stood up and let him carefully pierce a hole in the right shoulder of her dress. Bert stood back and nodded, and Annie pulled at the hole to make a more believable rip in the material. Bert smiled his approval.

'Maybe a slit near the bottom?' Annie suggested, and Bert handed her the knife.

'I can't bend down that far,' he explained as she cut into the material.

'Better?' Annie asked.

'One more thing,' Bert said, turning back to the stove and reaching his hand into the teapot sat on it. Annie squirmed as he rubbed sodden tea leaves over her dress. But she realised straight away what he was doing and she had to agree it was a grand idea. The dress looked filthy now.

'There you go,' Bert declared happily. 'I'll make a fresh pot of tea to warm you up and your new dress will be dry by the time we've finished it.'

Sitting back down wrapped in a blanket Bert had fetched for her, Annie felt a wave of excitement mixed with fear. She was really doing this. Once she walked out of that door and started talking to the women from the brothel, she would be completely on her own and her secret mission would be in full swing. If the pimps got their hands on her and tried to force her back to number 83, nobody but Bert would know where to find her – and he wasn't anywhere near strong enough to burst in and save her. He could go to the police, but would they listen to him after dismissing his previous claims? He was convinced they were in cahoots with the men in charge of the brothel, so it was unlikely he would turn to them anyway. Annie *had* to get this right – not just for the sake of the women being held captive but for her own safety, too.

24

Annie sat at the window to drink her tea and it wasn't long before she saw movement coming from number 83. She had just set down her cup when the front door opened. She leaned further forward, hoping to spot three figures emerging. But her heart fell when she saw the short man from the train station leaving with one of the younger girls – one who was never let out of sight.

'Another cup?' Bert asked, pouring himself some more tea at the table.

'I'd better not,' Annie replied, keeping her eyes fixed firmly on the brothel. 'I'm going to be doing a lot of standing around in the cold tonight and that will be much harder with a full bladder.'

Bert scoffed and Annie risked glancing round at him. Even in the darkness she could see him shaking his head. Knowing the men usually left at least thirty minutes between moving the girls out of the house, she decided to push Bert on his reaction. If she sat glued to the spyhole for another half an hour, she would surely lose her mind. Checking the clock on the wall before closing the hole back up and plunging the kitchen into complete darkness, she picked up her chair and took it back to the table to join Bert.

'Go on then,' she said teasingly. 'What do you have to say about my bladder?'

'Oh, it wasn't the reference to your bladder that made me react,' he replied, blushing slightly. 'You're a very strong-willed young woman, Annie. Very determined. You remind me of my Martha sometimes, is all.'

Annie was taken aback. She certainly hadn't felt either of those things recently – in fact, quite the opposite. Maybe this mission was doing her good and boosting her confidence already without her even realising. She couldn't see Bert's face properly – just the outline, but she could feel the smile in his voice as soon as he said his late wife's name.

'Tell me about her,' Annie said gently. She had been curious about Martha since she had met Bert but an opportunity to ask him about his wife had never come up. Annie was sensitive about such things and she liked them to come up in discussion naturally.

'She was my world,' Bert replied sadly. His eyes glistened in the darkness and Annie waited patiently for him to continue when he was comfortable. 'We were childhood sweethearts,' he said a few minutes later. 'I knew from the moment I met her she would end up as my wife. She was beautiful and I never looked at another woman from the day we met. I didn't need to – I had everything I could ever have hoped for in Martha.'

Now Annie's eyes were glistening, and she was grateful for the lack of light in the room. Bert's words reminded her of everything Richard had written in his letter to her. She had always thought Richard was one of a kind, but listening to Bert speak about Martha, she understood he was clearly made from the same mould.

'She wasn't just beautiful on the outside,' Bert added. 'Her soul was one of the most magnificent you will ever come across. I'll never meet another women like her, of that I'm certain.'

Annie could make out his thumb running gently over his wedding band and realised that she was doing the same thing with hers. Annie remembered then with a start that she had meant to leave her ring in a safe place in her room at the section house. She hated the thought of parting with it, even if it was just for a few hours, but she needed to look the part if she was going to gain the trust of the prostitutes. Of course, there were enough married women on the game in these times, but she needed to come across as inexperienced and naive. When Bert continued talking Annie pushed her own thoughts aside to listen.

'Martha's sister was struggling as the war went on,' he explained. 'Glenda was fifteen years younger than Martha. Their mother died when Glenda was just a few years old, so Martha had always been like a mother to her little sister. Glenda never married. She looked up to Martha so much and she always ran her potential suitors past her, but Martha was so protective of Glenda that nobody ever even came close to getting her approval.'

Annie smiled to herself. There wasn't so much of an age gap with her sisters, but she definitely had the same attitude towards anybody who wanted to court any of them. Betty had told her once that she was more worried about introducing boys to Annie than she was to their father. Even before she had joined the WPS and experienced a surge in confidence, the one place Annie was outspoken was when it came to her sisters and the opposite sex.

'Martha wanted Glenda to move in with us when the air raids started. She knew they would target London soon enough and she was terrified for her sister. She hated the thought of Glenda being stuck in her tiny flat all alone as the bombs fell. But Glenda was independent and stubborn and she refused to give up the small space she called home. She said that would be letting the Germans win. And the papers were saying an attack on London would be doomed. They had so much faith in our defences.' Bert sighed and took a gulp of his tea. 'I wish I'd done more to try and persuade her to join us here,' he said sadly. 'We have the basement, you see, so she would have been a lot safer under our roof.' He paused. 'It would have meant Martha stayed safe, too.'

Annie didn't like where this was going. She felt a rush of guilt for secretly longing for more air raids so she could experience more excitement and feel a little more alive.

'All through May the Zeppelins attacked locations along the Thames Estuary. Martha kept on at Glenda to move in with us, but she stood firm. The bombs hadn't managed to do much damage, so although they had spooked Martha, Glenda still felt confident any attack on London would fall flat. I'm afraid to say I got fed up with it all – Glenda was a grown woman and if she wanted to take her chances in her flat then I said Martha should just let her.' He looked pained as he went over the memory. 'Martha was so caring she just couldn't give up on her. So, she started spending some of her evenings with her sister in her flat in Stoke Newington. It was a few miles away from us here but Martha enjoyed the bus ride. Often, they'd have dinner together and Martha would fall asleep there and come back to me the following morning. I didn't mind because it was better than Martha travelling home in darkness because of the light restrictions.

'When Martha went to visit Glenda on the last night of May it was just like any of her other visits. I went to bed early, expecting not to see her until the morning. But as I lay down I heard the distant sound of the first bombs landing. I took myself down to the basement and convinced myself the girls would be all right. After all, what would I have been able to do from here? This was the first air raid on London but everything I'd read and heard told me our defences were ready for it.' Bert closed his eyes for a few moments.

'I was so tired that night that I ended up falling asleep in the basement. When I woke up in the early hours of the next morning I hauled myself up to our bedroom expecting to find Martha peacefully asleep in our bed and ready to make fun of me for being able to fall asleep anywhere. When I found our bed empty and unslept in, I knew.' Bert paused again and Annie wiped a tear from her eye.

'Even though I knew, I had to see it for myself,' Bert continued. 'It took me hours to walk to Stoke Newington with my bad leg. I was exhausted but thoughts of Martha kept me going. As soon as the block of flats came into view I could see half of it had been ripped off by the blast. It was still smoking and Glenda's window was gone. Most people would have accepted at that point that Martha was dead and turned around and left. But I'm a stubborn old fool.' Annie smiled to herself.

'Somehow, I made it to the rubble without collapsing with exhaustion. I rummaged through that wreckage with the rest of them for hours, desperate to find Martha miraculously alive, buried underneath something that had shielded her. Or maybe she had popped outside for some reason just before the bomb had hit. It's crazy the stories your mind will feed you to keep that little piece of hope alive.'

Annie thought back to all the explanations she had come up with for Jeremy's visit before she had finally accepted the truth.

'I was hoping for a miracle when there was no hope in hell that I was going to get one,' Bert sighed. 'But I just needed to see her face one last time. It was only when night fell and one of your lot came and guided me away that I finally gave up.'

The pair of them sat in silence while Bert's words hung in the air between them. Annie couldn't help herself. She knew more than anyone that there wasn't anything she could say to make him feel better or take his pain away. But she couldn't let him sit there swamped by his grief. She got to her feet and walked around to his side of the table. Bert stood too and he held out his arms just as Annie reached him. As they embraced Annie felt a rush of love for Bert. They stayed like that for a long while. Finally, Bert pulled away.

'I've kept you long enough,' he said. Annie walked back to the window and pulled down the tab of cardboard to let a glimmer of light into the room. She looked back and checked the clock – it had been twenty-five minutes since the last couple had left number 83.

'There's just one more thing I need to do to look the part,' she muttered, making her way back to the table again and running her thumb over her wedding band.

'It will be safe here,' Bert assured her, and Annie realised she felt better leaving it with her new friend than she would have done leaving it in her room on its own.

She went to slip it off, tears rolling down her face. It was the first time she had taken the wedding band off since she had put it on after it had fallen out of the envelope Richard had stored it in for her along with the letter. It was so special because they had both touched it – it was one of the last things her fiancé would have handled before his death – and she had kept it with her ever since losing him. It broke her heart to remove it now, but she knew he would understand. It stuck a little when she got it to her knuckle. Awkwardly, she wriggled it around to loosen it. She really had filled out in the last few weeks, she thought to herself. Annie looked down at her bare finger on her left hand and took in the slightly reddened, flattened flesh where the ring had lived for so long. A part of her. A constant reminder of her love for Richard, and his love for her. Her comfort over the last few months.

'You won't be without it for long,' Bert said softly.

It was just what Annie needed to hear. She handed it over to him and he slipped it into his pocket with a nod. Annie took a deep breath.

'You look perfect,' Bert commented. 'And I realise that's a strange compliment to give, given the circumstances.'

Annie had to laugh. She went back to her spot by the window and no sooner had she sat down than there was activity from the brothel.

'Someone's coming out,' she whispered urgently. It was Maggie's attacker – Annie recognised his tall, wide stature and almost bald head immediately. He had two girls in tow and one of them was one of the older prostitutes who Annie had seen going off on her own at least a couple of times now.

'This is it,' she said, trying to keep her voice calm as nerves took over all of her senses.

'Keep safe,' Bert rasped as she left the house. Annie didn't answer, though. She wasn't sure it was going to be possible to keep herself out of harm's way and she didn't much like lying, especially to her friends.

25

When Maggie's attacker led the women straight up Matilda Street, Annie had an inkling where they were headed. She had noticed that the more trusted prostitutes tended to be dropped off at Thornhill Square Gardens before the men carried on with the women who they wanted to keep a constant eye on. It was close to their base so it made sense but even so, Annie still couldn't understand why the women left there alone didn't flee as soon as they had a chance.

Annie held back as the threesome entered the gardens. She nipped inside the entrance and then tucked herself in between the railings and a bush and watched as the man appeared to talk at the older woman before leaving with the younger one trotting closely behind.

Annie emerged from her cover as soon as he was out of sight. She didn't want to waste any time; he would surely come back and check on her at some point. From her previous observations, she knew potential clients seemed to stream through regularly, and she couldn't be sure which ones might send back information to the men in charge.

Annie crept up to the prostitute so quietly that the woman let out a little yelp when she tapped her on the shoulder.

'What on earth are you up to?' the woman hissed through gritted teeth. She stared at Annie with wild eyes before doing a quick scan around them. It remained quiet and still. She glared at Annie again, who suddenly lost a lot of her confidence. She hadn't expected the women to be hostile towards her.

'I'm sorry I . . . I didn't mean to make you jump, I just . . .' Her words trailed off as she took in a big, dark bruise covering the left side of the woman's face. It looked awfully painful.

'If you're looking for help or advice then don't bother,' the older woman snapped, turning her head away to conceal the dark mass covering half her face. 'The sooner you leave me alone, the better. For your own sake as well as for mine.'

Annie stood rooted to the spot. She didn't want to give up straight away but she hadn't prepared herself for this type of reaction. She fumbled around for something to say to get the woman to soften towards her.

'Please, I just . . . I think I can help you. I know you're being made to do this,' she tried. She was staring at the woman's face, but she refused to meet Annie's eyes, instead constantly scanning the gardens and looking back to the entrance.

After a moment of silence, the woman scoffed. 'You can't help me,' she laughed bitterly and shook her head. 'The best thing you can do for me is to leave me well alone,' she spat.

Annie could feel the venom in her voice and it sent a shiver running down her spine. She retreated. Maybe she had taken on more than she could handle. She could only help the women if they wanted to escape. Could it be that they were happy doing what they were doing? They certainly didn't look it. Confused, Annie crept back into the undergrowth. She watched as just a few minutes later a soldier greeted the woman like an old friend. They had a brief conversation before leaving the gardens hand in hand.

Annie was about to give up and head back to Bert's, defeated, when she heard footsteps approaching the garden entrance. She sat still and held her breath as three more figures walked past her. It was one of the other men from the brothel, with two more of the prostitutes. He walked away with one of the women, leaving the second one in the same location where Annie had just failed to get the previous prostitute to engage with her.

She couldn't give up yet, she decided. She had to give it another shot now that another prostitute was standing, unguarded, right in front of her. Besides, she didn't want to go back to Bert with her tail between her legs.

Annie made sure to drag her feet as she approached this time, so that the woman wouldn't be taken by complete surprise when she emerged out of the darkness. She wanted to get off to a better start with this one. Hearing her coming, the woman turned around as Annie approached and gave a small smile. Annie recognised this woman, too. She was middle-aged with long brown hair. She looked extremely tired, Annie noticed when she stood next to her. She also looked dead behind the eyes – like all the life had been drained out of her.

'I wouldn't hang around here for too long if I were you, dear. You'd be better off moving on to another area if you're looking for men,' she said. The woman looked around her shiftily. 'You don't want to get caught up in what I'm involved in.'

'I think I can help you,' Annie said quietly. She was conscious of the fact that Maggie's attacker hadn't passed back through yet, so there was a double threat of being caught out. The woman smiled. Annie thought she might be on to something here and her hopes raised with that one small encouragement. The woman looked around again and then turned back to Annie, pulling all of her hair over one shoulder to reveal a line of small purple bruises running around her neck. Annie gasped in shock as she studied them.

'If I get caught talking to somebody who I can't make any money out of, Stevs will do it properly next time,' the woman whispered. 'Please, just go before one of them sees you.'

'Who's Stevs?' Annie asked, desperate for any kind of lead she could get her hands on. The woman sighed impatiently but described the man who had attacked her. Annie knew straight away the man in question was Maggie's attacker. 'Why do they call him Stevs?' she pushed. A full name would be a lot more useful to her, especially if it might end up being all she got out of this evening.

'I don't know his first name, but his surname is Stevens and everyone calls him Stevs,' the woman hissed. 'Now, leave me alone before they see me talking to you.'

'But they're not here, we have time,' Annie said urgently. 'I've been keeping an eye on how they work. Please. Let me help.'

'That's what they want you to think, dear,' the woman sighed. 'But somehow, they are always here. Always watching. Do you think I would come out here countless times every day and night and put myself through these terrible things if I thought I could get away? How do you think they keep us all in line?'

'But they leave you on your own,' Annie tried. 'I know you say they're watching but I've been following you all for a few days and I've seen where they go.

'They're never far away, dear,' the woman said. 'I had the same thoughts as you when I first arrived. But then one of the girls who was brought here at the same time as me – she made a run for it one afternoon. There was no big commotion or fallout and I was so happy for her. I even considered doing the same thing.' She fell silent and Annie could see her eyes were glistening in the moonlight. 'That evening none of us were sent out and we all breathed a sigh of relief,' the woman went on. 'But later that night she was dragged back into the house by two of the men holding us there. Then Stevs came in and kicked and punched her in front of us until there was no breath left in her little body. We had to sit there and watch as she screamed for mercy and begged us all for help. But there was nothing we could do. We couldn't overpower him, and it was obvious we would meet the same fate if we tried anything. We either stay or we die.'

Annie was astounded. She had known these men were dangerous, but she'd had no idea of the scale of the horror they inflicted on their captives.

'I've heard of other girls, the younger ones, disappearing when they step out of line. It's nice to think that they escaped to a better life, but we all know the truth. There's a lot of money to be made out of women like us abroad. As soon as you do anything that makes them think you're a risk or could cause them any problems, you're either dealt with like my friend was or you're packed off in a car with Claude, never to be seen again.'

Annie finally understood what kept the women here – violence and fear, and it made her more determined to bring these men down. 'Who's Claude?' she asked.

'I've said enough. Now, please clear off before you get me shipped off or killed,' the woman snapped.

Annie didn't want to push her luck, and she certainly didn't want to put this woman in any danger. 'I'll find a way to get you out of this. I promise,' she said. 'My name is Annie, by the way,' she added as she turned to leave.

'I'm Marie,' Annie heard the woman croak as she left the gardens to make her way back to Bert's house.

Annie was shivering and exhausted when she arrived back at Bert's. He was waiting up for her and insisted she take a warm bath as soon as she'd walked through the door. Annie was desperate to discuss what she'd discovered but the thought of the warm water soothing her trembling limbs was too much to resist.

When she finally climbed out of the tub she found Bert

had left a pile of clothes outside the bathroom door for her. She assumed they had belonged to Martha and she felt honoured that Bert felt comfortable loaning them to her. She wasn't sure if she would ever be able to stomach seeing another man in any of Richard's clothes.

When she joined Bert back in the kitchen she saw emotion flash over his face as he took in the brown dress and thick black cardigan, which swamped Annie's frame. He didn't make any comment, though. It felt nice to Annie to be wearing something that wasn't so tight, for once.

They sat down together over a pot of tea and Annie filled him in on her chat with Marie.

'That's who you need to focus on,' Bert said eagerly.

'I don't know,' Annie sighed. 'She was helpful but she seemed determined not to discuss it any further with me. She's terrified. And it sounds as though she has good reason to be. I don't want anyone to get hurt because of me.'

'She's already opened up to you a little,' Bert said. 'And that was before she knew just how much you could help her.'

Annie played with the wedding band she had put back on as soon as she had come downstairs following her bath, unsure how to proceed.

'Look,' Bert said, 'you've said yourself that you don't have much time. The rest of the women will all be just as scared as Marie is, but it seems like she's pretty damn brave if she gave you all this information on your first meeting.' Annie had to agree. 'She sounds like the perfect woman to get some of the others on-side for you.'

'What do you mean?' Annie asked, intrigued.

'Think how long it would take you to convince enough of these women to testify against their captors. First of all, you would have to wait to get them on their own, then you would need to gain their trust and goodness knows how long that would take. I suspect most of them will react like the first woman did this evening and it will take time to get to the point where they'll talk like Marie did. Only then would you be in a position to try and convince them to give evidence.'

'It would certainly take a long time if I was going through all of that with each one of them,' Annie agreed.

'So, focus on Marie. Gain her trust. Tell her you're with the WPS the next time you see her and then reveal your plan. Once she's agreed to take part you can leave it to her to round up more women who might be willing to talk. She's the one with regular access to them and she'll have a good idea of who will be likely to be willing to get involved.'

Annie couldn't help but grin. 'Thank goodness for you, Bert,' she said, shaking her head in wonder.

'You were certainly determined to make a meal out of a sandwich for a moment there,' he laughed. 'Now that's sorted, are you going to get your head down before the sun rises?'

'Oh goodness, yes I had better get going,' Annie cried, panicked. With the spyhole covered up, Bert had put the kitchen light on when Annie had returned and she could see from the clock on the wall that it was now almost two o'clock in the morning. She had another day shift with Poppy and Maggie to prepare for in just a matter of hours.

'I'm not letting you walk home at this time, especially not in the freezing cold,' Bert said firmly. 'You'll sleep in our spare bedroom. I'm always up early so I can wake you in time to get back and changed before your friends knock for you.'

Annie's heart twinged at the way Bert referred to it as 'our' spare bedroom. Martha was still a part of his life even though she was no longer alive. She accepted the offer graciously, knowing there was no question that she would turn the offer down. The thought of going back outside right now filled her with dread. It would still be freezing when she eventually had to head back to the section house but she felt like she would be able to face the cold after a solid sleep.

Bert knocked on Annie's door just after seven o'clock that morning, as promised. She had been in such a deep sleep that it took her a few moments to wake up properly and remember where she was. Then she leapt up and flew down the stairs as fast as her legs would carry her. She had to get back to her room before her friends woke up. She had already agreed with Bert that she would leave her ripped and dirty dress at his house. She felt uncomfortable wearing Martha's clothes home but she didn't have any other option. If Poppy or Maggie caught her creeping back into the section house in Martha's clothes then she could probably just about manage to explain it away by claiming she had visited her parents the previous evening and ended up borrowing some of her mother's more casual clothes after falling asleep on the sofa. There was no explaining away her undercover outfit.

Annie struggled to keep her eyes open during that day's patrol. And she couldn't stop thinking about what Marie had told her the previous night. It was more important now than ever to rescue the women from the brothel. And she was reminded of the fact that her Christmas deadline was fast approaching every time they passed somebody carrying a Christmas tree or hanging up decorations outside a shop.

'Is everything all right?' Maggie asked when they popped back to the section house to grab some lunch that afternoon. 'You seem a little distracted.'

'I've just been thinking about Richard a lot lately,' Annie replied, staring guiltily into her soup. 'It's getting harder, what with Christmas coming up.' She hoped her friend wouldn't see through the fib or notice the shame plastered across her face. She hated lying to her friends, especially as she was using Richard's memory in vain. But she needed to buy some time away from them without raising suspicions, and the idea that had suddenly popped into her head seemed like her best option. 'I might actually take a few days off, if the chief will let me. I think I need to spend some time with my mother,' Annie said quietly. Maggie and Poppy nodded in understanding and Annie felt even more ashamed.

'I'll get you a pen and paper and you can pop the written request in at the station when we head back out,' Poppy offered. As the idea had only just come into Annie's head, she hadn't had a chance to discuss it with Bert but she was confident he would be happy to let her stay with him for a few days. After all, he had told her she was welcome to use the spare bedroom whenever she needed it. She needed to focus all her time and attention on this operation if she was going to get it all tied up before Christmas, and after just one night undercover she knew it was going to be impossible to keep up with her patrols at the same time. This was the perfect solution as it meant she would be excused from patrolling and she also wouldn't have to worry about sneaking around behind her friends' backs.

Happy with her new plan, Annie wrote out the request for 'personal time' while Maggie and Poppy sat in a sympathetic silence. As soon as it was approved, she would pack a small holdall and head over to Bert's, ready to put her secret mission into action full-time.

26

C hief Constable Green was sitting at his desk when Annie went in to deliver her request. To her relief he read it quickly and nodded.

'You can have four days,' he said brusquely. 'I trust your colleagues can look after things until your return. You won't need a replacement?'

'Oh goodness, no,' Annie replied. 'I'll be back before you know it and Maggie and Poppy will do a great job without me.

'Very well,' he said, putting the piece of paper to one side before picking up his pen and beginning to write in his notepad. Annie took that as her official approval and her cue to leave his office.

'I'll cook you a special dinner this evening to say goodbye,' Poppy offered when Annie caught up with her friends to fill them in on the development. Normally, Annie would have jumped at the chance; she loved Poppy's cooking, especially at the moment. And she had a feeling she wouldn't be eating very well at Bert's. But the thought of sitting at the table with them both, clouded by her deceit, filled her with dread.

'I was hoping to slip away quietly,' Annie confessed, rubbing her wedding band. 'Besides, it's not a big deal because I won't be gone for long. It's just four days. And there's only a couple of weeks left before Christmas and we need to work out what we're doing. Maybe I can use this time to plan that with my mum – it would be a good distraction and having a fun few days with you two and my family to look forward to will stop me missing Richard so much during that time.'

'That sounds like a great idea,' Maggie pitched in, beaming from ear to ear. Annie knew she would have to go and visit her parents at some point to check it was all right to bring her friends over with her on Christmas Day. But that could wait.

In the end, Annie clocked off from their patrol early at Poppy's suggestion. She commented that Annie seemed distracted and maybe it was best she went home for some rest and family time. 'The sooner you leave us the sooner we'll get you back where you belong,' she declared sincerely.

Annie's heart ached as she bid her friends goodbye. They may have been under the impression that she was only leaving for a few days to retreat to the safety of her family home, but she knew just how dangerous her undercover mission was going to be. There was a possibility she might not see them again. She might not have been bothered about putting herself in danger but the thought of how upset her best friends would be if something awful happened to her made her feel that her actions were quite selfish. She tried to push the thoughts aside as she pulled each of them in for a hug.

'We'll see you soon, silly,' Maggie laughed as Annie clung on to her a little longer and tighter than was necessary. Annie managed to hold back her tears until she was back at the section house packing her bag. Once ready, she wiped her eyes and walked out with her head held high, feeling more confident with every step. She had no outside distractions to worry about now so she could focus on the operation fully. Thoughts of Richard flooded her mind and she wondered whether it would be such a bad thing if this all went wrong. Although all of this had given her a great diversion from constantly thinking about him, she still missed him more than she could bear.

If this all went to plan then she would feel great about saving all the women, getting justice for Maggie and getting the vile men behind the brothel behind bars. But if the worst happened and she was caught by the men and forced to become part of their disgusting set-up, she decided there and then that she would fight back with everything she had. From what Marie had told her, that would surely lead to her death – but that had to be better than the alternative. At least then she would be reunited with Richard again.

Annie's thoughts might have turned dark but her new relaxed attitude to her fate was expelling all her nerves. She needed to keep this frame of mind because nerves or any form of hesitation could send all her plans crashing down around her.

Bert was delighted to see Annie again so soon and only too happy to let her stay with him for as long as she needed.

'I had better get some more food in,' he commented mock-glumly. 'I've been living on soup and bread since Martha died but a strapping young woman like you will need something a little more substantial, especially if you're going to be out in the cold all day and night.'

Annie had indeed noticed from the pots and pans they had washed up together that first night that Bert's diet consisted mostly of soup. She smiled awkwardly at his reference to her being 'strapping'. He wasn't being nasty about her figure – Annie knew Bert didn't have that in him. He was a man without a bad bone in his body. But her waist was certainly filling out more with every day that passed. Annie still much preferred her fuller figure to the frail one she had been left with following Richard's death, but even she had to admit things were getting a little out of hand now. She felt uncomfortable in everything she wore and she was even thinking about asking Bert if she could keep hold of Martha's dress and cardigan to wear around the house while she was staying with him. She hoped he wouldn't find it too difficult. Maybe a few days away from Poppy's cooking would do her good.

They sat down together and studied Bert's notes along with the log Annie had kept over the previous days. They managed to identify Marie in Bert's papers from his descriptions, and Annie knew where she was in all of her own notes.

'She's certainly a good one to target,' Bert commented, rubbing the white, prickly stubble on his chin thoughtfully. 'They seem to use her a lot during both the day and the night.'

Annie nodded. 'I think it might be best if I hide out in the bushes in the gardens at Thornhill Square,' she decided. She could see from all their notes that Marie was hardly ever used anywhere else. 'Maybe she has some regulars who know to find her there,' she mused. 'That could be why she's always there and they don't take her anywhere else like they do with the other women.'

Annie wanted to head straight out to get started but Bert insisted she wait until the evening. 'You'll be safer going out at night,' he stressed as she tried to argue with him about it. 'And you had a long day and night yesterday. You need your wits about you for this. It's been a tiring week or two for you – I can see it in your eyes.'

Annie instinctively looked away from him and down at the table. It was true, she was exhausted. But she felt like she needed to keep going. If she stopped for too long then she wasn't sure she would be able to get started again. In the end, she agreed to go up to the spare bedroom for a lie-down to ensure she was fully rested and ready to go once it grew dark.

When Annie woke it was to the noise of pots and pans banging and clashing together. Confused, she climbed out of bed and made her way down to Bert's kitchen. Her stomach growled as the unmistakeable smell of fish reached her in the hallway, and she smiled. She hadn't eaten fish in a long time.

'I didn't think you cooked,' she said when she reached the kitchen to find Bert leaning over a big dish of fish and potato pie. Steam rose off the top and Annie took a deep breath in to savour the aroma. Bert jumped at the unexpected intrusion.

'An old bugger like me needs some warning. You can't creep up on me like that,' he wheezed, pressing his hand to his chest.

'Sorry.' Annie laughed. 'I didn't realise you were so engrossed.'

'Well, they do say that cooking is an art,' he said proudly, straightening his back and gesturing to the dish. Annie took a seat at the table and waited for Bert to continue. 'I stopped cooking when I lost Martha,' he said eventually. 'It was something we always did together, and it lost its . . . magic, once she was gone.'

Annie reached for her wedding band yet again. One of the things she had been looking forward to after marrying Richard was living together. She had made a list of all the meals she wanted to cook him once life was back to normal. He would never have cooked *with* her. She had never heard of a man preparing dinner with his wife before – but Bert was unique.

'Well, I'm very honoured that you have started cooking again just for me.' Annie smiled. 'You really didn't have to.'

'Oh, you'll need your strength for this,' Bert replied, turning around again to face her, his expression grave. 'It's freezing out there and you're about to go and stand in the cold for hours without a jacket.' Annie shivered at the thought. 'Besides,' he said thoughtfully, turning back to place the dish back in the oven, 'it's been lovely to get back into it again. And I've felt like Martha has been here with me.' Annie watched as his shoulders rose up and down as he let out a big sigh. 'It's just a shame she can't do the washing up,' he added before looking round at Annie and giving her a wink.

'I had a feeling that part might have been her job,' Annie laughed.

She had to admit Bert was a good cook. The pie was almost as good as one of Poppy's dishes.

With her bulging stomach satisfied, Annie went back upstairs to get changed into her undercover outfit. When she came back downstairs she handed Bert her ring – for some reason, she felt better giving it to him to keep in his pocket rather than leaving it in the spare bedroom. Then she bid her friend farewell and hoped the washing up would all be done by the time she returned.

Hiding in the undergrowth waiting for Marie, Annie rubbed her hands together and blew on them to try and warm herself up. Even with her WPS uniform on she tended to pace up and down to keep warm if she needed to stay in one spot for too long. But she didn't want to risk making any noise or draw attention to any movement in case anyone from the brothel turned up, so she stayed put. There were hardly any leaves left on the bushes so she had to crawl quite a way in to make sure she was hidden.

After what seemed like hours but was probably only about twenty minutes, one of the men entered the gardens with two women in tow. As usual, he left one woman behind and left with the second.

Annie waited a few moments before approaching the woman. It wasn't somebody she had spoken to before, but she looked familiar so she knew she had been in the men's clutches for a short while at least. She was aware she had planned on only focusing on Marie but she figured she may as well try and talk to other women if opportunities arose.

'Leave me alone. I'm busy,' the woman snapped when she turned and saw Annie approaching from behind. Annie immediately retreated back to her hiding place. Since talking to Marie she was wary of pushing things with anybody else. Now she knew their reasons for being so hostile towards her, she had to respect their wishes. They were frightened for their lives, after all, and she didn't want to be the one responsible for getting them shipped off abroad, or worse. She was taking enough of a risk focusing on Marie. She shuddered as the thought of the men harming Marie because she had been talking to her ran through her mind. She was going to have to be extremely careful if this was going to work.

The next few women who were dropped off over the course of the evening were just as unreceptive as the first had been, so Annie decided to hold out for Marie after all. As the hours drew on and she didn't appear, Annie started to panic that their conversation the previous evening had already landed Marie in trouble. But they hadn't spoken for long and she had been certain none of the men had been anywhere near. If Marie's captors knew about their brief talk then Annie wasn't sure how she was going to be able to help the women.

Annie was getting so cold that she started running a few laps around the gardens as soon as every woman had left with a customer. She knew from the regular pattern of movement that she had enough time to get at least three laps in before the next group turned up and it was just enough to get the blood pumping through her veins so that she didn't collapse from the extreme cold.

When Marie was finally dropped off, Annie watched the clouds of steam that flowed out of her captor's mouth as his words hit the icy air. He was obviously giving Marie the usual instructions but Annie couldn't hear what he was saying. As soon as he was out of sight, Annie grabbed a handful of soil and threw it towards Marie's feet. Marie jumped and looked around, confused, before shrugging her shoulders and turning to face the other way again.

'Pssst! Over here!' Annie hissed, lobbing a small stone in Marie's direction. Marie shook her head and grumbled something incomprehensible. Annie had to get her closer to her so that they could talk for longer without it looking obvious what they were up to.

'If you don't come to me then I'll come over to you!' Annie whispered as loudly as she could manage. Marie let out a big sigh, did a quick scan of the rest of the gardens, and then slowly walked backwards to the bushes. Annie let out a sigh of relief.

'What do you want?' Marie asked quietly but firmly. She was facing away from Annie, looking out into the gardens. Anybody peering in wouldn't have known she was talking to somebody hidden in the shrubs. 'I told you, there's nothing you can do to help me,' she added, sounding irritated.

'I'm with the police,' Annie whispered through chattering teeth. She had been taking slow, deep breaths to try and focus her mind away from how cold she was feeling but now she had to talk she found she could barely do so. Marie spun her head round and searched through the branches until her eyes, full of fear, landed on Annie. When she took in Annie's face, she relaxed.

'You had me worried there. I thought I recognised your voice from last night. Don't scare me like that, you silly little girl. You need to run home and leave all of this well alone,' Marie snapped.

'No, honestly, I'm a member of the WPS,' Annie hissed. 'I'm only dressed like this because I wanted to fit in. I didn't want to spook the men in charge into doing anything hasty if they spotted a police uniform hanging around where they're operating.'

Marie was facing away from Annie again. She started tapping her foot. Annie knew she didn't have long to hold her attention and get her on-side – she was getting impatient now.

'If the police know about the brothel then why haven't they stormed in and rescued us all yet?' Marie asked.

Annie quickly relayed her conversation with the chief to Marie. 'I need to get as many of you as possible to agree to give evidence against these brutes,' she concluded. 'Then they'll have to believe you've been forced to sell yourselves. If they go in now it will be you and the rest of the women getting locked away and the men will go free.'

'Maybe I'd rather be in prison than stuck where I am,' Marie replied quietly. 'At least in prison I wouldn't be forced to do *this* every day,' she added, gesturing around her. Annie had to admit she had a point. As terrible as prison was for women it would probably be a welcome change from the life Marie was currently living.

'Yes,' Annie agreed. 'But your captors would be free to start this all up again in another location. And I have no doubt that they would. If you're brave enough to speak out against them then you won't just be saving yourself and all the women they're currently holding – you'll be saving countless women in the future.'

Marie stood in silence for a long time. Annie was growing anxious. She wasn't sure if she should push further or let her mull over what she had said for longer. When Marie started walking away, Annie nearly leapt out of the undergrowth after her, but she stopped herself just in time.

'I'll think about it,' Marie called back behind her.

Annie couldn't help but grin from ear to ear, even though the action made her cold face sore. Not thirty seconds later, a man Annie hadn't seen before entered the gardens and started talking to Marie. After a few seconds, Marie nodded and they linked arms and left together.

Annie was desperate to run all the way back to Bert's. She needed to get the blood pumping around her body again, plus she was desperate to fill him in on her progress. But she held back for five minutes to give Marie time to get back to the brothel with her customer. She didn't want to risk catching up with the pair in the street.

From her hiding spot, Annie walked through the journey in her head. Once she was certain Marie would be back indoors, she shuffled out of the undergrowth and ran back towards Bert's house as quickly as her feet would carry her. She had to admit the night hadn't been the success she had hoped for – Marie could still say no to her. But the important thing to focus on was the fact she hadn't turned her down outright, so there was some hope this would work.

And if there was one thing this war had taught Annie it was that she had to cling to hope wherever she could find it.

27

When Annie turned into Copenhagen Street she stopped dead as she spotted a group of figures ahead. They were standing just a few doors between her and the brothel. She ducked into the nearest garden and poked her head out to try and get a better look without being spotted herself. It appeared as though they were talking and before long she heard some light laughter and then the two groups broke away and wandered off in separate directions. Now they were moving she could see that one half of the group had been a man and a woman – it looked like Marie and her companion. Her suspicions were confirmed as they turned to walk into number 83.

Annie set her sights back on to whoever the couple had been talking to. They were walking towards her now. Maybe it was one of the men in charge at the brothel, heading out with another prostitute? But as they drew nearer she could see clearly that they were both women. Confused and intrigued, Annie slipped out of her hiding spot and continued her journey along the street towards them with her head bowed so she looked as though she hadn't seen them. If two prostitutes from number 83 were out with no supervision then they were definitely worth speaking to. Annie looked up again as she heard their footsteps getting closer.

'Good evening,' one of them said pleasantly, and Annie studied them both for any indications as to who they were.

They were smartly dressed but even in the dark she could tell they weren't wearing a formal uniform. They did, however, each have on an armband. A quick glance told Annie they were with the National Union of Women Workers. Her heart dropped. She had finally come across the WPS' rival patrol – and she was out on her own in the middle of the night dressed as a prostitute. How on earth was she going to talk herself out of this one?

All kinds of excuses started running through her head as she heard the second woman introducing herself and asking her what she was doing out so late on her own. She had to think of something plausible – and quick – if she was going to avoid a night in a police cell and maybe even worse long-term. The truth was out of the question. She was running this amateur operation completely on her own and without any authorisation from the chief. If Annie gave the game away before getting the results she was after, she would be in a hell of a lot of trouble with him, and her secret mission would surely be shut down before it had even had a chance to get started properly. All her hopes of saving the women in time for Christmas and getting justice for Maggie would be dashed.

Then she remembered what Poppy had told her about the NUWW patrols. She had called them a waste of space. Annie had certainly never come across any of them the whole time she had been part of the WPS. They were apparently operating in and around Holborn, but this was the first time she had come face to face with any of them. Poppy's words played back in her head: *'They don't want to step on any toes and they just lurk on the sidelines.'* Annie decided to take her chances.

'I was out delivering some food to a neighbour for my grandfather,' she said to the two women who were now staring at her expectantly. She realised she must have left them waiting for an answer for quite some time while she debated what to do in her mind.

'It's very late,' the first woman said casually.

'Oh, I know. We were just getting ready for bed when my grandfather remembered we hadn't taken any food over to Doris down the road for a few days. The poor love has been struggling since her husband died and we've been trying to do what we can. I was meant to drop off our leftovers and go straight home but she got me talking and I ended up stopping for a cup of tea.'

'It couldn't have waited until morning?' the second woman asked. She didn't seem that bothered; it was as though she was just going through the motions.

'Doris doesn't really sleep since she lost Ron,' Annie replied, making her voice as sad and subdued as she could, 'so, we knew she would be awake. And we're not sure she eats unless we drop meals round. We had lots of stew left over so I thought it was best to drop some round to her before I got ready for bed. I couldn't stand the thought of her going hungry.'

Annie knew that if these women wanted to verify her story then she could take them to Bert and he would go along with it. But if they asked to meet Doris then she was in trouble. She decided to pre-empt them. 'Would you like to come back with me and meet my grandfather? He'll still be up. We only live a few doors down, which is why I came out without my jacket.' She rubbed her hands up and down her upper arms dramatically and bounced from foot to foot. 'I'm rather regretting that decision now,' she added pointedly.

'No, no, there's really no need – you get yourself back home to the warm,' the first woman said cheerfully, and they continued on their way. Annie stood for a moment, dumbstruck. That had been so easy. No wonder the NUWW patrols were looked down upon by the WPS. She and her colleagues would have been immediately suspicious of an excuse like that. They definitely would have followed up on it, with both 'Doris' and Bert. But those two had simply shrugged and wandered off into the night. And they had clearly stopped Marie just as she was about to step into the brothel with her customer – and they had let her carry on! Annie couldn't wait to tell Poppy and Maggie all about this when the dangerous gang were safe behind bars.

Back at Bert's, Annie filled her friend in on everything that had happened that evening, up until her run-in in the street. She held back from telling Bert about bumping into the women from the NUWW because she was worried about admitting to claiming he was her grandfather. He was certainly old enough to have that role, but she didn't want to offend him or make him feel uncomfortable. She felt close to Bert already and it had seemed natural to describe him as her grandfather – but would that description make him feel awkward? Annie would be over the moon to have somebody like Bert as her grandfather. She had only met both sets of her grandparents a few times. They had all died when she was still young and she had always longed for the special relationship with them that she had seen her friends enjoy with their parents' parents.

'That's not bad going for your first proper shift,' he remarked, looking impressed, and she pushed her thoughts about grandparents to one side to enjoy the sense of pride and achievement his approval gave her.

'Will you go out again tomorrow?' he asked.

Annie took a moment to consider. 'I'd rather go slowly with Marie and give her a few days to think about it. But I don't really have the time for that. I don't want to push her too much by turning up again in the morning, though.'

'Why don't you leave it until the evening again? It's easier for you to keep hidden in the dark, anyway,' Bert suggested.

'That sounds like a good idea,' Annie smiled. And she had to admit that she was looking forward to a whole day of rest.

The following day felt luxurious to Annie. She woke up late to the smell of simmering porridge, and her mouth immediately watered in anticipation. She was looking forward to being able to savour the flavour for once instead of rushing the meal before having to get out on patrol.

The thought of the WPS made her think of her friends and her heart suddenly ached for them both. She missed them already. But she reassured herself that she was making good progress and she was confident she would have everything wrapped up in time to spend Christmas with them and her family. Maybe she would even be able to invite Bert to join them.

She spent the rest of the day getting to know Bert better in between taking short, unplanned, naps on his sofa. Annie felt guilty and lazy but she found she just couldn't help it. Every time she sat down she found her eyelids growing heavy and her limbs felt like heavy weights.

'I don't know what's wrong with me,' she said groggily as she came around from an afternoon doze to find Bert sitting on the sofa opposite her, reading a book. 'Maybe it's because I've spent so long on the go. Now I've finally stopped my body is giving up.'

Bert nodded and gave her a sympathetic smile. 'It does sound like those patrols are hard work,' he said. 'All that time on your feet in the cold. And now you're standing around in a flimsy dress all night. Your body needs time to recover.'

Annie felt better after that and indulged in another nap until dinner time. When she heard Bert crashing and banging in the kitchen she had a little stretch before going to offer some help.

'I wouldn't dream of it,' Bert replied. 'You sit down and

have a cup of tea and keep me company while I cook for us.'

Annie took a moment to appreciate how much Bert had changed in the short time they had been getting to know each other. He had gone from a grumpy, quiet man to cheery and energetic.

'I'd given up on life after I lost Martha,' he suddenly said out of nowhere. It was quite a thing to say and he continued with chopping vegetables instead of turning to look at Annie while he spoke. 'Helping you, and these women, has made me realise that life is worth living again. I'm not sure what would have become of me if you hadn't turned up on my doorstep that day.'

Annie heard a quiver in his voice and tried to think of something light to say. Bert may have changed recently but she knew he would feel uncomfortable showing emotion in front of her. 'My waistline is certainly grateful you've redis-covered your love of cooking,' she joked, rubbing her belly and giving Bert a quick wink when he turned to look at her.

'You've got a beautiful figure,' he remarked. 'You're all woman.'

Annie blushed furiously and poured out the tea while Bert went back to his chopping. She had to admit she was getting used to her fuller frame. Maybe she would just buy a whole new wardrobe instead of trying to slim down so her clothes were more comfortable again. Besides, it wasn't like she had a husband to keep happy. The thoughts of Richard prompted her to remove her ring once more ahead of the night's activities.

'Try and drink more water during the day,' Bert commented as she struggled to wriggle it off her finger. 'I've no idea why, but it does help. Martha used to suffer with the same thing,' he added knowingly.

When darkness fell, Annie set off for Thornhill Square Gardens once more. She ran there this time, knowing how cold she was going to get standing still waiting for Marie to arrive. She didn't bother trying to speak to any of the others this time, instead blowing on to her hands quietly while each of them waited for customers and then running her laps around the gardens to warm up before the next one was dropped off.

Thankfully, she didn't have to wait too long for Marie. As soon as the older woman's chaperone had left the gardens Annie took a handful of dirt and skimmed it across the ground towards her. She heard the tut Marie let out even from a distance.

Annie waited patiently, willing Marie to approach her. Eventually, she sighed and started slowly walking backwards, checking around her as she went.

'You again?' she hissed into the undergrowth when she reached the edge.

'Hello,' Annie whispered, trying to sound cheerful.

'You really aren't going to give up, are you?' Marie said, her voice agitated.

'I want to help. You have a way out of this,' Annie replied. Marie sighed again and started tapping her right foot. 'Please,' Annie tried. She wasn't sure how this was going to work without Marie – the only prostitute who had given her a chance to explain herself.

'Okay. I'll see what I can do,' Marie relented. Annie had to supress a yelp of joy. 'You'll have to give me a few days to talk to the others. We don't get a lot of time without one of those bastards breathing down our necks.'

Annie's feeling of triumph was wiped out instantly. It was nearly the middle of December – she needed the women to speak out as soon as possible if she was going to get these men behind bars by Christmas.

'We don't have much time,' Annie stressed. 'Is there any way you can get the word around by tomorrow evening?'

Marie sighed again. 'It will be risky but I'll see what I can do. I'd love to see some of the younger girls free by Christmas.' Marie fell silent and Annie was just about to thank her when she hung her head and started talking again. 'I'm not so worried about myself. I've nothing left to go back to anymore. But some of those girls – they have loving families who must be missing them more than anything. They have no idea where their daughters, sisters and nieces are. Some of them have no hope of returning no matter how much their families miss them. They know they would never be accepted back once the truth of what they've been forced to do is revealed. But getting them away from this life is more important than anything.' Marie kicked at a bit of dirt on the path. 'How can it be fair that they are the ones to shoulder the shame for what they've been made to do?'

Annie stayed silent. She didn't know what to say to comfort her.

'But something like this . . .' Marie turned suddenly and leaned down to peer through the twigs and branches to seek out Annie. Once she locked eyes on her she held her gaze. Annie could see tears gathering in the corners of her eyes. 'Do you really think this could work?' she asked, suddenly sounding hopeful. 'If the men are prosecuted for making us do this then the families of those poor girls might understand they didn't run away to become prostitutes. They might welcome them back if we can prove they were forced into it.'

'I have to believe it will work,' Annie said firmly. 'It *has* to work.' She felt choked up with emotion but she did her best not to let it show.

There was a sudden noise from near the gates and Marie spun around to check if there was somebody there. Annie held her breath. She just needed a few more minutes with her. There was no further movement but Marie stayed facing away from Annie now.

'I've lost all of my family to this war. I don't care what happens to me,' Marie whispered into the cold night. 'I'll speak to as many of the girls as I can before tomorrow night. See you then.'

Annie was desperate to talk for longer, to find out more about what had happened to poor Marie. But she knew she had put her at enough risk as it was. She watched sadly as the older woman walked away and back to her spot to tout for custom. A couple of men approached her over the next hour or so but neither left with her. Annie wondered what was putting them off. Were they looking for someone younger? She wondered if Marie was relieved or upset to be turned down. Who knew what her captors would do if she failed to make some money tonight?

Eventually a soldier turned up who led Marie away. Annie watched as she took one final glance over towards the bushes. Her eyes glistened in the moonlight and even in the dark, Annie could see a whole world of sadness behind them. She wondered again what had happened in her past to make Marie so unconcerned about what might happen to her if she was caught trying to get the other women to speak out about their captors. She certainly knew where she was coming from – she had had the same feeling of recklessness since losing Richard. She wasn't entirely sure she would be here now, doing this, if she hadn't lost him. Maybe her life wasn't so different from Marie's, she thought sadly as she got ready to run back to Bert's house.

But she had helped Bert see that life was worth living again. Maybe if she saved Marie and the other women, she could do the same for them.

28

The next evening Annie was full to the brim with anticipation as she got ready to go and wait for Marie. She was so hopeful of Marie having news she had to stop herself from running to number 83, banging on the door and asking to speak to her.

'How many of them do you think she will have managed to speak to?' she asked Bert as he prepared a hearty dinner for them both. 'I think once I have five women ready to give evidence that should be enough, don't you?'

'I don't know, dear,' Bert said evenly. 'Try not to get carried away. I don't know how they operate over there but I would imagine it's going to be extremely difficult for her to talk to anyone else properly without any of those men being around.'

Annie felt deflated and her face must have given as much away as he stopped what he was doing to add, 'I don't want you to get your hopes up, is all. You're asking a lot of this woman and she needs to tread carefully if she's going to get this done safely.'

Annie felt a sudden rush of shame and guilt. She had told Bert that Marie had promised an update this evening but not that she had pushed her into speaking to some of the other women so quickly. 'I'm just so desperate to get them all out of there by Christmas,' she muttered.

'I know,' Bert replied sagely, getting on with his cooking again. 'But you might need to let go of that. This is delicate and if it needs more time . . . well, it would be dangerous to force it.'

Annie nodded. This evening she would tell Marie to take her time. Now she had her working for her she didn't really need to be at Bert's full-time anyway. She could move back to the section house and get back out on patrol and come to check in with Marie every few days. If she couldn't have the men behind bars for Christmas, then she could at least enjoy the hope over the festive season. That might be enough to get her through it without Richard by her side.

'Besides, I'm quite enjoying having the company again now you're here,' Bert added quietly.

'Don't worry, you won't get rid of me that easily,' Annie laughed. She already knew Poppy and Maggie would love her new friend. Once this was all out in the open she couldn't wait to bring them round to meet him. She envisioned long Sunday lunches together and was even hopeful the three of them could persuade Bert out to enjoy an afternoon tea with them all.

Once they were sitting down to dinner, Bert suggested that Annie sit by the spyhole once it was dark and look out for Marie from there. 'It seems silly for you to sit out in the freezing cold for hours on end waiting for her,' he explained. 'It was different when you were trying to talk to all the women, but it would make sense now to only head out once you see her going on her way.'

Annie had to admit that his plan made sense. She had been dreading another long night in the cold so she was only too happy to agree to this idea. When they had finished eating she helped him wash up the dishes before pulling a chair over to the spyhole. As soon as Bert had turned off all the lights, Annie opened up the gap in the cardboard and waited for a sighting of Marie.

Bert sat at the kitchen table to keep Annie company and they chatted away as she watched the men and women coming and going from Number 83. There was a lot of activity this evening but no sign of Marie, and Annie started growing anxious when she hadn't emerged after hours and hours of watching.

'Maybe you missed her?' Bert asked cautiously as Annie started tapping her foot nervously on the floor.

'No. Even if I missed her earlier this evening, she would have been sent out again by now. They always use her at least twice every night. I noticed that when I went through our logs tracking her.'

'I'm sure she's fine. Perhaps they gave her a night off?' Bert suggested.

Annie snorted. 'She's never had a night off, Bert. For goodness' sake! They're not adhering to employment laws!' she exclaimed. She felt Bert shrink back into his chair and immediately a stab of guilt pierced her chest for speaking to him so harshly. She had to explain to him why she was feeling so agitated. 'I'm so sorry. I shouldn't have shouted at you like that,' she said, staring intently through the gap in the cardboard. She ran him through her conversation with Marie from the night before, word for word.

'Ah,' he said in quiet understanding.

'I've got to do something,' Annie cried, bursting out of her chair and darting towards the door.

'Wait!' Bert shouted. He had never raised his voice and it made Annie stop in her tracks. 'What are you going to do?' he asked, calm again. 'Go and knock on the door and ask to speak to your informant Marie?'

'No, I . . . I don't know,' Annie said. But the fear and anguish and responsibility were bubbling over in her and she knew she had to do *something*.

'Don't be hasty,' Bert advised. 'We need to think this

through. It's only one night where she hasn't made it out. You can't go rushing in there. You might blow everything up when there's a simple explanation for her absence tonight.'

'It's only one night – but it's the night after I persuaded her to talk to as many of the women as possible,' Annie fretted as she walked over to take a seat at the table opposite Bert. The spyhole was still open, and the tiniest bit of the sunrise was streaming through it. 'What if I pushed her too far? What if she was so keen to get names for me that she got reckless and one of the men heard what she was up to? I should have given her more time. We know what they do to anyone who plays up, Bert.' Annie burst up out of her chair and started pacing up and down the small kitchen. She was full of nervous energy and worry. If Marie had been hurt then it would be all her fault.

'Let's try not to panic too soon,' Bert said evenly. 'We know from the log that she goes out during the day, too. Let's keep a lookout today and then if she still doesn't show you'll have to spend the evening in the shrubs and speak to the girls who turn up. I know they weren't keen on talking to you previously but they're bound to know if anything has happened to her, so you'll just have to find a way to get it out of them.'

Annie stopped pacing and nodded her agreement. 'Okay, I think that's the only option we have,' she replied. She was grateful she had Bert to talk this through with. Left to her own devices, goodness knows what kind of trouble she would have got herself into by barging round there looking for Marie.

'She could have been poorly this evening,' Bert tried to reassure her. 'Or maybe they got some new girls in they wanted to try out and there wasn't enough time to get Marie out as usual. We know there's only so many men available and they don't let the women leave the house without an escort. There's also the possibility she was held back for one of the more important clients who go straight to the house.'

Annie wanted so much to believe him – she had spotted a few unfamiliar figures leaving number 83 so perhaps he was right. She let out a big yawn and walked back over to the chair by the spyhole, ready to recommence her surveillance.

'I don't think so, missy,' Bert said firmly. Annie spun around, confused. 'You've been up all night and you're set for another long night ahead. I'll keep a lookout now while you go and get some rest.' She nodded gratefully and they agreed to take shifts for the rest of the day so they each got some sleep, with Bert insisting that Annie take as long as she needed before relieving him of his first one. She didn't think she would be able to sleep with all the thoughts of Marie and the terrible things that could have happened to her running through her head. But sleep found her as soon as she lay down on the bed.

When she stirred, Annie felt immediately full of emotion. She didn't know how long she had slept for but her dreams had been full of images of Marie in pain. In every one, Marie was staring at Annie as if to say: 'this is all your fault'.

Annie got dressed and rushed downstairs, hopeful of some good news from Bert. But when she burst into the kitchen he looked round and shook his head sadly. It was the same for the rest of the day. By the time the sun started to set, Annie was itching to get out to Thornhill Square Gardens to speak to the other women who were trusted on their own there. Bert insisted she eat first, although her appetite had all but disappeared with all the feelings of guilt and worry boiling inside her. Somehow, she managed to eat enough to satisfy Bert and then set off for her usual hiding spot.

Annie tucked herself away among the bare branches and twigs, far enough back so that anybody walking past would struggle to spot her. When Stevs entered the gardens, she held her breath. She was desperate to see Marie with him. But she was overcome with disappointment when the two figures accompanying him drew closer and she saw that neither one was Marie.

Annie waited patiently while Stevs spoke to one of the women. She couldn't make out what he was saying but the exchange appeared to be harsher than usual. He was leaning in towards her more than normal and his body language looked to be more threatening. Annie tried not to read too much into it. She was certain she was seeing something that wasn't there because of her fears for Marie.

When the man left with the second woman following behind him, Annie waited a few moments before emerging from the undergrowth. She didn't have time to waste trying to lure the woman over – she needed answers quickly and if any of the men appeared then she would throw herself at their mercy to save the prostitute. She was so anxious to find out what had happened to Marie that she wasn't thinking about her own safety.

On hearing footsteps approaching, the woman turned around and looked Annie up and down as she drew nearer. Once she was close enough, Annie could see the woman was probably around her age and her heart ached to think of someone so young caught up in something so terrible. Her long blond hair was tangled and dirty and she was shivering from the cold.

'This my patch,' she said through chattering teeth as she held Annie's gaze with a piercing stare. She had an accent, but Annie wasn't sure where it was from. She wondered if she had been a Belgian refugee, whisked away from the promise of safety as soon as she had reached London. 'You go now. Leave,' the woman ordered, turning her back on Annie.

'Do you know Marie?' Annie pressed, undeterred. 'She's

older than us, with brown hair.' The woman didn't react. 'She has bruises around her neck,' Annie added. She was certain she saw the woman flinch, even from behind and in the dark.

She turned around to face Annie again. 'You leave me alone. You get me killed,' she hissed through gritted teeth. Annie held up her hands and backed away.

She got a similar reaction from the next few women she approached. Back in the undergrowth, Annie wondered if she would ever find out what had happened to Marie, and if she would ever get another opportunity to infiltrate the brothel and bring down the men running it. No one else had been willing to give her the time of day before and it seemed clear that hadn't changed.

Annie felt close to giving up. It had been silly of her to think she could do this on her own. Feelings of foolishness swept over her as tears began to well in her eyes. Maybe she should admit defeat, go back to Maggie and Poppy and put all of this behind her. But would she be able to live with the knowledge that Maggie's attacker – Stevs – was still out there and inflicting misery on so many other women? Could she keep it from Maggie? And one thing was for certain: she couldn't walk away from this without knowing what had happened to Marie.

When the next woman was dropped off in the gardens, Annie approached her with a renewed sense of purpose. Gone was her softly-softly approach. She needed to know where Marie was and she wasn't going to give up until she had an answer.

'I know you don't want to talk to me, but I'm not going to stop approaching you all until I find out where Marie is,' she said firmly as the woman looked the other way, pretending that Annie wasn't there. 'I mean it,' Annie said, louder this time.

'Please be quiet,' the woman said. She spun around, grabbed Annie by the arm and yanked her towards the undergrowth. Panicked, Annie got ready to defend herself with some of the ju-jitsu she had learned during training. They didn't often have to use it against the prostitutes themselves but she was more than willing to if absolutely necessary.

The woman glanced all around her quickly and then let go of Annie's arm. 'I take it you're the woman polly who put the silly ideas into Marie's head?' she spat angrily. Annie breathed a sigh of relief that this woman was English and that she knew who Marie was. Although, it didn't sound as if anything she had to say was going to be positive.

'What's happened to her? Please tell me. I know it must be bad,' Annie begged.

'It's all your fault,' the woman said, folding her arms and peering around the gardens again.

'What do you mean it's all my fault? Please – what happened to her?' Annie tried again.

'You shouldn't have tried to get involved. This is bigger than you realise. You have to leave it alone now. You've done enough damage as it is,' the woman said. She still sounded angry, but there were tears running down her cheeks. She brushed them away and then folded her arms again. 'Marie is dead,' she whispered.

Annie put her hand over her mouth to stifle the cry that had escaped her.

'You can cry all you like, but be thankful that you didn't have to sit and watch the life drain away from her, bit by bit, like I did,' the woman said quietly. Tears were streaming down her face, but her voice was strong and even.

'What happened?' Annie croaked. She was staring at the ground. She couldn't stand to look this woman in the eye when they both knew that she was responsible for Marie's death.

'I can't talk about it,' the woman said sharply. 'It's too painful. And if I'm being honest, I don't think you deserve to know.'

Annie couldn't argue with that. This was one death that she would have to leave to her imagination.

'Those ideas you put into her head – well, she fell for them. She really believed you could save us all!' The woman laughed spitefully and shook her head. 'She tried to get us involved too but of course Claude caught wind of it. I don't know what she was thinking.'

'I'm sorry,' Annie whispered, wiping away her own tears roughly.

'Just leave the rest of us alone. Unless you want more blood on your hands,' the woman snapped before walking back to her pick-up spot.

Devastated, Annie wandered the streets. She couldn't face going back to Bert's. How could she explain that her actions had led to Marie's murder? A woman was dead and it was all her fault. Yes, she had only been trying to help but she had been too pushy. Her selfish need to get the brothel closed down before Christmas had taken over and she had put that before Marie's safety. All so that she could take the glory and have some positive news to distract her from the fact she was spending her first Christmas as a 'widow'. She groaned as she thought of all the other poor women gearing up for their first Christmas without their loved ones by their side. Some women had lost brothers and sons as well as husbands – yet they weren't running around putting innocent women in the firing line so they would have something to distract them from their grief over the festive season.

Hours later, Annie looked up and realised she had no idea where she was. Her aimless pacing had led her to a part of London she didn't recognise. Standing in the middle of the street trying to get her bearings, she spotted two figures approaching her. She could make out the WPS uniform straight away and instinctively she ducked into an alleyway to avoid being seen. As the two women walked past, she heard part of their conversation.

'I'm really pleased we helped her,' one of them said happily.

'Just think of what might have happened to her if we hadn't stepped in. I'll never get over the look of relief on her mother's face when we dropped her home,' the other responded.

Annie sunk to the ground and burst into tears. That was the kind of feeling she was supposed to be getting out of her role with the WPS. That was why she had joined up in the first place. It's what she had enjoyed for so many months previously. Instead, she was now consumed with guilt because she was responsible for a woman's murder.

As she sobbed, she came to realise that she couldn't in good conscience carry on with her role with the organisation. She had gone against everything the WPS stood for by taking actions that had led to a woman being killed in cold blood. As soon as she found her bearings, Annie decided she was going to make her way back to Bert's and write her letter of resignation. It was the only thing she could do after what had happened.

Annie was shivering so much by the time she had made her decision that she had to get up and move around. She started jogging to try and warm up, and as she started to finally get feelings back in her limbs her mind seemed to come alive, too. With blood pumping through her veins once more, she started thinking clearly. An image of Richard came to her mind, and she stopped to close her eyes and watch him as he wrote his final letter to her. He had been so proud of her in his last days. How could she give this all up now? She had to give it one final go.

Suddenly, her eyes shot open when a crazy idea pushed

its way into her thoughts. But she quickly shoved it to one side, telling herself it was too insane to entertain.

When the clock tower at King's Cross came into view Annie knew where she was. Making her way towards Copenhagen Street, her idea gnawed at her. She tried to ignore it, but it wouldn't go away. Instead, it kept pushing at her, niggling at her thoughts. It kept growing and growing – it was out of her control, until before she knew it, it was a full-blown plan.

With Copenhagen Street in view, Annie stopped and started walking in the opposite direction. She had to work out what her next step was going to be before heading back to Bert's house. She needed to have it straight in her head before she spoke to him. Annie blew on to her cold hands to try to warm them up. Then she stopped dead in the street. Surely, she couldn't go ahead with this? It was preposterous – a suicide mission! But it was the only thing she could think of that might work, and for that reason she felt compelled to try. If she gave up now then it would all have been for nothing – including Marie's death.

The only alternative she could come up with was leaving the WPS, and if she did that then she would be losing her two best friends while at the same time letting Richard down. Not to mention how disappointed her mother would be with her. With all that in mind, she didn't feel like she had anything to lose with her new plan.

Annie realised with a start that she was so keen to go ahead because she truly didn't care about what happened to her now. She stopped in her tracks and took a deep breath. It was decided. This was either going to go to plan and she would bring down the brothel, save all the women trapped there and get justice for them and Maggie and Marie – or she was going to fail miserably and perish along with Marie.

29

Annie felt terrible about lying to Bert, but there was no question of her telling him what she was about to do. He would only try and talk her out of it – he would think she had lost her mind. And she didn't want to upset him. If this all went wrong, which was a very real possibility, then she would rather he think that she never came back to see him out of choice. They hadn't known each other for long but she had a feeling that losing her in such a way would break his heart. It was better that he simply thought she had returned to her old life and she was too busy to come back and visit him.

Bert was relieved when Annie claimed to have found Marie. She hoped he didn't detect the quiver in her voice as she spouted her made-up story about how she had asked for more time to talk to the other women and they had decided to reconvene after Christmas. She would have given anything for her story to be true. All Annie could see in her head as she lied were images of the poor woman being beaten to death.

They agreed that Annie would go back to the section house and patrol with her friends as normal until the new year. 'I'll come back and see you and catch up with Marie in January,' she smiled, trying not to let her real feelings of sadness break through her pretend chirpiness. She couldn't bring herself to ask Bert about his plans for Christmas. With no family or friends to look after him, she already knew he would be

spending it on his own. She consoled herself with the fact
that if she managed to pull off her wild plan, then she would
be able to come back and invite him to spend the festive
period with herself, her friends and her family.

As soon as Annie got to the end of Copenhagen Street
and she was confident she was out of Bert's sight, she broke
down in tears. She had planned on going home to see her
mother and sisters before putting her plan into action, but
she couldn't face it now. If she had found it hard to keep
her composure in front of Bert then doing so in front of her
family would be impossible.

As she walked back to the section house she contemplated
sneaking in and back out again before Maggie and Poppy
realised she had returned. But she decided that, as painful
as it was going to be, she needed to see them one last time
before she did this. She owed them that, at least.

Maggie and Poppy were nowhere to be found at the section
house so Annie assumed they were out on a day patrol. That
worked well for her as it meant she could put her head down
and get some rest ahead of seeing them again. She would
sneak out that evening once they were in bed. She had decided
it was better to throw herself into this before she had time
to change her mind.

She drew the curtains to block out the weak winter sunlight.
As she lay awake in bed thinking of all the things that could
go wrong on her dangerous mission, she contemplated forget-
ting all about it and getting on with life as usual. But she
dismissed the thought almost as soon as it entered her mind.
She couldn't let Marie's death be in vain – and what did it
matter if her own life was sacrificed in the process?

'You're back!' Maggie cried when she walked into the
communal kitchen with Poppy following their shift. She
hurtled towards Annie but stopped in her tracks when she

took in the sight before her. 'And you're . . . cooking?' she exclaimed.

'It's good to see that you put your time away to good use,' Poppy said approvingly as she brushed past Maggie to pull Annie in for a hug. When they were finished, Maggie took her turn for a cuddle and then they all sat down at the table together while Annie left the stew she'd thrown together to simmer.

No wonder Maggie had been surprised; Annie hadn't cooked for her friends the whole time they had lived together. Growing up, she had been waited on hand and foot by her doting mother, so she had never needed to learn to look after herself when it came to cooking. But she had watched Bert closely in the kitchen during their time together and he had encouraged her to help him on a few occasions. So much so that she felt confident enough to cook a basic stew herself for her friends. It felt like the least she could do, considering what she was about to put them through. But she tried not to think about that as they started talking.

'We're so happy to have you back,' Maggie said. Then her demeanour changed. 'Are you feeling better?' she asked solemnly.

'Yes, don't you worry about me.' Annie smiled as best she could.

'It seems that all you needed was something to distract yourself with, and from the smell in this room I would say your mother is a good teacher,' Poppy said. 'I must say it will be rather splendid to have somebody to share the cooking with,' she added, looking between both Annie and Maggie with a raised eyebrow. Annie giggled. If she had been unenthusiastic about the kitchen before, then Maggie had gone out of her way to pretend it didn't exist. All the hours she had spent talking to her family cook Flo in the kitchen growing up, and she hadn't managed to pick up anything about fending for herself.

'I can just about manage a basic stew so I wouldn't get too excited,' Annie mumbled. She wished she could tell them about her real teacher. It felt unnatural to keep such a big part of her life back from them. But she reassured herself that it was for the best. And she would be able to tell them all about Bert soon, if everything went according to plan.

Annie didn't go into detail about her time away 'recuperating'. She felt bad enough lying to her friends without going over the top with it all. Given the circumstances of her leaving, they thankfully didn't push for information on what she had been up to. Once Maggie and Poppy had told her about what they had done over the last few days on patrol, they all agreed on an early night.

'See you tomorrow,' Annie said as brightly as she could on her way out of the kitchen.

The following morning, Annie got up extra early to make sure she didn't bump into either of her friends on her way out – or any of the other police officers, for that matter. As she put on her trusted 'undercover' dress, she thought back to how Bert had helped her make it tatty enough so that she would pass for a prostitute. Then she remembered she needed to look a little bit more presentable if her idea was going to work. She took it off and dressed instead in a plain, understated dark green dress, remembering that she needed to look poor and not privileged. She decided she'd had enough of braving the freezing cold temperatures and threw on her thickest shawl. Thankfully, it was old and in need of a good wash, so it finished off her look perfectly.

Next, Annie pinned her hair up. She pulled some of the hair around the sides down so it looked scruffy. She needed to pass for somebody who had been travelling for days.

She picked up the empty holdall she had unpacked the previous afternoon and crept out of her room as quietly as she could. She had to get past Poppy's room to make it out undetected and she knew she was a light sleeper and an early riser. Holding her breath, she tiptoed past and exhaled slowly when she reached the end of the corridor and had the main door in sight. Without a backwards glance she opened it and started running as soon as the cold, fresh air hit her. There was no turning back now.

When Annie got to King's Cross Station, it was bustling with people making their way to work and soldiers coming and going from their leave. She smiled to herself – it was the perfect time for the men from the brothel to try and pick up more victims. The busier the station was, the easier it would be for them to blend into the background and go about their business undetected.

She knew there was a train due in with Belgian refugees at some point that morning. Searching the platforms, she found a group of smartly dressed women waiting patiently. By eavesdropping into their conversations, she ascertained that they were waiting to escort the foreigners to their medical checks before taking them on to a dispersal centre, so she knew she was in the right place.

Annie ducked behind a nearby pillar to keep an eye on things. From her hiding spot she looked out for men from the brothel while quietly practising her 'broken English'. She needed to sound genuine for this to work and the men needed to believe she was confused and vulnerable.

When a train slowly pulled up to the platform Annie squeezed her eyes shut and brought her favourite image of Richard to mind. It was not long after they had met, and he had picked her up after work with a picnic. It was the most basic of dinners, and he hadn't been able to afford anything fancy to drink, so they had shared some water. But none of that had mattered to either of them as they had been delighted to be alone in each other's company. They had walked to one of the local parks and found a quiet spot to enjoy the balmy summer evening together. Annie pictured Richard's face as she told him about her day and she savoured the glint in his eye and the obvious interest he always showed when she was talking, no matter what the subject was.

'I love you,' she whispered into the air, and then she fell into line with all the refugees piling off the train.

30

With the official-looking women still in sight, Annie peered around the rest of the platform as discreetly as she could manage. She needed to catch a glimpse of the men from the brothel before she was 'checked in' and sent off to the dispersal centre.

She stayed at the edge of the crowd that was being guided towards the women, then stepped to the side and ducked down, pretending to adjust the laces on her boots. Searching around her desperately, she was about to give up and sneak away ready to try again later when she spotted two big pairs of boots just off to her left. Her eyes swept up the legs and her heart pounded almost painfully when she saw the black jacket Stevs always wore. When she got to their faces she was terrified but at the same time elated to see the now familiar almost-bald head of the man who threw her friend in front of a car, and the full head of dark hair belonging to his shorter companion.

The pair of them were watching the refugees closely. Now and then they nudged one another and muttered between themselves. Annie stayed crouched on the floor as the crowd of Belgians traipsed past her. When the bodies started thinning out she got to her feet and walked straight towards the two men. Putting on her best confused expression, she kept glancing around her as though she was looking for somebody or something. She risked a glance at the two men and caught them exchanging a knowing glance as she drew nearer to them.

'I go for medical?' she asked them, clutching her holdall to her chest and looking worried. 'You take me? Woman on train say look for right man,' she added, pointing back towards the train she had watched pull into the station just minutes before. Annie hoped her stilted English was authentic enough to convince them. She had gone over and over the way some of the prostitutes from the brothel had spoken to her out in the gardens, but most of them hadn't spoken to her for long so she didn't have a great deal to go on. The men looked at one another again, smirking slightly, and Annie felt a rush of apprehension as she realised her plan was working.

'That's right, you've found us,' Stevs said, grinning from ear to ear. But it wasn't a friendly smile – there was something sinister in it, like a wolf regarding its dinner. 'The car is this way,' he added as he took her bag from her and started walking off towards the exit she had seen them leaving from on previous occasions. Annie looked to the second man and he nodded reassuringly, holding his hand out in front of him to guide her into following his colleague. He had the same menacing glint in his eye despite his smile and Annie couldn't help but feel uneasy even though she had chosen to put herself in this position.

Annie stood frozen to the spot for a moment. This was it: her last chance to change her mind and back out. She could turn and run right now and be back in the safety of the section house with her friends before they had even realised she'd left. Or she could walk off with these men into what she knew would be a very dangerous situation – one that she might not make it out of alive.

'Come on, love, the car's waiting. The doctors have lots of people to see,' the shorter man said impatiently. Annie snapped herself back into the present moment and nodded apologetically before scurrying to catch up with Stevs.

Before she knew it she was walking along, wedged between

the two men and feeling like a lamb being led to slaughter. As her nerves kicked in she thought again of Richard in the park, smiling over at her and listening intently to everything she had to say. Then Marie's face took over. The soothing calm she had felt when she was thinking of Richard was replaced by anger. *That* was the feeling she needed to hold on to in order to carry out her plan effectively. She couldn't allow herself to feel scared of these men, despite the things she knew they were capable of doing to her. If she could keep herself feeling angry and focused, she would be able to make it through this safely.

The men led her to the all-too-familiar red car. Stevs threw her bag into the boot while the other man opened one of the passenger doors and motioned for her to climb in. When Annie peered inside she saw two other women already sitting waiting, looking confused and nervous. Squeezing herself in next to them, she tried to give them both a reassuring smile.

The door was closed behind her and she watched as the men had a quick exchange before they both got into the seats in the front. The shorter man was driving today and the whole car remained in silence as they took the route Annie knew would lead them to number 83 Copenhagen Street.

As soon as the car pulled up outside the brothel, the men got out. Annie tried to open her door but Stevs slammed it shut on her. He held a finger up and mouthed 'one minute'. He walked around to his companion and as they started talking, Annie strained to try and hear what they were saying. It was quieter in the street than it had been outside the station, so she was able to make out snippets of the conversation.

'Can I just have a go on one of them before we start sending them out?' she heard the short man pleading.

Annie felt sick. She looked to the two other women to see

if they had heard what she'd heard but they were both staring blankly ahead. One of them whispered something to the other in a language Annie couldn't understand. *Of course!* Annie thought to herself. They were from the train full of Belgian refugees, so they didn't understand much, if any, English. The men had assumed Annie was in the same position and so they were talking freely, unaware she knew exactly what they were saying.

Stevs growled menacingly. 'How many times do I have to tell you? These ones are for the high-bidders and . . .' but the two women beside Annie had started a panicked conversation and Annie couldn't hear the rest of the sentence over them. She shushed them and they fell silent, and Annie managed to pick up more of the discussion outside.

'. . . brown-haired, curvy one looks just right for me,' the short man was saying now. Annie glanced at the other women again – one had black hair and the other was blond. He meant her. She felt her pulse quicken and suddenly she was feeling warm and queasy. She closed her eyes and thought of Marie again and suddenly she was ready to fight this brute off if he tried anything at all with her. She would rather die than allow that to happen.

'We're not sending them out and we're not giving them a go ourselves,' Stevs snapped. 'They're to go straight to the holding rooms, away from the other girls, until the chief arrives to pick one. Claude promised him the first go – so just keep your hands to yourself for once.'

Chief? Annie thought, confused. She had thought the man called Claude was in charge, so who was this chief they were talking about now? Was there more than one boss? Either way, this was not a good situation for her. Her plan had been to talk to as many of the other women as possible before she was sent out on the game, at which point she would escape. But it sounded as though they had different ideas for Annie and her new companions . . . Annie felt a sick swoop of fear in the pit of her stomach. This was bad.

She took a deep breath and forced herself to think. She needed a new plan that would get her out of the house before she was violated. She would just have to convince the women to turn on the men together, she decided in desperation. Annie knew how many women they were holding here and she was confident the men wouldn't be able to do anything to stop them fleeing if they all agreed to charge out at once. At twenty women against four men, their captors might be able to grab hold of a few of them but the women would have the advantage, and she was certain they would be able to overpower them if they all fought back at once. They would also have the element of surprise on their side. The men would never see it coming.

Annie had just finished putting together this new plan when the car door next to her flew open. She jumped and then peered out to see the shorter man staring at her impatiently.

'Out,' he barked. He was obviously upset he wasn't going to have his wicked way with her. Annie hadn't imagined for a moment that she would ever feel grateful to Stevs, but right now she did.

She clambered out of the car and joined the other two women, who had been escorted out the other side, on the pavement. When Stevs started walking up to the front door of number 83, one of the girls suddenly turned on her heel and tried to run in the other direction.

There was a loud THWACK as the poor women was punched in the face. She fell to the floor with a thud and her friend screamed in horror. Annie was shocked. She had expected the man to grab hold of her and force her into the house, not use such extreme and unnecessary violence. Knowing these men would do anything to avoid a scene in the middle of the street, Annie quickly grabbed the second girl by the hand and put her hand gently over her mouth. She stared straight into her eyes and willed her not to make another sound. Thankfully, the woman nodded slightly and she remained silent when Annie slowly pulled her hand away. She squeezed her other hand reassuringly and they both stood back and watched as Stevs walked back towards them, scowling.

'What are you doing?' he hissed under his breath at his companion as he grabbed the girl splayed on the floor under both her armpits and hauled her to her feet. She was out cold but she was tiny compared to him, so he simply picked her up like a baby and carried her over the threshold. Annie could see tears running down the other woman's face as she watched her friend being carried inside. Suddenly, she felt a nudge from behind; the short man was trying to get them inside the house too. She squeezed the woman's hand again and as they stepped over the threshold, she could feel the man's breath hot on her neck.

Once they were in the hallway with the front door shut behind them, Stevs fixed a steely glare on his accomplice.

'What are you playing at?' he demanded. Now they were out of view of any prying neighbours, he had raised his voice and the volume made Annie jump. She remembered that she wasn't supposed to be able to properly understand what they were saying and so she stared directly at the floor. 'We can't present her to the chief with a bruised face. I'll put her in with the others while you take these two upstairs. And no funny business!'

The short man led Annie and the other woman up some steep stairs. The house was a lot bigger than Bert's and although the upstairs was in complete darkness, she could make out the doors to five rooms – all of them closed. She flinched as she heard panting coming from one of the rooms when they walked past. The short man let out a quiet chuckle in response to the noise and a chill ran down Annie's spine. He *enjoyed* the fact that women were being abused behind these doors. As Marie's face flashed into her mind again, she started to look forward to bringing him and his no-good accomplices down.

The man stopped at the door furthest away from the stairs and took a set of keys out of his pocket. Annie's heart sank as she realised they were probably going to be locked up inside until the chief, whoever he was, turned up. When he flung the door open and gestured for them to go inside, leering at her all the while, she braced herself. Stevs may have warned him against any 'funny business' but he was clearly not very good at doing what he was told and he had made it clear he was keen to do unthinkable things to Annie. She had already decided that if he tried anything then she would throw some ju-jitsu moves on him and suffer the consequences rather than endure any abuse at his hands.

He slammed the door shut behind them as soon as both girls were in the room and Annie let out a big sigh of relief. She looked around her in disgust. The room was dark and dingy. At first, she didn't think there was a window but then she realised it had been boarded up. She ran up to it to see if she could pull any of the covering away, but it was nailed tight to the window frame. From what she could see of the room from the light coming in under the door, it was filthy and there was rubbish strewn across the floor. On one side were two mattresses, covered in dirt and stains. Annie shuddered at the thought of what terrible things must have taken place between these four walls.

'Can you speak any English?' she asked her new roommate urgently. She needed to get out of this fix as quickly as possible and it would help if she had someone on her side to give her a hand. The girl just stared at her with fear written all over her face. Sighing, Annie gave up on that idea. It was clear she was going to have to carry her new plan out alone and come back for this woman later.

But when she looked at the woman's face again, she noticed tears pooling in the corner of her eyes, which were wide with fear. She was terrified. Annie felt a flash of guilt for being so abrupt with her. She had to remember that she had put herself in this position, whereas this woman had believed she was being led to safety when in fact she had walked straight into the lion's den – and on top of that, she couldn't understand a word anyone was saying to her. Of course she was going to be shocked and upset.

Annie pointed to herself, smiled warmly and whispered, 'Annie.'

The cloud lifted from above the Belgian woman and she smiled gratefully before pointing to herself. 'Amelia.'

'It's going to be all right, Amelia,' Annie said with more confidence than she felt. She knew she couldn't understand what she was saying but she hoped her tone would reassure her. Then Annie pulled out some of the sharp hairpins she had expertly placed in her hair earlier that morning. She silently thanked the Annie of that morning for pinning her hair up, hopeful the tools would come in handy now she was staring at a locked door. She put a finger to her mouth to warn Amelia to stay quiet and then started trying to pick the lock with the pins.

Annie had no idea what she was doing, of course. She had read about criminals picking locks in books and newspapers, but she had never had any cause to learn herself. She silently cursed herself for assuming she would be able to do it. What had she been thinking?

'Damn!' she whispered angrily, throwing the pins down on to the floor. Richard's face popped into her head and tears welled in her eyes. How could she have been so stupid to come so unprepared? What was she going to do now? She had just put her head in her hands to have a quiet sob when she felt a tap on her shoulder, and she looked around. Amelia was standing behind her holding one of the hairpins and motioning for Annie to move aside. Intrigued, Annie slid her body out of the way of the door and watched on in awe as the young woman got down on her knees and unpicked the lock in a matter of seconds. She couldn't believe her luck when Amelia set to work with an almost professional air. How had she learnt to pick locks? She hoped she would get a chance to ask her once they were both safe.

When it snapped open they both froze, terrified one of the men might be in the corridor. But when there had been no movement after a minute or two, Annie let out a quiet sigh.

'Thank you,' she whispered gratefully as the woman handed her hairpin back to her and nodded. It seemed they didn't need to speak the same language to be able to communicate.

Annie turned the doorknob as slowly and quietly as she could, petrified that any tiny noise would bring one of their captors racing to the room. Pulling the door open, she held her breath. As she went to step into the corridor, she felt Amelia moving behind her. Annie spun round and held up both her hands to stop her, shaking her head at her and hoping she understood that she wanted her to stay in the room.

Amelia nodded sadly and retreated to the back of the room, hanging her head. As Annie watched her from a distance, Amelia's coat fell open and for the first time since they had met Annie was able to see her round, bulging belly. There was no question that this woman was heavily pregnant. Annie had been too preoccupied to notice before. Besides, her frame was so slight that her heavy jacket had kept the tell-tale bump expertly hidden. Annie wondered if the men had realised.

Now there was no question that she was going to leave her in the room while she carried out her new plan, which was far too risky to drag a pregnant woman into. With no way of communicating to her that she would come back for her, Annie hoped she would take reassurance in the friendly smile she gave her as she backed out of the room. It was more important than ever now to get this done properly. Annie didn't care what happened to her in all of this, but she couldn't let an innocent baby suffer because she had messed up.

31

Tiptoeing along the hallway, Annie froze every time one of the floorboards creaked. When she got to each bedroom door, she put her ear up against it and as soon as she heard movement inside she crept on to the next. She shuddered when she heard a woman cry out in pain. The noise was swiftly followed by the sound of a loud slap and then whimpers. Annie tried not to visualise what was happening behind the door – she had to keep her focus.

Now she knew it would be impossible for her to speak to any of the other women being held here, she was hoping to find a room that the men worked out of – some sort of office or living room. In the absence of girls willing to testify, she needed to get her hands on evidence of the activities that went on here. If they kept any kind of record at all then she needed it in her possession before she broke out. Otherwise it would all have been for nothing.

Annie thought back to the smarter-looking men she had watched turning up at the property alone through the spyhole, and Stevs' reference to the 'high-bidders'. She realised that this set-up wasn't just a case of thugs pimping out prostitutes on the streets with the promise of somewhere private to carry out their seedy desires. No, there was a second arm to the seedy business, where women were hired out to men who could afford to pay extra for the privilege of not having to take the risk of picking them up on the street. And there had to be a record of that activity somewhere, there just *had* to be.

Annie was at the top of the stairs now and she felt certain that if there was some sort of office, it would be downstairs. She couldn't stay in this hallway too long. One of the men in these rooms would surely be done with their victim soon, and she couldn't risk getting caught out here on her own.

Just as she was about to put her foot on the top step, she heard a door opening below her. She jumped back up and ducked around the side of the bannister out of sight. *Please don't come upstairs,* she begged silently.

'Yeah, room two's time is up. I'll go and let him out,' she heard a man's voice saying. Panic ripped through Annie. Someone was about to come up the stairs! She couldn't let herself be seen.

Reluctant as she was to go back to the room she had just been locked in, she decided it was her only choice. The door below her slammed shut and under the cover of the noise she scurried to the other side of the hallway so that she was as far from the railings as possible and hopefully out of sight as the man came up the stairs. When she heard heavy footsteps on the stairs she used the noise to mask the sound of her running back to the bedroom at the end of the corridor. She turned the doorknob as carefully and as quietly as she could, stepped back into the room and then closed it again. She rested her head against the door and let out a long breath. Only then did she realise she had been holding her breath the whole time.

Annie suddenly remembered that she had left Amelia behind in the room and she spun round with her finger to her lips, silently urging her to stay quiet. She didn't want the man coming to investigate any unusual noise. If he found the door to their room unlocked there would surely be trouble. Amelia was sitting on one of the filthy mattresses stroking her bump. She looked absolutely terrified, but clearly understood the need for silence. Turning back to the door, Annie rested her ear against it to try and listen to what was going on in the hallway. She heard the jangling of keys followed by two sets of deep, mumbled voices, which she assumed belonged to the man who had come upstairs and the client he had come to let out of the room.

'I'll have the same one next week. Same amount of time,' she heard as footsteps made their way down the stairs. *Not if I have anything to do with it*, Annie thought angrily. The voice had certainly belonged to an upper-class gentleman, and he seemed to be booking his next appointment. Annie knew now that she must be right – there had to be a log being kept somewhere in this house of all the visits and the payments. Or at least a diary of appointments so they could keep track of it all. She kept her ear up against the door, listening out for the sound of the front door closing. Soon after, an internal door was opened back at the other end of the house. Then, finally, she heard the same door opening and closing before somebody went back into the room from which the man had originally emerged when she had been stood at the top of the stairs.

Annie crept along the corridor a lot quicker this time. There was no doubt in her mind that she needed to get to one of the rooms at the back of the house if she was going to gather her evidence. And she couldn't dally about it. She knew from her own logs how often people came and went from this house, even during daylight hours, and someone else in one of these upstairs rooms was certain to be finished soon.

When she heard male voices coming from the room at the bottom of the stairs she crept down, hopeful that they would drown out any noise she made. She paused at the bottom of the stairs. If they had heard anything and were coming to investigate then she was right next to the front door. She could fly through it before they even realised what was happening and be at Bert's house before they got to her. She wasn't sure if they would give chase in broad daylight for all the neighbours to see, but she had to have an escape route just in case.

Annie waited on tenterhooks for any sign of movement. When none came she had a big decision to make. She could walk out of that front door unscathed right now. Or she could put her life on the line to try to get hold of the evidence she needed to save these women. Now she was confident the evidence would be here, she briefly considered leaving and reporting the brothel to Chief Constable Green. But, while she was fairly sure his officers would find the evidence needed to prosecute the men in charge instead of putting all the blame on the women, she couldn't be certain. And what was to stop one of these men bribing the police or getting rid of the records before they could find them? No, she couldn't take the risk after making it this far.

Now she was here it was clear to Annie this was most certainly the suicide mission she had hoped it wouldn't be. She would have to be the luckiest girl in the world to make it into the office at the back of the house and out again with the evidence she needed without coming across any of the dangerous men in charge. But she had to take her chances and do this for Marie, for Maggie and for the unborn baby she now knew was in the room upstairs.

On hearing the men's voices start up again from the other side of the wall, Annie decided to take her chance and dash along the hallway, past the door to the room they were in. She held her breath all the while, only releasing it when she was a good few feet past the door. Her heart was hammering and she took a moment to compose herself – and to gather her courage for the next hurdle.

When she was ready, she took in her surroundings. She was at the end of the hallway now, and in front of her were two doors. Taking one last quick look behind her to make sure the coast was clear, she leant down to look through the keyhole of the door on the right. What she saw took her breath away. The room was full of terrified-looking women – she managed to count fifteen but she couldn't see all the way around the room so there could have been more. Some of the women had their hands bound and some were shaking through what she could only assume was a mixture of cold and fear. She wondered if this was where the men held the women who were sent out to solicit in between their trips out to pick up business. In the middle of the room she spotted the second girl from the car – still unconscious. She realised none of the other women were helping her because they must have been too scared of the consequences.

This was the room Annie had hoped she would be led to when she arrived. She contemplated trying to get inside so she could go ahead with her plan of inciting a revolt and getting them all outside to safety together, knowing the police would have to listen when there were so many of them telling them they had been held against their will. But they all looked so scared.

Annie suffered a moment of self-doubt: would she be able to convince enough of them to leave with her before being discovered? Glancing as far as she could through the tiny keyhole to the left, her breath caught in her throat when she spotted a big pair of boots. One of the men was in there with them! No wonder Marie had been found out so quickly – they were being watched the whole time. Marie must have been truly desperate to have tried talking to the other girls about Annie with him there.

Backing slowly away from the door, Annie knew her only chance now lay in finding some concrete evidence. She exhaled slowly and tried the door to the other room. She almost burst into tears when she found it locked. Wishing she could have brought her lock-picking companion along with her, she pulled out one of her hairpins and thought about the steps Amelia had taken to unlock the door upstairs. She was just about to try and recreate the trick when she heard voices coming from the room at the front of the house again, moving towards the door. There was a coat and umbrella stand leaning against the wall to Annie's left and she leapt behind it, grateful it was winter and there were lots of heavy coats hanging from it to conceal her.

Peering out, she watched Stevs leave the room. He stomped up the stairs and, from what she could make out from listening to his footsteps, unlocked one of the rooms in the middle of the corridor.

'Time's up, Justice Cromwell,' he said after coughing very loudly. Annie could hear a second set of footsteps, then the door was closed again. Keys jangled and then the two men made their way down the stairs. Annie watched on from her hiding place as the men shook hands by the front door, her heart beating painfully. She had recognised the man's name and now she could see his face she knew he was one of the senior judges she had seen at court. She was appalled.

'You'll find it's all there,' the client said as he handed over a pile of notes. Annie wondered what on earth the poor woman in that room had been forced to endure in order for that amount of money to exchange hands. Justice Cromwell was dressed in a fancy suit and he held a walking cane in one hand.

'Very well,' Stevs replied. 'And I'll book you in for two o'clock on Thursday.' The judge nodded his appreciation before opening the front door. No wonder they ran appointments from the house, Annie thought. High court judges couldn't risk being seen picking up prostitutes in the street.

There was going to be some real trouble when she revealed what was going on here.

'Good day,' the judge called out behind him as he walked off along the street, leaving Stevs to close the door behind him.

Annie breathed a sigh of relief that she had been disturbed before she had managed to get into the room she believed was the office. She was certain Stevs was about to go inside to store the cash he had just been given. She stood still as a statue with her back pressed right up against the wall, holding her breath as he made his way towards her. When he was standing outside the door to the room she so urgently needed access to, he was within touching distance. She could see his muscles bulging through his top and it made her wince to think about the amount of power he possessed. His companion was shorter and slimmer than he was and he had wiped the girl from the car out cold with one punch. Annie had no desire to learn how much more damage this man could cause.

Annie watched on in shock as, at the same time as unlocking the door, he slipped one of the notes the client had just given him into his pocket. Annie wasn't sure why she was surprised. He was clearly a terrible man with no morals and stealing was one of his lesser crimes. She listened hard as he entered the room, trying to work out from his footsteps which direction he moved in. She heard him open a couple of drawers, then there was some banging and some rustling before they were closed again. Annie tried not to breathe when she heard him making his way back towards the door. She was so close to gathering her evidence that she couldn't get caught. The man locked the door and as soon as she saw him go back into the room at the end of the hallway, she emerged from her hiding place, hairpin in hand.

Concentrating fiercely on the memory of what Amelia had done upstairs, Annie fiddled with the lock as quietly as she could. She was all too aware of the large man sitting on the other side of the door just to her right. She willed the lock to click open, trying not to get frustrated with her lack of success. She was trying not to panic but it was hard when she knew she didn't have a lot of time. She was sweating and her hands were shaking so hard she could barely hold the pin. Was she going to have to give up? Surely she didn't have long before someone else disturbed her. Would she be able to make it upstairs again to ask Amelia for help?

As panic surged through her, Annie tried her best to keep calm. She froze when she heard a noise coming from the room at the other end of the house. When nobody emerged, she gave the pin one last twist and it clicked open. It took all she had not to cry out in joy. Instead, she did a little dance on the spot before opening the door as quietly as she could, and shutting it behind her.

There was a big wooden desk in the middle of the room and Annie went straight to it. There was a set of drawers on one side and as far as she could see, there were no other drawers in the room. These had to be the drawers Stevs had been rifling through. Trying not to disturb the contents too much, Annie flicked through the big pile of paperwork but she couldn't see anything incriminating. A few bills, some official-looking invoices and betting slips, but nothing that showed what went on in the house. Disappointed, she tried the next drawer down but still there wasn't anything she could use to put these men behind bars. When the final drawer failed to throw up anything useful, Annie started to feel sick with despair. But she gave herself a firm mental shake, and promised herself that she would not leave this room without something she could use against these awful men.

Annie threw herself down on to the chair next to the desk and folded her arms, letting out a big huff as she did so. She was certain she had heard the sound of a drawer opening and closing when the man was in here – but where was it? Then it hit her: of course they wouldn't keep incriminating papers in such an obvious place! She peered around the room, scouring every inch for a sign of anything remotely out of place or unusual. Just as she was about the give up hope, she pounced forwards and ran her hand over the top of the desk. Carefully, she prodded and poked around the top and the sides until finally she felt a latch on the underside of the desk. She pushed down on it and a hidden drawer sprung open. It was small in length but very deep.

Her pulse racing. Annie thrust her hand in and pulled out the first thing she touched. It was a notebook with '83 C. Street' scrawled on the front. She opened it up and what she saw made her gasp loudly. Silently cursing herself, she stayed frozen to the spot, waiting for the tell-tale sound of male voices or a door opening to signify that somebody was coming to investigate the noise. When nobody came, she continued reading.

The notebook was full of names, addresses, dates and times of visits and details of cash transactions for a lot of men – all with well-to-do names. She flipped to the most recent entry and found Justice Cromwell's details written down. Reading further back, Annie had to put her hand over her mouth to stop herself from crying out in shock and rage when she came across the name of another of the judges she had encountered during her work with the WPS. She kept her hand in place as she read the names of two prominent politicians, too.

Annie couldn't work out why on earth the men in charge would keep such detailed records like this – they had the potential to ruin their clients' lives if they fell into the wrong hands. But then it dawned on her: that was exactly *why* they kept the records. This notebook was their security if anything went wrong with any of the more high-profile men who used their services. They would never be able to turn on them once they discovered what they had on them.

Annie started shaking as it dawned on her just how powerful the notebook in her hand was. She needed to get out of here with it before anyone found her. God alone knew what lengths these men would go to to stop it leaving the house. But when she went to push the secret drawer back into place, she noticed more notebooks. Picking through them she saw lots of different addresses on their covers. This brothel was just the tip of the iceberg! There were at least a dozen more in operation across the city.

If Annie had been shaking before, she was nearly convulsing now. While she was delighted to have gathered more evidence than she could ever have dreamed of, it had become immediately clear to her that she was in over her head – even more than she had originally thought. She had come into this knowing it was dangerous but she was in a far more vulnerable position than she had realised. She had to leave as soon as possible.

Pushing down her panic, Annie reassured herself that all she needed to do was to make it along the hallway undetected. As soon as she was outside she would hotfoot it to Hunter Street Police Station and present Chief Constable Green with the notebooks. He would have no choice but to send his men to arrest the gang and free the women. She had to hope that they wouldn't notice her missing in the meantime and take their fury out on her roommate. Annie grabbed as many of the notebooks as she could carry and crept out of the office.

As soon as she had closed the door, Annie heard a loud shout from behind her. Her blood ran cold as she realised she had been caught. She had been so close! Standing facing the office door still, she panicked about what to do. Whoever had caught her was between her and the front door. There was no question of her escaping. She had to protect her evidence at all costs. She cast around wildly, and then it hit her: the umbrella stand. But if she moved to drop them in there now, the man would see her. As heavy footsteps started making their way towards her, Annie dived behind the coats on the rack. The man would think she was stupid to think she could hide from him now he had obviously seen her, but she hoped the action would give her a precious few seconds to hide her haul.

'I can see you!' his voice roared from right next to her.

Though she was more terrified than she had ever been in her life, Annie kept her wits about her and managed to stuff the notebooks into the umbrella stand and then jumped out from behind the coats with her hands up in surrender.

'I sorry, I panic,' she muttered, remembering just in time to put on her Belgian accent. She looked Stevs in the face and experienced a jolt of terror. He was so angry a vein on the side of his head was bulging.

'You stupid girl,' he roared, leaning down and putting his face right up to hers. Spittle hit Annie's face and she flinched, bracing herself for the fierce blow that was surely going to knock her out. But none came. Instead, he grabbed her arm so roughly her whole body jolted. Before she could even try and put up a fight he had hauled her over his shoulder and set off towards the stairs.

Annie knew there was no point in fighting back against this brute. He was huge and there was no way she was going to be able to free herself from his grip. She was lucky he hadn't used any violence towards her already, especially given how angry she had clearly made him.

When he started on his way up the stairs Annie was relieved he hadn't taken her into the room where the other men were. This meant he might still be saving her for the 'chief' – which meant she still had time to get herself out of this house before something truly terrible happened to her. Even if she wasn't able to get her hands on the notebooks on the way out, they were hidden now so she would be able to tell Chief Constable Green where to find them when he sent his men in to investigate.

Stevs kicked the bedroom door open and threw Annie down roughly on to one of the mattresses. As she landed a shooting pain ran up her back and she cried out in pain. She looked over to her left and saw Amelia cowering in the corner.

'You're lucky I need you looking presentable,' the man sneered as he leaned over her, both his fists clenched tight. 'I'd love to teach you a lesson right now'.

Annie was splayed on the mattress, helpless. She closed her eyes and used her hands and arms to try to cover as much of her face as possible, fearful he would lose control and lash out at her against his better judgement. But then she heard his footsteps moving back towards the door. Peering out through her fingers, she watched as he opened the door again to leave.

'I'll be standing outside on guard this time, so don't go trying anything else!' he snarled as he slammed the door shut behind him.

32

Annie paced for hours, cursing her own stupidity. Why hadn't she confided in anybody and asked for help? What had she been thinking, convincing herself that she could do this alone? If she'd told Bert her plan, he would know where she was and could have been on standby to let the police know if she didn't emerge from the brothel by the evening. A glimmer of hope that he had seen her enter the house flashed through her mind, but then she remembered he had sworn off keeping tabs on the activity from the brothel now she had told him she was picking things back up with Marie in the new year. If she had planned this through properly then she would be sat here right now safe in the knowledge that backup was on its way. She couldn't believe how naive and foolish she had been.

'You'll wear those floorboards out soon,' a deep, mocking voice boomed from the other side of the door. Stevs was still there. Taunting her. Refusing to budge so that there was no question at all that she might be able to escape. Annie ignored his comment and continued pacing, trying to work out what her next move was going to be. She stopped when she heard sobbing. In all her rage and fear Annie had forgotten about the woman in the room with her. It was easy to do; with the windows boarded up there was hardly any light once the door was closed.

Amelia was lying on the wooden floor cradling her baby bump. Annie walked over and sat next to her. She put a reassuring hand on her head and started stroking her hair comfortingly. 'I'm so sorry. I really thought I could save you,' Annie whispered. Before she knew what she was doing, Annie started telling the woman about everything that had led her to being here now. She knew Amelia couldn't understand a word she was saying but it didn't seem to matter. Getting it all out was helping Annie feel better and Amelia stopped crying, seemingly soothed by Annie's company and story.

When she was finished, Annie felt a little better. And she was pleased to see her new friend was asleep next to her. With her head clear, she started to think about what she was going to do when this 'chief' finally showed up. There was no way she could let him anywhere near Amelia. She would have to put herself forward.

From what she had seen of the way the gang operated here, Stevs was likely to show this important client into the room and then leave him to it. But there was no question of Annie allowing this man to do anything to her. She had come into this willing to die rather than let that happen and nothing had changed now that she was staring down the barrel of the gun. Suddenly an image of Richard flashed into her mind. But it wasn't the happy, smiling Richard she was used to imagining. He was sad. Disappointed, even.

'I'm sorry,' Annie said to him silently, her eyes closed as she pictured Richard sitting in front of her. 'I know I've let you down. I didn't feel like life was worth living without you and I got a little reckless. But I don't want to die.'

She opened her eyes as the realisation hit her. She might not have Richard anymore, but she had so much to live for still. She had her family and her friends. She had the WPS, she even had Bert. They had become so close over the last couple of weeks and she had been so happy to learn she had made him realise life was worth living without Martha. She had been so wrapped up in getting her secret mission tied up that she hadn't stopped to take in the fact that he had helped her, too. She could see now that as much as she would of course far rather have had a life with Richard in it, she still had one without him. She had a lot to live for, even though he was gone. She closed her eyes and brought Richard to mind once more.

'I'm still devastated to be living life without you,' she whispered. 'That will never change. But I know you wouldn't want me to join you just yet.' She paused to wipe the tears from her eyes. 'I promise if I make it out of this alive, I'll try my very best to move on and be as happy as I can without you. I know you don't want to watch me pining for you and putting myself in dangerous situations. You always wanted me to enjoy life and I know you still do.' Annie kept her eyes closed for a few moments more as she pictured Richard smiling and walking off into the distance. She finally felt that she had had the goodbye she had so desperately wanted.

When Annie opened her eyes again, she wasn't sure how much longer she had left until the client arrived but she knew she had to come up with a better plan before he got here. She still needed to fend him off, but instead of accepting that she would be beaten to death for refusing to comply with the gang's orders, she had to find a way out of this terrible mess alive.

She crept over to the windows and searched for any loose boards that might allow her to pull the wooden covering away. If she could make a gap big enough so she could see out into the street, she might be able to attract the attention of somebody below. Annie clawed around the edges and then slumped down on to the floor, defeated. These men were professionals – of course they wouldn't have left any room for somebody to be able to pull the boards away. It was all nailed in perfectly.

Annie crawled back over to sit next to Amelia again. She

had no other option: as soon as the door was shut behind this 'chief' character, she would use some of her best ju-jitsu moves on him in order to subdue him as quietly as possible. Then she would try to talk him around. Maybe she could convince him that she knew there was another woman here undercover and the police were about to arrive and raid the premises. He was clearly an important man and the thought of getting caught by the police with his trousers down would terrify him, even if he was confident the prostitutes would be the ones prosecuted. It was a level of shame no self-respecting man could live with. That's why the gang kept their records. If he believed her then she might just be able to convince him into taking her and Amelia with him when he left. If he was so important then the gang might just allow it. It wasn't a great plan, but it was the best she could come up with.

When Annie finally heard footsteps making their way up the wooden staircase, she listened intently in case it was the client meant for her. After a brief pause she heard Stevs talking and she knew this was it. The moment of truth. Nerves shot up her body, from her toes to the top of her head. Everything tingled as it dawned on her that what she did in the next few minutes would determine whether she made it out of this house dead or alive. She tried her best to stay calm but she couldn't stop herself from shaking. It was an elaborate ruse but she had to believe it could work. It was her only hope of making it out of here. She took a deep breath to try and calm herself down so she was able to think straight.

'We've held back two of good quality for you, sir. You can take your pick,' she heard Stevs saying. Annie felt bile rising in her throat. It disgusted her how he talked about women, as if he was working in a butcher's shop and presenting customers with his best cuts of meat. But it didn't surprise her in the least. She also knew for certain now that the gang had no idea that Amelia was pregnant. Unless this man had some kind of horrible fetish, of course. Annie shivered and pushed the thought away.

Despite her best attempts to stay calm, Annie's whole body pulsed with nerves as she readied herself for what was coming next. Amelia was stirring next to her, so she quickly ushered her into the corner of the room, her finger over her lips so she knew yet again to keep quiet. Amelia nodded silently, her eyes wide with fear as she scrambled along the floor.

'I won't let them hurt you,' Annie whispered. She positioned herself in front of her, ready to pounce on the client as soon as the door was closed. He was talking to Stevs and she strained to try and make out what was being said. He was speaking too quietly for her to make it out, but the voice sounded strangely familiar. She tried to place it – where did she know it from? She heard footsteps retreating along the corridor and knew Stevs was leaving. That was one thing, at least. The last thing she needed was for him to hear her trying to placate this man and burst in before she was finished.

When the door opened Annie instinctively found herself backing up into the corner. She was almost on top of Amelia when she came to a halt. With the door open, a shaft of light came into the room and for a split second before it was shut again she caught a glimpse of the client's face. Annie's breath caught in her throat. She couldn't believe what she had just seen. It couldn't be, could it? She wondered briefly if she was imagining things but she couldn't deny who was standing right in front of her. And now she knew where she recognised his voice from.

What was she going to do now? Her plan was completely useless now – he would know straight away that she was bluffing about undercover police. Because if the police were waiting to raid this place, he would be the one man who would know all about it. Bert had been right when he'd claimed the gang were in cahoots with the police when they had first met. And when the men here had talked about the 'chief', it wasn't some silly nickname they had come up with for one of their most important customers. Because standing in front of Annie right now, expecting to have his wicked way with her, was Chief Constable Green.

33

Annie stood rooted to the spot, waiting for Chief Constable Green to make a move. Even without his uniform on she could tell it was him from his short, round stature and heavy gait. He hadn't said anything yet and she thought that due to the darkness and her raggedy clothes, he must not recognise her. That was one good thing, at least. Maybe if she could keep him at a distance and change her voice slightly then she might be able to talk him round before he got too close and realised who she was. She was panicking too much to come up with a plausible story, though, and before she knew it he was making his way across the room towards her.

Annie yelped as he grabbed her arm roughly. Any hope she had entertained that he was here undercover himself had disappeared. The only thing she had on her side now was the fact that he was short and clearly unfit.

'You'll do just nicely,' he panted into her ear as she turned her face as far away from his as she could manage. 'Even in the dark I can see you've got curves in all the right places. I told them I wanted someone a little more substantial and they haven't let me down. I can't stand those skinny girls.'

Annie had taken as much as she could bear, and she was more angry and disgusted than she had ever been in her life. She brought her foot up and kicked the chief square in the groin with as much force as she could muster. There was a lot of power behind her kick and he let go of her arm to grab hold of the affected area as he stumbled backwards, groaning.

'You stupid little bitch!' he hissed. 'You'll regret that.'

Annie used the next few seconds he took to recover to work out her next move. She was just about to try to subdue him with some ju-jitsu when he launched himself in her direction.

'Come 'ere!' he raged as she jumped to the side to avoid his grasp. She spun back around to face him and they stood staring at each other through the darkness, each braced for the other to make another move.

'I know who you are,' Annie said as calmly as she could. The chief's head twisted to the side slightly, as if he was trying to make out her face in the limited light. 'And now I know why you were so keen to dismiss me when I came to you with details about this awful place. You're one of their biggest customers!'

He peered into the dim light. 'It's you!' he said. He started laughing as the realisation hit him. 'You really are a stupid little girl,' he spat. 'You really thought you could bring this operation down all on your own? I was right when I said women should be staying at home. All this going out to work gives you ideas above your station.'

He was edging closer as he spoke and Annie was shuffling backwards to try and keep him far enough away so that he couldn't reach out and grab her again. She had purposefully backed up away from Amelia and she was relieved that he hadn't seemed to have noticed her yet. But she knew she must be due to back into the wall soon. As soon as her back hit the wall she was going to lean forwards and try to get the chief in one of the tightest ju-jitsu holds she knew.

'You're just angry I found out about your dirty little secret, you corrupt bastard!' she said, her voice dripping with disgust. It was the strongest language Annie had ever used but these were extreme circumstances and she found herself relishing it. She reached her hand out behind her, searching for the wall, but Chief Constable Green jumped forwards and before she had a chance to react he had one hand firmly on her shoulder and with the other he grabbed a chunk of hair before forcing her head backwards.

As the back of Annie's head connected with the wall she was overcome with a sharp pain that ran all the way down her body. She felt herself go limp despite the fact every inch of her wanted to fight back.

The chief threw her body to the floor and stood proudly over her. She groaned and tried to focus on his face. She panicked when another man suddenly turned up next to him, but as the figure merged back with the chief, she realised she was seeing double.

Annie wondered if she should just give up. The chief was never going to let her walk out of here alive – he simply had too much to lose. And she felt like all the fight had been knocked out of her. But when he started undoing his trousers a feeling of strength suddenly ran through Annie again. Her whole body was in pain but she couldn't let this happen without a fight.

She was about to kick out at him when the chief laid down on top of her suddenly, pinning her down. She tried her best to hit out at him but he was so heavy she could barely breathe, let alone move. She clawed frantically at his face, refusing to give in. She could tell he was getting frustrated. Having to fend off the constant swipes to his face was distracting him from what he wanted to do to her.

Suddenly, he bunched his hand into a fist and raised it above his head. Annie instinctively moved her head to the side and squeezed her eyes shut, bracing herself for the blow about to come. But when she heard a loud THWACK, she didn't feel any pain. The chief's grip on Annie loosened and when she opened her eyes she saw him topple on to the floor next to her. A figure was looming over them with a large object in its hand.

As her eyes readjusted to the light, Annie realised it was Amelia who had just saved her. In all her panic and stress she had completely forgotten she was still in the room with them. The chief hadn't seemed to notice her at all – and thank goodness for that.

Annie tried to sit up but her head was still fuzzy. Amelia dropped her weapon and as it crashed down next to Annie she saw that it was a large piece of wood. Confused, she looked over to the window but it was still completely boarded up from what she could tell. Amelia got to her knees next to Annie. She stroked her forehead before placing her hands behind her shoulders and gently easing her up to a sitting position.

'Thank you, Amelia,' she said quietly. Then she rubbed the back of her head and winced when she felt a sticky liquid. She was bleeding. No wonder she felt so dazed. But she forced herself to concentrate. She had to make sure the chief wasn't in any state to jump up and overpower them again.

She leaned over him tentatively. He was out cold. Annie exhaled slowly, trying to come up with yet another new plan. Her first instinct was to flee the house and run for backup. But something was niggling at her. What was to stop the chief from turning this all around and laying the blame on her? He could claim *he* had been the one entering the brothel undercover and that he'd discovered her here turning tricks in order to fund her WPS volunteering role. Who was going to believe her over him? No, it was no good – she needed the evidence from the umbrella stand. She was going to have to risk sneaking back towards the office to retrieve the note-books before making her escape.

Knowing there was no way she could leave Amelia behind,

Annie slowly got to her feet and motioned for her to do the same. She looked over at the chief again and noticed the wood on the floor next to him again. She looked to Amelia for an explanation, who walked over to one of the mattresses and lifted it slightly. Annie followed her over and peered underneath. There were two more planks sitting there. Whoever had sealed up the window had chosen to try and hide the leftover wood rather than dispose of it properly.

Annie gestured for Amelia to follow her. As they crept across the room, Annie still felt a little unsteady on her feet from the blow to her head but she did her best to stay focused. When they reached the door she was thankful to find it unlocked. Stevs had obviously assumed Chief Constable Green was more than capable of dealing with two frightened refugees on his own. She laughed to herself at his arrogance, before realising he had very nearly been right. If it hadn't been for Amelia and the discarded wood, she certainly wouldn't be making her way out of this room now.

The two of them crept down the stairs. Annie was conscious of the fact that a lot of time had passed since Stevs had dropped the chief off in their room. She didn't know when somebody might come up to check on them. She grappled over whether to go straight out of the front door or take her chances with going back for the notebooks. If she had been on her own she probably would have taken the risk to make sure she left with the evidence. But she had Amelia in tow. Not only did she owe her life to this woman, but Amelia was carrying a baby and Annie had no desire to be responsible for any harm coming to an innocent woman because of her, let alone her unborn baby.

When they reached the bottom of the stairs, Annie glanced back down along the hallway at the umbrella stand with a heavy heart. But it was just too risky. There were two rooms between her and the evidence – both containing men who

34

Amelia looked up at Annie with pure fear in her eyes. Annie couldn't understand what had happened. They had been so close to leaving and she had even sacrificed the notebooks to make sure her new friend made it out unscathed. So how was this happening? He must have slipped out of the room downstairs as Annie was opening the front door and pushed Amelia to the floor in a matter of seconds.

Stevs looked over at Annie. He was furious – his eyes were bulging with rage and hatred. He started rolling up his sleeves while holding eye contact with her. Annie knew the action was meant to make it clear to her that he meant business; he wasn't going to be letting anyone off this time. A cold breeze from outside entered the house and sent a shiver down Annie's spine, reminding her of just how close she was to freedom. She could, of course, turn around right now and run. But she dismissed that thought immediately. In the time it took her to get backup to the house and call for help, it would be too late for Amelia and she wasn't willing to leave her behind to save herself.

Annie took a deep breath and waited for Stevs to make his next move. She hoped he would come for her instead of turning on Amelia. She was prepared this time and confident her ju-jitsu would be enough to fight him off. But she would have to be swift – if any other gang members turned up and joined in then she would be in deep trouble.

Suddenly, he grinned over at Annie and then turned his

attention to Amelia, who was curled up in the foetal position with her arms crossed protectively over her belly.

Laughing, Stevs swung his leg back and kicked Amelia in the back so hard that her whole body jolted and she screamed out in pain. Then he looked over at Annie again. It was like he was goading her. He knew Amelia wasn't going to fight back so he was going to hurt her until Annie couldn't take any more and stepped in. He was spoiling for a fight and Annie was going to have to oblige him. But she was frozen to the spot. If she lunged towards him it would be too obvious. He was waiting for her to do that and he was ready to lash out at her when she did. He was so much bigger and more powerful than her that she wouldn't stand a chance. One blow from him could easily floor her.

The ju-jitsu Annie knew was all about incapacitating someone when they didn't expect it – it was more successful if she was using it in defence because they were coming at her and she could use their own momentum against them, or if she was jumping in to help somebody who was being attacked. She needed the element of surprise in order to overpower someone like this. He would just simply swat her away if he saw her coming.

He grabbed Amelia under her armpits and pulled her to her feet. Amelia stood in front of him, cowering and shaking, her face wet with tears. He looked over at Annie again before bringing his hand back and slapping Amelia's face. The noise of his palm against her cheek made Annie flinch and the impact sent Amelia flying backwards into the wall. As she hit the wall her coat flew open to reveal her unmistakable baby bump. Stevs' eyes lit up in shock as he took in the sight before him. As suspected, he'd clearly had no idea she was with child.

That split-second of uncertainty and confusion presented Annie with the perfect opportunity to take the brute by surprise. As he stared with wide-eyed shock at Amelia's stomach, Annie launched herself at him. Because he hadn't seen the attack coming and had time to defend himself, he toppled straight over as Annie threw all her weight against him. He ended up splayed on the floor on his front with Annie on top of him. Before he had a chance to react, Annie grabbed hold of his arms and twisted them up behind his back. She knew she wouldn't be able to keep him subdued for long so she looked over to Amelia and motioned for her to leave.

'Quick! Run!' Annie cried urgently, aware that other members of the gang could turn up at any minute. How the man in the room just feet away with all the other women hadn't come out to investigate all the noise she wasn't quite sure.

Just then, Stevs started fighting back against Annie's grip. She turned her attention back to him and pushed all her weight into his back to try and keep him on the floor. Why couldn't she hear Amelia leaving the house? She risked another glance around and saw Amelia's horrified face staring down at the floor below her. Annie followed her gaze and found a pool of water.

Realising that Amelia's waters must have broken, Annie was desperate to run over and comfort her and try and help her. But she had to deal with Stevs first and she couldn't risk any of the other men walking into this scene with Amelia still here.

'Go and get help,' she urged Amelia, battling her own panicked frustration. She knew she couldn't understand her but surely she must be able to pick up on the fact that she needed to get out of here. As Stevs continued fighting back against her and hurling profanities at her, Annie searched around desperately for something to help her. They had landed just shy of the umbrella stand and there was a large black umbrella just within her reach. Annie took a deep breath and reached out for it. The man tried to take advantage of the fact the weight upon him had reduced by flipping over, and Annie brought the end of the umbrella down against the side of his face with all her force. It didn't knock him out but it certainly left him dazed and confused.

As Stevs tried to regain his senses, Annie jumped up and ran to Amelia, who was still staring in horror at scene at her feet. Annie placed her hands on both her shoulders and guided her quickly to the front door. She had just pushed her over the threshold when a hand grabbed hold of a chunk of her own hair and pulled her back into the hallway.

Annie was flung against the wall and she groaned as the impact shot through her whole body. But she was buoyed by the fact she had managed to get Amelia to safety and she still had some fight left in her. She spun around to face Stevs, just in time to see his fist flying towards her head. She ducked out of the way and used all the energy she had left to kick out at him. Her foot connected with his groin and he cried out before doubling over in pain, clutching at his private parts.

Annie allowed herself to believe she might make it out of this alive and started running back towards the front door. But she hadn't even made it a few steps before she felt a blow to the back of her head. Annie lost all control of her legs and fell to the floor heavily. She tried to scramble to her feet but the man was looming over her and she didn't even get time to brace herself before his foot connected with her chest. The impact knocked all the air out of her and as she struggled for breath, she closed her eyes.

This was it – Annie was certain of it. He was too big and powerful compared to her and there was no way she could fight back against him now. He was going to kill her, but she refused to let his face be the last thing she saw before she died. Keeping her eyes firmly shut, she pictured Richard and found herself smiling through the pain. She had managed to save Amelia and her baby and now she was going to be reunited with the man she loved. Annie waited for the fatal blow. She just wanted to be released now.

All of a sudden she heard heavy footsteps approaching the front door. Annie's heart sank. She wanted this over with now. She was ready to go. If the rest of the gang burst in before Stevs could finish the job then she could end up enduring unthinkable pain and suffering before someone finally put her out of her misery.

'Just do it,' she groaned. It seemed surreal to be begging somebody to kill her but the alternative just wasn't worth thinking about.

When the front door burst open Annie wondered if she could get away with playing dead. She braced herself for more kicks and punches, or to be dragged off to one of the rooms upstairs. But instead of rough hands hauling her to her feet, a gentle pair eased her up slowly and when she finally opened her eyes again she was met with the face of a policeman instead of that of the menacing gang member she had been expecting.

Confused, Annie looked to her left and saw another two policemen tackling her captor to the floor. He was putting up a good fight and for a moment she wondered if, with his height and strength, he would be able to break free and flee. But the officers finally got him to the ground. The policeman who had helped Annie to her feet gently guided her out of the front door. She couldn't believe she was walking out of the house alive after so many failed attempts and having accepted such a grim fate just moments before. She almost expected to be dragged back inside again just before making it out on to the street.

When she saw Amelia standing in the street taking deep

breaths and screwing her face up in agony while clutching her bump, Annie couldn't believe her eyes.

'What is she still doing here?' she demanded of the police officer. 'She's in labour!' The man's face turned white as he took in what Annie had said and looked from her to Amelia. Annie rushed to Amelia's side and reached her just as she collapsed to the ground, letting out a huge, guttural groan. She looked up at Annie pleadingly.

'We need to get her to hospital,' Annie barked at the officer as she crouched on the ground next to her friend.

'The car's just over here,' he spluttered, pointing down the road but then looking desperately from left to right. Then his gaze fixed on the police car turning left at the end of the road. Annie looked over in the same direction and cursed when she spotted it – Stevs was sitting in the back, being driven out of view. She hadn't even heard the officers hauling him out of the house and into the vehicle.

Amelia screamed out in pain and Annie instinctively knew there was no time to wait for an ambulance.

'Help me get her to her feet,' she instructed the officer. He ran over and between them they managed to coax Amelia up. Her legs immediately gave way beneath her but they somehow kept her up and were able to drag her along the street.

'Where are we taking her?' the officer panted as Amelia let out another gut-wrenching cry. Sweat was pouring down the poor woman's face now, despite the freezing temperature. Annie knew she had to get her to take more deep breaths, but she was also aware of the fact she didn't seem able to understand a word of English. She craned her neck to make sure her face was in front of Amelia's and then she started taking deep breaths herself. She caught Amelia's eyes and Amelia nodded through the pain before imitating what Annie was doing.

As they continued slowly along the road, Annie knew there was only one place she could take Amelia now where they would be able to safely deliver her baby. She looked up towards Bert's house and felt relief wash over her. She was going to have a lot of explaining to do but that was going to have to wait. They needed to deliver this baby safely and then Annie could start thinking about just how she was going to deal with everything else.

35

Bert was waiting patiently at his front door when the group arrived. Annie had been hopeful that he would have heard the commotion in the street nearby and checked to see what was going on through his spyhole, and it looked as though she had been right. When they reached his house, Bert stepped aside to give Annie and the officer room to get Amelia inside. She had felt like a dead weight the whole of the short journey and, after everything she had endured beforehand, Annie was exhausted. Annie could feel Bert's eyes boring into her, awaiting some kind of enlightenment as to what on earth was going on. As far as he had been concerned she was safely back with her friends and patrolling far away from the brothel.

'I'll explain later,' she whispered, sure that he would accept that and continue to help. 'Let's take a break here then we'll move her to the living room,' Annie added, leaning against the wall to catch her breath.

'I don't think you have time for that,' Bert warned, looking down pointedly at Amelia. Annie followed his gaze and found her friend was now lying flat out on the hallway floor with both her knees raised. Propping herself up on her elbows, she looked up at Annie like she expected her to know what to do next.

Annie panicked. She had never delivered a baby before. She had been counting on sending the police officer off to find some medics while she and Bert kept Amelia comfortable. Surely they had time for that?

'You need to push, love,' Bert advised.

'She can't speak English,' Annie said, getting down on her knees in the cramped hallway and taking one of Amelia's hands in her own. Her heart was racing. This was all happening so quickly. 'What do we do?' she whispered, looking up to Bert for help.

'Where's she from?' he asked, remarkably calmly given everything that was happening around him.

'Belgium,' Annie replied. 'Her name's Amelia.'

She thought she was hearing things when Bert started speaking in another language. Through heavy puffs and pants, Amelia replied in what Annie assumed was her native tongue and Bert nodded his understanding. Bewildered, Annie looked up at him again with raised eyebrows.

'I'll explain later,' he said pointedly, and Annie laughed with relief as well as humour at his sarcastic retort. Serious now, Bert ordered Annie to remove Amelia's underwear while he went to fetch towels.

'And you, sir, need to get us some medical help. And fast!' he shouted back down to the police officer from the middle of the stairs. Annie wasn't holding out much hope now she knew how close Amelia was to giving birth. The Red Cross' motor ambulances were scarce and the City of London Police Ambulance Service only had three motor ambulances in operation. Would they be able to find one to make it to them in time? The policeman rushed out of the door and Annie turned her attention back to Amelia.

When Bert rejoined them he got shakily down on his knees and took hold of Amelia's other hand. Annie still had no idea what she was doing but she felt a huge comfort knowing Bert was here with her. He seemed to have a handle on the situation – he really was full of surprises – and she was confident they could help deliver this baby between them. Amelia managed to babble something through her moans and Annie looked straight to Bert for a translation.

'She says she feels like she wants to push,' Bert explained.

'She probably should, then?' Annie replied nervously.

'I think so,' Bert said. He laid the towels out on the floor in front of them before speaking to Amelia in a foreign language again. She started groaning again and Annie felt her grip tighten around her hand.

'Come on, Amelia. You can do this,' she said firmly. Her friend might not have been able to understand her but she was confident the encouragement in her voice would translate. They held eye contact as Amelia's groans became progressively louder, but then she suddenly fell silent and stopped pushing. She slumped to the side, panting.

'You have to keep going,' Annie urged her. Amelia whispered something.

'She's very tired,' Bert translated. Annie looked down between Amelia's legs. She could see part of the baby's head already.

'She's almost there,' she cried excitedly. 'Tell her, Bert! Tell her she's almost there! I can see the baby's head. She's so close. She just has to keep pushing for a little while longer. I know she can do this! I just know she can!'

Annie was overcome with excitement and emotion. This baby had to make it. They had beaten the odds to get to this stage together and Amelia had helped her twice now, so she had to do everything she could to help her through this. As Bert spoke to Amelia in the language Annie didn't understand, Annie moved around behind her and propped her back and head up with her body. She started stroking her hair and whispering in her ear. Suddenly, Amelia reached up behind her and placed both her hands around Annie's neck. Annie placed her own hands over the top and squeezed as Amelia cried out.

Annie thought the noise might have the whole street gathering around Bert's front door to find out what was going on. It sounded as if somebody was being murdered. But she could see the baby's head emerging now and tears filled her eyes as Bert guided it out. Annie had never witnessed anything so beautiful in her life and she couldn't believe she had gone from begging someone to kill her to this incredible moment in such a short space of time.

Amelia stopped to catch her breath and Annie stroked her hair again soothingly.

'She's almost there,' Bert said before saying something that seemed to rouse Amelia again. Her grip around Annie's neck tightened again and Annie knew she was gearing herself up to push again.

'One more push,' Annie said firmly. Amelia cried out again and all of a sudden there was a baby in Bert's arms. He quickly wrapped it in a towel and wiped its face down. When the first little cries came out of its mouth, so tiny but so powerful, Annie found herself breaking down. She was so happy the baby was all right and that she and Amelia had made it out of the brothel alive, having come so close to dying at the hands of Stevs and his awful gang of thugs.

After having stayed so calm and collected during the birth, Annie noticed that Bert now looked uncomfortable with the baby in his arms.

'She's so tiny,' he whispered, holding her out to Annie. Annie gently moved Amelia around so that she was leaning against the wall, then she took the baby from Bert. Looking down at the wonderous little human in her arms, she felt a stab of pain when she remembered the fact she would never be able to create something like this with her one true love. But she snapped herself back out of it quickly – this was about Amelia, not herself. She offered the baby to Amelia but she shook her head and looked the other way.

'What's wrong?' Annie said, panicked. 'Is she unwell? I do wish those medics would hurry up.' Bert put a hand on Amelia's shoulder and the two of them had a conversation in the language that Annie couldn't understand. Amelia broke down in tears halfway through and Bert's eyes became wet as Annie looked on, desperate to know why the new mother was so distraught. They stopped talking and as Annie cradled Amelia's daughter, Bert explained.

'She says her life is over now that she has this baby. A German soldier raped her while her hometown in Belgium was being invaded and when her family discovered she was pregnant they disowned her.'

'But why?' Annie gasped. 'It wasn't her fault – she was raped.'

Bert shrugged. 'The same reason women are blamed for these things in this country, I expect,' he said sadly, staring at the innocent child in Annie's arms.

'You have to tell her it's not her fault,' Annie pleaded.

'I have done. She wishes that instead of fleeing the horrors of war in her country to come to England, she had just stayed there and died.'

Annie couldn't take any more. She nestled herself in next to Amelia against the wall and cradled her as they both wept. Slowly, she edged the baby nearer to her, until she was almost in Amelia's arms. She could almost feel the love bursting out of her new friend when she made that first contact with her daughter, and suddenly the baby was out of Annie's arms and firmly in Amelia's grasp. Amelia was smiling through her tears now.

'Tell her she can build a new life here with her daughter. She's survived so much already – this will be nothing in comparison,' Annie said, her voice thick with tears. Bert translated and Amelia nodded, appearing stronger already.

Suddenly, the policeman burst back through the door with two medics. Annie jumped out of the way to allow them room to check the mother and baby over. Then they scooped Amelia up, who now looked as though she would never let her daughter go. Annie did her best to hold herself together as they guided Amelia outside to transport her to hospital.

'We made a pretty good team back there,' Bert commented, breaking the silence that had fallen over the house as they both digested what had just happened.

'We always do,' Annie smiled. 'But I had no idea you knew any other languages. Were you speaking Belgian to Amelia?'

'No, they speak mainly Flemish and French in Belgium,' Bert explained. It turned out that Martha had been born in Belgium. Her family had moved to England when her father got work here when she was young. She had stayed fluent in Flemish despite learning English when they arrived. 'She had always longed to go back and visit and it's something we planned on doing together,' Bert explained. 'I let her teach me her language. She was a brilliant teacher and I couldn't wait to take that trip with her. But we kept putting it off – there was always something else to save for, you know what it's like. And then she died. I haven't spoken a word of that language since I lost her. Until today.' Bert's eyes were filling with tears again and Annie pulled him in for a hug. 'I always thought all my years of learning Flemish had been for nothing,' Bert said, pulling away now. 'But maybe it was all leading up to today. It felt like Martha was here with me, you know?'

Annie understood how he had kept so together now.

'Anyway, you need to tell me what on earth you were doing at the brothel,' Bert said, suddenly stern again. He wiped the tears from his eyes, blew his nose and fixed Annie with a stare, like a schoolteacher waiting for the answer to a particularly tricky question.

Annie started confessing, but when she got to the bit about breaking into the office she suddenly stopped. 'The notebooks!' she cried as she dashed out of Bert's house and back down the street towards number 83.

There was a swarm of police at the house now, and dishevelled women were being led out one by one. Everything was in chaos. Right outside the house, two of the gang members were wrestling with officers along with three clients and Annie took her chance to sneak her way past them. She knew they would all be protesting their innocence. They would probably be taken in for questioning but once they told the officers they were there as clients they would be sent on their way and the women would be prosecuted for selling sex. It made Annie's blood boil! She needed to grab the notebooks and show them to somebody trustworthy to prove what had been going on before the gang were freed.

Annie had just made it to the umbrella stand when she heard footsteps on the stairs. She looked around and saw Chief Constable Green emerge, swaying from side to side and holding his head where Amelia had hit him. There was blood running down the side of his face and covering his hand.

'Chief!' one of the constables shouted, full of concern. Annie watched as all the other officers stopped what they were doing and looked at their boss. She could tell they were all trying to work out what he had already been doing here – and out of uniform.

'There she is!' Chief Constable Green yelled, pointing straight at Annie. 'That's the WPS officer we let into our station in good faith! I came here to investigate the little slut and I was about to arrest her for prostitution when she attacked me!' He sounded outraged and Annie had to admit that, with the way he was telling it, his story sounded genuine even to her. That's how good he was at lying. And how else could she explain being here dressed as she was? But that wasn't her main concern right now, and she used the cover of his outburst to grab a small jacket from the array that were hanging above the umbrella stand. She shrugged it over her shoulders.

The whole house had gone quiet as everyone tried to get their heads around what was unfolding in front of them.

'Arrest her right now!' Chief Constable Green barked. Annie turned herself to the side so a coat was hiding her and she reached into the stand and grabbed the first couple of notebooks that her hands fell upon. She quickly slipped them into the pocket of the jacket resting on her shoulders before emerging with her hands out in front of her, ready to be cuffed. It was no use protesting her innocence here. These men all answered to Chief Constable Green. She would have to wait until she was at the station.

36

Annie was thrown into a holding cell at Hunter Street Police Station. They tried to get her to talk but she refused to be interviewed until Frosty was present. She had no idea if word of her arrest had reached her friends, but with the rate at which gossip seemed to spread through police stations she was certain they would have caught wind of it by now. She felt frustrated when she thought about how confused they must be by it all. But she was also confident they would give her the benefit of the doubt until she had a chance to explain everything to them herself. Surely they wouldn't believe she had turned to prostitution?

Every now and then Annie could hear Chief Constable Green ranting and raving further down the corridor. He was determined to have her sent straight to the magistrates and sentenced for her 'crimes'. But she had heard some of his officers reminding him that the case would be thrown out unless she had been officially interviewed before she was charged, and for that she was grateful. And so she continued to refuse to budge on her demand to have Frosty present before she would talk. Frosty was the only person higher up the command chain who she could trust – who knew who else in the police was corrupt like Chief Constable Green? She just had to keep the notebooks safe until Frosty arrived.

When the chief finally relented and sent someone to fetch Frosty, Annie started getting nervous. What if her sub-commandant didn't believe her? Or what if she was so ashamed of her 'actions' that she refused to come and help her in the first place? She paced her cell for what felt like hours. When she was walked to the interview room she almost collapsed when she laid her eyes on Frosty. The sense of relief was overwhelming.

'You have twenty minutes, then we'll be back to start the formal interview,' a male voice informed them before locking the door behind him. Annie didn't waste any time filling Frosty in on everything she had been up to, starting from the first sighting of Stevs and ending with her dangerous run-in with Chief Constable Green. She left out the part about sneaking down to the office and finding the notepads. They were short on time and she thought it would be better to just show her the evidence once she was finished, to back up her story.

'And now I'm here talking to you, as I didn't know who else I could trust with all of this,' she finally finished, her voice hoarse with all the talking.

Frosty stared at Annie appraisingly for a few minutes. Annie desperately searched her face for some kind of sign she believed her or at the very least supported her. Finding none, her heart sunk heavily. Did she really think she was lying about it all?

'I believe you, Annie, I really do,' Frosty declared at last, as if she had just read her mind. 'But we need hard evidence. Surely you must be able to understand that Chief Constable Green's version of events is plausible – especially to anybody who doesn't know you personally. And with things being the way they are with the police as well as further along the justice system, he will be believed over you simply because he's a man and you are a woman. Add into the mix the fact he's your superior and, well . . . I don't know how we're going to manage to get you out of this.' She looked genuinely distraught by the circumstances, so her expression changed quickly to one of confusion when she looked up to see Annie grinning back at her.

Annie reached into the pocket of the jacket she had been wearing like a safety blanket since her arrival at the police station, terrified of letting it out of her sight for even a second in case the evidence was ripped from her grasp. She pulled out the two notebooks and laid them down on the table triumphantly. As Frosty opened the one relating to number 83 Copenhagen Street, Annie sat down again and studied her face.

Frosty gasped. 'This is . . . explosive,' she spluttered as she started reading through all the names, dates, times and cash exchanges. 'How did you get hold of these?'

'They were in a room at the back of the house that the gang were using as an office,' Annie explained. 'I managed to get in and grab a handful of them. I didn't want to hand them over to the police because I was worried they might end up being "misplaced" – especially if the chief caught wind of them. There are too many influential men involved in this to hand them over to anybody. The whole scandal could have been buried and I would have been left to rot in prison.'

'You did the right thing, Annie,' Frosty said as she picked up the second notebook and read the address on the front. 'So, there are more brothels?' she asked.

'At least a dozen,' Annie said. 'Will these logs be enough to show that the gang were holding all the women there against their will, and forcing them to have sex with their clients to make them money? We need to prove the men are at fault here and not the poor women they held captive!'

'I would say so,' Frosty replied, still eagerly reading through all the names and details. 'Chief Constable Green is in the first one a lot. It looks like he was one of their biggest clients. No wonder he was so keen to have you sent straight to the magistrates.' She shook her head. *And no wonder he had Bert's windows smashed when he dared to report the brothel to his men,* Annie thought to herself.

'It also explains why he warned me and the girls off patrolling at King's Cross Station. That was one of their prime pick-up spots from what I can make out,' Annie said.

Frosty sat back in her chair looking thoughtful for a few minutes. 'I will need to take these away with me,' she explained. 'Do you trust me to look after them?'

'Of course. That's why I demanded to see you,' Annie replied.

'I'll make sure justice is done, but you might have to spend a little while longer in the cell before I can get you out.'

Annie nodded in understanding. She had waited so long for that already that another few hours wouldn't make any difference. She was relieved to have Frosty on her side and she couldn't wait for the chief to get his just deserts, along with all the other gang members.

It was the early hours of the next morning before Annie was finally released from her cell. When Miller unlocked her door she was relieved and happy to see a friendly face.

'You caused a bit of uproar there, didn't you?' he said, grinning.

'Is the chief still here?' Annie asked nervously, cautiously poking her head out of the cell door.

'Of course he isn't,' Miller laughed. 'We had a call from the commissioner a few hours ago. Turns out that lady you sent for went straight to him after leaving here. Whatever you told her it did the trick. He sent officers to the chief's house to arrest him and we're getting a temporary replacement later this morning. He told us not to let you out until the chief was in custody.'

Annie exhaled slowly, her head spinning with relief. 'What about the women brought in from the brothel?' she asked.

'They've all been released without charge. A few needed medical attention – the poor loves had been beaten pretty badly.'

'And the men?' Annie asked nervously. She crossed her fingers that the gang members hadn't been set free after all of this.

'All still in custody.' Miller smiled. 'The chief was pushing for them all to be released last night but we just didn't have the manpower to do it properly. Now I know the full story I can understand why he was so keen to get them back out on the streets. No doubt they'll rat on him now they're all looking at prison stretches. Was the chief really in on it all?'

'I'm afraid so,' Annie said, but she didn't have time to fill Miller in. She had to get to the section house to see Poppy and Maggie. She had been gone for twenty-four hours now and she knew they would be worried sick.

She bid Miller farewell and ran down the street to the section house. She walked into the communal kitchen to find her friends sitting at the table. Poppy looked tense and strained and Maggie's face was red and puffy with tear tracks running down it. It broke Annie's heart to see them distraught, knowing she had caused the anguish they were suffering.

She cried out at the same time they both looked up to see her. The three of them rushed together and there was a scramble of hugs and kisses as they messily reunited. After a few minutes of relief Annie felt the atmosphere change. Poppy pulled away and as she wiped the tears from her face, Annie saw a growing rage taking over her face.

'Where on earth have you been? And what happened to your head?'

Annie put her hand up to the top of her head and winced when she touched the wound Chief Constable Green had inflicted when he'd hit it against the wall. It was encrusted with dry blood. She had been so caught up in everything since that she'd forgotten all about it but suddenly her banging headache made sense. As Maggie guided her into a chair, Annie wondered why nobody had bothered getting her any medical attention – but then she remembered she had been treated as a criminal up until just minutes ago.

'We've been worried sick,' Poppy fumed. But she wasn't angry enough to ignore her maternal instinct and Annie smiled gratefully as she started making a pot of tea and then gathered supplies to tend to her wound.

'We were just debating whether we should go to your parents to ask for help,' Maggie explained as Poppy clattered about behind them. 'We did our shift without you, assuming you had gone home again after realising you'd returned too soon. But we checked your room and saw that nothing was missing. What happened to you and why are you dressed like that?'

Poppy placed a cup of tea down in front of Annie and then sat down on the other side of her to start tending to her wound. Wincing through the initial pain as Poppy began cleaning up the site of the cut, Annie admitted everything she had been up to behind her friends' backs.

As Annie had expected, Poppy and Maggie were both shocked and angry that she had put herself in such a dangerous situation.

'I don't understand why you didn't think you could tell us,' Poppy said sadly. 'You could have been killed, Annie. It sounds like it came very close. We could have helped you!'

'You probably would have tried to stop me for a start,' Annie said sheepishly. Poppy raised her eyebrows and Annie knew she was right about the fact she would have tried to stop her. 'But also,' she added, turning to address Maggie who had gone deathly pale and not uttered a word since the first mention of her attacker, 'I didn't want to stir up all those terrible memories for you. I was desperate to get that brute behind bars, but I couldn't risk pulling you into it as your emotions might have taken over and it was just too dangerous for that. I wanted to be able to sit here and tell you I'd got justice for you, like I am now. I wanted that to be the first time you heard about him again.'

Maggie wiped tears from her eyes and pulled Annie in for another hug. 'Thank you,' she whispered.

'We're still angry with you,' Poppy said firmly.

'I had to do it for myself,' Annie said, pulling away from Maggie's embrace to face Poppy again. 'If I'm honest I didn't care about how dangerous it was. I wasn't really bothered about what happened to me. But coming so close to death has made me realise I have a lot to live for. And I helped somebody else realise that, too,' she added, and she smiled as she thought of her friendship with Bert. 'I hope you can forgive me,' she said tentatively after a few moments of silence.

'Of course we forgive you,' Poppy said, smiling. Maggie nodded her agreement and Annie laughed nervously.

'You had me worried for a moment there,' she admitted.

'Well, now you know how we felt last night!' Poppy cried, hitting Annie playfully on the shoulder.

'Ouch!' Annie winced, surprised at how much it hurt – but then she remembered how tightly Chief Constable Green had grabbed hold of her the previous day.

'Oops, sorry,' Poppy grimaced. She lifted up Annie's sleeve to reveal the start of a massive bruise.

'It's all right,' Annie said, trying to sound upbeat. I got off lightly.'

'What can we do to help?' Maggie asked.

'I haven't slept a wink, so all I want to do right now is rest,' Annie replied.

'It's the best way to help the body heal,' Poppy said. 'But first, you need some food.'

At the mention of nourishment, Annie felt her stomach grumbling. Rubbing the area gently she laughed. 'My belly agrees!' she joked. And so Poppy made them all a huge pan of porridge which they enjoyed together before Annie was sent to her room to clean herself up and get some sleep.

Poppy tried to get Annie to rest up for a few days before returning to patrolling, but she refused. After an initial long sleep she felt fidgety and eager to get back out on the beat with her friends.

A number of high-profile figures had been arrested off the back of her actions and the officers at the police station stopped her whenever they bumped into her to congratulate her on their efforts. Chief Constable Green's temporary replacement – a tall man with a moustache and greying hair called Chief Inspector Perry – had even called Annie into his office to heap praise upon her, which Annie had found slightly distressing, but very pleasing.

Although Annie was elated to have uncovered the brothels and brought down the gangs and the men taking advantage of the women, she couldn't stop thinking about Amelia and her baby. There were just under two weeks left until Christmas now, but she found she couldn't get into the festive spirit. She felt subdued and it was as if Amelia's words were haunting her. She kept going over what she has said to her: her life was over now she had a baby. It should have been the happiest time of her life but yet she had been devastated. What was Christmas going to be like for the two of them?

As Annie patrolled the gardens in the Holborn area with Poppy and Maggie one afternoon, she glanced over at the Foundling Hospital. The facility was over-capacity at the moment so that was out of the question for Amelia and besides, they didn't take in mothers and babies together so it wouldn't have worked for her friend anyway. She wanted to keep Amelia with her daughter.

Suddenly, an idea popped into Annie's head. She immediately tried to dismiss it, reminding herself that the last idea she'd had had nearly got her killed. But as the group continued with their patrol, Annie couldn't shake the idea. What if she could help Amelia and other women like her? She might just be able to stop some of them from having to suffer the lifelong consequences of other people's depravity. The more she thought of the idea, the more she knew she had to try and put it into motion. After watching that baby being born in front of her, her heart ached to think of her and others being abandoned or growing up in poverty and shame.

That afternoon, she rushed off at the end of patrol, assuring Poppy and Maggie that she wasn't up to anything risky this time. She promised to explain everything to them on her return – but she didn't have time right now as she needed to get to WPS headquarters before Frosty left for the day.

Racing up the steps to get into the building, she cried out with relief when she recognised Frosty's tall frame at the top. She had caught her just in time.

'What are you doing here?' Frosty asked. 'You haven't uncovered more corruption, have you?' She raised her eyebrows mock-sternly.

'No, no, nothing like that,' Annie panted, trying to get her breath back. Frosty walked back into the building with Annie in tow and once they were sitting down in her office, she waited patiently for Annie to explain the reason behind her impromptu visit.

Annie didn't want to waste any more time, so she thought she might as well just come out with it. 'I want to open a baby home, but I need your help,' Annie declared proudly. She was pleased to finally feel comfortable in her sub-commandant's presence and had stopped tripping over her words in front of her.

'A what?' Frosty asked, leaning forward and looking intrigued.

'So many children are being born as a result of rape and prostitution. There's no one to help their mothers, who are so desperate to survive that they end up abandoning the poor souls. Places like the Foundling Hospital can help the babies when they have space, but wouldn't it be better if they were able to stay with their mothers? Why should women be forced to give up their children? Of course, some will want to and in those cases we can take in the babies and leave the mothers to start afresh, safe in the knowledge their little ones are being given a better start in life than they could ever hope to offer them. But for the others, we could take them in together and help them build a new life.'

When Frosty simply stared at her, Annie felt deflated. She had been speaking so passionately but her superior obviously thought it was a silly idea.

'This is what the WPS is all about,' Annie said sternly. 'We're here to help women like this.'

'I'm sorry, dear. I don't mean to upset you,' Frosty said, patting Annie's hand fondly. 'It's a wonderful idea, it truly is. But the bit I'm struggling with is this: where exactly do you see the money for all of this coming from? You know we're a voluntary organisation – you're not even being paid – and we rely on donations from our supporters to keep everything running. We just about manage as it is without having to pay for somewhere to put up all these women you want to help.'

Annie smiled. She had thought about this on the way over. 'I would like to talk to some of your benefactors,' she declared. 'I'm sure if I put a proper plan together then I could convince enough of them to donate extra money to help cover this.

We would have to start small, of course. But then once everyone sees the success of the place, they'll be falling over themselves to donate more money to help such a good cause. Please, just let me try?'

Frosty rubbed her chin, deep in thought, and Annie willed her to agree. She knew from Chief Inspector Perry that Amelia had been discharged from the hospital with her baby and sent to the dispersal centre she had been headed for before the gang picked her up at King's Cross. If she could get this put together in time and reach Amelia before she was sent on somewhere else, she could welcome her in as one of the baby home's first mothers. What a way that would be to pay her back for saving her life!

'One of our donors has been in touch recently to offer accommodation for recruits struggling to pay rent while they volunteer,' Frosty said. Annie almost leapt out of her chair as she sat up straight, ready to hear more. 'She owns a big house just outside London and she's become very lonely since all three of her sons signed up to fight in the war. She was a widow long before the war started and her sons had been looking after her.' Frosty fell silent and looked to be deep in thought once more. Annie liked where she thought this was going, but she was wary of jumping the gun so she stayed quiet.

'She's too fragile to run things herself. She would need some help,' Frosty continued.

'I would be happy to run things,' Annie blurted, unable to contain her excitement any longer. She was bursting to get something in place to help women like Amelia, but to be able to be directly involved would be a dream come true. Her stomach fluttered again and she was momentarily distracted by the sensation. She wasn't hungry like she had been when it had last happened. She placed her hand on her abdomen and felt the flutter again.

'Are you all right?' Frosty asked, looking concerned.

'Yes, sorry I . . . I just had a strange feeling,' Annie said quietly, still feeling perplexed. 'But please know that I would be happy to help your lady in any way I can. And I'm sure Poppy and Maggie would want to be involved, too.' She couldn't wait to reveal her plan to her friends. Surely if they were all on board with it then there could be a way to run the baby home around patrolling, so they didn't have to give that up or separate. For the time being, they could take it in turns to stay at the baby home, and patrol in pairs.

'Let's not get carried away – I have to get my donor to agree to open up her home to strangers and their screaming babies before we start celebrating. It's very different to allowing respectable WPS recruits stay under her roof.'

Annie nodded, but still allowed a wide smile to spread across her face.

As she made her way back to Holborn, Annie was full of hope and excitement. She really felt as though she might have found her calling with the baby home. She rubbed the ring she had put straight back on since returning to the section house and thought of how proud Richard would be of her right now. They might not have managed to achieve their dream of starting a family together, but she was going to be able to honour that lost opportunity by helping count-less other women make the most of motherhood. As her belly fluttered again she took it as a sign that this was going to work out and she smiled the rest of the journey back.

Epilogue

Christmas Day

The sound of children singing carols outside in the street travelled in through the window as Annie opened it slightly to let in some air. Despite the frost outside, the room was positively balmy due to the roaring fire and all the bodies crammed together excitedly wishing each other a merry Christmas. Annie stood next to the huge Christmas tree in the big dining room. Watching everybody laughing and joking together, her heart swelled with love.

She still couldn't believe that in less than two weeks, she and Frosty had managed to get the WPS Baby Home up and running and that she was spending Christmas there with all her remaining loved ones. It was far from perfect – there were lots of tweaks needed yet, but they had welcomed their first few new mothers already and Annie couldn't wait to help the place grow and develop. Poppy and Maggie had been excited and supportive when she had shared her idea – as she had known they would be. And Lady Wright, the benefactor that Frosty had mentioned, had been only too happy to open her doors up to women who had found themselves with child through unhappy circumstances and unable to support themselves.

It had ended up falling to Annie to make most of the arrangements for the baby home but she had been more than happy to take on the responsibility. Maggie and Poppy had continued with the Holborn patrol and they had agreed to start a rota at the baby home in the new year that would see them all doing their fair share of shifts there while still spending time together on patrol.

Annie was looking forward to getting out on the beat again. Her appetite seemed to have grown even more in the last week and she was finding her clothes were getting even more snug now. She put it down to feeling happier now the gang and the chief were all behind bars awaiting sentencing for their crimes – the big boss, Claude, had even been hauled in when one of the gang members had given up all the sordid details behind his running of the operation to try and get a lighter sentence. Annie had also put her increasing size down to the lack of exercise she was taking while she focused on the baby home instead of patrolling. She was confident she would slim down once she was back to pounding the streets for hours on end.

When Annie had suggested such a big gathering for Christmas Day, she hadn't been sure if Lady Wright would be keen. She had already been so generous, after all. But Annie had been feeling torn about where to celebrate – on the one hand she'd been eager to be surrounded by family and friends, but on the other she didn't want to abandon the women at the baby home so soon after settling them in, especially as Amelia had agreed to move in with her daughter until she was back on her feet.

Filling up everyone's wine glasses before the dinner was served, Annie felt so grateful to have all her loved ones here with her. There was her mother and father and all her sisters – her aunt and cousins had decided to spend Christmas Day together at the Becketts' family home. Maggie and Poppy were there, of course, and Bert had almost fallen over himself to accept the invitation when she had issued it to him.

Now that everyone was here, Annie knew it had been the

best way to help her get through Christmas Day. She was still missing Richard like a lost limb, but with so many of the people she loved in one room together it was difficult to dwell on the fact that this should have been their first Christmas Day together as man and wife. She would never get over losing him, but she felt like she was finally learning to live with it. Processing those feelings made Annie think of Bert and Martha. She looked around for Bert now and found him sitting in the corner with Amelia and her baby and two of the other new mothers. Bert had been teaching Amelia basic English and she was getting on well so far. When Annie approached them Amelia looked up and smiled. She had been so much happier since moving in and her baby had thrived, although she hadn't named the little one yet.

'Merry Christmas, my friend,' Amelia said slowly and proudly, beaming now from ear to ear.

'Merry Christmas to you, too!' Annie announced cheerfully.

'Amelia has some news for you,' Bert said.

Annie suddenly felt anxious. Surely Amelia hadn't managed to arrange her own accommodation yet? She was just getting to know her and the new baby and she wasn't ready to send them out into the world on their own yet. Besides, she was the one who was supposed to help organise all of that.

'I call my baby Annie. Like you, Annie,' Amelia said, concentrating on every word and holding eye contact with her as she spoke.

Annie's heart filled with so much love and gratitude that she felt like it might just burst. 'Oh, that is so beautiful!' she gushed through tears of joy. 'I'm honoured, Amelia, I truly am.' It was the best Christmas present she could have hoped for.

Suddenly Bert was on his feet. 'Everybody!' he yelled, and the room fell silent while all eyes fell to him. 'I would just like to thank Lady Wright for welcoming us all into her home at such a special time. It means so much to be able to spend this day with such wonderful people.' He raised his glass towards Lady Wright, who was blushing in the corner. She was a quiet woman and Annie knew she would be cringing at the attention as everybody else raised their glasses towards her and a chorus of 'thank you's rang out in her direction.

Annie made her way over to Lady Wright to tell her the good news about Amelia's baby and check on whether she should start asking everybody to sit down ready for their meal.

'It's so lovely to have the house full again,' the older woman declared, placing a hand on Annie's shoulder. She had dressed up for today's celebrations and Annie thought she looked positively regal with her hair swept back and all her sparkly jewels on show. Annie was just about to reply when she came over all dizzy. As she swayed, she reached out a hand in order to steady herself and she felt the wine bottle slip from her grip. There was a loud clatter as it hit the floor.

'Sit down, dear,' Lady Wright said, gently guiding her to the table and pulling out a chair. Everyone had gathered round after hearing the commotion and Annie looked up to see a sea of concerned faces.

'Whatever's the matter?' her mother asked, pushing her way to the front of the crowd.

'I don't know I . . . I just came over all funny,' Annie muttered. 'I suddenly feel exhausted again.'

'Again?' her mother asked.

'She's not been herself since losing Richard,' Poppy stepped in to explain. 'Why don't we take her into the little room next to the kitchen?'

'Yes, good idea,' Bert declared. 'You ladies go and see to Annie and the rest of us will have a few more drinks while we wait for our dinner, eh?' he added jovially.

Mrs Beckett helped her daughter to her feet and guided her to the side room, where she sat her on a chair before Mr Beckett, Poppy and Maggie joined them.

'I've been wondering for a little while . . .' Poppy started tentatively before stopping suddenly when Mr Beckett coughed uncomfortably.

'I think this might be women's business. I'll be next door if I'm needed,' he muttered before making a swift exit. Poppy looked a little more relaxed as the door closed behind him. Annie was waiting expectantly. What was it that her friend wanted to say and why was she finding it so difficult to say it?

'It's just, well . . . you've been struggling since we started at Holborn and, you've been sleeping a lot and feeling unwell—'

'I've been grieving,' Annie said defensively. 'And then I pushed myself something silly to get to the bottom of what was going on at the brothel. I don't know what you're getting at but I think everything has just caught up with me, that's all.'

'But your clothes hardly fit you anymore,' Poppy said quietly.

Annie felt her face flush bright red. Why was Poppy being so horrible to her? Surely she understood pointing that out would embarrass her? Maggie had gone to the kitchen to fetch a glass of water. As she came back into the room and placed it on the table next to Annie she caught Poppy's last sentence.

'We think you might be in the family way,' she blurted out, in true Maggie style. Then she looked round at all the shocked faces. 'Well, someone had to say it,' she declared defensively. 'Otherwise we'd be sat here dancing around the issue all day and I don't know about you lot but I'm hungry!'

Annie would have laughed if she hadn't just been knocked

for six by her friend's announcement. But as she went over everything in her head, she realised Maggie could be right.

There was the sudden loss of appetite and queasiness a few weeks after Richard's death. She had put it all down to grief, but had there been more to it? She had also attributed her out-of-character tiredness to grief, but could she have been feeling so exhausted because her body had been so busy trying to build a new life while she insisted on pounding the streets? Then there was the return of her appetite paired with her swelling stomach and breasts. Was the weight gain down to more than just Poppy's delicious meals? And she was always so tired despite the extra sleep she had sneaked in. She had put that down to her extra work on the brothel but, now she thought about it, she had only had a few long days and nights and she had more than made up for lost sleep. And those flutters in her belly recently – had they been a baby making its first movements inside her?

'You lost so much weight through grief to begin with that there was no way of telling,' Poppy said quietly. 'And when you started putting it back on, we were happy you were eating and thriving again. But with all the sleep and the queasiness, we knew something was up. Then when your clothes started getting tighter, something didn't add up. Yes, you were eating more – but we were both eating the same things as you and exercising just as much and we weren't putting any weight on.'

Annie's head was spinning.

'We hoped you'd work it out for yourself and come to us,' Maggie added. 'We were going to say something in the new year if you hadn't broached the subject by then. We weren't sure if you knew about it and were keeping quiet on purpose, or if you really were oblivious.'

'But I don't understand. When . . . who?' Mrs Beckett

spluttered. Annie was grateful her father had left the room but now she wished her mother had, too.

'The re-proposal,' Annie whispered, looking shamefully at the floor as she tried to work out the dates. She would be almost five months gone if Maggie was right. She realised now that she couldn't remember the last time she'd had a period but she certainly hadn't had one since those stolen few hours with Richard. She had always planned on waiting until she was married, but they had both been so carried away . . . Annie had been so wrapped up in everything since then that she hadn't given her missed periods a second thought. But how had she not realised there was a life growing inside her?

'Oh, Annie,' Mrs Beckett sighed. She knew her mother would be disappointed she hadn't waited until she was married. But with everything that had happened since, she hoped she could forgive her. She wouldn't be getting a grandchild if Annie had insisted on waiting, after all. As the realisation dawned on her, Annie came over all faint again. She took a sip of the cold water on the table next to her and instinctively placed her hand on her belly. As the cold liquid hit her stomach, she felt the unmistakable sensation of a kick. It was more than just a flutter this time. Annie gasped.

'You're right,' she whispered, tears filling her eyes.

As she thought it all through, the revelation made her feel both soaringly happy and achingly sad. She had thought she'd lost all hopes of starting a family with her beloved Richard when he was cruelly taken from her all those months ago – but now those lost dreams had been restored and there was a part of her one true love growing inside her; she would always have a part of Richard with her. But she was also facing motherhood alone as an unmarried and disgraced woman. Annie twisted the wedding ring around on her finger.

'You were as good as married, my dear,' Mrs Beckett said, stepping forward to place a comforting hand on her daughter's shoulder. 'You've been wearing the ring anyway and telling people you were married. Plenty of women are bending the truth in these times.'

'That's right,' Maggie chipped in. 'As far as anyone is concerned, your husband died in battle.'

'It's very nearly true,' Poppy added.

Annie suddenly felt a huge weight lift. She had thought Amelia naming her daughter after her was the best Christmas present she could have hoped for, but this surpassed all expectations.

'It looks like I'll be turning that wedding gown into a christening outfit after all,' Mrs Beckett said warmly. The thought brought tears to Annie's eyes.

Annie beamed, but then fear shot through her as she remembered she still had to explain all of this to her father. 'What about . . .?' she started, staring up at her mother's face.

'I'll deal with your father,' Mrs Beckett said firmly.

Relieved, Annie rubbed her belly and felt a strange kind of comfort from the action. It was similar to the feeling she'd had when she'd rubbed her wedding ring for comfort. It felt strange to know that she had turned to an inanimate object for comfort when she had had part of Richard with her all along.

'It looks like my patrolling days are well and truly over,' she said, looking over to Poppy and Maggie with happy tears in her eyes. 'For now, anyway.'

'You'll still be a part of the WPS.' Poppy smiled, gesturing around her. 'It's almost like you set this place up for yourself,' she joked.

'And you'll *always* be a Bobby Girl,' Maggie declared proudly, picking up her wine glass and raising it in a toast.

Poppy and Mrs Beckett both did the same, and Annie picked up her water again.

'Bobby Girls forever!' Maggie, Poppy and Annie chanted together, and then they all clinked glasses and took a sip of their drinks. When Annie's belly rippled again she thought of Richard and realised she was the happiest she had been in months – and it was all because of him.

The Bobby Girls' War, the next book in Johanna Bell's gorgeous Bobby Girls series, is available now.

I love this photo of some of the WPS recruits chatting to soldiers at a London train station during WW1. It's great to see them all smiling and getting along after reading about the negativity the women received from other police officers.

Acknowledgements

As always, I would first like to thank my editor, Thorne Ryan – for trusting me with your Bobby Girls and for your constant support and guidance.

To my wonderful agent, Kate Burke at Blake Friedmann; thank you for always being there. And to @SquareMilePlod on Twitter – I don't even know your real name, but you went out of your way to help me make sure my description of Holborn's police station in 1916 was authentic and for that I am truly grateful!

Big thanks to all of my family for putting up with me while I immersed myself in the world of the Bobby Girls once more, but particularly to my mum for entertaining a toddler with endless energy and a lot of spirit while all the places she loves were closed. There is no way I would have finished this book without your Nana Daycare!

Last but not least, I must thank Beverley Ann Hopper, Janice Rosser, Deborah Smith and Louise Cannon; my online cheerleaders who I am sure have sent many, many new readers my way. And of course, you, reader – thank you for joining the Bobby Girls on their latest adventure.

Bookends

When one book ends, another begins...

Bookends is a vibrant new reading community to help you ensure you're never without a good book.

You'll find exclusive previews of the brilliant new books from your favourite authors as well as exciting debuts and past classics. Read our blog, check out our recommendations for your reading group, enter great competitions and much more!

Visit our website to see which great books we're recommending this month.

Join the Bookends community:
www.welcometobookends.co.uk

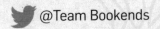 @Team Bookends   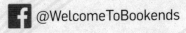 @WelcomeToBookends